TRACKED

OTHER TITLES BY DR. REBECCA SHARP

The Kinkades

The Woodsman

The Lightkeeper

The Candlemaker

The Innkeeper

The Gentleman

The Beekeeper

The Glassmaker

Reynolds Protective

Archer

Hunter

Gunner

Ranger

The Vigilantes

The Vendetta

The Verdict

The Villain

The Vigilant

The Vow

Covington Security

Betrayed

Bribed

Beguiled

Burned

Branded

Broken

Believed

Bargained

Braved

Carmel Cove

Beholden

Bespoken

Besotted

Befallen

Beloved

Betrothed

The Odyssey Duet

The Fall of Troy

The Judgment of Paris

Country Love Collection

Tequila

Ready to Run

Fastest Girl in Town

Last Name

I'll Be Your Santa Tonight

Michigan for the Winter

Remember Arizona

Ex To See

A Cowboy for Christmas

Meant to Be

Accidentally on Purpose

Hypothetically

Save Me the Trouble

Mr. Sandman

Winter Games

Up in the Air

On the Edge

Enjoy the Ride

In Too Deep

Over the Top

The Gentlemen's Guild

The Artist's Touch

The Sculptor's Seduction

The Painter's Passion

Stand-Alones

Reputation

Redemption

Revolution

Passion & Perseverance Trilogy

(A *Pride and Prejudice* Retelling)

First Impressions

Second Chances

Third Time is the Charm

TRACKED

DR. REBECCA SHARP

OFF THE GRID

Montlake

This is a work of fiction. Names, characters, organizations, places, events, and incidents are either products of the author's imagination or are used fictitiously. Otherwise, any resemblance to actual persons, living or dead, is purely coincidental.

Published by Montlake, Seattle

www.apub.com

Amazon, the Amazon logo, and Montlake are trademarks of Amazon.com, Inc., or its affiliates.

EU product safety contact:
Amazon Media EU S. à r.l.
38, avenue John F. Kennedy, L-1855 Luxembourg
amazonpublishing-gpsr@amazon.com

ISBN-13: 9781662541940 (paperback)
ISBN-13: 9781662541957 (digital)

Cover design by Eileen Carey
Cover image: © Wander Aguiar Photography; © HamzGRPHC, © THP Creative, © Minii Ho / Shutterstock; © Mr. Music / Adobe Stock

Printed in the United States of America

For everyone who watches NCIS, Reacher, Tracker, or Criminal Minds and secretly wishes there was a spicy NSFW version. This one's for us.

To my husband, the love of my life.

Chapter 1

Calder

Rule #24: The easiest path is usually a trap.

"On the count of three," Colby said, grinning just a little too wide. *"Three."*

My younger sister scrambled up the rock face, her lean frame and braided brown hair moving up the cragged cliffside with the swift skill of a spider.

She had a half-second head start on me from her method of . . . counting. But that was Colby—always trying to outmaneuver, outsmart, and outperform the rest of us, her five older brothers. Maybe that was why her nickname, even now that she's twenty-four, was the Dynamo.

Digging my hold into the practically sheer rock, I lunged after her, leaving a trail of chalk fingerprints in my wake.

There were higher, more treacherous cliffs buried in our family's thousand-acre ranch, which was tucked away into the Wyoming Tetons, but this wall, dubbed Free Fall for its paralyzing vertical ascent and sparse holds along the way, was our litmus test. *Part of our legacy.*

My hands found their familiar rests, pulling me closer to Colby as my eyes scanned for my next hold; they always had to be one step ahead.

Rock climbing was both a physical and mental exercise. The combination of strength needed to hold yourself and a steady mind to calculate your next safest step made it one of the most important skills Cassius Stone had impressed on his children. And ascending Free Fall was graduation.

Cassius's rule—one of many—was that his children were allowed to attempt the thirty-foot climb when we turned fifteen. None of us had waited that long, though Colby, of course, snuck out to summit Free Fall at the youngest age of thirteen.

The scar on Colby's left brow marked her accomplishment; she'd lost her footing on the climb back down, gashing her head before she caught herself and landed on her feet. The injury was nothing compared to the victory, which she'd worn with a wide smile and a slash of blood streaked like a laurel wreath across her forehead.

The Free Fall at Fifteen was one of the few rules Cassius was proud to see his children break.

"Your counting could use some work," I taunted, my fingers sinking into my next hold as I pulled myself almost level with my sister. I had the natural advantage of height and strength, so my delayed start only attempted to even the playing field.

"Your *climbing* could use some work," she countered, and made a quick scramble that put her back in the lead.

We'd all made the Free Fall summit countless times in the last decade—or almost two, in my case. The cliff provided endless courses to the top as nature's elements evolved the rock with every passing year. The challenge of the topography was never as interesting to Colby as the competition for who could peak the fastest, a record I'd always held and she'd always wanted to claim.

She shifted and stretched above me, desperate to keep her lead. There was only about ten feet left to the top, and while she was moving quickly, I was still going to win.

"You sure about that, Dynamo?"

"Shit." I heard her rough mutter and the scrape of her shoes as I rose beside her, then above her. There were a few more curses that followed me up the rock face; she'd chosen a shorter path, but the ledges were less reliable at the top, a risk she was now paying for.

Colby's climbing was just as impulsive as the rest of her, always exploding toward the next step rather than evaluating the best step, which was why I caught up to her with fewer but more well-placed hooks. Climbing, like survival, was a chess game, necessitating thought before action.

I reached the top and hauled myself up over the edge of the cliff. Sitting on the ledge, I smiled down at Colby and wiped my hands together. "I think my technique is still working out pretty well."

She reached the summit a few seconds later, taking a seat beside me and letting her head fall forward with a heavy groan.

"It was those last holds that screwed me," she muttered, her irritation settled squarely between her bunched shoulders.

"They're too shallow on that section of the wall."

"I know, but it's the fastest way to the top."

"Only if it were reliable," I rumbled and nudged my elbow to hers. "Maybe next time."

Determination creased her expression; she was already plotting her next attempt, hopefully along a more thoughtful path.

The only way to counteract Colby's instinct toward impulsiveness was to make her lose. She loathed losing to any of us, so it was the only thing that forced her to stop and proceed with a little more caution the next time around.

Rule #29: Train your siblings as if their lives depend on it, because someday, they might. Cassius didn't mince words when it came to his rules of survival, especially in this. To go easy on Colby because she was smaller or because she was a girl or because she was our sister gave her an advantage the real world wouldn't guarantee.

While I made sure the Dynamo didn't get in over her head, none of us held back during any kind of challenge. If she lost, she learned. And when she learned, she got better.

"Calder!" a deep voice from below boomed.

Creed stood at the base of the wall, his arms crossed over his chest. Stone sibling number two was not unlike the cliff Colby and I sat on:

extra large, inexorably hard, and naturally silent. Drawing water from a stone was easier than drawing words from *this* Stone. Though only a year younger than me, Creed was an inch taller than my six-foot-one frame and forty pounds of muscle broader, and he carried himself like he was still in the military police, ensuring he was consistently mistaken for the eldest of our clan.

"Be right down," I called back.

Turning to Colby, I jerked my head toward the base. "Let's go, Dynamo."

She remained boldly still, her mouth pinching tight in a way that instantly reminded me of our mother. Annie Stone was murdered when Colby was six, and her only daughter had inherited every last gene of defiance, boldness, and grit. That, combined with being the youngest and the only girl, meant Colby got away with things that Cassius never let the rest of us do. Even as adults, she was the only one who got to break his rules.

Case in point, the cell phone she quickly pulled out to snap a photo of the panorama in front of us: a horizon of mountain peaks married to meandering plains, our childhood home the single solitary structure for as far as the eye could see. One of Cassius's staunchest rules was no technology in the house. Especially cell phones. Until he caved for Colby and her photography.

Granted, her cell was encrypted seven ways to Sunday, but still—Colby was allowed while the rest of us had to deposit ours, turned off, in a signal-jamming lockbox on the front porch.

Rule #10: Cell phones are tracking devices that happen to make calls.

Growing up Stone meant growing up survivalist. Even the name of Dad's property, Stonewall Ranch, advertised both its literal and figurative meanings: surrounded by mountains, and outsiders weren't welcome. He wanted to live off-grid, so the house had its own sources of energy and water. However, being completely cut off from the world was harder the older we got.

We descended Free Fall's face, Colby's feet landing on the ground with the first thud, followed by my own. Thankfully, only Creed caught my grimace. I might still beat her to the top, but at thirty-three, and with a knee injury from a wrestling match in college, my days of jumping the last ten feet to land were coming to a swift end.

"No luck?" Creed grunted, our sister's disappointment as marked on her expression as the scar on her forehead.

Colby jutted out her chin. "Not yet." Looking to me, she added, "Same time next month." It wasn't a question, and if it were up to Colby, we'd be out here again tomorrow for a rematch. *But I'm not twenty-four anymore.*

"Sure." I chuckled and brushed some of the leftover chalk from my hands.

"All right, I'll see you guys at the house." She headed for the path back.

"Colby . . ." Creed stopped her. "What happened to Creighton's tea?"

Her eyes flicked wide, the unmistakable sparkle of mischief—and merriment—lighting in them. "Why?"

I banded my arms over my chest, waiting to hear the newest torture our sister had inflicted on our grouchiest sibling.

Stone sibling number five was a doozy. At twenty-six, Creighton was the second youngest and was as surly as Creed was stoic. He was the most . . . different from the rest of us. A genius with an off-the-charts IQ, he was covered in self-inflicted tattoos and possessed the irritable demeanor of a septuagenarian. He was more analytical than practical, but even that didn't spare him Cassius's survivalist training and having to summit Free Fall.

While the rest of us left Creighton to his solitary pursuits, Colby loved nothing more than to torment him with practical jokes, insisting that misery needed comedy, not company.

"He was aggravated. Looking for Donnie."

Donnie was Colby's pet duck. Her hobby of rescuing injured wildlife from every corner of our property meant we'd had an array of unusual pets over the years. Donnie had had an injured wing when she found him three years ago, and after she'd nurtured him back to health, he became domesticated. He roamed freely through our family home, much to Creighton's dismay. But the duck, like the cell phone, wasn't something Cassius would forbid his youngest.

Colby shrugged far too nonchalantly and offered, "Maybe Donnie likes tea, too." And then she disappeared down the path, a little extra pep in her step.

Creed looked back at me, his eyebrow cocked like a silent question mark.

I blew out an exhale and shook my head. "I absolutely think she trained Donnie to steal Creighton's tea."

Creighton was a character of extremes. A disorganized disaster in some lights, a savant of specifics in others. One of his extremes was his obsession with exotic teas. Some he grew. Some he imported. And none he shared. Especially with a duck.

"What's up?" I asked, and went over to the large boulder where I'd set my cell before attempting the climb.

"New case," he grunted, staring expectantly at me as I opened my phone and scanned the details.

A $20,000 reward for an Alabama State college student who'd gone missing on vacation with friends in Florida. "How long has she been gone?"

"Four days."

We hadn't grown up thinking our unusual upbringing would equip us for anything more than being experts at survival. Cassius certainly hadn't anticipated we'd someday monetize our abilities to track people or prey in the wilderness, hunt as well as the most expert marksmen, or survive for days in the harshest of elements. However, just as my interest in law school had waned, Creed was injured overseas. When he came back, circumstance and happenstance collided, and I'd realized there was a market for our shared, specialized skill set. And so, Stone Tracking Services was born. Over the course of the last decade, our other three brothers joined our business venture for one reason or another.

We were retrievalists—a term Creighton hated because it wasn't a real word, but since Creighton hated most things except for tea and tattoos, we kept it in spite of his protests.

As retrievalists, we found what was missing for those who offered a reward and, in special circumstances, for those who didn't offer one. Our cases were usually missing persons. Sometimes missing valuables: Jewelry. Paintings. A relative's missing will. Rarely missing pets, but never fugitive criminals. An important distinction between what we did and bounty hunting, albeit one people generally struggled to understand.

"I know you just got back from California, so if you want me to take it, I can—or if you want to go. It doesn't matter."

Where Colby was the Dynamo, Creed was the Drifter, always needing to be on the move. I usually gave him preference when a new reward came through, especially one that was across the country.

The distinct rumble of an approaching quad paused our conversation. Within seconds, a four-wheeler appeared from the path to the house with Cassius at its helm.

Cassius Stone was a hard man. A wild man. All muscle and grit. Exactly the kind of man one would expect to find living off-grid on a thousand acres of wilderness. Once upon a time, he'd been a secret service agent at the very heart of technology and world events. It was because he knew that world that he'd moved here, not just to escape it but to also hide himself and his family from it.

Cassius stopped beside us but left the engine running as he said, "Calder, I need you to come back to the house. There's someone here to see you." His voice had the quality of worn leather, abraded from prolonged wear and tear but still supple from its lasting strength.

If it weren't for the gray hair and beard, one would be hard-pressed to believe the fifty-eight-year-old was a father of six rather than the eldest of seven. And a single father, no less, for the last eighteen years.

"At the house?" Whoever this visitor was wasn't my first concern.

Few people ventured onto Stonewall Ranch, and even fewer did so without an invitation. The ranch was *family only*. Though it wasn't one of Cassius's written rules, it was an unspoken one.

I could count on one hand the number of people who'd been invited to our home. Uninvited guests, on the other hand, were usually hunters or hikers who'd missed the posted PRIVATE PROPERTY and NO TRESPASSING signs; they were welcomed by Cassius's stiff warning and the even stiffer shotgun strapped to his back as he patrolled the perimeter.

"Yes." Cassius jerked his chin, the salt-and-pepper gray of his beard framing the harsh slash of his mouth as he ordered, "Get on."

I shot Creed an apologetic glance. "If you want to wait—"

"No, I'll go," he said without a single inflection of emotion. But that was Creed. He just did. Went. Lived off the back of his massive Harley like staying in one place too long—even here—put him in peril.

I climbed behind Cassius, who hit the gas before I was fully seated.

"Who is it?" I called over the howling wind at my ears.

Cassius didn't answer me, and it was on purpose. Whoever was here, it was my fault they'd invaded our sanctuary. Just like it was my fault my mother had been killed.

The house appeared ahead to the squawking of a fleeing, furious duck.

Donnie flapped out of the open attic window belonging to Creighton's room, landed in the grass behind the house, and waddled his way toward the blow-up pool Colby had fashioned into Donnie's own personal pond. I was fairly certain there was a small bag of tea leaves clutched in his beak.

Well, that answered that.

The home I'd grown up in was large by any account. With six children, Cassius Stone had spared no expense in building the appreciable stone-faced, large-windowed, two-storied compound to comfortably house our wild brood. The footprint then expanded to accommodate Cassius's expansive library, from which we were all required to read, and Mom's spacious kitchen and attached greenhouse, which Cassius now religiously maintained.

Cassius rounded the front of the house, and my attention went to the unfamiliar dark-red sedan parked next to Creed's modified F-250. It had Wyoming plates. Numerous dents on the bumper. And as we pulled up next to it, I saw a barcode sticker in the front window. *A rental.*

Was it someone from a recent case? I'd been to Colorado, Nevada, and Texas in the last three months, but no contacts from there seemed likely. We never gave out the ranch address. Ever. *A rule.* Maybe someone local who'd moved away? Someone who'd worked with Mom?

I climbed off the four-wheeler, running through the possibilities the same way I'd scanned Free Fall's rock face for my next hold. *What were my options? What made the most sense? What had the highest probability of being correct?*

I entered through the front door to Creighton's taut warning aimed at our sister down the hall: "This brings a whole new meaning to *fowl* play, Colby. That duck better watch out."

Colby called back, "It's not Donnie's fault your room is a disaster and you keep losing your tea!"

It was, 100 percent, Donnie's fault. However, it was equally true that Creighton's domain was a complete disaster. It was the kind of thing people wrote off for a genius who must have a method to his mess and madness.

Driving a tattooed hand with ink-stained fingers through his shoulder-length hair, Creighton glowered at her and then at me, and then thundered back to his attic.

"Library," Cassius said, and turned, heading to the kitchen. It was almost lunchtime, which meant he'd be making cold-cut sandwiches for whoever was home before taking his afternoon patrol through the property.

I walked in the opposite direction through the living room, past Colby's photographs on the walls, the aged leather couches worn from six wild children, and the stone hearth that yawned for winter's daily log fires, all the way to the pocket doors that sequestered the cerebral domain of the library at the end of the house.

Whoever it was, it wasn't a friend; I'd determined that much. My friendships came in quality, not quantity, and also came at a distance. Most of those I would have considered close had been from college or my law-intern days, and all of them lived out of state.

I stepped over the threshold, scanning the bookcase-covered walls that had always made this my favorite room of the house, until my eyes landed on her.

Her.

Small frame. Slim jeans. Short boots. Loose blazer. Red hair. She turned, and I felt the unmistakable, unrepentant slam of my heart as it detonated in my chest.

Green eyes and full lips greeted me, along with a familiar smattering of freckles over her nose, more numerous now in the summer. But it was the hair . . . I would know that copper-drenched hair anywhere. Even after . . . Damn. *Even after twelve years.*

"Lara." I broke the silence and took a step forward, noting the instant flicker of distrust that hardened her face and the slight downturn of her invitingly pink lips.

I couldn't remember exactly the last time I'd seen Lara Crane, but whenever it had been, my body had responded in the same exact way. That had never changed. The undercurrent of heat. The hum of attraction in my veins. The ache for someone so wholly inappropriate, especially then but even now.

"Calder."

All the pieces clicked into place. The rental car. A visitor who was from here but didn't live here any longer. How she knew where to find me.

There was one time—*one single time*—in college when I'd brought my ex-girlfriend to the ranch. It wasn't to see my home or meet my family, but to help her. Unfortunately, my attempt to help had only ended in disaster.

That ex-girlfriend was Rachel Crane. *Lara's older sister.*

Judging from the sharp edge in Lara's emerald gaze and the way she held it like a knife to mine, she didn't want to be here. *Didn't want to see me.* And I didn't blame her.

"What happened?" I asked, cutting to the chase as I folded my arms over my chest.

She wouldn't be here if she had any other choice, which meant she didn't.

Pain seared her expression. "Rachel's missing."

Chapter 2

Lara

Calder Stone was wildly, ruggedly handsome. *Still.*

My heart thundered against my ribs as I stared at the proverbial cardboard cutout of my memory of my sister's college boyfriend. Everything from his clipped dark-brown hair and murky hazel eyes to the trimmed stubble of his beard was all familiar. Even his style—dark pants and plain gray tee—hadn't changed in all these years.

But had Calder always been this tall? This broad? My chest tightened as I met his stare. *And had his eyes always had those gold flecks?*

Maybe there was some kind of *Tuck Everlasting* fountain of youth hidden in this wilderness, because the silver-haired man who'd greeted me at the front door, with a slight frown eerily similar to the one his son wore now, was also age-defyingly handsome.

Calder's jaw clenched, and my breath snagged, watching the flex of his *masseter* highlight the hard edge of his jawline and the pulse of his *temporalis* echo his frustration.

God. Even after a dozen years, it was hard not to lose myself in the mental anatomy lessons that would run through my premed head every time Rachel had brought him around.

Human musculature as taught by a bare-chested Calder Stone was far more captivating than any textbook illustration or lab examination of dissected cadavers from class.

Though I'd tried to frame my fascination as educational, there was no denying my attraction to my sister's boyfriend. Not even now. But attraction was biology, not rationality. If physical chemistry were logical, I wouldn't feel warmth in the presence of the man who'd broken my sister's heart.

"What do you mean, Rachel's missing?" His calm voice rippled through the room.

Calder was always calm. No. *Calm* wasn't the right word. Calder was a mutation of confidence, composure, and just a hint of coldness topped with a charming smile. It was that slight aloofness that had made him attractive to Rachel . . . and destroyed her when they broke up.

I shook off the surge of anger. It wouldn't get me anywhere, especially since Calder was my best chance at finding my sister.

"I mean she's missing. I haven't heard from her in weeks. She's not answering her phone. She's not at her apartment. And I think her new boyfriend might have something to do with it."

His stance widened and his dark brows furrowed.

"Okay. Missing and in danger are two very different scenarios," he said, explaining the shift in his demeanor. His voice, however, still remained calm. "Why don't you start from the beginning?"

He motioned to the closest of the two recliners in the room, silently offering for me to take a seat, but I declined with a shake of my head; I couldn't sit. Even at the hospital, I'd dictate my notes at the end of my shift while pacing along the hall. I needed movement to keep my thoughts on track—to keep them from running away from me.

"Three weeks ago, Rachel FaceTimed me just as I got off my overnight shift at the hospital. She wanted to tell me she was going on some big camping trip with her new boyfriend, Brandon." I took a few steps along the shorter side of the room, reaching the chair, and then turned and walked back. "I was . . . not supportive."

Wordlessly, Calder stepped behind the opposite recliner and rested his hands on the back, subtly opening a path for me to pace the full length of the room.

"We argued. Brandon got involved and got angry and hung up on me. She didn't answer when I called back, so I figured I'd give it a few days and then check on her again. I texted and then called. No response. Straight to voicemail. A few more days, same thing."

"Has she done this before?"

I stopped, my back to him, though I was sure he caught the slight dip of my head. "Yeah," I confessed, forcing myself to cauterize any emotion from my answer, though I couldn't remove the thickness from my voice. "We argued frequently about her relationship choices, and there've been a handful of times where she'll just stop talking to me for a little."

"So why is this time different?"

I didn't realize how tense—how braced—I'd been until I heard no trace of doubt in his voice and all the stiffness in my body suddenly released. It was the complete opposite from the response I'd received from the Jackson police earlier today. All they'd had for me was doubt. Doubt and dismissal.

She's an adult. She told you she was going on a trip. There's probably just no service. All I'd heard was *She's not important enough.*

I turned and my eyes connected with Calder's hard stare, a shot of heat injecting into my veins.

"Because usually when I threaten to come and see her, she responds right away to stop me. And this time . . . well, I'm here." I held my hands out from my sides because I was the proof. Because me being here meant Rach had never responded to stop me, which she would've done if she were okay, which meant she wasn't.

My sister wasn't okay, and I felt responsible.

"Okay." Calder nodded. "I'll need all of her information. Phone number. Address. And what about the boyfriend? What's his full name, and do you have a phone number?"

"I don't know his last name or phone number," I admitted, guilt and regret wrapping my throat in a caustic blanket. "Rachel doesn't share a lot about her relationships with me anymore. We're not as close as we used to be."

The bond between sisters was a funny thing. At times, it was the strongest tether two people could have, and it had been strong for us growing up. Our dad left when we were young, and after that our mom wasn't home much, and when she was, her own traumatic relationships pushed Rachel and me even closer.

Unfortunately, as we'd grown older, strong became brittle. When I'd seen my sister falling into the same toxic traps our mom had with men, I spoke up. I confronted her. I told her she deserved better. But instead of avoiding the traps, she'd started avoiding me. An easy feat, when my residency took me to Arizona.

"I have her information in my phone," I offered and reached for my purse. "I took a screenshot of Brandon while we were on FaceTime when he started yelling, because I just knew something bad was going to happen." My fingers paused on the zipper, remembering my phone wasn't inside. "But your dad . . . took my phone."

Calder's lips thinned into a straight line. "Right," he muttered. "Come with me."

He led us back through the house and then outside. Crouching, he unlocked the discreet metal box that, on first glance, looked like a mailbox next to the door. He retrieved my cell and his, leaving at least one more phone still inside.

"Sorry about that," he said and handed me back my phone. "Cassius's house rules."

Cassius. I wasn't sure what I found more interesting: the extent of these rules or that Calder called his father by his first name.

"Rachel always said your family took being off-grid seriously."

"Any technology that can find you can be used against you," Calder returned like he'd been made to repeat the mantra hundreds of times before. *Not a mantra—a rule.*

Back then I'd assumed my sister was exaggerating, since Calder lived more or less like a normal college student on campus, aside from the not drinking and rarely partying part, which was only abnormal when compared to the college experience my sister wanted to have.

Rachel was extroverted and loved to go out. Loved to dance. To drink. To have too much of a good time. And for a while, the only thing she enjoyed more than partying was the attention she got for being Calder's girlfriend.

Calder was considered a wrestling prodigy at Wyoming State. I couldn't tell you how many championships he'd won, but it was enough to earn him campus-wide fame, shooting him to unexpected celebrity at a school where football was king. What my sister initially relished about that celebrity—all the invitations to exclusive campus parties—quickly soured when Calder never wanted to take advantage of them.

Almost religiously, she'd call me every week complaining that Calder didn't want to go to some party—or if they did go, how boring he was because he didn't want to let loose.

I should've said something then, when it was easy. Suggest maybe they weren't right for each other. But I'd stayed out of it because I thought Calder was a good influence on her. I'd thought he could calm her. Steady her with his reserve. Instead, it'd only gotten worse.

I hit the power button on my phone and waited for it to turn on.

"This way," Calder said, and walked down the three steps leading off the porch.

I stared at first, thinking he had to be going to my car or his truck—if that was even his truck—because there was nothing else here, but he turned and walked right by them.

Jogging to catch up, I followed him along the front of the house, unable to stop myself from admiring how those pants fit his *gluteus maximus.*

Like cosmic punishment, my boot caught on a rock and made me stumble. Calder glanced over his shoulder. If he caught me staring at his ass, he didn't let on.

I really needed to stop cataloging every well-defined muscle belonging to my sister's ex-boyfriend.

"I take it Rachel told you where my family lived," he said, heading deeper into the property until the gravel drive tapered into wild grass.

"She mentioned . . . described coming here." *That one time.*

My sister hadn't been a model girlfriend by any stretch of the imagination, but that didn't absolve Calder for how he'd treated her that night. Even days later, when she'd told me what happened, she could hardly get the words out over her sobs. She'd had many breakups before, but I'd never heard her devastation quite like that.

"And I assume you've gone to the police?"

"They were my first stop." My hand balled in a fist as I recounted how that had gone. "When I didn't find her at her apartment, I went straight to the station to report her missing. When I explained what happened, they told me to wait and that not every crappy boyfriend who takes a girl on a camping trip intends to murder her."

There wasn't a time when I'd ever not been professional, but that moment sure came close. It was like the national coverage and publicity of the case where that *had happened* turned the two officers I'd spoken to bitter instead of better.

Calder muttered something under his breath; it sounded like a frustrated *of course*, but with the wind blowing across the property, it was hard to be sure.

"As I was leaving, the receptionist mentioned there was a private company in the area that specialized in finding missing people. She said you'd rescued a young girl who'd been stranded in Yellowstone for over a week when even the park rangers had given up. Well, maybe not you—"

"Maddie," Calder interrupted. "Her name was Maddie, and it was me."

I swallowed. "I asked for the name of the company, and as soon as she told me Stone Tracking Services, I realized who it was—that it had to be you."

"Had to be me?"

"Maybe not you, but your family." Last I knew, he'd been heading into a law internship. "Rachel told me that your family was big into hunting and tracking. Plus, there was the time you found Pebbles." The grass started to thicken, turning from yellow to green as we walked farther from the house.

Calder slowed and looked over his shoulder. "That's right. I was surprised she made it all the way to the next town over."

"All the way into a tree in the next town over." Heat fizzled along my spine when I remembered, quite vividly, those minutes as he climbed to reach the escaped cat and bring her back down.

How both heads of his *biceps brachii* visibly flexed as he grabbed those first branches. The curve of his *deltoids* and *trapezius* muscle bulging against his shirt as he hoisted himself higher. Then there was the broad sweep of *pectoralis major* from his sternum to his shoulders as he reached out and plucked Pebbles from the end of the branch and held her to his chest. And, of course, no lesson was complete without recalling the reveal of his *rectus abdominis* when his shirt snagged on a twig on the way down, lifting the fabric to reveal twin stacks of tightly bricked abs.

The way he'd looked at me when he returned Pebbles to my arms wasn't part of the lesson, though. *An imagined look, of course, because he was Rachel's boyfriend.*

"So you knew it had to be me because I saved your cat a dozen years ago?" He chuckled, the sound feeling like a luxury for a man who lived so sparsely.

"She was technically Rachel's cat," I corrected without thinking, and Calder stopped.

Procerus, corrugator—his brows knotted tighter as he stared at me. "She said Pebbles was yours."

Oh, Rachel.

It had been twelve years, but it was these stupid little lies of hers that hurt the most. The ones that reminded me of the lengths she'd go to hide who she was to please the person she was with.

"She knew you didn't like cats, so she asked if I could keep Pebbles at my place," I explained, wishing this little lie was the extent of it, but it was nothing compared to the bigger ones.

After a few months of dating, Rachel had started telling Calder she was staying at my house off campus for the night when she was really at frat parties with her roommate. I wasn't complicit in the lies, just a casualty after the fact. An obligated *If Calder asks, Lara, I was with you last night* alibi. I'd told her to leave me out of it, but she never did. And because she was my sister—always the two of us against the world—I'd protected her. Maybe more than I should have.

Back then, I hadn't known enough or had enough foresight to give my sister relationship advice. It was only after their breakup that the guilt hit me.

I was an analyzer. A diagnostician. *A doctor.* And I couldn't help but diagnose the cause of my sister's increasingly problematic relationships as symptoms stemming from a single traumatic injury: that first devastating heartbreak inflicted by Calder Stone.

There was a flash of something on his face—maybe regret, but it moved too quickly, too slightly. Like the rush of a breeze. There and gone, before I could be certain.

It didn't matter what it was. I wasn't here to scold a grown man for the lasting consequences of a choice he'd made twelve years ago. Neither my lingering resentment nor my frustrating attraction for Calder made any difference to the reality that he was my best shot at finding my sister.

Glancing back, I saw how far we'd walked from the house, the structure now small and sitting at the base of the shallow but measurable hill I hadn't even realized we'd been slowly climbing.

"What's that?" I asked, pointing to another, smaller cabin I could see beyond the Stone homestead; it looked to be about the same distance from the main house as we were, though the terrain between the two buildings appeared much flatter.

Calder didn't even look before answering, "Watchtower. Where my brother Callum lives."

"Watchtower?"

"He does all of the technological tracking, communications, and case management for the business."

Squinting, I could just make out the large wraparound porch and the several satellite dishes attached to the roof. And then it hit me—the memory of the message Rachel had sent me a few years ago.

"Wait. He was the storm chaser?"

Bits and pieces of the news article about the *Widowmaker*, a massive tornado that had wrecked through Wyoming not that far from here, claiming the life of one storm chaser and paralyzing another. A picture of the famed tornado wrangler known for his easy smile and characteristic cowboy hat: *Callum Stone.*

When Calder didn't reply, I yanked my head back in his direction and found he'd disappeared.

There was a row of ancient evergreens lining the top of the hill in front of me. Behind it was the only place he could've gone. Rounding the trees, I stopped short, realizing their purpose: to conceal the massive Airstream parked behind them.

Calder stood, holding open the silver door, waiting for me. "Come in."

Chapter 3

Lara

"Coffee?" Calder offered, moving to the kitchen counter directly inside the massive camper's front door.

"Sure. Thanks," I said and scooted behind him into his mobile home. Another coffee would be good right now; I was long overdue for my second cup of the day.

Inside, natural light streamed through several small windows, illuminating the gray wood-paneled interior. The dining table had been converted into his workstation, his laptop closed on one side, folders and a notebook strewn across the top.

"French press or pour-over?"

I turned to my right, seeing the array of coffee makers, ceramic filters, and a digital scale positioned along the counter. And then Calder . . . rolling up his sleeves to reveal a rugged topography of strength and sinew.

My mouth parted, my eyes roaming greedily. If muscles and tendons were protected like mountains and trees, Calder Stone would be the first man honored for his anatomical beauty. *And I would be the first person caught trespassing over boundaries I should've abided.*

Crap. I snapped my jaw shut and hoarsely picked the first option. "French press sounds great." The only question I'd ever considered when it came to coffee was *How many cups?*, and my answer lately had been *Never enough.*

Calder started the electric teakettle and then grabbed the glass press and a bag of grounds, scooping them into the container.

Get it together, Lara, I chided, diverting my gaze to the rest of the space—to anything that wasn't Calder's arms at work.

Beyond the dining area was a living space, followed by the bathroom at the far end. In the living room, a couch faced a wall where a TV should've been but wasn't. Instead, a bookcase claimed the surface, the shelves lined with slim little notebooks. I wondered whether they corresponded to each of his cases. If so . . . My eyes widened at how many there were.

Abutting the bookcase were two frames. The first held a photograph of the Tetons, and on the second one below it, a hand-drawn topographical map, the word STONE was scrawled in the corner. Looking closer, I saw distinct handwritten notes marking certain spots: *Free Fall, Tree House, Watchtower, Lima Bean Lake.*

The kettle beeped, and it had to be me, but the violent alert sounded just like our vital signs monitor in the hospital. I spun on instinct, an instant grip of panic around my throat. Calder looked at me, concerned, and I quickly buried the reaction.

"So, this is where you live?" I said, unsure whether it was a statement or a question or simply a distraction.

"You thought I lived at the house?" he rumbled, pouring the steaming water onto the coffee grounds and setting a timer on his phone.

Who knew making coffee could be as precise as surgery?

"Why wouldn't I?" I countered, heading back toward the kitchen.

What struck me wasn't the compact efficiency of the Airstream, but the unexpected sense of warmth it held inside its silver fist. The bookshelf. The coffee machines. The map and handwritten notes. And even on the table, a crossword sat on top of some folders, half completed. It was all . . . Calder. All cozy ruggedness packaged in a perfect, hard shell.

I lifted my eyes and noticed the second door at this end of the camper that I'd missed when I'd walked in. *Calder's bedroom.*

Rachel had never shared any details about that part of their relationship, but, standing here, I couldn't help but wonder whether there was a ruggedness beyond that door, too.

"Fair," Calder returned, and I faced him just as one corner of his lips twitched like he wanted to smile. "Yeah, I live here. Only Creighton and Colby, my two youngest siblings—and sometimes Colton, the third oldest—live at the house."

I made a sound of acknowledgment. "Well, you have a really nice camper."

Camping, to me, was a tent in the woods. Growing up in Wyoming, sleeping in a tent was something Rachel and I had done plenty of times when we were younger, especially when Mom had dated Ronnie; he'd been a creep, and it felt safer to sleep in the backyard. Thankfully, Ronnie hadn't stuck around beyond summer.

"Thanks." His timer went, and he shut it off, pushing the plunger of the French press through the liquid. *Pronator teres*, *flexor carpi ulnaris*, and *flexor carpi radialis* reported for duty.

Stop, Lara. Sister's ex's anatomy class is done for the day.

I sank onto the bench seat at the table and reached for the crossword puzzle—a new distraction—and scanned the clues for the few unsolved spaces. Number fourteen stopped my eye: *the path between nose and lips.*

"Here you go."

I looked up as Calder put his hand on the back of the seat and set the mug in front of me, and my breath jammed in my throat.

The camper had felt pretty roomy until this moment. Until he stood between the table and the counter and tipped forward to deliver my coffee. Too tall. Too broad. *Too close.* Instantly, the space felt as small as a cell. *And as hot as an oven.*

It wasn't the first time his proximity had stolen my breath or blasted goose bumps over my skin, nor would it be the last that he seemed oblivious to it.

"Cream or sugar?" he asked, like his closeness wasn't causing me a cardiac event.

"Philtrum." I blurted out the only word on my mind after watching his mouth trace over the words.

"Excuse me?" He cocked his head, a crease forming between his brows.

I pointed to the puzzle and read the clue aloud. "'The path between nose and lips.'"

He leaned closer to look, and out of some instinct toward insanity, instead of pointing to my own *philtrum* to illustrate, I turned and touched his. My index finger landed flat on the valley between his nose and his upper lip, his skin rough from his short beard. *Rugged but warm.*

Calder's pupils blew wide, and I felt his sharp pull of air like a hot blade along my finger. *What was I doing?* I choked back to reality.

"Sorry." I jerked my hand back and pushed the crossword away, mumbling, "*Philtrum.* It's the answer to fourteen." And my excuse—*explanation* for touching him.

He said nothing and spun away, so I added, "No cream or sugar. Thanks." Maybe the last thirty seconds could be erased if I just pretended they didn't exist.

Get it together, Lara, I thought as I grabbed my mug and breathed in the strong aroma. Closing my eyes, I took a giant sip and dissolved into the rich taste. *Wow, this was a good cup of coffee. Really good. Maybe the best.*

Calder Stone. Anatomy specimen. Coffee-making god. *And careless heartbreaker.* That last was the one I really needed to focus on.

A throat cleared, and my eyes flipped open to find Calder seated opposite me at the table. Staring. *Had I moaned out loud?*

"Can I get Rachel's phone number and address?" he asked.

After pulling up my sister's contact, I slid my phone across to him.

"I'm going to have Callum see if he can get a location on her cell, if that's all right?"

I nodded and watched him snap a photo. "It goes straight to voicemail, and has been for weeks," I said. "At first, I thought she was declining my calls, but now I'm worried her phone is either off or dead."

I picked up the warm mug again and clutched it close to my chest like it could buffer the chill from the word.

Rachel was alive. She had to be. Even with my science background and medical degree, I still held an unwavering belief that if something truly bad had happened to my sister, I would know it. Deep down, I'd know if she was dead. *Wouldn't I?*

"If she went camping, she could also have no service." Calder's voice broke through my tangled thoughts. More than the suggestion, his soothing tone settled my unease.

I'd always appreciated Calder's steadiness, especially for Rachel, whose emotions tended to swing wide. Unfortunately, she hadn't felt the same; his composure had only aggravated her, to the point where she did things only to try to get a rise out of him. Lying. Partying. The more she did, the greater the wedge between them. The greater the wedge, the more she did to try to make him fly off the rails to prove he cared. It spiraled and it wasn't good, and it had ended even worse.

Calder's unwavering calm when he'd broken up with her, even in the face of her devastation . . . she took it as he'd never cared. Maybe if he could've fluctuated just a little, the damage wouldn't have been so deep. So lasting.

"Can you still track it, if that's the case?" I asked, shoving the past back into the recesses of my mind where it belonged. All that mattered now was finding my sister.

"Sometimes."

Calder finished his message to Callum and set his phone down.

"I take it you're not as averse to technology as your dad?" The work they did would be nearly impossible to do without it.

"He has his reasons—his rules for the way he is. For the way we grew up." A shadow passed over his face.

I repeated his caution from earlier with a nod. "Any technology that can find you can be used against you."

"Rule number seven."

"He's not wrong," I murmured, willing to bet that if I opened any social media app on my phone right then, I'd be bombarded with ads for Airstream campers and French press coffee makers.

"No, he's not. He's also not wrong that a weapon you can't or don't know how to control is a weapon that controls you," Calder stated simply, running his thumb along the handle of his mug. "Cassius refuses to accept the middle ground between those two things. The rest of us don't."

"You call him Cassius." *Not Dad.* And for all the insight into Calder's childhood, it was this that intrigued me the most.

"That's his name." *And the only answer I was getting.* "What can you tell me about the boyfriend? Brandon?"

"They've only been dating a few months, I think. At least, it's only been a few months since she's told me about him, though it couldn't have been too much before that, because she broke up with her previous ex six months ago."

I'd never regretted more not pushing Rachel to give me details about Brandon—even a last name.

Calder slid a notebook out from underneath the crossword puzzle; it was the same as the ones that filled his bookshelves. He unclipped the pen from its cover and opened it to a blank page.

"And the camping trip they were going on—she didn't tell you where specifically?" He began to scribble down notes.

I shoved aside the tinge of awkward irony, talking about my sister's ex-boyfriends with one of them, and answered, "No."

"Was it tent camping or camper camping?" he probed, and at my confused expression, clarified: "Many of the parks around here, you'd need a permit to camp with any kind of camper, but not for a tent."

"Oh." That made sense, though I didn't know anything to make it helpful. "She didn't say what kind of camping," I admitted and shook my head. "It's my fault. When she told me, the first thing I did was caution her. She hasn't known Brandon for that long, and to go into the wilderness . . . I just . . . I don't know. Maybe I've watched too many documentaries, but it didn't seem like a good idea." *But that was Rachel: jumping headfirst into relationships with guys who were bad news.*

I blew out an exhale of frustration and took another gulp of my coffee.

"You said she FaceTimed you?"

I nodded and picked up my phone again, searching for the screenshot I'd taken during the call.

"They were at some diner I didn't recognize. I assumed it was around here, but who knows—they could've been anywhere, going anywhere." I tapped on the image of Brandon's angry face.

Rachel's boyfriend had a thick beard and a scar on his cheek. His features were heavyset, but it was hard to make out anything else about his face from underneath the obnoxious red hat he'd continued to wear even though they were inside.

"Here." I showed my phone to Calder. "He wasn't at the table when she called, because it seemed like he'd overheard only the last bit of our conversation when he grabbed the phone and . . . hung up on me."

"What exactly did he say?" He scrutinized the image.

I swallowed. "Does it matter?"

His gaze caught mine, the gold in his eyes a little brighter. "It might."

To whom, I wasn't sure, but I answered anyway, bleeding all emotion from my voice as I air-quoted the asshole. "He told me to 'stop being a stuck-up doctor bitch' and that I 'shouldn't judge my sister's relationship when I've never had one of my own.'" I frowned. "There might've been a *fuck you* at the end, too, but that was the gist of it."

"Sounds like a"—Calder grimaced—"real winner."

If only he knew about the ones who'd come before Brandon. This *real winner* wasn't even the worst.

"Wait." Calder grabbed my wrist when I started to pull back.

My eyes snapped to his, heat searing from his fingertips like an IV straight into my veins.

Roughly clearing his throat, he released me. "Sorry. Can I see that again?"

Like I was handing him an organ transplant rather than a cell phone, I carefully passed it over to him, watching as he zoomed in on the screen.

His brows creased, his *masseter* firing spectacularly. "That's the Antlers Diner. I recognize the logo." He zoomed back out. "I'm going to send this to my phone," he said and waited for me to nod before doing just that and then returning my phone on the table. *In the safe zone.* "It's right up 1-91 before the elk refuge."

I knew where the elk refuge was . . . "Is it new?"

Calder quirked his head. "Maybe three years."

"I've haven't been back since college. No wonder I didn't recognize it."

"Looks like we have a place to start." Rising, he took his mug and mine to the sink.

Did that mean he was going to take Rachel's case?

I spun around and perched on the edge of the seat, my heart beating in my throat. "So you're going to help me?"

Calder turned, surprise breaking the veneer of his chiseled face before he rumbled, "Of course."

Air whooshed from my lungs, and I felt my eyes start to sting. He was going to help me. He was going to find Rachel. *Everything was going to be okay.*

Relief hit like a narcotic. Potent and psychotic. And it was the only explanation for what I did next—something I never would've or should've done otherwise: I lunged from the table and hugged my sister's ex-boyfriend.

What a careless mistake.

Calder Stone might have been calm and collected, but there was nothing *cool* about him. Nothing cold at all, in fact, about the six feet of hot male pressed like a statue against my front. Intense and imposing. All those muscles I'd cataloged now mapped in 3D to my chest.

I shouldn't have been doing that at all, but he was the only one who could help me find Rachel. If something happened to my sister . . . I couldn't lose anyone else.

"Thank you," I murmured with a trembled exhale and clutched him tight, holding on to his stillness like it could keep me steady.

Without hardly moving, Calder managed to lift one arm to give me the lightest pat on the shoulder, like being embraced by a client was nothing more than an awkward cost of doing business.

Except it was more.

He might have felt like a fortress, but there was no hiding the feral thud of his heart from my cheek. It wasn't still. It wasn't steady. His pulse boomed like I'd injected him with 1mg of epi and brought him back to life.

"Lara . . ."

I breathed in deep, filling my lungs with the earthy scent of him: cedar and coffee mixed with just a hint of something warm. Maybe amber. And then I pulled away and banded my arms over my chest like I'd keep them better restrained in the future.

And I would.

I shouldn't salivate over Rachel's ex. Too bad I knew, with more medical detail than most, that attraction was chemical, not rational, so there was no stopping this . . . electricity. No matter how much I shouldn't. No matter what he'd done.

"I can't thank you enough, Calder," I said quickly, creating some professional distance between us. "And I'll pay you, of course. I have fifty thousand—"

"Lara, please," Calder inserted gruffly, a glint of gold catching my eyes. "Let's just find Rachel first."

I frowned. I was definitely going to pay him. I wouldn't accept a handout as some kind of penance for how he'd treated my sister. That was between the two of them. This, between us, was business. *And a little bit of anatomy.*

"Okay," I agreed with a brusque nod, playing by his rules for now.

"Lunch rush should be dying down right about now, so it should be easier to ask around." He grabbed his notebook and pen from the table. "We'll take your rental, if that's all right?"

"Sure."

I followed Calder out of the Airstream and into the quickly warming August day, focusing on anything that wasn't him.

Maybe I needed my own set of Stone rules.

Rule #1: Don't salivate over Calder Stone or his gluteus maximus.

Chapter 4

CALDER

Rule #18: A weapon you can't control is a weapon that controls you.

Cassius taught me that rule when I was twelve, just before placing a hunting rifle in my arms.

It was a good lesson to learn, especially when it came to guns, but as I got older, I realized *weapon* was a broad term and guns weren't the only definition. Cell phones were a weapon. Technology was a weapon. Cars were a weapon. But even more than that, emotions were a weapon.

I'd watched Mom's fear shape how we lived at the ranch, always afraid a shadow from Cassius's past would catch up to us. Cassius had changed because he couldn't control his grief over Mom's death. I didn't know which emotion Creed carried with him since he'd been discharged, but it made him distant and drift away. Colton was haunted by ghosts like he still had cuffs around his wrists. Callum was abraded by anger after the accident, and Creighton by bitterness. Anger, grief, fear, bitterness—I'd seen what each of those *weapons* had done to my family over the years, and I refused to become another casualty.

Like hunting, rock climbing, and tracking, controlling my emotions was a skill I'd honed over the years. Perfected through diligence and the looming threat of destruction. But right now, I was unsettled by how little control I had over the desire soaking through my veins for the woman in the passenger seat. Desire that felt less like a weapon and more like a wildfire—a force of nature unable to be stopped.

And that was a problem. A big fucking problem.

"So, you haven't been back to Wyoming since college?" I asked, deciding small talk was preferable to tense silence.

"No," Lara answered, shaking her head. "I moved to Colorado for med school and then down to Phoenix for my residency. After my mom passed, I didn't have a reason to leave Arizona. Rachel was kind of all over the place after you guys graduated, and we weren't on the best of terms . . ." She trailed off, obviously not wanting to elaborate or for me to probe.

To say my relationship with Rachel had been tumultuous was like calling the Tetons tall: true, but vastly understated. And the way it had ended . . . Lara didn't know the real reason why I'd broken things off with her sister or what had happened afterward. If she did, she never would've hugged me. No, if she knew the truth, she never would've come for my help in the first place.

I tightened my hold on the steering wheel, reminding myself that Lara's personal opinion of me was immaterial, no matter how tainted it was. She hadn't come to me to fix the past. She'd come to me to find her sister, and that was exactly what I was going to do.

"What kind of medicine?" I asked, pulling out of the ranch's winding drive.

"Emergency." Her hand twitched where it rested on her knee.

Interesting. I would've pegged Rachel as thriving in that kind of environment. Reactive. Fast paced. High stakes. Lara, on the other hand, had always seemed more reserved—like she'd been the one to curb her older sister's enthusiasm even before I came into the picture.

"Do you enjoy it?"

"I did—*do.*" Lara stumbled over her answer and lowered her gaze for a split second. "And what about you? Weren't you going to law school?"

The redirect of the conversation wasn't subtle, just like her knee-jerk reaction to the teakettle; there was something there she wanted to avoid talking about, but it wasn't my business to pry. No part of her was any of my business—especially not the little slide of her tongue across her lips.

Wondering how my ex-girlfriend's little sister tasted was the very opposite of my business.

My job was to find Rachel. To treat this like any other case. To be professional. And like any other case, as soon as we were finished at the diner, we'd go our separate ways and I'd contact Lara once I had answers. That was how this worked. That was how *I* worked. *Alone.*

"I was. Interned at a law firm for a little and decided it wasn't for me." I let my gaze slip over to her, knowing my aviators masked my attention.

"So you decided to become a reward hunter?" Lara pulled her hair from one shoulder over to the other and then absentmindedly felt her wrist for a tie, making me think she wasn't used to wearing it down.

The first thing I'd noticed about Lara when Rachel introduced us in college had been her hair. The rich red was the same shade as the first leaves on the ranch that turned in autumn, and wholly different from her sister's dark brown. Even now, I remembered how hard I'd fought then not to stare—not to keep staring.

Wanting to stare at my girlfriend's younger sister should've been a warning sign that something wasn't right. *Not wanting to be at that sorority party in the first place should've been a warning sign that something wasn't right.* Unfortunately, those weren't the kind of warning signs we'd been taught to recognize on the ranch.

"Retrievalist," I corrected.

"Not the same as a rewardist?"

The smallest grin tugged one corner of my mouth. "Sounds like you've read Jeffery Deaver."

The popular author had a series in which the main character made a living by seeking missing persons rewards and called himself a rewardist. Sometimes that was what we did. Sometimes the reference helped explain our business model. But no matter how small the distinction, the terms didn't feel the same.

"I've been listening to one of his books between patients at work. Probably why it's taking me forever to get through it, but I'm really enjoying it and the narrator is phenomenal," she said, her lips curling at the ends.

Damn dimples. I gritted my teeth as my pulse charged and my cock stiffened. How could I have forgotten those soft dimples and the way they framed her full lips? The sight dragged me right back to the painful state of arousal she'd inflicted when she hugged me. *Uncontrollable and unexpected.*

Cassius had raised us to be prepared for the unexpected, but I was having to accept there was no preparing for her. No preparing for how *not in control* I was of my desire around her.

I cleared my throat and then kept talking, hoping to curb my currently unmetered response. "We take jobs. We retrieve people. Things. Information. It doesn't always come with that kind of reward," I explained. "So . . . retrievalist."

"Fair." Her head bobbed. "So then how do you go from prelaw to retrievalist?"

Normally, I ended this story at the beginning: that growing up survivalist had made becoming a retrievalist an easy and profitable career choice. It was a clean, simple answer: *Nothing could get messy if you didn't let people in.* But talking to Lara, being around her, the things it did to me . . . It was all the very definition of *messy*. And that was how the truth slipped out.

"Creed, my younger brother, was in the military police. He suffered a head injury on a mission and was recovering at Walter Reed, and one day, something triggered his PTSD and he disappeared from the hospital. Just gone . . . without a trace." I hit the blinker, turning onto the local highway. We were still about five minutes out from the diner. "I dropped everything to find him. It took me six weeks, but I finally tracked him down. He'd made it through three states and couldn't remember what happened, how he got there, or why he'd gone."

"Oh, wow."

Avoiding the sympathy in her gaze was a trap, one that diverted my focus to the distracting O of her mouth and the smooth column of her throat as she swallowed. An ache unfurled from the center of my chest. A craving for something I couldn't want. Not then. Not now.

Dammit. I forced my stare back to the road and finished the story. "He was okay. Physically. He just needed a familiar, quieter place to recuperate."

"You searched for him on your own?"

When she looked out the window, I shifted carefully in my seat to ease some of my discomfort. *Apparently, I was thirty-three going on thirteen.*

"It was better that way," I grunted, forcing my guard back up. "What's that saying about too many cooks in the kitchen . . . ?"

My siblings and I had been raised to be lone wolves, that was true, but not the answer to her question.

I'd gone looking for Creed on my own because Colton was in prison, Callum was chasing a storm, and Creighton and Colby were still in high school. My only other resource would've been Cassius, and he wouldn't have been a resource, but a ticking time bomb. After Mom's death, his severe caution had morphed into straight paranoia, and I hadn't been sure what actions he would take or lengths he would go to to find his son.

But none of that was anything Lara needed to know.

"I brought Creed back to the ranch, and over the course of the next couple of months, people I'd met during my search began contacting me. A nurse from Walter Reed whose husband went missing. A sheriff from Virginia who didn't have the resources to help parents looking for their runaway son. A lawyer from Tennessee whose witness disappeared in a Mob case. They offered me rewards to find people the same way I'd found Creed. I had no desire to go back to law, so I agreed."

"And brought your siblings along for the ride?"

I arched an amused brow. "Do you think anyone brings any of the Stones 'along for the ride'?"

Her expression scrunched and she shook her head. "No."

"Creed got stir-crazy and liked the idea of being constantly on the move. The rest of them eventually ended up in the fold for one reason or another." My hand tightened on the steering wheel as I held back that almost every reason was traumatic. "All of us except Colby. She does her own thing, unless you count her knack for *retrieving* every injured animal on the property."

"Ahh, so you *are* still in the cat-rescuing business."

The tension broke, a low chuckle rumbling from my chest. "Retrieving business," I corrected lightly. "And no, I think that retrieval was a one-time deal."

"An exception to your rules?"

My gaze collided with her bright-green one, and all lightness evaporated, dispersed by the bolt of heat that went straight to my groin.

"Yeah," came my hoarse agreement as I turned into the Antlers Diner. "An exception."

Like everything else about her . . . and what she did to me.

The parking lot was dotted with only a few cars, the lunch crowd mostly cleared out as expected. After swinging the Toyota into a spot near the entrance, I killed the engine and turned to Lara.

"I know the owners, Ron and Teddy, so let me handle the questions." I sounded sterner than I'd intended, but it was for the best. *For business.* Better to set the tone now than when we were inside and emotions could take hold.

Lara's eyes pinched ever so slightly, but I got out of the car before she could argue.

I didn't let family members or friends or whoever had hired me come along on the case; the risks and overall hinderances were too numerous to count. So bringing Lara here was definitely an exception—*another one*—to my rule, but I told myself it was a calculated one.

In spite of her fears, there was no evidence to suggest something bad had happened to Rachel. So if a few questions to the right people could put this search to rest, then I could have Colby come get me and Lara could leave without needing to return to the ranch. *Without planting her memory in any more corners of my life.* As it was, it would take another decade—or longer—to erase the feel of her softness pressed to my chest.

I reached the entrance, eyeing the old security camera above the door that swung open to a familiar chime. I'd stopped at countless diners all over the country, and I swore that bell was the same in every one. Maybe that chime was legally required to put *diner* in your name.

"Thanks," Lara murmured as I held the door and then followed her inside.

On instinct, I took a quick scan of the room.

Rule #27: Know your exits before you need them and any threats before they become one.

The building had three exits—the main entrance and two rear doors—plus basement access through the kitchen with BILCO doors on the right side of the building. And in an emergency, any of the front windows could also be broken and climbed through.

On the ceiling, the security cameras collected dust on their covers, the system still the original from when they opened. I did a second sweep of the space, charting every person inside despite doubting any immediate threat; feelings were rarely a good indication of fact.

An older gentleman sat at the very end of the counter, sipping coffee and watching TV. In the perimeter booths, an elderly couple enjoyed a late lunch, and a family of four, on vacation, had their park maps spread over the table in the booth next to them. The middle-aged waitress, her blond hair like a pouf of cotton candy on her head, pointed to a spot on the map, likely giving them a recommendation.

I went to check the kitchen next, but my attention snagged on Lara's profile, her head tilted up and her jaw slack as she looked around.

How was it that over a decade later, I still couldn't stop myself from staring?

I gave my head a small shake and walked around her to the counter just as a familiar face came through the swinging door.

"Calder." Ron greeted me with a gap-toothed smile, wiping his hands on the towel slung over his shoulder before extending one over the counter. "Good to see you. It's been a while."

"Good to see you, too. How's Teddy?" I shook his hand firmly and then angled my back to the wall.

"Oh, good. Keeping busy—keeping me busy running around." Ron cocked his head toward his better half, whom I'd already tagged in the kitchen.

Ron and Teddy were restaurateurs from California who'd taken an early retirement, moved out here, and then came out of retirement to open up a quality local diner. The Antlers, however, looked anything but local once you stepped inside.

The place was covered from floorboard to ceiling with every piece of gaudy antler decor you could find. Chandeliers. Sconces. Table lamps. Wall decor. Wallpaper. It was all antlers, everywhere. However, while they stretched the definition of *local*, Ron and Teddy had succeeded in their quest for quality. The food here was pretty damn good, and it was a favorite takeout spot for Colton and Creighton. Neither of them liked to cook, and in Cassius's house, you ate what was made for you or you fended for yourself.

"Who's this you've got with you? Finally settling down?"

Shit. I stiffened. "No, nothing like—"

"I'm Lara Crane." My no-longer-silent partner stepped to my side, flashing a wide smile. "I'm a friend of Calder's."

Friend was quite an overstatement of what we were and an understatement of what the lower parts of me wanted to be.

"Lara. So nice to meet you. Can I get you both something to drink? To eat?" Ron instantly went into host mode.

"I wish we were here for pleasure." I spoke too quickly, grimacing at my word choice. "Unfortunately, we're looking for Lara's sister. She hasn't been able to get a hold of her for a few weeks, and we're just trying to make sure she's okay. When Lara last spoke to her, she was here eating lunch, so I was wondering if I could ask you and your staff some questions."

"Oh, jeez. That's terrible." Ron's expression sobered. "Of course. Anything you need."

Reaching for my cell, I caught a slight ripple of tension that went through Lara, her worried gaze quickly turning away. Maybe I should've asked her to wait in the car.

Yeah, she never would've agreed to that.

"Rachel was here on the fourth with this man." I opened the photo of Brandon and showed it to him.

Ron pulled his bright-red glasses from his head onto his nose, took my phone, and squinted. "The fourth, you said?"

I nodded.

"What day . . ." He trailed off and turned to the calendar on the wall behind him. Looking over the rim of his readers, he scanned the dates. "The fourth was a Friday. I had a feeling . . . Marlene!" he hollered across the restaurant.

The waitress who was chatting with the family in the booth looked up, and he waved her over.

"Thursdays and Fridays, we have Marlene working the tables so I can help Teddy in the kitchen. If anyone saw him, it was probably her—Marlene." He put his hand on her shoulder and pointed to me with the hand still holding my phone. "This is Calder Stone. His family lives up the way a bit, and he's looking for a friend of his."

"Nice to meet you, Marlene."

She beamed. "Pleasure to meet you, darlin'."

"Do you remember this man?" Ron pushed the phone in front of her face. "He would've been in about three weeks—"

"Oh, I remember him," she cut in, all the warmth with which she'd greeted me pushed out with a loud huff and barricaded away by the defensive fold of her arms. If that hadn't made her opinion of Brandon clear, the scowl on her face spelled out, in all capitals, her dislike. "He's the one I told you about. Sent back his eggs three times during the lunch rush, all so I'd have to take it off his bill—and then didn't even leave a tip."

Great.

"I do remember you mentioning," Ron muttered, handing back my phone with a shake of his head.

Trading my phone for my notebook from my pocket, I flipped the worn cover open to the marked page. Usually these notebooks averaged a five-case fill rate, depending on how involved they were and how many notes I took. For everyone's sake, I hoped Rachel's situation wouldn't be more than a footnote on a single sheet.

"Did he pay with a credit card?"

"Yes."

"Ron, could you—"

"Pull the charge from that day?" he finished eagerly. "Sure thing." He disappeared into the kitchen, a man on a mission.

Giving Marlene a smile, I clicked my pen. "Do you remember the woman he was with?"

The waitress pinched her red lips. "I do. Sweet-looking thing. Had the same green eyes as your friend here, and I remember because they looked just like my little niece's, and I told her that when she was sitting at the table."

Lara instantly drifted closer to my side, drawn to the recollection of her sister, and my muscles braced like they would for a fight—for a threat. *Maybe that was what she was. Not an exception to my rules, but a threat to my sanity.*

"Do you remember overhearing where they were going or what their plans were?" I pressed the pen to the paper, digging the black ink into a dot.

"Oh, no." Her head moved side to side so furiously, I was surprised we didn't hear something crack. "After he sent the eggs back the third time, I kept my distance and my quiet. Once my mouth opens, there's a good chance this baby won't stop, and the things I wanted to say to that man . . . Phew." She fanned herself with her hand, getting worked up over the memory.

"And the woman he was with, she didn't mention anything?"

Marlene's anger deflated in an instant, the very definition of someone who was controlled by their emotions. Fuming fury one moment and then abject pity the next.

"Oh, no. She was so sweet. Pulled me aside and kept apologizing for him sending the eggs back." As Marlene spoke, I clicked off my pen, growing less and less confident in the fruitfulness of this conversation. "She even tried to give me some cash for a tip from her purse, but I told her to keep it. Almost told her to use it to get herself a new man, but she had to rush outside because he was getting loud with the police in the parking lot."

I stilled. Maybe this was going somewhere after all.

One of the more fascinating aspects of the retrieval business was the wide berth in people's definitions of *important*. The things they thought were significant to tell me and the critical details they brushed off as unessential. *Like sharing that Brandon sent back his eggs three times, but not that he ended up in an argument with the police.* It was why I relied so heavily on observation, detailed questions, and following only facts I could prove.

"The police were here?" It was my next question, but it wasn't my voice.

I gritted my teeth, watching as Lara ignored my instruction and injected herself into the conversation. She didn't even wait for Marlene to answer before bombarding her with more questions.

"Why were the police called? Was it because of Brandon?"

This was why I didn't bring loved ones along, especially when that loved one was used to being at the center of deduction—medical deduction, but deduction nonetheless.

This wasn't the emergency room, and Lara wasn't the one treating this case. I was. And it was for the exact same reasons that family members weren't allowed in an operating room; her emotions were the kind of thing that could derail the surgical precision of my search.

"Oh, no, dear. Harry and Shelton were in here for lunch."

"Harry Stokes and Shelton Boone are part of the Jackson police force," I interjected, jotting their names in my notebook.

Harry and Shelton were stand-up cops and had known my family from back when Colton had been arrested. They were some of the solid few who didn't get territorial when we were hired to supplement a missing persons investigation, or insulted when we came up with more leads that panned out than they did. In fact, last I knew, Creighton still consulted with them on certain police cases.

"Here you go, Calder." The swinging door thumped forward and back as Ron came through it, his hand held high, a piece of notepaper suspended between his fingers. "I pulled the charge. The card belonged to a Brandon Westman."

I scratched the name into my notebook, copying the spelling from Ron's paper. "Thanks, Ron." I motioned that he could throw the note away; I had the information where I needed it. "Marlene, you said Brandon was getting loud with the police. Could you describe what you saw exactly in the parking lot?"

There was little point in asking her whether she'd heard what they were saying. Even if she'd been standing near the door where we were now, there was still a concert of other sounds going on around her. Cooking from the kitchen. The customers' conversations. The radio. The TV. Add to that the physical barrier of the building and then, during a busy lunch hour, a reasonable distance to where Brandon would've literally parked, there was no way whatever Marlene thought she'd heard was reliable.

"Oh, I didn't see much except the yelling."

No point in correcting her that one couldn't "see" yelling.

"Where were they standing? Close to the building? Farther away?"

"Oh, they were going back and forth by a camper parked at the very front of the lot by the road. The young man was hollerin', and the police were pointing to the camper; maybe they were arguin' about that, I can't be sure."

"Thank you so much, Marlene." I jotted down *camper*, underlined it twice, and then flipped my notebook closed. "You've been so helpful. We really appreciate it." I flashed her a quick smile and then waved at the owner. "You, too, Ron. Good seeing you."

"Anytime, Calder. Don't be a stranger."

My hand was on the door when Lara called, "Wait, Calder—"

I didn't stop or even slow my stride into the parking lot. There was no more information to be gleaned from Marlene, though emotion would drive a person to believe they could draw water from a stone. *No pun intended.*

I had fished my cell from my pocket, starting a message to my brother, when Lara's hand landed on my arm. *Unexpected.* I jerked away—*uncontrollably*—catching the flash of hurt in her gaze before she wiped it clean.

Dammit. I wasn't trying to be a dick, but my dick was being a dick every time she came close. And every time she touched me, it only got worse.

"That's it?" Lara demanded, her arms swinging wide. "Don't you want to see security footage? They have cameras around the building. One of them might have the license plate of the camper—"

"Lara, enough," I stopped her, my voice more growl than tenor. "Reverse the roles. How would you feel if I came into your emergency room and started questioning how you do your job?"

She blanched and bundled her arms over her front.

"You're right." Her throat bobbed. "I do know what it's like when patients and Dr. Google try to tell me how to do my job. It's just . . . my sister." Her voice broke at the end, and she turned away before letting her shoulders sag. *Like she didn't want me to see the weight she carried.*

An unfamiliar tightness banded around my chest as I watched her walk aimlessly away from me.

Lara was used to being the responsible one. The caretaker. Something she'd been long before she became a doctor. I recognized the trait because I felt the same for all my siblings, especially after what had happened to Mom; I felt responsible in a way that went too deep to be healthy. For all the years Lara had spent looking out for her sister, caring for her mom and then for her patients, when was the last time someone had cared for her? *When had she last trusted someone to care for her?*

"Lara."

She turned her head slightly over her shoulder, but not far enough to meet my gaze. I had a feeling if she had, I'd see the tears bottled in her eyes.

"I'm good at what I do, and I'm going to find Rachel. I promise." I heard myself carelessly break another rule. I never promised results. Not in this business. Not ever. It was for all the reasons easy to imagine, and yet I'd just made another exception. For her.

"I'm sorry," Lara murmured, running her hands up and down the sides of her arms, though there was no chill in the air.

A different kind of frustration bubbled against my skin. The urge to kiss her, to coax her mouth open and drain the tension from her body, hit me. *Unexpectedly.*

Shit.

"It's all right," I grunted and returned to my text, watching in my periphery as she moved a few paces away.

I quickly tapped out Brandon's name and sent it through to Callum. After two years of working with me, my brother knew exactly what information I needed and just how to get it.

When I looked up, Lara had started a slow 360 spin, scanning the parking lot like there were clues to be found if she just looked hard enough.

My gut clenched. Was this what everyone who hired me felt like while I worked? Or was it only her because she was here with me now?

Whatever the answer, I didn't like the heavy yoke of helplessness settled on her shoulders. I more than didn't like it. I felt a sear of anger burning through me, like I'd do anything to stop it.

So I did.

"Lara," I called before I could stop myself, and a second later twin green orbs glittered at me. "The security cameras—the brand, the model is cloud storage only, which holds footage for a maximum of two weeks, so whatever they captured would've already been overwritten." I cleared my throat, not used to having to explain my process, let alone *wanting* to. "To store anything older, they'd need a dedicated physical server in the diner." Which they clearly didn't have.

There wasn't reason to say more except her strain started to ease. Her shoulders softened and she looked at me with the same swell of gratitude that had propelled her to hug me. And like an itch that needed to be scratched, I wanted to push her to that place again. *The place where she couldn't stop herself from reaching for me.*

"I sent Brandon's information to Callum," I continued. "He'll be able to find any vehicles registered to him, including the camper."

"What about the police? Are you going to call and find out what they were talking to Brandon about?"

My cell started to vibrate, and I gave her a single "hold on" finger as I picked up the call.

"Hey, Callum," I answered, feeling Lara get closer to my back.

My brother's terse voice sped through the information. "Brandon Westman has two vehicles registered to his name. A 2008 Ford pickup and a Timberleaf camper. The Ford was tagged a few weeks ago for an expired registration."

"Got it. So police flagged him for the expired tags on the truck," I confirmed loud enough for Lara to hear.

"Yeah . . ." Callum grunted; it wasn't like me to repeat information back to him, but he wouldn't ask. For once, I was grateful for the dismal interest he held in anyone's life. "I also checked permits, and he paid for one three weeks ago at Bridger-Teton; his license plate registered as entering the park the day after it was flagged by the police as expired. The permit for the camper expires in three days, but he still hasn't upped the registration on the truck."

I hummed in thought. With expired tags, it was a safe bet Brandon would linger in the park as long as he could before renewing the registration or risking a fine rather than a warning from the police.

"Great. Thanks—"

"Calder, that wasn't the only permit that came up." Callum caught me as I turned back to Lara, about to hang up. "He also paid for a hunting permit for the park."

Shit.

"Got it," I replied flatly, holding Lara's increasingly narrow stare. "Anything else?"

"Don't go looking tonight. There's a storm coming." If Callum was warning me about it, then it was serious; he hadn't earned his nickname, the Daredevil, for nothing.

"Thanks—" The line went dead.

"What is it? What did he say?" Lara asked as soon as the phone vacated my ear.

"Brandon's plates on his truck were expired. That was what the police were arguing with him about." And thanks to Callum, I didn't need to make a second call to the precinct to find out more.

"Does he know where it is? Can he track it?"

"The model is too old for GPS, but Callum found a permit request to camp in the park, and a record of Brandon's license plate entering Bridger-Teton the day after Rachel called you."

"So he's in the park? They're in the park? Where do we—"

"His truck and camper entered the park," I interrupted, keeping my tone level in hopes it would steady hers. "His permit is good for another few days, which makes it likely he's still there but not a guarantee."

"But if he is . . ."

"There are only so many sites that allow campers to park—"

"So we'll start with those—"

"Lara." A frustrated growl edged from my chest. "I'll check out all the campsites first thing tomorrow and let you know what I find."

"No." She fired the word at me, suddenly pacing like a caged animal. "I'm going with you. If Rachel is with him, I need to be there—"

"You're not going to be there." I'd thought my tone was nonnegotiable, yet she didn't back down.

She strode right up to me and lifted her chin, her delicate features sharpened with determination. "Fine, then. I'll start the search by myself."

She lurched to walk around me, but I grabbed her arm to stop her. "Dammit, Lara. Brandon has a hunting permit for the park."

The anger that had colored her cheeks now drained completely, her freckles standing out like dark stars against a pale night. "So he has a gun," she inferred, all her determination hollowed out from her voice.

Without thinking, I stepped closer, the heat of our bodies colliding in the almost nonexistent space separating us. Lara's tongue darted out, the pink tip sliding along her lips. My eyes followed it as if it were a red flag waved in front of a bull. A dare to stop her. *To kiss her.*

I released her arm like I'd touched a hot stove. *No, a stove would've burned less.*

"It's a safe assumption."

Lara's head swayed, her eyes going vacant for a second. The danger was enough to make her pause and think, but inevitably not enough to stop her.

"I can't *not* be there, Calder. Not if Rachel is with him," she insisted.

"And I need you to let me do my job." *And let me do it alone.*

"If you find her, I don't know that she'll trust you. That she'll go with you," she countered just as firmly.

Shit. I'd never encountered a case where a missing person didn't want to be rescued. But then again, I'd never searched for a missing ex-girlfriend before.

I wanted to promise it would all work out, but the tenuous end of my relationship with Rachel made me hesitate. Would a dozen years be enough to dull any lingering anger she harbored for me? *Maybe,* if she was being held against her will. *But if she wasn't?*

"All right. Take your car and meet me here tomorrow morning at eight," I said, rubbing my hand on the back of my neck. Unfortunately, I didn't trust her not to go searching for Brandon on her own if I didn't agree to something right now.

"Wait, why not tonight?"

As if on cue, Callum's warning personified into a growl of thunder above us, storm clouds clawing through the fabric of the wide-open sky.

Lara looked up just as a heavy raindrop landed on her nose, the cold burst making it wrinkle. Seconds later, thousands of them darkened the pavement.

Taking her arm again, I propelled her toward her rental.

"You can't track them in a thunderstorm?" she demanded when we reached the driver's-side door.

"If we had information that she was in imminent danger, I would, but we don't, so going out in this is reckless, not a rescue."

Rule #3: Nature doesn't care about ego. The moment you underestimate it is the moment it will kill you.

The prelude of rain ended, and with a boom that shook the ground, the skies opened to the full production of the downpour. Cursing, I threw open the door and bundled her into the car, shouting, "Tomorrow morning," before closing her inside.

Sprinting back into the diner, I stopped just inside the door and stared through the glass. Somehow I found Lara's gaze through the onslaught of raindrops.

I might have been unwilling to underestimate nature, but I had a gnawing suspicion I was severely underestimating my desire for my ex-girlfriend's younger sister . . . and the danger I was in by continuing to be around her.

Chapter 5

Lara

I'd forgotten the bigness of Wyoming's wilderness. The vast saffron plains that spread endlessly. The scabrous viridian-swathed mountains that stretched limitlessly tall. The lightless midnights that boasted the galaxy's trove of stars. But the storms . . .

I'd forgotten more how summer thunderstorms rolled in at the end of every day like a curtain call of thunderous applause shearing the sky's serenity. Last night's storm hadn't woken me, but instead kept me company, its tumultuous trembling equal to the turmoil of my thoughts.

My sister was missing. Maybe she was in the park. Maybe she was okay.

Maybe she wasn't.

Worries deluged into fear. *What if I was too late? What if I hadn't done enough? What if I lost her for all the reasons I'd lost Ian?*

Twelve years from now, I'd still lie awake at night searching for all the signs I'd missed. All the things I could've done. All the ways I'd failed Ian Mercer as his doctor that day. *All the ways I worried I was now going to fail my sister.*

There was no escaping the feeling of helplessness that snapped taut like a tether twining my past to my present. It was why I'd been desperate to go with Calder to the park.

I needed to be part of this. I needed to be doing something to save her. And maybe . . . just a little bit . . . I needed Calder's steadiness to hold on to my sanity.

The sound of tires on gravel caught my attention, and I checked my phone. *Eight o'clock on the dot.*

I pushed off the hood of my rental as a black F-350 drove through the diner's parking lot and stopped behind the Toyota.

The window rolled down, revealing the same grim expression Calder had left with yesterday. *And the same rush of heat I felt every time I saw him, grim faced or not.*

"Good morning." The straight seal of his lips twitched.

"Morning," I greeted, holding his gaze for a second before I looked away.

Calder was nothing if not perceptive, and I didn't want him to see the dark circles around my eyes, because there was a strong chance he wouldn't just see exhaustion under my eyes, but the emotional evisceration that had caused it. I couldn't afford to give him more ammunition for why I shouldn't be going with him today.

"Ready? We'll take my truck."

My eyes cut back to him, his eyes narrowed enough to unnerve me. "Yeah, I just want to grab another coffee before we go."

I'd already had one cup before leaving the Betty B and B that morning, but I needed more. Preferably poured directly into my sleep-deprived eyes, but the usual absorption method would have to do.

"Lara," Calder called, stopping me before I even turned. "I made you a French press."

He held up a travel mug from inside the cab, and my jaw went slack. *He'd brought me coffee?*

My exhausted emotions tangled further. That was Calder. Honorable to a fault. Thoughtful to a fault. *Even when frustrated with me.* It was hard to both admire and abhor qualities that in this moment made me feel warm and protected, but a dozen years ago had torn my sister's heart apart.

In spite of all my anxieties last night, Calder hadn't been one of them. I hadn't worried that he wasn't going to show up this morning. I hadn't worried that he'd go to the park without me. I hadn't worried because he'd given me his word, which was as unbreakable as stone. Literally.

There was only one worry I had about him. One thing that had woken me for different reasons and consumed my mind like a fever dream: the way my body responded when Calder was near and the way I fantasized about him when he wasn't.

Calder cleared his throat, bringing me back to the moment. "I like Ron, but their coffee isn't as good as mine."

No, I imagined with all his gadgets and timers, it wasn't.

"Got it."

I locked my rental and rounded Calder's truck, climbing into the passenger seat.

With my purse in my lap, I buckled in, noting the back seat was taken up with utility duffel bags; only the first aid bag, red with a white cross, was readily distinguishable, though I could hazard a few educated guesses as to the kinds of survival gear in the others.

"Which one is mine?" I asked, pointing to the two travel cups in the console.

"Back one." Calder spun the wheel and steered out of the lot.

Dorsal venous arch. Dorsal metacarpal veins.

I grabbed my cup and brought it to my lips, forcing my eyes shut as I downed the first welcome sip.

Stop thinking about Calder's anatomy. There wasn't a test. Not when the answer to every question would simply be *wrong.* Wrong to think about my sister's ex. Wrong to fantasize. Wrong to want. *Wrong to everything.*

The diesel engine growled as we headed toward Grand Teton National Park. The tops of the iconic mountains propped up the morning blanket of clouds like poles to a circus tent, the bright-blue sky underneath holding no trace of the ugly storm that had swept through last night.

"How was your night?" Calder asked stiffly, his eyes on the road.

"All right," I answered as a speed limit sign flew by. Two, actually. Another thing I'd forgotten about Wyoming. There were two speed limit signs posted inside the park: one for during the day, and one for after dark.

"Storm keep you up?"

"Yeah," I lied. "I forgot how bad they can be."

They always said that to become a doctor, especially an ER doc, you acquired the ability to sleep anywhere, anytime, and it was true. Two weeks ago, I would've slept through a storm like that without any problem. Now, every time I tried to sleep, I was back in the emergency room, staring at that man's face, feeling a kind of panic like I'd never known.

I had to wonder whether I'd ever be able to sleep well again.

I went to put my cup back in the holder just as Calder reached for his. Our hands brushed, the hot static stumbling the pattern of my pulse. Our eyes connected with a bolt of lightning that split wide all my thoughts for him to see.

"Sorry." I quickly pulled away before he saw too much.

I'd prepared for a gamut of emotions yesterday on the way to see Calder. I'd prepared for anxiety and uncertainty over whether he'd be able or willing to help me. I'd also prepared for anger and distrust. For the twelve years since they'd broken up, I'd watched my sister's romantic relationships devolve and destroy her. She might not have told me every detail of what had happened, but I saw enough of the aftermath to prepare for more than a modicum of resentment toward the one good man who'd broken her heart.

But I hadn't prepared for everything else.

Not the tingling in my skin, like his gaze inebriated my nerves. Not the uneven unspooling of my pulse whenever we touched, nor the warmth in my veins as though my body were fighting an infection—a disease of inappropriate desire. And definitely not the way I trusted him. Instinctively. *Wildly.*

"The storms get worse as the summer goes on," he remarked. "Where are you staying?"

"The Betty bed-and-breakfast in Wisdom."

Calder made a sound of acknowledgment, one I assumed was an approval, since he said nothing else. The Betty was adorable. Quiet. And only about twenty minutes to Jackson. The owners were an older couple. Very welcoming and sweet. Hopefully, they didn't hear my cries that always woke me from my nightmares.

I sat up taller, quickly compartmentalizing those thoughts as the large sign for the Moose Entrance flew by. "Wasn't that what we wanted?" My head swiveled to follow the turn-off.

"No," Calder replied and then paused, giving me a front-row seat to his internal debate over how much to explain. "There are three entrances to the park, and a campsite within range of each, but there are only two designated areas for elk hunting close to the park. Zones seventy-five and seventy-nine. Seventy-five is to the right of us but back closer to the Moose Entrance. Zone seventy-nine is farther north than the Moran Entrance, which is where we're headed."

"You think he's staying at one of those two because he has a hunting permit," I mused, my fingers drumming on the to-go cup. "Why start at the north one?"

It would've been easy to stop and check the one we'd just passed on the way.

"The Moose Entrance is the main entrance. The busiest and the most patrolled by rangers. With an expired registration on his truck—"

"It would be riskier," I finished, a thrill running through me when he nodded.

"Track the person, not just their footprints," he instructed with a low voice. "Understanding the mindset of your target usually reveals where to look next."

Another rule.

I took another swig from my cup. Calder's thought process was as satisfying as his coffee. It was sharp without being bitter. Smooth without being watered down. It was a treat. *An anomaly.*

"Do you think Brandon's that smart?" I dragged my tongue over my lips.

Calder's *masseter* flexed, his beard rippling. "I think people who regularly brush up against the law get pretty smart on ways to avoid it."

"He's been in trouble before?" I straightened, unease resting on my shoulders. "Did you talk to the police?"

Calder's knuckles whitened where he gripped the wheel. "Minor stuff. Mostly parking violations and a few charges for possession."

"Drugs?" I croaked.

"Just marijuana, but it's illegal here, so he was tagged for it."

My exhale escaped with just a little bit of tension.

Calder hit his blinker and let off the gas, approaching the Moran Entrance. Every time he turned the wheel one-handed, I stared for just a second too long and clenched my thighs a little tighter.

"Did you check his record because of me? Because I insisted on coming with you?" I had to be the reason for the added caution.

"I checked because the information changed," he said, his smooth voice filling the weighty silence as he drove through the lot, following signs for campground parking. "Confronting a man who is camping with expired tags is different than confronting a man with a weapon. Tracking a person means knowing your target, and if Brandon has a license to carry, I needed to know if he'd ever used that weapon in ways that were problematic with the law. Weapons charges. Assault."

"Oh."

Calder's attention flicked to my mouth when the sound escaped, and then snapped back. "But yeah, I also wanted to confirm I wasn't putting you in unreasonable danger by bringing you with me."

I put a pause on the conversation as we entered the next clearing, the perimeter of the tree-lined lot dotted with campers of all shapes and sizes. "What kind of camper does he have?"

Calder slowed to let an older couple cross the lot in front of us; they waved their thanks, their hiking poles tethered to their wrists.

"Timberleaf teardrop camper. Wyoming plates 23R9-V9," he recalled without missing a beat, and continued forward.

I scanned each passing vehicle on the right, while Calder took the left. Spot after spot passed, none with the right size or shape vehicle, and no one who remotely resembled the barrel-chested, bearded man who'd grabbed my sister's phone to curse at me.

The slow thump of my heartbeat rolled almost to a complete stop when we reached the far end of the lot with no luck.

"And if I was in unreasonable danger? If Brandon did have a history of violence?" I couldn't help but ask, my frustration peaked at the precipice of another failed lead.

"Then you wouldn't be here," he said and drove into the secondary lot marked as overflow.

Anger lashed like a hot whip on my spine. *He would've left me behind even though he'd agreed.*

"You would've gone back on your word?"

"The only word I gave was to meet me at the diner at eight."

My mouth opened, but no sound came out. He was right. He hadn't promised I could come; I'd only assumed.

"You don't have to like the way I do things, Lara, but you do have to understand why." The piercing look in his eyes gutted me. "I will never agree to something that could put you in danger. Ever. I won't spare your feelings at the expense of your safety."

It was the greatest unfairness, when chivalry could feel cruel.

"There."

My head snapped forward, all argument forgotten as I zeroed in on the rust-scarred pickup in the farthest corner of the overflow lot; hitched behind it, the teardrop camper was backed discreetly into the woods, shielding it almost completely from view. *Along with its expired registration tags.*

Calder slowed and pulled off to the side, making sure it was his door that was closest to Brandon's truck.

He turned to me, the hard angles of his face even more severe. *Even more beautiful.* "Violent record or not, once we're out of the truck, you do exactly as I say, understood?"

Goose bumps spread over my skin. It was a question but not a request. In the hospital, I was responsible for every choice. Every decision. I was the one calling the shots. But not here. Not with him. I'd unpack why that wasn't as unnerving as it should be later.

I nodded mutely, and he continued. "Even if Rachel is there, Lara, if Brandon is hostile, I need you to still obey me."

The way he said "obey" made me shiver for all the wrong reasons, the tremble severe enough to make my chin dip.

Calder growled, "I need to hear you say it."

"I understand," I confirmed, my breathless response spurring him into action.

Without pausing, he reached across me and extracted something from the glove compartment—*his weapon.* Lifting the back of his shirt, he clipped the gun in its holster to his waistband and then flipped his jacket over it, concealing it from sight.

He opened the door and climbed down from the truck, gravel crunching under his feet, while I sat there reeling from his sequence of movements that was, quite possibly, one of the hottest things I'd ever seen. *Right up there with the one-handed turn of the steering wheel.*

Realizing just how crazy that thought was, I scrambled out and around the back of the truck, almost running into Calder.

His face, a mask of focus, didn't even falter. "Stay behind me," he instructed quietly and gave me his back.

We approached Brandon's truck from an angle. It was hard to see much from behind him, but I realized Calder kept a very specific, tight path where there wouldn't be a clear view of us, either through the front windshield or the side window.

We were a few paces away when Calder tilted his head and reported, "Truck's empty."

An exhale blew through my lips, though I couldn't say it was with relief.

He confirmed through the driver's window and then headed for the trailer, stopping at the hitch.

"Wait here."

My feet immediately stopped, my eyes darting around the trees like I expected Brandon to jump out from the brush. Wind swished through the leaves. A pair of birds cooed a morning melody in duet. But every sound, even the soothing ones, set my pulse further on edge.

Steady, I cautioned, grappling for the mental tools I deployed in the hospital to excavate adrenaline and metabolize it into a purposeful calm.

My breathing slowed and my focus lasered in on Calder as he made his way to the camper's door. Avoiding the small window with a larger stride, he tactically positioned himself between the window and the door, his back flat to the exterior panel.

While there was no reason to expect Brandon to be hostile, Calder wasn't taking any chances. Keeping his body away from the door, he reached out and knocked firmly. "Brandon Westman?"

My heart thumped, the following silence like a ticking bomb.

"Brandon?" Calder said and knocked louder. "Anyone home?"

The birds flew out of the tree. Branches snapped like the cracking of knuckles preparing for a fight. Leaves crunched in the tightening fist of footsteps.

I gasped and Calder looked back at me, the moment freezing us in its thrill, when a rough voice shouted from the trees.

"Hey! What the hell are you doing? Get the fuck away from my camper!"

Brandon.

The beard. The same flannel shirt. The bitter snarl. I'd seen him only for a few seconds, but I instantly recognized him.

He stalked out of the woods wearing sweatpants and a pair of Crocs, and if I had to guess, we'd arrived at his camper just as he'd gone to relieve himself.

Heart pounding, I whipped my eyes over him, looking for any sign of a gun and coming up empty. *Hopefully.*

"Brandon Westman?" Calder asked calmly, stepping slowly away from the man's door so as not to startle him, one hand lifted to signal peace.

"Who the hell are you?" he sneered, looking every bit the bully as he lumbered closer.

"I'm Calder Stone, and this is Lara," Calder answered, his voice steady, as though he were talking down a wild animal. His raised hand lowered, the other resting on his hip close enough to his weapon in case the *talking down* didn't go as planned. "We're looking for Rachel Crane. Is she with you?"

"Rach—" He stopped with a curse, planting his hands on his hips, which quickly disappeared under the roll of his stomach. "Is that what she told you? Fucking cunt—"

I stiffened, my teeth sinking into my tongue to stop myself from speaking.

"Mr. Westman, is Rachel Crane with you?" Calder demanded again, the edge of his tone cutting through Brandon's labored breathing.

"Does it look like she's with me?" His gaze swung between us like the unsteady gait of a drunk. "And who the fuck are you, and why do you—" He broke off, his eyes locked on me.

I felt the second he recognized me the way anesthetic hits a nerve—the instant tingling. The paralysis. The buzz of epinephrine. Adrenaline in my veins.

"You. You're the bitch sister I talked to that day." He pivoted and started in my direction. I backpedaled instinctively until my shoulders collided with his truck. "You're the reason she turned into a cunt—"

"Hey!" Calder's shout detonated through the clearing.

Moving in the span of a single blink, Calder put himself between Brandon and me, flattening his palm on Brandon's chest like a wall not to cross. "Mr. Westman." His voice rumbled with a threatening kind of calm. "You smell like a growhouse, and your registration is still expired, so either I make some calls and get you in more trouble or you tell me where Rachel Crane is."

"Fuck you." Brandon knocked Calder's arm aside and shoved him like this was some high school playground and he was going to give Calder a beating. Calder stepped back and steadied himself. "I don't have to tell you a fucking thing about that cunt," Brandon spat, and then he swung.

"Calder!" I couldn't stop my warning, but he didn't need it.

Calder easily ducked out of the path of Brandon's fist. Using the momentum of the attack, he grabbed the back of Brandon's shirt and propelled him into the side of his camper. There was a sickening thud, followed by a roar of pain and a definite dent left in the metal exterior.

"Fuck, man. *Fuck.* I think . . . you broke my fucking nose!"

Brandon didn't get a chance to stumble or collapse to the ground before Calder was behind him, wrenching one of his arms behind his back and pinning him to the camper with a forearm wedged to the back of his neck.

His nose was definitely broken, the bulbous end angled unnaturally to the side of his face, blood streaming from his nostrils, but I kept my professional assessment quiet.

"Where is Rachel?" Calder demanded.

"She's not here," he snarled. "Go ahead and fucking look. My camper's open."

Calder jerked his gaze to me and nodded, a wordless instruction to check inside.

The handle was unlocked. A dense wave of marijuana hit me as soon as I opened the door and slammed me back to the hospital that day, the thick scent of pot oozing from every fiber of Ian's clothes.

Coughing, I covered my mouth with my sleeve and held my breath, choking off the memory as I looked inside.

There was a bed, bags of weed, smoking paraphernalia, and no sign of my sister.

"It's empty," I said, gulping in fresh air as the door shut.

"I fucking told you—ahh," Brandon whimpered as Calder lifted his arm and increased the strain on the man's shoulder. "Come on, man. I fucking told you—"

"When was the last time you saw Rachel?"

"I dunno. Two weeks ago, maybe?"

"Where?"

"Here."

"So she was here with you?"

"Yes, and then she fucking left me."

Left him. My breath hitched, my eyes connecting with Calder's. Maybe my sister had listened to what I'd told her that afternoon after all.

"Do you know where she went after she left?"

"Did you not fucking hear me? We broke up. Why the fuck would I know or care where she went after—ahh. Fuck, fuck, fuck!" Brandon rose on his toes, seeming desperate to escape the pressure Calder put on his arm, his shoulder on the brink of popping from its socket.

"I did hear you, Mr. Westman. However, you don't seem to be hearing me. You were the last person to see Rachel alive and alone in these woods. If you need me to spell out more clearly how bad that looks for you—"

"All right, fuck." Brandon spat, blood and spit running from his face down the side of his trailer. "I don't know where she went, but she left because she wanted us to go to some touchy-feely kumbaya retreat instead of coming here and hunting like I'd planned."

I moved closer, the threat of him nothing compared to the information he had. "What retreat?" I asked before I could stop myself, feeling the heat of Calder's warning stare.

"I don't fucking know." His lip curled, but he'd clearly learned his lesson, because he kept talking. "Some couples thing in the BLM around here. She tried to talk me into it, saying it would be good for our relationship, help us work things out." His voice took on a mocking whine. "I told her that bullshit was for pussies and there was no way in hell I was going. We argued. She said she'd go on her own and find a better man, and I said fine, because honestly her pussy was too fucking high maintenance anyway, and then she left. Haven't seen her since."

Red rimmed the edge of my vision, a shocking notion entering my mind: I wanted to do this man harm. Not lethal harm, but memorable harm, for the way he talked about my sister.

"Do you remember the name?" Calder demanded.

"Wilder something, or Wilderness . . . I don't fucking know. She had some brochure."

"Do you still have it?"

"No, she took that shit with her."

My chest tightened. It wasn't a complete loss, I reminded myself. We had an idea of where Rachel had gone. We could search online, find a list of the retreats around here—*Which would be innumerable, given the vast marketability of nature retreats in areas like this,* the pessimist inside me whispered.

"I don't know why the fuck you're asking me. Maybe you should ask the fucking waitress who gave her the brochure. She could tell you."

"Waitress?" Calder and I said in unison.

"Yeah, the bitch who couldn't get my eggs right thought she'd get back at me for not tipping by passing that shit to Rachel."

Marlene. Calder and I looked at each other, coming to the same simultaneous conclusion.

"All right, Mr. Westman. Thanks for your cooperation—"

"Fuck—"

"If you continue to go about your business here without further incident, I won't call the rangers and the police and tip them off to your activities," Calder threatened with an olive branch as he pulled Brandon off the camper.

"Wait." I put my hand on Calder's shoulder, stopping him from releasing Brandon. He glared. "I can't leave him like this."

Calder's stare hardened as I walked in front of Brandon. If he wanted to, he could have stopped me, but he didn't.

"Hold him still."

Brandon's beady brown eyes narrowed on me, full of hatred. "Your sister's a cunt."

I exhaled slowly. Do no harm. Giving him a fake smile, I reached for his face and replied, "And you're a very small man."

Brandon's shout shook through the forest as I reset his broken nose without warning.

Chapter 6

Calder

Rule #19: Never draw a weapon you don't intend to use or aim at anything you're not willing to kill.

"Why didn't Marlene tell us about the brochure?" Lara asked as soon as we reached the truck.

I slid my Glock 42 in its holster back into the glove compartment and hit the ignition. "We're going to find out."

"You didn't pull out your gun," she said, not bothering to hide her surprise.

"I didn't intend to use it," I countered. Shifting into reverse, I cupped her headrest and looked over my shoulder, catching her gaze along the way.

"Not even to warn him?"

"Never pull out a gun you don't intend to use or aim at anything you'd regret shooting."

Being homeschooled at Stonewall Ranch was different in a lot of ways. In addition to the basics, we got the . . . not-basics, including firearm lessons.

Cassius had been trained in Hōjutsu, the Japanese martial art of gunnery, so our lessons went beyond target practice. We started from the bottom. Everything from cleaning, assembling, disassembling, diagnosing problems, and repairing, all the way to tests on different kinds of rounds and which guns they were used for. And eventually, once Cassius was satisfied we'd mastered respect for the incredibly dangerous weapons, lessons on how to actually shoot them.

"You would've regretted shooting him?"

Lara wanted to sound serious, but she wasn't. The woman who couldn't stop herself from helping the man who'd called her sister a cunt about a half dozen times in the same number of minutes wasn't the type of person who could ever be serious about causing a person harm.

"The same way you would've regretted walking away without setting his nose. Sometimes what you want to do and the right thing to do aren't the same," I answered, and her eyes snapped to mine.

Suddenly, it felt like I was talking about a different kind of harm: the kind that came from wanting her and knowing I couldn't do anything about it.

"If I can avoid the hassle of discharging a firearm in a national park, I will," I continued roughly and drove us out of the lot, fighting against the tightness in my chest.

"You don't think there's any way he's lying, do you?" Lara picked up her coffee, gulping down several mouthfuls like it went beyond a pick-me-up into a hold-me-together.

"He's a lousy human being, but he wasn't lying," I said. "Why?"

"Just wondering."

My gaze flicked to the passenger seat. "Wondering" wouldn't have left a crease in her brow.

One of the more common hurdles in my line of work was when friends or loved ones refused to believe where the evidence led me. Normally, I (politely) ignored their emotional reactions because it had no bearing on my search. But in this case, it had a bearing on her, and that, I was having a hard time accepting, let alone ignoring.

"Is it the retreat? Do you think her wanting to go was out of character?"

"I'm not sure," Lara said, her gaze dropping to where her hands were knitted around her coffee cup. "A few weeks ago, I would've said yes. I'd told her—begged her—so many times to talk to someone, to try any kind of therapy because every one of her relationships has been worse than the last. But she wouldn't listen."

Even though there was no malice in her voice, guilt still pricked at the lining of my chest. Her sister's instability wasn't Lara's responsibility, but that wasn't what she needed to hear right now, especially coming from me.

"And now?"

She sighed. "Now I'm worried I finally got through to her and she signed up for something that was at best a scam and at worst . . ."

I couldn't—and wouldn't—speak to the possibilities because I didn't have enough facts. Instead, I heard myself reply with something even worse: "Whatever it is, we're going to find her."

"Is that a promise?"

Never guarantee results. It was more than just a rule—in this business, it was a commandment.

But all I had to do was look at her, all green eyes and glimmering hope, to break it. "Yes."

The drive back to the diner went much quicker, and we pulled into a lot that was very different from the one we'd left earlier. Almost all the spots were full, and by the time I'd parked and we walked to the entrance, there were people sitting outside the door, waiting for a table.

"Lara." I stopped and turned.

"I know." She winced. "Let you do the talking."

My fist flexed and released at my side. When she'd spoken up earlier—when Brandon had started toward her—it had been a long time since I'd felt anything akin to panic. *Control your heart rate, control your fear.* In that split second, my heart rate had gone wild. *Because she wasn't supposed to be there.* Because if something happened to her—

I grabbed the door and swung it wide, flooding my mind with the task at hand.

Unfortunately, the lunch rush was just ramping up. Ron was behind the counter, volleying back and forth from one end to the other. He waved when he saw me but couldn't afford much else. I spotted Marlene as she pushed out of the kitchen, her hair just as big as yesterday, her lips a little redder, and her arms filled to the brim with plates. Muttering excuses to those standing, waiting for a seat, I headed in her direction, Lara like a warm shadow at my back.

"Marlene."

"Oh, hey there, darlin'," she greeted and then handed out four plates of burgers to the booth in front of her like she was dealing cards rather than delivering food. "What can I do you for? Did you find your friend?" She tried to sidestep me, intent on heading to her next table, but I blocked her path.

"Did you give the woman we asked you about a brochure when she was here?" I didn't waste either of our time. "For some kind of relationship wilderness retreat?"

Her brows furrowed and then exploded wide with her exclamation. "Oh!" It was a good thing there were no longer any plates in her hands, the way they plunged to her chest. "Yes—no. I mean, you see, I was in the kitchen, and when I came out, she was standing over there by the register, looking at the pinboard. I went to see if she was okay, given the commotion outside, and that was when she apologized to me for her boyfriend. She was waitin' for me to come back into the dining area."

"And the brochure . . ." I led her along.

"Yes, well, I didn't give it to her. She was looking at one on the board when I went over to check on her; she was reading it, engrossed, and I told her she was welcome to take it if she was interested. Then she started apologizing to me and wanting to give me a tip—"

"Marlene, what was the brochure for? The name of the retreat?"

"Oh, well, I don't remember that, darlin'," she chided with a chuckle, and my jaw locked. "But you know"—she squinted—"there might be another one pinned over there. I think whoever posted it left a couple—"

"Thanks." I turned and Lara was already back at the entrance, scanning the corkboard. I reached her just in time to hear her mutter, "There," and then shoot up on her toes to reach the pamphlet tacked near the top.

There was no way she could reach it, even on tiptoe.

"Let me," I huffed and came up right behind her, reaching over her head and past her straining fingertips. *Damn woman just couldn't wait a second for help.*

I unclipped the brochure just as she lowered her arms and spun—directly into the enclave of my body. Her gasp ricocheted off my chest. All my muscles turned to stone. Lara angled her head up, her full lips peeling apart when her gaze met mine, verdant green hazing with forbidden shadows.

God, she was beautiful. So beautiful. *And too damn close.*

Oxygen dumped into my chest as I lowered my arm slowly, afraid any sudden movement would close whatever abysmal space existed between us. I was a restrained man. Too restrained, maybe, but it served me well. However, restraint only succeeded with recognition—awareness of the things that were dangerous and avoiding them with intention. But Lara . . . she was an exception, not just to my rules but to my restraint, too. I recognized every inch of her soft, tempting danger to me, and yet I continued to put myself in her perilous proximity. Like I didn't care about the devastation it could bring.

Like I'd forgotten the destruction it had already caused.

Unfortunately, all my caution became worthless when the door swung open and two kids, followed by their parents, barreled into the restaurant, one of them knocking right into me.

"Shit." My hand shot out to stop me from falling forward, anchoring on the corkboard at the same moment her hand landed on my chest.

Desire exploded in my veins like a chambered bullet accidentally fired. A decades-old ache lodging itself in my ribs.

Her eyes crashed into mine. Our breaths tangled into an inextricable knot of need, promising the only way to loosen it was to get closer.

Without moving—without even trying—things became messy. Lines started to blur.

I'd trapped her against the wall rather than crushing her into it, but somehow crushing seemed less catastrophic than . . . *this*. My body wedged to hers. My heart charged like a caged beast against her hand. Her head so close, the freckles on her nose became a map that led my gaze to her lips.

Lara's eyelids dipped. *An invitation.*

Her fingers curled into my jacket. *A plea.*

"Oh, I'm so sorry. So, so sorry." The moment shattered, the crash as sharp and jarring as a breaking glass. A hand landed on my shoulder, accompanying the effusive apology from the mom whose kid had bumped into me.

I pushed away from the wall, and from Lara, giving my full attention to the woman. "It's all right." She could barely give me a weary smile before she was pulled away, trying to wrangle her kids back to her side.

"Let's go outside," I muttered and moved a little desperately toward the exit.

The cool breeze did little to dull the heat surging through my blood. Or the frustration.

Attraction wasn't a new feeling to me. Like everything else, it had a purpose. An appropriate time and place when I could indulge in something casual, usually with someone I'd meet while on a case. It was easier that way. Safer not to risk the complications of an involvement with someone local.

But this . . . what I felt for Lara . . . was unfamiliar. An exception to even the rules I had for attraction.

It lacked all reason and rational sense, and made me want to shove her against the wall in the middle of a crowded diner and kiss her senseless. One would think my relationship with her sister would've created at least a mental barrier if not a physical one, yet there was nothing. *Less than nothing.*

I could hardly even remember kissing Rachel or what it had felt like, let alone wield that memory like some kind of shield.

I stopped next to Lara's rental, which had a prime parking spot from earlier. Her shoulder brushed my arm as she came to my side, and I stiffened, regretting for the millionth time my decision to bring her along.

Wordlessly, I opened the brochure, the front having no information besides *Wilderness Within: A Relationship Transformation.*

"'Reconnect with your authentic self to attract authentic love. At Wilderness Within, we believe the path to meaningful relationships begins with self-discovery,'" Lara read aloud, and though unnecessary, I was grateful for something to fill the silence other than the drum of my warring heart. She continued reading below the photo montage of loving couples and smiling faces: "'Singles: Discover why past relationships failed, discover your true desires, and learn how to attract a partner who truly sees you. Couples: Rekindle what brought you together through guided experiences that create lasting bonds.'"

Reaching over me, she pulled the flap open, bypassing the rest of the promotional text.

"'The journey to partnership excellence begins with a single step into the wild. Let us be your guide. Call for more information . . .'" The phone number was the only concrete detail included in the brochure.

"Hold on," I said and handed her the paper. Drawing my cell from my back pocket, I used it to snap a photo and sent if off to Callum with the message 411, meaning I needed all the information he could find. "Let's see what they have to say," I muttered and entered the phone number from the back, making sure I set my phone on speaker after I hit the call button.

"Hello, thank you for calling Wilderness Within, where the path to meaningful relationships begins with self-discovery." The receptionist regurgitated the headline on the brochure. "This is Brielle speaking. How can I help you connect today?"

Man, they laid it on thick.

"Hi, Brielle, my name is Colter Shaw," I introduced myself with the overtly fake name, catching Lara's raised brow. "I'm looking for a friend of mine who I believe might've signed up for your retreat, and I was wondering if you could confirm that for me? Her name is Rachel Crane."

"Good afternoon, Mr. Shaw." If she picked up on the fictional alias I'd chosen, she didn't let on. "Unfortunately, we take our clients' privacy very seriously. In addition, as part of our program, we provide counseling with our therapist, Dr. Julia Maxwell, so we are also under strict patient-privacy laws as well."

Great.

"I fully understand," I replied genially and then switched tactics. "I just haven't heard from her in a few weeks, and we're all starting to get concerned. I don't want to file a missing persons report or send the police out searching if she is just immersed in your program."

Sometimes the threat of police intervention loosened lips.

"I also do understand, Mr. Shaw," she said, her exaggerated sympathy already telling me my tactic wasn't going to work this time. "Unfortunately, I still can't disclose any information more than the details of our program, which is two to four weeks long depending on whether you are coming in as a single or as a couple. In addition, we do mandate a no-cell-phone policy during the length of the retreat and collect those devices at the start of the seminar, so that could explain the lack of communication from your friend if she were participating."

While it filled in another missing piece of Rachel's disappearance, it wasn't enough.

"I appreciate the information, Brielle. Would it be possible to visit the retreat as a prospective guest?" I probed, holding back the part where we'd look for Rachel while we were there.

"No, I'm sorry. Growth and confidence in relationships blooms from the bedrock of security, so unlike other offerings, we don't do gimmicky tours or guest visits during a running session in order to preserve the sanctity of our clients' vulnerability while they are with us."

Either she'd read the words enough times to own them, or she truly believed in what the retreat offered. Not that there was anything wrong with what they espoused to provide, but I was naturally wary of programs like this—promising self-help, secluded in nature, closed off to the public.

You only have to rescue one person from a cult to become skeptical of anyone promising miraculous transformations in the middle of the wilderness.

"We do offer limited tours between sessions," she added, almost as a by-product of my silence.

"And when would that next opportunity be?"

"In two weeks."

I turned away, hoping the speaker hadn't caught Lara's sharp gasp. "Great, thank you so much for all your help."

"Of course. Thank you, Colter, for considering Wilderness Within, where every relationship starts wild—"

I hung up before she could finish.

"We can't wait two weeks to look for Rachel," Lara declared, folding her arms staunchly over her chest.

"Wasn't planning on it." I flipped open my messages and frowned, seeing no response from my brother. "I sent a photo of the brochure to Callum. He should be able to find a location."

Lara turned, biting her bottom lip as she kicked a small stone around with her foot. "I can't believe they won't let you contact anyone there or even just confirm someone is okay."

"It's not uncommon for these types of places. They really try for that off-the-grid vibe," I muttered, attempting my own search online for Wilderness Within, but their website was a carbon copy of the brochure. Lots of photos, little information.

"Maybe you should start hosting a retreat at the ranch," she grumbled. "Show them how it's done."

I lifted my head and stuck her with a flat stare. Those who really lived off-grid didn't host retreats to advertise it.

"It was a joke," she clarified at my unamused expression, and then her brows popped up. "Also, Colter Shaw? Really?"

One corner of my mouth kicked just a bit higher. If she'd just started Deaver's series, she was in for an ironic surprise when she reached *Hunting Time* and heard the pseudonym Mr. Shaw used.

"They say Michael Jordan uses the names Clark Kent and Bruce Wayne to stay anonymous when he travels."

"Because that's not suspicious," she murmured, rolling her eyes. "Although one time, I did have a patient come in insisting his name was Frank Sinatra."

I chuckled. "A legend."

"In many ways," she replied, and, when I cocked my head, added, "He came in around the holidays with a tree-shaped ornament stuck in a place it didn't belong." Now it was my turn to raise a brow. "Like I said. An ER legend."

"I usually pick something more innocuous, but I thought you'd enjoy it," I said and immediately tensed. Why would I admit to that—to using the main character's name from the novels she'd mentioned reading?

In the retrieval business, it was pretty standard to use an alias for one reason or another. I had several, with varying degrees of credibility, but for a phone call, I could pick anything.

"So, is the singles' program two weeks long and then it's couples after that? Because it's been longer than two weeks since I've heard from Rachel . . ." Lara pulled her bottom lip between her teeth, her focus back on the brochure like it could tell her something new.

"Let's see what Callum can find, and if we have a location—"

"I'm going to call them again."

"For . . ." My protest faded because her cell was already at her ear.

Regardless of the retreat's intentions, they weren't going to give out any more information on their clients, no matter what she asked, but maybe she'd feel less helpless finding that out for herself.

Opening my message to Callum, I sent a string of question marks, hoping to urge him along. If he didn't respond by the time she was off the phone, I'd call him. When I looked up again, Lara gave me a thumbs-up, which I guessed to mean the receptionist had answered.

"Hi, Brielle, my name is Lara Croft." Our eyes connected, hers mischievous. "I'm calling because I picked up one of your brochures, and I'm interested in your program."

I frowned. Tomb Raider . . . *more like troublemaker.*

"I see. That sounds wonderful. When is the soonest I could join the retreat?"

My head jerked up, shaking wildly as I mouthed, *No.* Lara turned away, presumably to ignore my warning. *Dammit.*

There was no way she was joining the program. That wasn't the solution.

"Lara," I warned low, knowing she could hear me.

Going undercover for information was risky and unpredictable, especially with no confirmation Rachel was even there. The safest, surest plan was to get a location for the retreat and surveil it for any sign of Rachel.

"So the singles' introduction to the course started two weeks ago, and you can't join afterward?" she confirmed to the woman for my benefit.

I let out a tight breath. *Good.*

My phone buzzed. Callum had texted back.

Two minutes.

"Oh, so the couples are just joining the program now."

"Lara," I growled and reached for her.

The wild woman scampered around the other side of her car like this was some kind of game.

"Yes, I'm sorry. I misunderstood the process. Silly me." Lara faked a laugh, but her eyes were as serious as sin the way they pinned mine. "Correct, it's not just me. My boyfriend, Calder, and I would like to enroll in the couples' portion of the retreat."

Boyfriend.

Couple.

A red fog came over me, whatever she said after drowning in the drone of my furious pulse.

"Lara . . ." Her name cracked from my chest as soon as she ended the call.

"They bring singles into the retreat for two weeks and then add in people who are already in relationships," she said, defending her rash decision. "It was the only way for us to get in."

"No, it wasn't," I said, my jaw spasming. "We don't even have solid proof that Rachel is there—"

"I know she is, Calder." She glanced at the brochure. "I know it."

My breathing labored as I fought for reason. "Okay, say she is—you think the best way to get to her is to go undercover as my girlfriend? Yesterday, you said you had to be involved because Rachel wouldn't trust me, and now you want to show up and have her think we're dating?"

The corners of her mouth turned down. "It's not ideal, but it's the only way we'll know for sure. Plus, Rachel would know—would realize—that I would never . . . with you . . . after how—" Her mouth snapped shut, red flushing her cheeks.

Even as she cautiously verbalized the wreckage between us, there was no denying both of us were thinking about what had happened in the diner. Despite our past. Despite how her sister felt about me. Despite her own opinion of me . . . of what I'd done . . . of what she needed from me . . . we'd almost kissed. We'd both *wanted* that kiss.

Even now. I was furious, and still I wanted nothing more than to kiss the hell out of her.

"Dammit, Lara." I drove my fingers along my scalp.

This was why I worked alone. Growing up Stone meant growing up under the perpetual test of worst-case scenario. And the worst-case scenario invariably meant that help was never guaranteed.

"Give me a better idea and I'll agree to it," she offered, her stance firm and her chin defiant. "I saw an opportunity and I took it."

"No, you were desperate and you reacted—there's a difference," I ground out, my jaw locked tight. "It's better to move at the pace of observation rather than desperation. When you rush, you miss critical details."

"And when you don't act, you miss opportunity," Lara volleyed back, the green in her eyes glittering.

"Making up your own rules now?"

Her chin lifted. "Sometimes it's better to beg for forgiveness than to ask permission."

Desire rocketed straight to my groin. *Oh, the way I'd make her beg . . .*

I stifled a low groan and banded my arms over my chest. "How long do we have?"

Before we had to go along with Operation Insanity.

She slid her tongue along her lips, armoring them for the answer she knew I wouldn't like. "Brielle said she would message me the address tomorrow morning at eight, and we're to arrive by nine."

My lungs deflated with a hot hiss. Less than a day was a pretty poor timeline.

I rattled off my plan like I was bailing water from a sinking ship. "If Callum can find a location before then, we'll send one of his drones out to surveil. To confirm Rachel is there first."

"Once Brielle sends the address, could he . . ." She trailed off, seeing me shake my head.

"It's not the address of the retreat," I said, wishing it were that easy. "Places like this usually have some lot where you leave your car and all your traceable belongings before they bring you on-site." At least in my experience with programs like this, that was how they'd worked every single time.

"Oh. That makes sense." She folded the brochure absentmindedly. "Did Callum get back to you?"

I checked again. "Not yet." He'd said two minutes, but it had been ten. "I'm going to head back and check in." My truck beeped when I unlocked it.

"I'm coming with you," she said, quickly elaborating when the low, gravelly sound I'd buried rose from the dead. "We should probably prepare just in case we have to go tomorrow and pretend . . ." Her throat bobbed.

"To be dating." My voice was as hard as my glare.

Folding her arms, she refused to back down. "I'm sure you have some rule about being prepared."

I frowned.

Rule #1. The essence of survival is preparation. But for some reason, what she was suggesting didn't feel like preparation, but purgatory. *Pretending to want a woman who couldn't know I actually wanted her, for how long?*

"Just look on the bright side," Lara added when I didn't respond. "It's not like we have to pretend to have a good relationship. I mean, that's the point of the program. So we won't really need to pretend very much. We can just go and be our incompatible selves."

Incompatible.

"Yeah," I said gruffly, even as my eyes roamed over her again.

It didn't feel incompatible the way she made my body heat. It hadn't felt incompatible when her body was pressed to mine or when her mouth was poised and parted for my kiss. And it definitely didn't feel incompatible to claim her as my girlfriend even though it should've felt worse; it should've felt illegal. *Illicit.*

Her weak smile flashed wide with bravado. "It'll be easy."

I almost choked. Easy . . . *Tell that to my cock.*

Decades spent being raised as a survivalist, and as I pulled out of the lot, the only thing I could think was that I might not have the skills to survive a fake relationship with my ex-girlfriend's little sister.

Chapter 7

Lara

Pretend to be dating Calder Stone.

I wouldn't say it was my finest moment, but while I was on the phone with the receptionist, my skin had started to tingle the way it did when a trauma case came into the emergency room, and I had split seconds to make calls that could be life or death. While I hoped—desperately—that wasn't the situation Rachel was in, I couldn't shake the feeling that something wasn't right.

So I'd administered the lie . . . and watched Calder turn from calm stone into a churning volcano. Glowing. Smoking. *And about to erupt.*

After instructing me to leave my rental and get back in his truck, we rode—in taut silence—back to the ranch.

I'd never seen him look so intense before. Not then. Not now. Calder wasn't used to playing by anyone else's rules but his own, and now I'd just gone and changed the entire game. I knew it wasn't ideal—that I'd stepped on his proverbial professional toes. *And signed us up for a couples' retreat.* But I didn't have a choice. My gut told me this was the only way to find my sister.

My gaze flicked to the man stewing beside me. If I looked closely, I'd see the smoke of frustration coming out his ears. The problem was, if I looked too closely, I'd see other things: the knot of his jaw muscle about to snap from the tension and the gold flecks starbursting from his pupils from our almost-collision inside the diner. With the way he stared at me—at my mouth—any other doctor might have diagnosed that look as desire, but I couldn't; I wasn't a specialist in my sister's ex-boyfriend's emotions. *I couldn't be.*

As we pulled into the driveway, the sun dipped low in the sky, a yolk drooping toward the jagged, lofty mountains that would puncture its vibrancy and spill its soft warmth over the towering steeps. This time, the Stone homestead appeared like a gem nestled in a forested fist—a sanctuary tucked into its surroundings, protected and picturesque.

I could see why Cassius Stone had chosen it. Why anyone would choose it.

Instead of going to his Airstream, Calder drove past his dad's house to the second building I'd spotted from the top of the hill: his brother Callum's house.

The Watchtower, he'd called it.

Without speaking, on par for the drive, he parked and we got out of the truck. While Calder strode straight toward the entrance, my pace was slower as I took in the building.

It was newer construction, a wraparound porch that enclosed the whole building and provided a 360-degree vantage point to the fields and mountains that stretched in every direction.

Calder walked up the handicapped ramp to the front door, and I noted how the ramp wasn't in addition to the stairs, but in place of them. My vague recollection yesterday was now confirmed: Calder's younger brother had been the famed storm chaser who'd barely survived his last encounter with a tornado.

I moved to catch up and almost missed the home's most striking feature: the glass-encrusted dome in the center of the roof, perfect for viewing stars and storms.

"Callum!" Calder called and banged on the front door.

A dog tore around the corner, emitting a single bark of greeting before wearing a circle around my legs. I recognized the breed—a blue heeler, just like my neighbor's dog back in Phoenix.

"Hey, buddy." I smiled and crouched, giving his wet nose my open palm to sniff.

"Lara, meet Twister," Calder grumbled.

"Hi, Twister," I said as he licked my palm, and then slid my hand back to scratch behind his ears. "Is he your brother's?"

"Sort of" was the only answer I got before the door opened.

I stood, my eyes widening when there was no one on the other side.

"Cal?" Calder called again, stepping into the house.

I followed, seeing that the other side of the door was rigged with various sensors and a large pistonlike control that allowed for a remote command to not only unlock the door but also open it.

"Coming," a terse voice sounded from a distant corner.

Calder folded his arms while we waited, clearly intent on maintaining our no-talking atmosphere. *Fine with me.* I crouched and continued to love on Twister while I took in the inside of the house.

From end to end, the large open space flowed from the kitchen and dining area, through the living room, to an office at the far side. I admired how it was designed intentionally to accommodate its handicapped inhabitant—and couldn't miss how it was furnished to be unaccommodating to everyone else. The kitchen had a table but no chairs. The living area: a TV and a single recliner, but no couch. And in the office, three desks spanned the wall, with no fewer than seven computer monitors between them and no desk chair.

I wondered whether the intent was to discourage unwanted guests or to reflect a lingering bitterness toward the reminder that his life would now be lived from a wheelchair. Maybe it was both.

Between the living room and the office was a staircase to the glass-domed loft. Except it wasn't stairs, but ramps, I realized as Calder's brother flew down them and came to a turbulent stop ahead of us.

Something it was clearly built for. The custom wheelchair reminded me of a fancy race car with its cambered wheels, bright-teal decals, and missing armrests. And the man in the driver's seat looked equally as reckless.

Callum's short hair fell unkempt on his head, a shade lighter than his brother's. Like Calder, he wore a plain tee that stretched over a strong upper body that now compensated with additional muscle for legs that rested motionless in navy sweatpants.

"You never got back to me," Calder greeted.

"I was busy, and you never said it was Category 5 urgent," Callum replied before turning his attention to me, his cold blue eyes narrowing severely.

"Callum, this is Lara. I'm searching for her sister."

Callum regarded me like a stranger, something that he knew existed in the world but was both unexpected and unwelcome.

His chin jammed down in a brusque nod—the only greeting I was going to get—before he said to Calder, "I have info on that retreat."

Grabbing one wheel tight, Callum whipped his chair around so fast, I was surprised the tires didn't screech as he headed for his computers, clearly expecting us to follow.

Calder turned to me and muttered, "Don't take it personally."

I didn't—*wouldn't.* I'd worked in medicine long enough to recognize when someone's rudeness wasn't a reflection of me, but of the pain, physical or emotional, of their own circumstance.

We joined Callum and my eyes roamed over the theater of information displayed on the computers. Some of them had weather maps on steroids, one had some kind of simulation program running, and another had paused on drone footage of the bird's-eye view of a mountain face.

"Wilderness Within was incorporated three years ago by Dr. Julia Maxwell, licensed psychologist originally based out of San Francisco, specializing in relationship therapy," Callum said, a woman's headshot appearing on the monitor directly in front of him. "There was no address on the website or anywhere on the internet that I was able to find. However, there's a property owned by the corporation."

A new window opened up with an aerial photo pulled from Google Maps of a small building and parking lot about thirty minutes east of Jackson.

Callum zoomed in. "The building is maybe only two thousand square feet, and the lot can't be more than an acre."

"So, not where they have the retreat," I huffed.

"Most likely the address they'll send you tomorrow," Calder said. "It looks like where they have participants park and check in. There's probably some kind of storage area where we'll leave our phones, and then they'll transport us to the actual location."

"'Us'?" The singular word was the only interest Callum had shown in anything other than delivering the details he'd found.

Calder ignored him. "Do you have a recent image of the property?"

"I did a drone sweep, but it looks nominally the same. Maybe a fresh coat of paint on the building." Callum pulled up a video on the left-hand screen, the camera approaching the building and then zooming down on the lot.

"Wait!" I blurted out and moved over to point at the footage, brushing Calder's arm in the process. "That's Rachel's car."

I pretended not to notice how he stepped to the side, creating some clearance between us, as he said, "Do you have a better angle, Callum? We should run the plate—"

"You don't have to. Zoom in there." I pointed to the back windshield, the Wyoming State decal sharpening into focus. Below it, one for the University of Colorado School of Medicine. "I gave Rachel my car when I moved to Arizona; those are my stickers." I turned to Calder. "This means she's at the retreat."

His frown angled so deep, I was surprised the corners of his mouth didn't strike gold.

"It means her car is parked at this building," Callum corrected, instantly sobering my hope.

He was right, though. This didn't explain where Rachel was now. The singles' program had ended two days ago, and there'd been no word from her. Would she have stayed for the couples' session? Was that even allowed? Had she met someone else at the retreat? I shuddered. That would be diving in pretty deep with someone she'd just met. I hated to say—to think—it wasn't beyond the realm of possibility, especially because the alternative . . .

"Zoom out again," Calder directed. "The land it abuts here to the east—"

"BLM."

Calder swore under his breath.

BLM was the designation for land belonging to the federal government's Bureau of Land Management. I didn't know exactly how many acres of public-use lands they held in the state, but it was in the millions, and it was popular with campers and hunters because it came with very few rules.

"I can fly a drone out there, but even in this smaller pocket between the national park and the reservation, we're still looking at tens of thousands of acres."

"No, that'll take too long." Calder massaged the hard edge of his jaw with his hand. "This is the only property owned by the corporation?" He didn't wait for confirmation before tacking on, "What about Maxwell? Does she have property in her name?"

"Well, that's where things get interesting. For Wilderness Within, everything from their legal status to tax filings, even down to the reviews left online, is legitimate. But I had the same thought as you, so I looked into Maxwell and found this." Callum clicked, and documents appeared next to the doctor's image on the monitor: Schedule C forms filed with the IRS for the last three years. "According to their website, Wilderness Within runs two retreat cycles: one at the beginning of summer and one at the end. Based on what she filed with the IRS, Maxwell is bringing in roughly ninety thousand a year after expenses from Wilderness Within, but when I looked into her personal assets, I found a mortgage for a

$3 million home just outside of Jackson, a lease for a brand-new Porsche that she's upgraded every year for the last three years, and a $1 million condo in West Palm Beach that I can find no record of on any third-party-rental listing website, so she's not renting it out."

"Does she have a private practice? Would that account for the spending?"

"No," I scoffed and bit into my cheek when Calder glared at me. There was no way a psychologist could afford all that, even in private practice, without some external source of funds.

"No, she doesn't. She had a practice in California, but she closed it when she moved to Wyoming."

"Family money? Investments?"

"Not that I've found."

"So she's getting money from somewhere to afford her lifestyle, but somewhere that she's not reporting it."

"Maybe she asks for gifts or donations from participants at the retreat and then doesn't report them," I suggested.

"That would be a lot of gifts."

"I might've found something else on Maxwell." Callum leaned forward. "I thought it was odd that she closed up shop and moved to Wyoming. She has no family or any other ties to this area. I looked into her practice thinking the reason was financial, but I didn't find any hardship there."

"Something with her license?"

"Still valid." Callum clicked and opened a clipped image. "When I was looking for information on her office, I found this review cached on one of those provider-aggregate websites."

You did this to Hannah. She's gone because of you. You're a monster.

"What does that mean? Who's Hannah?"

"Great question," Callum drawled, his sarcasm barely contained. "Except for a great-great-aunt who is deceased, I couldn't find anyone named Hannah associated with Julia Maxwell. The only, most likely option is that Hannah was—"

"A patient."

"Right." Less sarcasm this time. "I did a search crawl for any article or blog from around the time of this post that mentioned *Hannah, Maxwell, tragedy, psychologist* . . . anything along those lines, and this is what showed up."

An article from a university newspaper appeared.

Sophomore Suicide Shakes Campus

"'Sophomore Hannah L., found dead in her dorm Wednesday morning from apparent suicide,'" Calder read aloud. "How does this have anything to do with Maxwell?"

Callum clicked, enlarging a section of the article.

> Family of the deceased claim she was seeking psychological treatment regularly before her passing.

"You think Maxwell was treating her, and the person who left that review blamed her for Hannah's death," Calder inferred.

Just like someone blamed me for Ian's. Instantly, my throat clogged and my vision blurred. Ian's face—his eyes bright and wild in front of mine. My heart slugged against my chest, seeing the way he looked at me—

"Lara." Calder's hand touched the back of my arm, and I flinched, snapping out of the memory.

"Doctors get blamed for many things that aren't their fault," I murmured, a telltale catch in my voice.

"True, but do they all pack up their successful practice in the city and move states away to run a wilderness retreat?"

No. I swallowed but didn't say anything. It did seem off—but then again, I'd up and left for Wyoming after Ian, even though Rachel was my reason.

"I have a call out to the student who wrote the article for the paper to see if I can get more information. He's still at the school getting his master's, so I should hear in the next day or two."

"All right. In the meantime, keep following the money—"

"It has to be coming from somewhere, I know," Callum finished, not bothering to hide the drip of bitterness in his voice. "I know how to do my job, Calder. You don't always have to be the director."

Calder winced. "You're right."

"I know," he said, and then one of his computers on the other end of the desk started beeping, and it must have been something important, because Callum spun his chair around and almost ran over my foot to check the alert.

He squinted, zoomed in on one of the weather models, and then whistled. "Gotta go. Come on, Twister."

The dog bounded over, waiting for the door to the back side of the porch to open. Callum grabbed a baseball cap off the nearby coatrack, several of them adorning the rungs. At the very top, and well beyond what he could reach from his chair, was a cowboy hat. *The* cowboy hat he'd been pictured wearing in the news. I had a feeling it was out of reach for a reason.

"Looks like we're going to the retreat," I murmured.

Calder's expression remained almost unreadable as he looked me over. *Almost.* Ever since that moment back at the diner, the glint in his hazel eyes had burned like embers he couldn't put out.

His jaw flexed. "Then I guess we better learn a little bit about each other so our"—his jaw flexed—"incompatibility isn't mistaken for ignorance."

Following him back outside, I pretended like I hadn't heard how his voice hit a speed bump over the word *incompatibility.*

Chapter 8

Lara

"Who taught you to cook?" I asked, watching Calder at his stove from the same seat I'd taken earlier.

After leaving Callum's, we'd made a pit stop at his dad's; I'd waited while he went inside the greenhouse abutting the far side of the house. When he returned, it was with two sweet potatoes and a handful of kale.

It was these moments when my sister's disappearance didn't feel like the only mystery I wanted to solve. The Stone family was a puzzle of so many incongruous yet interconnected pieces, each just as intriguing as the next. But none so much as the eldest. I'd be lying if I didn't admit the latent silver lining to my impetuous plan was to have an excuse to learn more about Calder. About his life. His family. *About why he seemed so alone.*

"Cassius," Calder answered, volleying several jars of spices from the cabinet to season the meat hissing in the frying pan. "But growing what we cooked and knowing what was safe to eat was my mom's domain." The way his hands moved suggested he'd made this meal a thousand times. "Survival means knowing the difference between what can sustain you and what will kill you."

Another rule.

I propped my elbow on the table, resting the side of my head on my hand. "So, the greenhouse was hers?"

He pressed his lips together and nodded. "Cassius mostly tends to it now, with some help from Colby and Creighton. The rest of us can get by but never quite mastered Mom's green thumb the way they did. Ironic, since they had the shortest amount of time with her." He stiffened at that, like he hadn't meant to say it.

I vaguely remembered that Calder's mom had died when he was young. "How old were they when she passed?"

Talking about his mom was a sore subject. I could see him pull away from the topic just as surely as if I'd physically pushed on a pressure point.

"Six and eight."

"Wow." I swallowed, feeling my throat start to tighten. "I didn't realize . . . I'm so sorry." The words felt awkward. Insufficient. I'd never been good at sympathy, even at the hospital. Not because I didn't feel it, but because as soon as I expressed it, it started to swallow up my thinking. My judgment. My composure. "How old were you?"

"Fifteen." He reached for the kale left drying in the sink.

"That must've been hard," I murmured, blinking rapidly. "I was twenty-six when I lost my mom. I couldn't imagine losing her at only six. Or with my sister only being six."

"We survived." *Survival* implied both perseverance and grit, but also scars.

I wanted to ask what happened. Like every other piece of his family, there seemed to be more to the story. Unfortunately, I wouldn't risk rocking the proverbial life raft that was barely floating on the sea of civility between us.

He changed topics, and I let him. "Do you cook?"

If my small snort wasn't a clear enough answer, I replied, "I microwave. And DoorDash."

"Those are the kind of things that sustain you while also slowly killing you," he grumbled and began cutting up the kale, the thump of the knife rocking on the cutting board echoing the thud of my heart.

Extensor carpi ulnaris. Extensor digitorum. I stared, the wavelike ebb and roll of his wrist mesmerizing me. My eyes grew hooded, and for a second, the lack of sleep and the eventful day drew me into exhaustion, but then he tossed the green leaflets into the pan and their sizzle jerked me out of my stupor.

"I aim for the healthiest I can make work with my schedule," I said, taking a deep breath of the amazing scent filling the Airstream. "I have to say, it's several steps up from my childhood menu, which consisted of Rachel making us PB&J for lunch and microwaving SpaghettiOs or Chef Boyardee for dinner because Mom was working."

The toaster oven dinged that the sweet potatoes were done. Giving the ground beef one last toss, Calder shut off the burner and grabbed a towel to pull the potatoes from the oven.

"Your mom was a teacher, right?"

I sat forward, impressed, though not surprised, by his recall. Meanwhile, I wasn't sure whether I'd ever known what Calder's parents had done before . . . survivalist-ing.

"When you met Rachel, she was, but when we were younger, she waitressed and cleaned houses, and sometimes she'd bartend on the weekends." It had been on most weekends, and the ones that she didn't were only because she wanted to spend it with whatever man she was dating at the time. "She did what she could . . . what she had to do as a single mom. When we were in high school, she started taking night classes to get her teaching certificate."

"Impressive." Admiration colored his tone as he filled our plates with the sweet potatoes, topped with the meat-and-kale mix.

In so many ways, she was, but like most people, Mom's greatest strength had also been her greatest weakness. For as hard as she'd worked to provide for us, she was equally as driven to find the person who would provide for her. Maybe financially, but mostly emotionally.

Rachel and I were all she'd had, and we were her children. Her dependents. She'd tied shoes and kissed boo-boos. Had made sure our clothes were clean and there was always food in the fridge. But when things got hard or money got tight, she'd had no one to hold her up. Not in the way an adult needs. So while I admired like hell the way she'd loved us,

I pitied her desperation to find someone to love her, not because being loved wasn't a worthwhile aspiration, but because the way she'd settled for things . . . for the way men had treated her . . . broke my heart.

"She was an amazing mom. She worked hard to take care of us and pursue her own dream," I conceded and stood, needing some physical movement to shift me away from a topic that touched too close to my sister's own struggles.

I cleared Calder's files, laptop, and crossword puzzle from the tabletop. Hands full, I turned and almost crashed into him, his hands also full.

"Sorry," I said, a strong whiff of dinner piercing my nostrils and making me moan. "Wow, that smells good."

Our eyes connected, his injected with the same look he'd had at the diner. Hunger. And not the kind that was satisfied by the *"things that would sustain you."*

Calder moved around me without a word, setting the plates on the table while I moved his things to his desk, noticing his notebooks standing proudly on the bookshelf.

"Are these from all your cases?"

Calder looked over while tearing off two paper towels from the roll. "Yeah."

"It's a lot." I joined him at the table, each of us taking a seat on opposite sides. "You've done a lot."

"I like to stay busy." He picked up his fork and scraped up a bite.

"Have you worked in every state?"

Calder shook his head. "No, I tend to stick to the Midwest and Northwest. Creed usually volunteers for retrievals that are farther; he gets restless staying in one place. We call him the Drifter."

"What do they call you?" The question jutted out, my fork poised in front of my mouth as I waited for the answer.

He looked at me like I'd just asked one more thing I wasn't supposed to know. *But now I needed to.* "If we're going to be—pretend to be a couple, I should know if you have a nickname."

His eyes narrowed. "The Director," he grunted and went back to eating.

The Director. Now Callum's comment earlier about Calder *directing* his work made so much more sense. In fact, the entirety of the male specimen in front of me made so much more sense. His initiative. His command. His skill for calm disregard. *And his frustration when I changed the direction of our search.*

With my first bite, the desire to talk faded. Like most of my meals, I hadn't realized how hungry I was until I started eating. There were days when I'd go a whole ten-hour shift without anything more than a protein shake. It wasn't healthy, but to me, that was being in health care. I gave my all every second I was in the hospital and only returned to myself and my well-being as an afterthought.

But this . . . Calder's dinner was delicious. The sweet starch of the potatoes, the savory spiced beef, and the slight crunch of the kale.

"This is incredible," I barely managed to get out between bites, scarfing down everything on my plate.

"Thanks," Calder drawled, and it took me a minute to realize he was staring.

Heat flushed my cheeks, and I quickly dropped my fork onto my empty plate, noting how his was still half full. "Sorry," I mumbled, wiping my mouth with a paper towel and searching for the right words to explain why I ate every meal like I was going for gold in Olympic speed-eating. "I don't get a lot of time to eat on my shifts, so I've gotten good at eating . . . quickly."

I tried not to think about how much of my life outside of work was lived in short bursts. Eating. Sleeping. Reading. I didn't slow, let alone stop, and maybe that was why I never saw my crash coming.

Calder made an indecipherable sound. "So, Colorado State for medicine and then ended up in Arizona?"

Right. This exercise in preparation couldn't be one-sided.

"My residency was there, and then I decided to stay."

"What hospital?"

"Sunrise Medical Center," I answered and felt a delayed sting of worry. *What if he looked it up? Or saw the story in the news?* I didn't want to talk about what had happened any more than he probably wanted to talk about his brother's accident or his mother's death.

"What did you tell them?"

"I'm sorry." My heart slammed into my ribs so hard, I swore one cracked. "What do you mean?"

Calder frowned, gathering the last of his food on his fork. "For why you're here? Did you tell them about your sister?"

"Oh. No." I swallowed. "I'm just taking personal time."

"This would be hard on anyone, Dr. Crane, but like the rest of your team, you have the full support of the hospital. However, you need to take the four weeks off. It's not negotiable while legal does what they need to do."

I turned my head away, unable to stop the memory of Dr. Morgan's face when he'd put me on leave. Nor the way he couldn't give me any confidence that I'd still have my job when these four weeks were up.

"I guess maybe we should figure out some basics? For tomorrow?" I blurted out, trading my own demons for the ones who'd taken my sister. "We'll need to be on the same page."

"Okay," Calder said and looked up, waiting for me to go on.

"Well, I think we should come up with a different job for you. I'm guessing being any kind of investigator / retrieval specialist is going to bring more questions than answers. So what job do you pretend to have when you're someone other than Calder Stone?"

"Rancher."

"Right." I blew out a breath. *Maybe his nickname should be Captain Obvious.*

Calder sat forward. "So, you're worried about my fake job but not about the fake relationship we'll need to have?"

"No—I mean, yes. I mean, I thought we'd keep that part simple. We met in college, went our separate ways, and then connected again back in Wyoming . . . The best lies are the ones closest to the truth, right?" I bit into my bottom lip, and his nostrils flared like I'd bit him.

"And what about us is 'simple'?" Calder asked, the huskiness of his voice settling into my veins the way an anchor sinks to the ocean floor.

Nothing. Nothing about Calder, nor the way I was attracted to him, was simple. Not then. Not now. Not in this fake story and not in reality.

"We just have to fake enough to get to the retreat. It should be easy enough then to find Rachel, right?"

I didn't like the way his mouth drew into a tight line.

"And if she's not there?"

"Her car is there. You can't tell me that Rachel *not* being there is the more likely scenario." Defensiveness saturated my voice. I knew we'd been through this, but I also knew she had to be there.

"I'm not, but it is a possibility, and one we should be prepared for." The way his jaw fired, I'd be shocked if it wasn't sharp enough to split the hairs of his short beard.

"Where else would she be?"

"And what if she's been at the retreat the whole time and hasn't contacted you because she can't? Or what if she still doesn't want to talk to you?"

His words weren't meant to harm. They weren't accusatory or denigrating, like what Brandon had said earlier. But like the blade of a scalpel wielded to flay damaged tissue from healthy, they still cut a painful path to the tenderest of flesh.

Still, he was right. That was also a possibility, and one I should be prepared for.

"Then I guess our relationship will be no worse off than it already is," I said with defeat. "As long as she's safe, I don't care how she feels about me."

At least that sentiment, I knew he'd understand.

"Let me clean up quick, and then I'll take you back to the Betty," Calder said, standing and stacking my plate on his.

"Okay."

As he washed the dishes, I moved to the small couch, wanting to put my feet up for just one minute. Already feeling my eyes turn heavy, I reached for the crossword puzzle from the pile of Calder's things. Hopefully, this exhaustion meant I'd sleep soundly tonight.

PHILTRUM

I paused on the neatly printed letters, the only answer in all caps.

For the first time since I'd set us on this path, I really let my mind dip its toes into what I'd signed us up for. *What would this fake relationship really entail?* Talking—therapy, I assumed. But what if there was more? What if there were physical exercises? *Intimate exercises?*

My heart charged forward as I forced those thoughts back.

Resting my head on the back of the couch, I pushed my brain to focus on the black and white squares in front of me—an easier puzzle to solve than my simmering attraction to my sister's good-looking, good-cooking ex-boyfriend.

It wasn't long before the soothing rush of water from the sink, the soft cushion of the couch, and the simple abundance of exhaustion was enough to send me over the edge into sleep.

"Lara!"

Gasping, I grabbed my chest to catch my heart as it tried to escape. Ian's red eyes and dilated pupils as he lunged for me freshly imprinted on the inside of my eyelids; it wasn't what had happened that day, but my nightmares didn't care how much they twisted the truth, as long as it made it more traumatic.

"Lara." The deep velvet of Calder's voice was like a warm weighted blanket over my trembling consciousness, his hand on my shoulder, anchoring me in the midst of the storm. "Are you all right?"

No.

"Yeah." I nodded quickly, fighting to steady my breathing and keep my eyes away from his hunting gaze.

If Calder looked too closely, he'd know something was wrong, and if he knew something was wrong, he might change the plan for tomorrow. His words—*I won't spare your feelings at the expense of your safety*—rattled around my head like a grenade waiting to explode.

"Yes, sorry. I just . . . I must've been dreaming," I insisted, sitting up straighter and taking stock of my body. My vitals. My racing pulse. My damp skin.

Just breathe. I coached myself like I was talking to a patient. The adrenaline, the panic, the fear . . . it wasn't unlike many of the patients I'd treated in the ER with severe injuries, their bodies going into overdrive to compensate.

In my case, the only injury I'd sustained was to my mind. Dr. Morgan had strongly recommended therapy during my time off, but my invisible demons weren't nearly as important as my missing sister, so therapy would have to wait.

"I don't think it was a dream. You were panting and crying—" His voice caught. "It reminded me of when Colby had nightmares after our mom died."

The ball in my throat swelled. At least I hadn't yelled Ian's name . . .

"I'm sorry, but it was just a bad dream. They happen to everyone," I murmured and cupped my hands over my face so he couldn't look me in the eyes. Normally, I would've just closed them, but if I did that now, I knew what I'd see. *Ian. Angry. Dead. His father. Enraged.* And that would only make it worse.

"Don't apologize." Calder withdrew his hand, though his gaze roamed over me, the brush of heat searching for every confirmation I was okay. "Do you remember what you were dreaming about?"

"No." I shrugged and shook my head. "I'm sure it's just from the stress of Rachel being missing. Of not knowing . . ."

I didn't want to talk about the hospital or the death of my patient, and I definitely didn't want to talk about them with Calder.

Feeling my heart rate start to level off, I lowered my hands. I wasn't prepared to see Calder crouched in front of me in gray sweatpants. *And shirtless.*

I was too shocked to keep my mouth from dropping. The humming in my veins solidified into something heavier. Something hotter and infinitely more electric.

My gaze slid down the taut band of his *sternocleidomastoid*, which ran from the base of his ear down to his sternum. That, I'd seen before. But lower . . . his *pectoralis majors* bulged as he hunched forward, defining both the *clavicular* head and the *sternocostal* body, and with only the dim light from . . . somewhere behind me . . . the shadows played tricks on my mind, hinting at the rise and fall of more abdominal muscles than there should be.

Why was his shirt off? Had he dirtied it while cleaning the dishes?

I turned to the counter, processing the cleanly stacked dishes next to the sink, and then, farther, found the source of light was coming from Calder's bedroom.

My head whipped back. "What time is it?"

Hazel-gold orbs pinned me with concern. "Almost midnight."

"Midnight?" I choked and sat up. "Why . . . You were going to take me back to the Betty—"

"And then you fell asleep on the couch in .2 seconds and were more or less dead to the world," Calder said firmly. "Figured it was better to let you sleep."

Oh my god. I'd fallen asleep on his couch and he'd let me. He . . . *he'd put a blanket over me.* And there was a pillow . . . "I'm sorry. I guess the travel and everything caught up to me." I threw the blanket off my legs. "I know it's late, but can you take me back to the Betty? I'm sure they're worried that I didn't come back—"

"I called Jerry earlier and let him know you wouldn't be back for a few nights."

"You—" I snapped my mouth shut, realizing I sounded mad. Was I mad? I was the one who'd fallen asleep here, and it wasn't like we weren't going to meet up again first thing in the morning. No, I wasn't mad, but I felt . . . unsettled.

Like my mother, I took care of everyone around me. I took care of people for a living. But unlike my mother—*because* of her—I didn't want anyone to take care of me. It was safer that way. And not only had Calder taken it upon himself to care for me tonight, but he'd also just witnessed me at my most vulnerable. And that was as reckless as holding up a metal rod in the middle of a lightning storm.

"I'll need to go back in the morning. To get my clothes . . ." *Clothes. Toiletries.*

"We'll leave early and stop on the way."

He had an answer for everything.

"Okay." My chin dipped, an acquiescence to the situation. "I guess I'm staying here, then."

Calder stood, and my attention took another direct hit: His abdomen and waist were now at a perfect viewing angle from my seat. The definition of his *inguinal* creases, the "V," as it was colloquially known, confirmed he had less than 5 percent body fat; the ridge wasn't formed by muscles as they grew bigger, but by ligaments that became more defined the less body fat a person had. However, if I followed those lines beneath the waist of his sweats, there was a muscle—

"You're welcome to take the bed, but I didn't want to move you."

"No." I fired the word out as fast as I could. "The couch is fine." There was no chance I was sleeping in Calder's bed. Not with him. Not without him. Not on his pillow. Not with his scent. *Not with my fantasies.*

I didn't want—couldn't want—anything from this man except his expertise and help in finding my sister. Not his secrets. Not his story. Not the feel of his touch, nor the taste of his lips. And definitely not the way that wild gaze promised to devour me if it was ever unleashed.

His intense scrutiny brought goose bumps to my skin. "Okay."

"Thank you," I said softly, pulling the blanket back over my legs and turning away from him.

This time when I closed my eyes, all I saw were endless planes of hard, tanned muscle and hungry hazel eyes.

Chapter 9

Calder

Rule #30: Move at the pace of observation, not desperation.

"Don't," I warned in a low voice as Lara strayed toward her former rusty red Volvo in the parking lot.

I placed my hand on her lower back and drew her close. "There are cameras facing the lot and no reason for you to be snooping around a car you shouldn't recognize," I murmured, making sure my head blocked the sound and the view from the footage.

This was why she shouldn't have been here—why *we* shouldn't have been here. She wasn't prepared for this kind of work. *And I wasn't prepared for her.*

Her determination. *How my resistance faltered in the face of it.* Her questions. *The ease with which I wanted to answer them.* Her sleeping on my couch. *The way I wanted her in my bed.*

It was no surprise when the GPS coordinates sent to Lara's phone this morning had directed us here, to the unmarked lot from Callum's video. In spite of the full parking lot, the small building had no business sign, and the exterior didn't promise much: chipped paint, cracked window frames, all the shades drawn like there was nothing more to see. It wanted to fly under the radar.

Sketchy strike one.

Lara turned and smiled wide. "Got it."

We continued toward the building, Rachel's car intentionally forgotten. I should've removed my hand but I couldn't. Sure, it was part of our cover story, but I was having a harder and harder time keeping myself away from her. Especially after last night.

Since Mom died, I'd never been a great sleeper. Even on the road, away from any concern for my family or their safety, I still slept light. So when the first strains of Lara's cries bled into my room, I was out of bed with my sweatpants on in seconds.

I'd reached her quickly, quick enough to know she was having a nightmare, to hear her whimpering someone's name, but not quick enough to hear what it was. She knew, though. Just like she knew the reason for the nightmare. Something haunted the woman at my side. Maybe it was her sister's disappearance, but that wasn't the only thing.

The door to the small building swung open as we approached, and Lara stiffened. *We were being watched.*

"Lara?" There was no mistaking Brielle's voice from our call yesterday.

The brunette receptionist was petite and wearing a tight skirt and blouse. Professional attire, yet her hair was pulled into two buns on either side of her head, each tied with a bow. The choice made her look young—young enough to make me wonder, with concern, just how old she was. *Sketchy strike two.*

"Yes, hi." Lara inched ahead to greet the woman and then introduced me. "Brielle, this is my partner, Calder."

"Welcome, welcome. Please come in." She ushered us inside, the polished interior a Mr. Hyde compared to the exterior's tattered Dr. Jekyll.

Bright professional paint. Big, fake floral arrangements. To the right, a cushy waiting area that could've passed for the lobby of a fancy spa, its green velvet sofa looking untouched. Photographs of happy couples decorated the walls, and I recognized some of them as stock images like the ones Callum had manipulated to create our fake backstories.

The reception area was a mannequin made up in luxury, masquerading to the clientele who paid, according to Lara, $8,000 per person for their two-week retreat.

At the desk, I clocked two security cameras: one behind reception and facing out, the other mounted behind a hanging plant on the far side of the room. That was the important one. I followed its line of sight to a short hallway on our left ending in two locked doors with keypad handles that advertised something worth protecting.

"Welcome to Wilderness Within. We're so glad to be working with you toward achieving ultimate happiness." Brielle bubbled another canned response as she moved behind the desk and motioned to two tall glasses on the counter, both filled to the brim with a green mixture. "I have our proprietary matcha smoothies here for each of you. Beginning this journey with healthy intentions and an open frame of mind is the first step to success."

"Thank you." Lara took a glass and a sip before I could stop her. When both women looked at me, I declined with a sharp shake of my head.

Lara glared, and my hand balled into a fist as she took another sip. *Dammit.*

"I received the forms you filled out via email, Lara. I do have some final consents and waivers here for both of you to sign. Since you're joining us a day into the seminar, Dr. Julia doesn't want to delay your arrival, so I'm going to ask that you take them with you and fill them out on your way to the retreat or later this evening."

She set the small stack of papers on the counter.

"Sure," Lara said as I slid the forms in front of me. Liability waivers. Confidentiality notices. And nondisclosure agreements. *Interesting.*

It was possible that they genuinely wanted to protect all conversations and proprietary methods used during the retreat. But the gut feeling I had wasn't one of legitimacy.

"And I see we brought no bags, which means you followed the instructions in my message perfectly," she continued, genuinely thrilled that we'd followed the orders to not bring any clothing or personal belongings with us, indicating that they would be provided. *That was a new one for me.* We'd just finished picking up Lara's things from the B and B when the message came through, so now our bags sat in the back of my truck.

"At the retreat, we want everyone to feel like they're in a safe space to be vulnerable and that all of our guests are on equal footing while with us. So in order to eliminate any distractions or unproductive judgments, we provide all participants with the same uniform, so to speak. Do you have any questions about anything so far?"

"No," I answered. *None she'd be able—or, more likely, willing—to answer.*

"Wonderful." She extended her arm in the direction of the hallway, Vanna White–style. "Beyond the door at the end of the hall is a locker room. There, you'll find two things. First, there are shelves for men and women containing sized bundles of our Wilderness Within wardrobe that you will need to change into before you head to the retreat."

A metal key clicked onto the counter, a tag with the number 19 attached to the ring.

"After you've changed, you can secure your clothes along with any personal effects in locker number nineteen. Cell phones. Wallets. Everything." When neither Lara nor I made a comment, she went on. "I can assure you, this building is very secure and is monitored by twenty-four-hour surveillance. Also, as you've experienced, we are very selective about handing out our location, only doing so to those who have pledged their commitment to the retreat."

Meaning anyone who forked over enough cash to prove they were worth admittance.

"The code for the locker room is 0129. Once you've changed and secured your things, I'll be waiting for you here and will escort you to your ride."

"Great." My frown deepened as I watched Lara lift her glass, her intention to drain the rest of the drink before heading back to change.

Shit. I shot my hand out for the key and purposely knocked into Lara's arm, sending the glass flying from her fingers.

"No!" Lara let out a choked cry, attempting to catch the cup, but all that did was send it spinning toward her, spraying the front of her shirt and blazer and jeans with green goop.

"Damn. I'm sorry." I feigned dismay, picking the glass up from the floor; the rug under the desk had prevented it from shattering.

"Do you have tissues or something?" I asked, seeing Brielle just standing there, eyes wide, hands over her mouth like she'd just witnessed a car crash, not a spilled smoothie.

"Oh, y-yes. Yes," she stammered, darting from one side of the desk to the other like a squirrel stuck in the middle of the road, unsure which way to go. "I . . . I'm sorry. I guess we must be out."

"Maybe in the back?" I prompted.

"I have to change anyway . . ." Lara said, her glare barely tethered behind her calm facade.

"I'll check, but changing is just easier," Brielle said with a nervous laugh. "The code is 0129," she reminded us as we moved down the hall, her voice carrying the distinct edge of panic.

"You did that on purpose," Lara accused as soon as the locker room door closed behind us. "Why—"

I silenced her with a hard look and a finger to my lips. Mercifully, her whole demeanor became compliant, begrudgingly, as her head swiveled to follow me while I scanned the room.

A video camera in a changing area was illegal, but I wasn't willing to put it past them.

Moving along the perimeter, I scanned the corners of the ceiling and then stopped in front of the shelves of individually wrapped clothes. I slid the bundles side to side, confirming there was no camera behind them or some kind of peephole from another room. Taking a pack of clothes labeled *Small* from the women's rack, I held it out to Lara along with my explanation.

"I don't trust that they didn't put something in the smoothie." I kept my voice quiet. No video surveillance didn't implicitly imply no audio recording.

Her eyes rounded and sank to her wet shirt. "It tasted like matcha . . ."

"How do you feel?" I asked when she took the clothing bundle from me. I turned then to pull a large one down for myself.

"Nervous but otherwise fine so far," she admitted honestly, tearing open the plastic and pulling out what amounted to a loose T-shirt and matching pants.

"Good." I opened my own pack, relieved it was only clothes we had to change, not shoes. When I looked back, Lara was staring at the shirt she'd held up in front of her, her brows knotted. "What is it?"

"Nothing, I just can't believe I paid eight thousand dollars to wear scrubs for two weeks." She tried to brush off the question with uneasy humor, like I hadn't noticed her hesitation and the shadows staining her eyes. "I need to change, can you . . ."

"Yeah," I clipped and strode over to the locker marked 19.

Keeping my back to her, I unlocked it and began putting my things inside. Backpack. Empty wallet. Phone. I'd already left my Glock in the truck because there was no chance—legitimate or not—they'd let me take a weapon to the program.

"Do you think they're going to go through our things?"

"Probably," I said without hesitation, attempting to ignore the sound of fabric separating from her skin. *Attempting and failing.*

"But if they check our wallets, they'll see our IDs—"

"We're not going to leave them," I told her, biting my cheek when I heard the zipper of her jeans pause. "Just take yours out when you're . . . done, and I'll handle it."

The metal teeth continued to flay apart, simultaneously unzipping the seam between reality and fantasy in my mind. And when I closed my eyes, it only gave that fantasy a highlight reel. Her top gone. The denim unwrapped from her legs, leaving her in nothing but—

"Calder." Lara's voice, and her soft hand on my shoulder, made me jerk. "I'm done."

Fuck, so was I.

Bracing myself, I turned, unable to stop my eyes from sweeping down and taking her in.

If the goal was for everyone to be in uniform attire that wasn't a distraction for any reason, then Lara had failed. Or maybe I had. Because I could still track down every dip and curve of her body beneath the supposedly ill-fitting clothes. The bland blue-gray color even set off the vibrant shade of her hair and the pink in her cheeks—a pink that deepened the longer I looked.

Maybe it was the smoothie. Had to be. But she was the doctor; she'd know whether something was wrong.

"You can add your stuff," I said, and stepped behind her so I could change.

"Where are you going to keep our IDs?"

"With us," I grunted, moving as quick as I could, but hiding a hard-on underneath too-thin clothes wasn't an easy feat.

"How?" she asked as I came up behind her, setting my clothes on the top shelf where she couldn't reach.

Lara spun around, her eyes wide when they landed on my chest.

"Give them to me. I'll show you," I rumbled, my voice dropping lower.

She extended her hand, her license and two credit cards in her palm.

Taking them, I lined their edges up with my own and then bent down with my back to the wall of shelves like I was going to tie my shoe.

Tipping forward onto the ball of my foot, I grabbed the heel of my work boot and turned it to the side, revealing a hidden compartment. I looked up at Lara, my gaze conveying everything I needed her to know—and her blank expression told me she received the message.

After tucking all forms of our identification into the carved-out slot, I slid the heel back in place.

"Wow," she said when I straightened. "What other gadgets do you have hiding in your clothes?"

We both froze. The catch of her breath marked the tear of lust as it arrowed into my chest. What she'd said . . . *what we both heard.* It was a mistake. A misspeak. But she didn't correct it.

I waited, seconds peeling away like rings of a centuries-old oak, yet she didn't try to correct herself—to overexplain. Just like at the diner, we found ourselves shoved together in a way that neither of us wanted to untangle.

But we had to. *I had to.*

"We should go." I held out my arm, channeling all my energy into stopping a certain *gadget* from turning to stone.

"Wonderful." Old Brielle was back, and it appeared she'd found a roll of paper towels from somewhere in the bowels of the building to clean up the smoothie. "I can take you to your ride. Would you like a water for the drive? It'll only be about fifteen minutes."

Shit . . . Maybe Callum's drone could've found the retreat in short order.

"No, thank you," Lara answered this time, my caution clearly affecting her decision.

"Okay. Then if I could just have your key . . ." She trailed off as I set the key ring on the desk. "Great. This way, please."

We followed her outside, her heels rocking on the uneven dirt path that led around the side of the building.

"Hold on one second," I called before we reached the corner. Brielle and Lara both stopped and looked at me, confused. "I just want to make sure I locked my truck."

Brielle nodded but looked impatient.

I jogged over to my truck, my feet kicking up dirt as I checked the driver's-side door. I let the handle land with a thud so everyone heard the confirmation.

"All good," I said, returning with another apology. "Sorry about that."

Without comment, Brielle directed us around to the back of the building, where I noted the second egress point. Two exits, as I'd expected for a building this size. One out front and one out back. Why we were brought around the building rather than straight through was an inconsistency I filed away for further consideration.

Behind the building, an early 2000s Jeep Wrangler was parked on the other side of a small thatch of trees, the engine running at a low hum. Mud caked the tires and wheel wells, and the windshield had only a patch where the wipers had cleared the grime.

The driver's-side door swung open.

"Lara, Calder. This is Matthew." Again, Brielle's display hand swung out to introduce the large man striding toward us.

He wasn't wearing scrubs, instead sporting boots, jeans, and a black polo underneath a black jacket. I had a feeling he was around Creighton's age, but with his bald head and intensely serious face, he appeared older.

"Matthew is our head of security and will be escorting you to the campsite."

"Security?" I asked, extending my hand along with an easy smile and a feigned laugh. "Do we have something to worry about?"

"Oh, no—"

"We're heading into BLM lands, Mr. Calder," the man rasped, not only cutting off Brielle but also completely ignoring her as he took my hand, his grip dominating. "There are lots of dangers in the wilderness—bears, wolves, cougars, bison. Someone has to be prepared."

And that someone was apparently him.

He drew his hand back and rested it on his hip, revealing a glimpse of his holster inside his jacket. I forcibly stopped myself from raising an eyebrow; the Beretta 9mm would be useless against all the mammals he'd listed. Like an umbrella in the middle of a hurricane, the small-caliber handgun would hardly put a dent in most of the animals that roamed the BLM. *A person, on the other hand . . .* My jaw screwed tighter.

"We need to get going. Dr. Julia is waiting." His terse tone was followed by an equally abrupt about-face.

"Enjoy your journey!" Brielle called after us, to which Lara returned a thank-you.

Taking the path behind the vehicle, I noted the missing license plate from the back. Bold. There must have been a plate for it somewhere; they wouldn't risk driving on the road without one, but out here . . . the BLM lands were the real Wild West. No one policed them, let alone checked license plates. Then again, if you had nothing to hide, there was no reason to have no plate.

Sketchy strike three.

I opened the passenger door, lifting the seat forward for Lara. We shared a glance as she slid into the back, her pupils more dilated than before.

"You okay?" I asked quietly once she was seated, waiting for her nod before I pushed the seat back and climbed in.

The inside of the vehicle was spartan. Not quite as dirty as the exterior but certainly not luxurious. The center console displayed the incorrect time and was set to *Cassette* mode; whatever year the Jeep was had to have been one of the last when they still put cassette players in the dash.

"Buckle up. The ride out is bumpy," Matthew ordered and then hit the play button. As he shifted the manual transmission into reverse, a woman's voice came through the speakers, low and melodious.

"Hello. My name is Dr. Julia Maxwell, and today you are embarking on your journey toward a transcendent relationship, a journey that begins by stripping away the distractions and expectations of the world we live in and finding the wilderness within . . ."

Chapter 10

Calder

Rule #31: Learn to see what doesn't belong. The human presence creates patterns that disrupt the natural world.

A few years ago, we'd been hired to find an Idaho woman who'd gone missing while on vacation in Florida. Creed had taken the drive down to Miami, while I'd been tasked with looking into the time-share company that owned the condo she rented. Despite growing up on the ranch with Cassius's repeated endurance trials, I'd been surprised to find how ill prepared I was to withstand the desperate determination of a time-share sales pitch. The ninety minutes was nothing short of indoctrination rather than information.

And that was exactly what I was reminded of while listening to Maxwell's introduction to the retreat: thirty minutes of carefully crafted indoctrination for a decision we couldn't get out of. At least, not easily.

Pretending to be engrossed in her slow, soothing proselytization, I monitored the direction and distance from the parking lot. We headed east for about five miles and then, maneuvering through a stretch of trees, turned a little northwest, following preworn tire tracks through the mud I presumed the Jeep had made over the last several days.

When we finally stopped, it was in a pocket of dense forest that couldn't have been more than seven or eight miles from the main road—a relatively short distance, considering all the doctor's emphasis on wilderness immersion. Then again, in Wyoming, you didn't have to go very far into untouched land to feel light-years away from civilization.

Matthew parked and turned off the engine just as Maxwell's introduction ended. "We're here," our impassive guide announced and exited the Jeep, seemingly expecting me and Lara to follow.

I pulled the passenger seat forward and froze. Lara's skin was flushed, from her cheeks to her chest, her pupils the sharpest of points. Wisps of her hair had worked their way out of the tie holding them back.

"You okay?" I held out my hand.

She nodded, but as she clutched my hand and stepped out of the Jeep, she murmured, low enough for only me to hear, "There was something in the smoothie." Anger shot through me, and she felt it. "I'm fine." She gave my fingers a hard squeeze as if to order, *Don't say anything.*

Say anything? The anger I felt was lethal, not conversational. *Drugging the people who came here?* I tried to bury the emotion, knowing it wouldn't serve me, but I couldn't. The way I . . . thought . . . about her wouldn't let me.

"Calder," she pleaded softly, but my feet stayed rooted—fossilized to the ground. *I should stop this now.* It didn't matter whose plan this was. When she was with me, she was my responsibility. *Mine.*

She tugged on my hand, and against my better judgment, I moved. I went with her. *I made another exception to my rules.*

"This way," Matthew said, not bothering to wait before leading us through the trees.

Even with the crunch of footfalls on foliage shed to the forest floor, the cool breeze still quivered with the very faint hum of cars through the woods—audible if you were listening for it—confirming my assessment.

After about twenty yards, the trees opened to a small clearing with a woman, her dark hair braided down her back, sitting cross-legged on a giant blanket in the center, her eyes closed and her hands on her knees in apparent meditation.

"Dr. Julia."

She had to have heard our approach, but Dr. Julia Maxwell didn't open her eyes until Matthew called to her.

"Lara, Calder." She came to life with a broad, staggeringly white smile and rose to greet us. "Welcome to Wilderness Within." Her voice resonated with authority and warmth, an invitation to trust.

Now in her early fifties, Maxwell looked a decade younger, her features frozen with unnatural assistance. Like Matthew, she wasn't wearing the uniform, but instead loose pants that landed at her ankles and a long cardigan draped over a plain top, all in beige.

"Welcome," she repeated and took my hand. "I'm Dr. Julia Maxwell."

She wasn't wearing any rings, but the tan lines on several of her fingers suggested that bare skin wasn't her norm—and neither was the Wyoming climate. Unless she was outside working on a ranch from sunup to sundown, but even if I hadn't known about her condo in Palm Beach, her hands were too soft to suggest days spent outside doing any kind of manual labor.

"Is this the retreat?" I assumed the part of skeptical boyfriend, figuring it was common.

Beside me, Matthew tensed, and the larger man's arms folded slowly over his chest; he didn't like that I'd questioned the doctor. *His leader.*

Maxwell lifted a staying hand, though her gaze was so intent on mine that I almost missed the wordless order to stand down.

"This," Maxwell began, her extended hand flattening and sweeping around to indicate the glen, "is the Sanctuary. It's where all of your private counseling sessions will occur with me over the next two weeks. It's a reassuring distance from the center of the retreat, where you don't have to worry about any infringement on your privacy."

As I followed her hand, the tracker in me picked up on the subtle but slightly depressed browner grass that led through the trees to the east, worn down from the trek of couples back and forth from the base of the campsite to *the Sanctuary*.

While that bruised earth was by far the most defined on the ground, it wasn't the only path from the glen. A mar of footprints led north of the clearing, much fainter, probably only traveled by one or very few persons. *That was the path I wanted to follow.*

"I always start every retreat experience here with each couple individually," Maxwell continued, and I returned my focus to her. Exploration would have to happen later. "I find that beginning this journey in a safe, intimate, and secluded space is a critical first step to connecting to our true, wild cores. So the three of us will be resting and reflecting here for the next hour before I bring you to the campsite and to your lodgings."

"I see," I murmured, my pulse thudding just a little harder when Maxwell reached for Lara's hand.

"Hello, Lara. Did you enjoy your welcome smoothie?"

"I did, thank you." Whether or not the words were true, there was no disguising the subtle change in Lara's voice. It was a little lower. A little slower.

"It's my own proprietary blend of all-natural ingredients. I designed it to help my clients relax and start to break through those barriers that hinder us from reaching our wild core," Maxwell explained, her head turning, eyes lingering on me for an extra second, making sure I knew that *she knew* I hadn't taken the offered drink. But there wasn't chastisement in her gaze—only confidence. Like she enjoyed breaking disbelievers down.

Releasing Lara's hand, Maxwell turned to the security guard. "Thank you, Matthew."

It was equal parts gratitude and dismissal, yet the security guard hesitated, watching the woman with a look I recognized as longing. I pretended my interpretation wasn't from acute familiarity.

When Matthew realized I was observing him, he quickly lowered his head in a strange kind of subservient bow and murmured, "Yes, ma'am."

Maxwell's expression was frozen in a placid smile until her guard was gone from sight.

"Please, join me." She motioned to the blanket.

I moved my hand on Lara's back and guided her over. *Part of the ruse.* It was part of the ruse that my hand slid to her waist, then up along her back, her shoulders as she sat, and that my chest thumped extra hard when she turned her face up to mine. *Part of the ruse.*

Lowering to join her, my uncomfortably stiff dick reminded me that the only person I was fooling was myself.

"Welcome again to Wilderness Within. It is my honor to be a part of your relationship journey and transformation over the next two weeks." Maxwell sat on the pillow that had been hidden under her before, placing her a level above us. "Since you've listened to my introduction on your ride here, we can begin taking those first important steps to finding our wild cores. Only once we access that inner wildness and nurture it, can we truly connect with one another."

If I were here because I'd wanted what her retreat promised, it would be easy to believe her. Whether she believed it herself or was that good of an actor, Dr. Julia Maxwell presented her platform with a conviction that was almost hypnotic. Maybe it was hypnotic, I thought, glancing at Lara, with her wide eyes and blushed cheeks, her attention rapt on the smooth-talking doctor.

"Where we begin today isn't with the basics, but the essentials. Not the details of your relationship history, but the depth. When you leave the Sanctuary today, you should leave uncomfortable," she warned. "Like a muscle you haven't used in some time was just exercised to its limit."

Lara shifted next to me, her knee bumping against mine. We'd rehearsed details this morning. Fast timelines and essential facts. All the things Maxwell had just said she didn't care to know.

"Your wild core isn't soft or tame. It's been caged. Locked away and silenced." Her eyes drifted slowly between Lara and me. "I used to ask couples why they'd come here—what brought them to Wilderness Within. I don't need to ask anymore." Her confidence continued to spread, smooth like butter from her mouth, and hunted for any trace of ego.

Growing up on the ranch meant limited contact with the outside world beyond a monthly trip into town for groceries, clothes, and to visit the library. After eighteen years of survivalist living, going to college and being around so many people had been a shock to my system.

Cassius might not have prepared us for society, but as in all things, adaption and evolution was still the key to survival. So I'd signed up for an introductory psych course my first semester.

As it had turned out, reading people and understanding their motivations was, at its core, very similar to tracking in the wilderness. They both involved seeing disruptions in nature's patterns. Like how the bent blades of grass heading north from this small glen, and the subtle injection of self-importance in Maxwell's altruistic air, suggested there could be more to the story.

Was she a full-blown narcissist like most cult leaders? *Maybe. Maybe not.* I'd found narcissism harder to detect in women, mostly because narcissistic men tended to be grandiose: overt, egocentric, and needing attention. Whereas women presented more covertly. In Maxwell's case, the appearance of altruism and a desire to help could be simultaneously masking and fueling her need for superiority.

"I know you're here because you feel like there is something missing in your relationship. Something broken. Well, I'm here to tell you not to worry; nothing is missing, just buried under the trappings and trauma of society, and it's my job to reach inside the both of you and break that wildness free." She acted out the notion with her hands, stretching them out as she spoke, locking her fingers tight together, and then yanking them apart. "There can be no secrets here. No hesitation. The only way this will work is with wild honesty. Wild intimacy. And wild trust."

I listened, feigning complete focus. What kind of secrets did she coax her clients to reveal? Anyone who could afford $8,000 for a two-week retreat was the kind of person who could afford big secrets.

Was that where her money came from? Drugging her clients and then blackmailing them with the protected information they gave her?

"Are you ready to break free, Lara? Calder?"

I nodded as Lara answered, "Yes."

"Wonderful." Maxwell's smile spread. "Then let's begin."

Chapter 11

Lara

I could see how easily my sister would've been swept away into this experience. How catastrophically eagerly she would've believed the promises Wilderness Within made about the retreat and what it would do. The steps they took to insulate you from the world. And I could imagine how fluidly Dr. Julia's words would've reached her. A life raft amid a sea of bad relationships.

If Wilderness Within were a real program, I'd be grateful.

If it were real, I doubted there'd be a bad feeling in the pit of my stomach like there was now.

"We'll start in the shallows of your relationship. An oath to each other. A warm comfort we can wade back to once we enter into the deep." Dr. Julia's dulcet voice glided through the clearing like a bending breeze.

I wanted to *wade* into the campsite and look for Rachel, but I'd picked this path. Subterfuge versus stakeout. Ruse over restrained reconnaissance. *A fake relationship with Calder Stone.*

It was that part that filled the pit of my stomach with a swarm of butterflies.

"If you could both turn and look at each other," Dr. Julia continued, her smile hardly moving.

My head tipped as I looked at the man beside me, only to find his gaze was already rooted around me like the arms of a tree, strong and decades deep. I shivered.

"Good. Now, Lara, if you could repeat after me: Calder, I promise to you my wild honesty and my wild intimacy."

Oh god. My throat constricted. Forget subterfuge—this was sabotage. *Self-sabotage.* Admitting to things that I should never admit to. I tried to swallow, but my nerves clawed at the sides of my throat. What had I said? *The best lies were rooted in truth.*

"Calder." I inhaled. "I promise to you my wild honesty and my wild . . . intimacy."

Was it the breeze that made his shirt tighten over his shoulders right then?

"Now, Calder. If you could repeat the same back."

"Lara, I promise to you my wild honesty and my wild intimacy." His collected tone skipped over the words like a rock across the water's surface, hardly disturbing the tension that had tangled them on my own tongue, and yet there was still a ripple of . . . something. Something he wanted to ignore.

"Wonderful. This is our tether—your promise to each other to move through this program with heroic honesty," Dr. Julia continued, and I welcomed the reprieve to turn back to her.

My gaze roamed a slow path over her placid face. She was very pretty—more so in person than in the photographs Callum had found online. She was the kind of person one would say had aged gracefully, but *gracefully* wasn't enough for her. No matter how calmly she spoke or how slow her movements, her forehead never creased, and no crinkles formed at the corners of her eyes when she smiled.

"Lara, I want you to share what draws you to Calder. Presently. Every day. Not the initial spark of your relationship, but the wick in his core that continues to make you burn for him."

Burn for him. What a way to put it . . . and what a truth it carried, even in our bed of lies. My lips peeled apart, letting my breath whoosh out but leaving the heat stamped in my cheeks.

"Share with him," she added, the open flat of her palm directing my attention back to my fake boyfriend.

Calder's face was expressionless, though the rest of him was anything but. The stubble of his beard whispered at the tension underneath, the cords of his neck pulled taut where they moored to his clavicles. Frustration honed every rugged inch of him, from his shoulders to his fingertips, the ends denting the fabric of his pants where it gripped his knees.

"What draws me . . ." I repeated slowly. *His anatomical encyclopedia of perfect muscles.* An easy answer, but not real enough. My gaze caught in Calder's once more, secured in his bearings, and the answer tumbled unbidden off my tongue. "His intentionality."

Heat burned through my cheeks, and my heart pounded a mile a minute. "And it's not a wick, but an anchor that pulls me toward him when things are calm. When they aren't . . . his intentions are always steady."

To help me. To protect me. *To take care of me.* Even in the span of the last few days, his every decision fell into this category.

"I can see that," Dr. Julia murmured, waiting until she had both our attention to continue. "The way you've looked to him this entire time is the way a captain seeks the lighthouse anchored to the shore."

My throat bobbed as I swallowed. *For show. It was all for show.*

"And, Calder, will you share what draws you to Lara?"

"Her determination," he replied smoothly. *Zero hesitation.*

My eyes snapped wide.

"You're surprised by that, Lara?"

Crap. Whatever he said shouldn't have mattered, just like he shouldn't think—*could never know*—that what I'd said was the truth. But I couldn't take it back now.

"I . . . yes."

"Why?"

The best lies were rooted in truth. "Because he doesn't always agree with all my decisions."

"Good," she praised me, her bright white smile flashing briefly. "One of the biggest chains imprisoning our wild core is perceived weaknesses. A weakness can never be completely hidden because they are intrinsic to our wildness, and to free it, we must embrace our vulnerabilities, not only in ourselves but in our partners."

She turned to Calder.

"Let's start with you this time, Calder. What do you perceive is your biggest weakness?" she asked, then added, "And remember, this is your safe place for wild honesty."

Calder grunted, and I didn't have to feign my interest in his forthcoming answer. *What would he think his weakness was? Would he even share something that was true?* Probably not. He did this—he deceived—as a part of his job. Why would he hesitate to deceive me?

"My need to be in control."

My brows popped up. Well, that was certainly true, *Mr. Director*.

"I see." Dr. Julia hummed, her attention turning on me for a brief moment, cataloging . . . something before she looked back to Calder. "And where does that need come from?"

Calder hesitated, and I caught the single fire of his *masseter*. "I'm the oldest of six. Our mom passed away when some of my siblings were pretty young, so I was responsible for them."

"Very understandable," she agreed and tilted her head. "But needing to be responsible and needing to be in control are very different things. I need wild honesty, Calder, if this is going to work. What about that event made you need control?"

While she may have been a lot of things, Dr. Julia's training, her counseling, wasn't a sham. She'd recognized that Calder was holding back and called him on it. She asked for our honesty and wasn't afraid to demand it when necessary.

I couldn't help but glance at him, wondering whether this was where he'd draw the line—if this was where the lies would start.

"My mother was murdered."

"I'm very sorry about that, Calder. How old were you?"

"Fifteen."

"Still a child."

"But old enough." His insistence was unrepentant.

Dr. Julia linked her hands in her lap. "So, you have a need to be in control because you're afraid if you're not, something could happen to the people you care about like it did to your mother?"

"I guess." His voice cracked for the first time, the slightest blemish to the calm he'd maintained up to now.

"Is that how you are with Lara?"

I won't sacrifice your safety for the sake of your feelings. I'd thought I understood before, but I hadn't. Not even close.

His answer fired from his lips. "Yes."

I waited for the next question, knowing what it was—where she was going. I was prepared to answer the same question and offer up my weakness. And then she asked me something completely different.

"Lara, I couldn't help but notice you were surprised by Calder's answer," she remarked, and I stilled. Maybe if I hadn't drunk her damn smoothie, I could've been better about hiding my reactions. *Would've been.* "Do you perceive Calder's need for control as a weakness in your relationship?"

Even if I wanted to say yes—to add another lie on top of the one about our relationship—I couldn't. Yes, Calder took control, but it wasn't a weakness. It was a relief. A respite from the person I otherwise had to be. *The person I'd been for so long.*

"No," I answered softly, my gaze caged in the magnetic trap of his.

Dr. Julia wouldn't let it go. "How do you feel about his need for control?"

"I . . ." My throat bobbed as I swallowed. It didn't matter what I said. Truth or lie, it didn't matter because this wasn't real. "I appreciate it."

Calder's disbelief ripped through him. The slight tightening of his grip on his knees. The ricochet of his clenching jaw. And his almost imperceptible inhale as it breached the firm line of his lips.

"You appreciate it," Dr. Julia repeated, slightly louder. "Good. This is good. Do you see how important this is?" Her enthusiasm was genuine, though her question rhetorical. "What you perceived as a weakness, Calder—what has kept you from letting your relationship with Lara deepen—is actually something that brings Lara closer to you. Now, Lara, I want you to explain why you appreciate it, but I want you to look at Calder when you share."

Look at . . .

My body began to comply, though my mind was rife with concerns. *Just say what she wants to hear from you,* I mentally coached myself. I shouldn't have been nervous to tell him. It didn't matter *what* I told him, because this wasn't real.

This was nothing more than a placebo effect. A chemical reaction to a well-crafted ruse.

He. And. I. Weren't. Real.

Dredging in a deep breath, I scooted on the blanket to face Calder, Dr. Julia fading into my periphery.

"Take his hands," Dr. Julia interrupted gently, the instruction poking another hole in my confidence.

Touch him? Wasn't it enough that he could hear how my heart had started to beat harder against my chest? Wasn't it enough that he could see the way my lungs strained against my ribs? *Now she wanted to let him feel how the truth trembled behind the construct of this lie.*

His eyes goldened like autumn-approaching leaves preparing for their downfall, and his palms turned up. *I could do this. I had to do this.* I slid my fingers into his. *Thenar. Hypothenar. Extensor pollicis longus.* The Latin blurred like fingerprints scorched of their design. It was fine. A glorified handshake. *That altered the fabric of my identity.*

Calder gave me a reassuring squeeze, and my head jerked up from our locked hands.

"I appreciate when you take control, Calder," I began again. *See? You can do this.* My tongue swiped over my lips, and I didn't miss how his gaze lowered to my mouth. "I appreciate when you take control, because I'm in control of so much that I don't know how to let go. I'm afraid to let go—afraid I don't know how to." *Afraid of what I'd lose . . . who I'd let down again if I did.* "When you take over . . . it's a relief."

"Why can you let go with him? Why do you feel safe letting go with Calder?" Dr. Julia's soft prompt wove through my ears.

"Because I trust you. I trust . . . your intentions." I tried to swallow but couldn't. The way he looked at me was like he could read between the beats of my pulse. Like he could see that there was so much more I'd . . . trust him with. *If things were different.*

"Wonderful, Lara. Wonderful. I really think we're onto something groundbreaking here," Dr. Julia praised, and the soft press of her hand on my shoulder snapped the bubble that had absorbed Calder and me. I quickly drew my hands back and wiped my palms on my knees. "Now, tell me what do you believe is the critical weakness holding back your wild core? What keeps you from unapologetically grasping for what you want in your relationship with Calder?"

The fact that it can't be real. My jaw dropped, and I quickly snapped it shut.

My weakness . . . His perfect anatomy. The slow curl of his lips. The way he takes care of me even though he hardly knows me.

The way I wanted the man who broke my sister's heart.

"My need for control?" I blurted out.

"Really?" Her tone made it clear she didn't believe me. After regarding me for a long second, she turned to Calder. "Do you agree?"

"No," Calder answered flatly. The way he saw right through me was as sharp as a knife through my chest.

I glared at him. *Why couldn't he just go along with it?*

"Good. We welcome wild honesty, don't we, Lara?" *Great.* I was being chided by a therapist about how I was treating my fake boyfriend.

"Yes," I said through tight teeth.

"So, tell her, Calder—what do you believe her weakness to be?" Man, this woman wasn't pulling any punches. As soon as it sounded less than honest, she dug her hooks in and demanded the truth. *Ironic, since all this truth was built on a single lie.*

And of course, Calder wouldn't hold back; I knew he wouldn't. "You always take care of everyone before yourself."

I gaped. "I'm a doctor. It's my job to take care of everyone else."

Dr. Julia spoke first. "An honorable defense, Lara, but I doubt Calder was referring to your priorities while working."

It didn't matter, I chanted in my head. *It didn't matter.* "It's not a weakness to take care of people you care about."

"Putting other people first is natural and can be healthy and even necessary in certain scenarios, but in a relationship, it creates a barrier around your wild core. Tell me, who do you prioritize in your relationship with Calder?"

My mind started to spin. From the drink. From everything. It tumbled my thoughts until I could no more distinguish real from fake than I could between up and down.

I prioritized no one because there was no relationship. No me and Calder. The only reason we were here was—"My sister," I blurted out, a train wreck in two words.

Dr. Julia leaned back. Calder froze.

Crap. Emergency code CRAP. I should've said Calder. That was the right answer. She'd asked who I prioritized in our relationship, and I should've said him. That was where this whole thing was heading. Instead, I'd answered with another truth.

"Your sister?" Dr. Julia repeated. I wished there was some way I could backpedal—some correction that would make sense. But there wasn't. "Can you elaborate?"

My mouth parted. This was my fault. I was the one who'd put myself in this position. I was the one who'd insisted we join the retreat as a couple. *I was the one who brought up Rachel.*

"I . . ." My voice trailed off. *Pull it together, Dr. Crane. This is an emergency, and your lies are about to bleed out.* I had to give her something—something that wouldn't make her question why we were here. "Calder and my sister dated back in college. I guess . . . I guess I still put her and how things ended between them above my own feelings."

It took a few long moments for the dust my words had kicked up to settle. Long moments in which Dr. Julia said nothing, probably recognizing that she'd just pulled our fake relationship off its proverbial life support. Long moments that turned the magnetic gold in Calder's eyes molten with something I couldn't decipher, didn't understand. Like there was something he wanted to say but was intentionally silent. Not because of Dr. Julia, but because he was protecting me from something else.

"Thank you, Lara," the doctor said softly, reaching out and resting her hand on my shoulder. She did the same with Calder. "Thank you, Calder. I honor and appreciate your honesty and vulnerability. I can see the connection you two have. It's very primal. Very promising. I can't say I've had too many couples so willing to open up about themselves on the first attempt."

Maybe because there was no relationship for us to lose.

"I believe we have taken a significant first step here today to unburdening the wild core of yourselves and your relationship together." It was only when she stood that my vacant attention finally broke. "Now, the truth is only part of reaching our wild core. Like a worked muscle, it needs to be stretched so it doesn't lose that openness."

Calder rose with her and then extended his hand to help me. Without thinking, I sank my fingers into his, where the warmth I'd felt in his gaze became tangible again.

"Ben is going to take you to your lodgings." Dr. Julia extended her arm, beckoning a very different security guard from the trees.

Ben looked around our age, though with a kind of baby weight to his face and thinning blond hair. He wore the same attire as Matthew, but filled it out with bravado rather than muscle. With more smirk than smile, he barely spared Calder a glance before looking at me in a way that made my insides cringe. The only thing that made it worse was the way he rested one hand on the gun at his waist like it was glued there—and to the power trip that having a weapon gave him.

"In your tent, you'll find a schedule of events for the next two weeks, along with two journals, where you should spend the next two hours reflecting on our session. We touched on a lot of deep and important things, and it's critical to give yourself that alone time to process and respond to what we've uncovered."

She walked us over to Ben, and Calder stopped in front of me, partially shielding me from the other man.

I guess I wasn't the only one who noticed his leer.

"I encourage you to spend your reflection outside, in nature. There are several open paths you can explore around your tent. My only request is that you respect the privacy of the other guests." Dr. Julia's pleasant voice took on an edge. "Everyone has received instructions to remain separate until our first group session tomorrow morning, and the guards will be around to make sure everyone honors those instructions. It's critical that the initial stage of this experience not be overwhelmed with too many external factors."

Great. So even if Rachel was here, we wouldn't find out until the morning.

Chapter 12

Calder

Rule #20: The best weapon is the one between your ears.

Whistling the tune of that piña colada song, Ben led us roughly a quarter of a mile along the foot-worn path away from Maxwell's sanctuary.

Fresh branches and fallen leaves crowed under our footsteps, the grass a tired yellow from the consistent battering. Through the trees, slivers of large light-brown tents tucked into the enveloping foliage. I created a mental map as we walked, the details of our surroundings marred only by the distraction of who walked ahead of me.

Lara was on edge. Her shoulders were pinched. Her head snapped from side to side, and her hands continued to comb through the red-drenched waves of her hair, as though searching for a place to moor her thoughts. I had a feeling they oscillated on the same tipping point as my own.

"After how things ended between them."

Her answer haunted me like a midday shadow. The way she'd looked . . . the way she'd talked . . . the things she hadn't mentioned. Lara didn't know a fraction of what had happened between Rachel and me. *Something that didn't matter now,* I forced myself to remember.

What we discussed with Maxwell. . . it might be the truth, but it wasn't something to fix. *We* weren't something to fix.

"Here are the bathrooms. Toilets. Showers." Ben pointed to the portable structure that gave some semblance of the comforts of indoor plumbing.

We followed another path to the left, passing two more tents that sat several yards off the worn ground.

"Tent seven," came our introduction at the end of the narrowed walkway, a cabin-size sandy-colored tent that terminated that portion of the trail.

Ben unzipped the flap and held it back for us to enter.

No lock on the tent door. Common, but not comforting.

I followed Lara closely inside, my balled-up fist resisting the urge to make a statement to the guard who still openly tried to get a look at her ass.

For all the luxury promised with the high price tag, the residence we were given for the next two weeks was surprisingly sparse. A small table and two chairs on one side of the tent and a bed on the other. A single queen-size bed.

I looked at Lara at the exact moment her eyes swung to me.

One bed for the two of us.

Heat thumped down to my groin. *Dammit.* Had I really thought they'd give us each a sleeping bag? It was a couples' retreat. Was I really that naive?

"A gong will sound when it's time to return from reflection to your tents. Dinner will be brought to you at five thirty. At six thirty, Dr. Julia will do an evening reflection, which will come through your speaker." Ben jerked his chin to indicate the Bluetooth speaker hanging from the top of the tent. "When Dr. Julia is finished, you'll have an hour to journal and use the bathroom or shower before curfew," he continued to drone from the tent-flap doorway, his eyes lingering on Lara. "Curfew is eight p.m. unless there's an evening activity taking place. The schedule and your journals are there on the bed."

Lara turned and bent to examine the papers, oblivious to the crude gaze of the guard as it roamed over her ass. Like his authority vacated our right to privacy and Lara's right to decency, Ben stepped inside our tent for a better view. And it took only two steps to put me right in front of him.

"Anything else?" I asked with only a thin veneer of calm coating my voice.

His frustrated glare clashed with my furious one.

I'd dealt with plenty of men like Ben in the retrieval business. Cops, federal agents, or any kind of head of security usually bristled at my assistance on a case. Give a man any kind of badge and weapon, and far too many times an inflated sense of ego followed. But never had that egregious ego tempted me to violence the way it did now.

I stepped closer, and instantly he removed his foot from inside our tent. Nostrils flaring, Ben frowned like a spoiled child and looked me up and down.

"Curfew is strict. Don't let me find you roaming outside the tent after hours," he grunted, puffing out his chest and casually strumming his fingers on his gun. "It can be dangerous out there."

Subtle. I doubted it would amount to any real threat.

I stayed in the entrance as he walked away, whistling that same tune, and waited until he was completely out of sight before I faced Lara again.

"What was that about?"

"Nothing." I shrugged it off and then quickly swept the tent for any kind of bug or recording device. After confirming there were none, I took my turn examining what was left for us.

Two journals. Two pens. And the next day's itinerary.

1. 8am—breakfast
2. 9am—morning reflection hour
3. 10am—Group Intimacy Trust Session #1

I stopped reading. *What the hell had I agreed to?*

"I'm sorry."

I replaced the paper and turned.

Lara sat cross-legged on one of the chairs, her bottom lip pinched between her teeth. She looked younger like this. Uncertain. Wholly unlike the woman who'd shown up at the ranch with her almost reckless determination to find her sister, and very much like the woman who'd fallen asleep on my couch only to be woken by her nightmares.

"For what?"

"For bringing up Rachel," she answered, tucking her arms to her chest. "I felt like Dr. Julia was searching . . . like I had to give her something, and it just came out."

The urge to walk over and take her face in my hands, promise her I was going to fix this, and then kiss her overwhelmed all rationality. I wondered whether giving in to the ache was exactly what Maxwell had meant when she talked about freeing your *wild core.*

I cleared my throat—and my thoughts.

"Don't apologize. The best lies are the ones closest to the truth." I repeated her own words back to her and handed her a notebook. "It would be a real barrier if . . ." *If we were really dating.*

"Yeah." Lara pursed her lips, flipping through the blank pages of the journal. "So, we're supposed to reflect . . . for an hour . . . What are we really going to do?"

Her eyes lifted to mine, and instantly I imagined her bent over that bed. Naked. Legs spread wide. Obeying my every command.

Fuck.

"I'm going back to the Sanctuary." I grunted and grabbed my journal, needing to get my dick under control. "There was another path leading away from the clearing. Since Maxwell didn't follow us when we left, I'm assuming her tent is separate from everyone else's."

"Okay, then I'll explore the campground—"

"Lara—"

"Don't tell me to stay. She told us to walk around, so I'm going to wander around . . . and look for my sister."

"I thought you appreciate when I take control."

Her eyes narrowed. *"Sometimes."*

Determination. My exhale pushed through my nostrils. I was the one who'd said I admired it; I'd made my bed, and now I had to sleep in it. My gaze homed in on the singular, ominous structure. Another problem to be dealt with later.

"Fine," I caved. "Walk the trails. See who you see, but don't talk to anyone. I don't want us to get kicked out before we have a chance to find answers."

Lara stared at me for an extended second and then agreed. "Fine."

"We'll meet back here at the gong." It wasn't a question, but I waited for her nod of acknowledgment anyway. "And stay away from Ben," I ordered, my voice devolving into a base growl, and left before I could gauge her reaction. *Or before I could think too long about mine.*

Leaving our tent, I cut a path behind it and parallel to the trail we'd taken from the Sanctuary. Normally, I'd follow existing paths and overlay my footprints on already damaged underbrush, but with a dozen couples, plus Ben, Matthew, Maxwell, and possibly other guards roaming the woods, I opted for my own course. For today, privacy trumped obscurity.

About twenty yards east, the tree line opened to windswept prairie bordered by a highway and the slopes of the Tetons in the distance. Setting my back to a large tree trunk, I scanned the perimeter and listened. *Alone.* I braced my back against the tree and lifted my left foot onto my knee.

While my and Lara's IDs were hidden in my right boot, the left held a satellite phone with a two-week-long battery. The number pad slid out from beneath the screen. Thankfully, the only number I needed was on speed dial.

"I was about to send out the search drones," Callum answered gruffly.

"No, you weren't." It hadn't been nearly long enough for that. "Are you tracing my location? We're near Route 1-91. I see Tetons to my north and Glover Peak due east. I'd say we're about fifteen or so miles south of Bondurant."

"12.2."

Close enough.

"You meet Maxwell?"

"I can see the connection you two have. It's very primal. Very promising."

"Yeah." I sounded hoarse. Hell, I felt hoarse. *Raw.* "So far, it's just been Maxwell and two of the security for the retreat, Matthew and Ben. Any word from the reporter?"

"Yeah. Lots of them."

"Well, that sounds ominous." I rubbed my hand along my jaw.

"Hannah is Hannah Layman, and the rumor on campus was that even though Hannah had a serious boyfriend at the time, she was involved in something with her therapist and her therapist's boyfriend."

"What kind of something? Like a relationship?"

"A sexual kind of something. Her roommates thought she was being groomed, but had no proof."

"Shit." I blew out a tight breath. "Did he confirm it was Maxwell?"

"No, but Hannah's parents did." Callum paused as one of his weather alerts went off in the background. After silencing it, he continued, "Once I had her name, I looked them up. They moved after her death, so it took me a minute to track them down, but they confirmed Maxwell was Hannah's therapist. Apparently, she taught a one-day seminar on managing college stress to the incoming freshman, and Hannah was in that lecture."

"Did they know what was going on?"

"Not until after her death. Apparently, Hannah left her boyfriend a letter alluding to what had happened and he brought it to them. They hired a private investigator to look into Hannah's death and Maxwell's involvement."

"But he didn't find anything," I assumed with a growl.

"No, he did. Just not enough." No matter how guilty a party looked, without proof, an accusation was nothing more than defamation. "Maxwell's boyfriend at the time was a lawyer. James Braun. According to Mrs. Layman, he threatened them with a pretty hefty defamation lawsuit if they publicly insinuated anything criminal about him or Maxwell without proof."

Damn.

"Proof they didn't have."

"They weren't going to stop looking, but then Maxwell up and disappeared."

"Here," I murmured, shaking my head.

"No one named James there?"

"Not yet."

"I'll try to find a more recent photo for you."

"Maybe she left the boyfriend behind, too." Especially if he'd almost cost her her license. "I'll do a sweep over your coordinates tomorrow morning and keep you updated with anything new."

"Things start up here at eight," I informed him.

Callum preferred to gather footage either at dusk, when his drone could be mistaken for some kind of bat, or at dawn, when few would be up and looking at the sky.

"I'll be gone before then. Also, there's another storm cell coming through tonight. Hope your shelter is sufficient."

The closest Callum came to a warning.

"Thank—"

The line went dead.

I replaced the phone in my heel and headed toward the Sanctuary.

When the outhouse peeked through the trees, I started counting the tents I'd marked between the Sanctuary and bathrooms. When I saw the third, I dipped back into the forest and walked south, paralleling the slope of the highway.

Thirty yards brought me back to the empty clearing. In the opposite corner, I crouched and examined the recently trod packed dirt and crushed leaves. Rising, I carefully followed their trail into denser woods, a mix of lodgepole pine and spruce. Ahead, something white and unmistakably unnatural caught my attention.

A camper, the name *Tiffen* scripted onto the side. A luxury RV, and this one was at least as big as my 33FB, though not towable.

There was no way that thing took the same path to get here that we did.

Veering to the right, I circled the motor home from the safety of the trees, taking note of the license plate still attached to the back; I memorized the number to send to Callum later.

As I backtracked to the other side of the camper, I saw the clear, flat path the RV had taken to this plateau—a direct shot from the road. Maybe a ten- to fifteen-minute drive.

The door to the RV swung open, and I stopped instantly as Maxwell stepped out, a cell phone pinned to her ear. I wedged against the nearest tree and stilled to listen.

"Another one? I thought we decided only one per session." Her exasperation carried like a cloud of dust.

One what? And what agreement?

A branch snapped near me and Maxwell spun around. *Shit. Was that*—I looked over my shoulder and saw Matthew coming from the Sanctuary. Neither of them saw me.

Maxwell went back to her call, and the security guard's pace increased when he heard her worry.

"Will it be better, my darling?"

Darling. I went on alert. *Was she talking to James?*

Matthew continued closer until she held up a finger to stop him.

"I know. You're right." Her head lowered in defeat. "There are a few prospects. I will need a little more time to find the very best for the Garden."

Garden? I didn't get the feeling that Maxwell had a green thumb. Not from her luxury camper, nor her soft, tanned hands.

She ended the call and lashed out at her right-hand man. "Yes, Matthew?"

"Do you want to stay here tonight, Julia?"

Where else—

"No. I want to go back to the Garden tonight and see Adam." *Adam. Not James. And again, this garden.*

Shit. I added the key words to my mental list of more questions for Callum.

Maxwell rubbed her hand across her brow. "I'm going to have to sleep out here tomorrow and probably the following few nights. I need to have more private therapy sessions with the couples to screen them for admission to the Garden. The one from yesterday—the two who argued. I'll start with them."

There was definitely something more going on here. Maxwell was using Wilderness Within as a sieve, filtering couples through some kind of assessment, then inviting ones with certain characteristics to this "garden."

Was that where Rachel had gone? *The Garden?*

"Is that what you want?" Matthew questioned her, and I saw her flinch, her real answer a blip over her face before she masked it and went to him, lifting her hand to his cheek.

"Of course, dear Matthew."

I pressed into the tree, hearing her instruct him to head back to the office and pick up dinner for the participants. I watched her disappear inside and waited for Matthew to leave before moving from my post.

My eyes lingered on the camper. Maxwell had to have notes on her clients in there, which meant I had to take a look inside. And it sounded like tonight might be my only shot. *Storm or not.*

Chapter 13

Calder

Rule #33: Know your exits before you need them. Whether it's a room, a tent, or a conversation, always have an escape route planned.

"Bathroom. Tent. Tent. Our tent." Lara drew her finger along the map she'd sketched into her journal, tapping twice on the spot that marked our current location.

We'd both returned to the tent just as the dinner gong sounded. Within moments, the thud of approaching footfalls terminated in Ben's petulant voice announcing he had our dinner.

Neither of us said a word as he delivered the food, which was more promising than the accommodations: a chicken-and-quinoa salad layered in vegetables and a citrus dressing. Ben took one long look at Lara like he'd *almost* dug up the gumption to dare me to do something about it, but then cowered, reminded us about curfew, and left. I listened to his footsteps, nodding when it was clear for us to speak freely.

She immediately opened her journal again.

"I counted three more groupings of three tents, all branching off of this grassy area here." She'd created a map of the area in lines and shapes. "Beyond the last set of tents, there's a small overlook above a stream or river—I'm not sure."

"Probably a small stream off the Snake River." I closed her journal and handed it back to her. "Your map is good."

It wasn't detailed by any means, but I was impressed by her spatial awareness . . . and the fact that she'd thought to draw it out in the first place. Cassius would be impressed, too. My father had a thing for maps. A hobby . . . if Cassius Stone had hobbies. He made them. Collected them. Restored them. My old bedroom had become his map room.

"The history of the world can be deduced from maps alone. He who controls the land, controls the story." Not a rule, but a resounding truth.

"Thanks." She traded the notebook for her dinner bowl and sank onto the edge of the bed. "I only passed five couples, but none of them . . . I didn't see Rachel." She mixed everything with her cardboard fork. "What did you find?"

I wanted her to keep talking so she wouldn't hoover in her food, but it was too late for that. She'd finished almost half her dinner by the time I started mine.

"Maxwell has a motor home on the other side of the Sanctuary where she stays. She was on the phone with a man named Adam when I found it. He sounded like her significant other."

I'd stopped at the same point along my way back to message Callum again.

"What were they talking about?" She scooped up her last bite.

"It sounds like she uses Wilderness Within as some kind of recruitment platform for a place she called 'the Garden.' She mentioned inviting another couple or two from this session to whatever this garden is." I tipped forward and scraped together a bite, adding, "She did suggest one of the other couples who was arguing during their session with her yesterday, so it could be for some kind of advanced therapy."

Lara nodded and swallowed, setting her empty bowl on the table, her expression lost in thought.

"I also spoke to Callum."

Her head whipped to the side. "What? How?"

I dropped my fork into my bowl and carefully lifted my left foot.

My silence encouraged hers as I opened the heel and showed her the tiny phone.

Her voice dropped to a whisper. "Did he talk to the reporter?"

I nodded. "And Hannah's parents. It was Maxwell who was treating Hannah—who they believe she was involved in some kind of . . . relationship with."

"Relationship?" Her jaw dropped.

"A threesome, possibly coerced, with Maxwell and Maxwell's boyfriend at the time."

"Oh my god. That's so . . ." Horror rounded her eyes. "Is Adam . . . Was he—"

"No. Maxwell's boyfriend at the time was a lawyer, James Braun. He threatened to sue Hannah's parents if they continued to come after them. Didn't matter, because Maxwell disappeared out here not long after that."

"Oh my god." Her hand pressed to her stomach like she was going to be sick. "So they groomed Hannah, and then she committed suicide. I can't believe this." Her wild eyes found mine. "Do you think that's what she's doing here? Grooming people for this garden and then—oh, god. What if Rachel—"

"Lara. Breathe." I bent in front of her and grabbed her shoulders like I could hold her thoughts steady. "A good tracker moves at a pace of observation, not desperation. We can't get ahead of ourselves." *Again.*

Breathing deeply, she took a moment and then nodded. "What rule is that?"

"Thirty." I released her and sat back in the other chair, contemplating an additional tenet to my survival rules: *Remain at least three feet from Lara Crane at all times.*

Gripping the edge of her seat, she bent forward and hung her head. "Maybe I should get a copy of these rules."

"Why? Do you want to obey me all the time?" The words were out before I could stop them.

She didn't look at me, but she'd heard me loud and clear. Her shoulders stiffened, and I caught the fringes of pink spreading through her cheeks.

Ignore it.

Ignore me.

Of course, she wouldn't.

Lara lifted her head, her hooded eyes finding mine. "And if I do?"

There was a loud screech that turned to static. We both jerked our attention to the small speaker hanging from the top of the tent just as Maxwell's voice imbued the space.

I knew I was in bad shape when I welcomed this woman's intrusion.

"Good evening, my wild hunters. I hope you had a wonderful afternoon immersed in nature and encouraging your wild core."

We stared at the speaker like it would make a difference. Like ignoring a growing fire was an effective way to extinguish it.

"Tonight, our reflection will be on something critical to your wild core and the connection it has with others: physical intimacy."

Shit.

I didn't know who turned first, but in a second, my eyes pierced hers. Everything that shouldn't fade away did—where we were, who we were here for—and left only one thought: *Why was there so much space between us?*

"In the wild, animals don't disguise or hide their intentions or attraction, yet that is what society has taught us to do. Cage it. Restrain it. Compose it."

I should have turned away. Looked away. *Moved away.* But I couldn't seem to tear my gaze from her. And Maxwell spoke like she knew it.

"Physical intimacy isn't only about touch. It's about allowing your wild core to recognize its counterpart in another without barrier or restraint. When you find that connection with another person or persons, society teaches us it's a distraction, when the truth is that it's instinct. When you are hungry, you eat. When you are thirsty, you drink. And when your wild core connects with its counterpart, you give in."

My hand tightened on my knee. Believing Maxwell to be right or wrong didn't change my position. It didn't change my attraction to the woman in front of me. And it couldn't change my ability to act on it.

The last thing I could do was reach for Lara, no matter how my wild core or how my throbbing cock felt.

Stifling a grunt, I reached for one of the refillable steel water bottles that had been delivered along with the dinner tray, uncapped it, and downed several long dregs.

"That connection . . . you feel it now in your tents. The awareness between you and your partner humming like a current of electricity that needs to be grounded."

Current of electricity? More like the charge of a hydrogen bomb.

Lara stood suddenly and I went still, my body bracing for a physical attack. She dragged her chair toward the corner of the tent and climbed up on it.

"What are you doing?" I spun the cap back on the bottle and shot to my feet.

"Seeing if I can turn it off." She grabbed the speaker.

"The body knows what the mind denies," Maxwell continued, her voice contorting as Lara searched for a switch.

"Probably not," I replied and then cursed when she stood on her tiptoes.

In the span of a split second, I broke my tentative new tenet. Forget three feet—I put myself within three inches of her, worried she would lose her balance and fall.

"We will begin intimacy sessions tomorrow, but starting tonight, I encourage you to not censor your desires."

"Lara, let me," I growled as the chair wobbled on the unsteady ground.

"I think I found it." She ignored me and shoved herself up higher, leaning forward. *Big mistake.*

"Lara!" I lunged just as the chair toppled, her feet sliding off the edge and sending her straight into my arms.

She cried out as my arms locked around her waist, catching her as the chair tumbled to the ground, forgotten by the time it landed.

All that was left was her in my arms. Her body against mine. Her lavender scent. Her face inches above my own.

"No matter what trials you face in your relationship, resisting or restricting the primal urge for physical connection is dangerous."

We stared into our own destruction, face-to-face with our own lies. Maxwell's warning dumped gasoline on our fire.

I gritted my teeth. Heartbeats scrambled through my veins like I was at the edge of a cliff. At the precipice of peril by the press of her softness. I couldn't be doing this—shouldn't be feeling this. But I did, and I couldn't stop it. Couldn't contain it. No matter all my rules, she was their every exception.

Fuck. I should've let her fall.

A terrible thought, but she would've been fine. Eighteen inches off the ground wasn't catastrophic; a big step rather than a fall. But this . . . this wasn't saving her. Maybe Maxwell was right: Resisting this was dangerous, but giving in would be destruction.

Still, I couldn't let her go.

The soft pants of her breath drew me closer. The roam of her blush over her freckled skin and down her neck muddied my reason. And these clothes . . . they concealed nothing. Not the hard peaks of her nipples, nor the stretch of my stiff cock.

"Surrender the illusion of control and the weight of society's propriety."

Lara's hands on my shoulders began to move, sliding around the back of my neck and locking at my nape. Her deep-green gaze settled on my mouth. *Wanting.* And then her tongue slid along her lips, whipping a foreshock through me. A warning of something coming. A tectonic crash that only promised ruin.

"Welcome the wildness of want in all its forms. Sight and sound. Scent and the sensation of touch," Maxwell continued like she was only speaking to us. To me.

I was already drowning in the feel of her, but every inhale of her soft lavender scent only threatened to swallow me from the inside out.

"When it grips you, hold it right back. Latch on to the beast and let it consume you."

Was her goal of this to work everyone up? To send the campsite into a cacophony of cries and moans? Was that her power trip? Controlling others' intimacies?

Instinct forced my breathing to slow. *Control your heart rate, control your fear. Panic is a luxury survival doesn't afford.* The caution Cassius had carved into our bones reared its head now. Now, when I wasn't in the wilderness. When I wasn't facing a threat of nature or weather or beast. When the only danger I had to fear was my attraction to my ex-girlfriend's younger sister. Electric like lightning. Thudding like thunder. Drenching like a downpour. And gnawing as though made of the sharpest teeth.

"Here in the wild, there are no rules. Here in the wild, there is no propriety. Here in the wild, you can take what you want."

Lara's gaze unspooled into mine, netting us in a moment of stillness as her head drifted lower, her mouth on a clear trajectory for mine. A path so unmistakable, it might as well have been etched in stone.

What if I took one kiss? One taste so I would know how to survive this? How to survive her . . .

"Calder . . ." Want baked into her breathless plea, desperate and needy. And god, did I want to give in. To take care of her the way she wanted. *The way I'd always wanted.*

I went stiff—some parts of me more painfully than others. There were some things in nature humans weren't made to survive; the smartest survivalist recognized those things. Respected those things. And retreated from those things.

For me, Lara Crane was one of those things.

There was no having or taking, touching or kissing my fake girlfriend. There was no coming away unscathed from succumbing to the ache for my ex-girlfriend's little sister.

And I couldn't do that to her. Or to me.

"There is no off button," I grunted and loosened my hold. Every inch of her body, as it slid along mine, left only scorched earth behind until her feet touched the ground.

Even if there was a way to turn it off, I didn't trust whatever—or whoever—might be lurking to not take note that we'd silenced the very coaching we'd paid for.

"I'm sorry—"

"I'm going to step outside for a few minutes. Excuse me." I took myself, and my raging hard-on, through the flap to our tent and as far away from her as I could justify.

—

Shit.

I scrubbed my hands over my face and then adjusted my throbbing cock, heading away from our tent as the last dregs of dusk filtered through the trees.

For several long, assessing minutes, I did nothing but pace and listen to the breeze whirring the leaves. The rustle and crack of branches giving way under the scamper of small animals. The howls of wolves galloping over the open expanse in the distance.

What the hell was I doing?

I closed my eyes and saw Lara's face looking down at me again. Hoping . . . Wanting . . .

No. I turned in the direction of Maxwell's RV, clinging to my directive. *Finding Rachel—not falling for her sister.* The sooner we left here, the better.

We hadn't even made it a single night—*with one bed*—"Dammit." Another bridge we would need to cross soon. There wasn't room for someone to sleep on the floor. I'd admit that I'd toyed with the idea of sharing, respectfully, the bed, but now there was no way.

I'd sleep outside; it wasn't like I hadn't done it hundreds of times before.

Cassius and Mom had engineered countless "sleepovers" when we were younger. Not sleepovers at friends' houses like most kids. Sleepovers in nature. *Survival sleepovers.*

They'd started short, a night or two in the wilderness. Then they'd gotten longer, with no shelter. No prepared food. Nothing but what Cassius and Mom had taught. How to track. How to forage. How to hunt. How to find or make shelter.

The final "sleepover" was ten days in the wilderness. Ten days, at fifteen, to prove we were capable of survival. Callum's ten days were spent almost entirely in straight sequence of severe thunderstorms; we'd always said that was the crucible that had turned him into a storm chaser.

Mine had finished the day before Mom was murdered.

"Calder?" Lara whispered, and I turned, though not enough to get a good look at her; my body was still raw from the burn of having her against me. "Dr. Julia's done," she said like I had any interest in returning to my own personal purgatory.

"Okay," I acknowledged, but didn't move.

Of course, she didn't move, either. "Can I ask you something?"

All kinds of warning sirens went off in my head, and I ignored them. *A new, bad habit of mine.* "Yeah."

She quietly came over and stood beside me. "If Rachel isn't here. Do you think she's . . ."

"No." I wasn't going to go down that path. First, because a tracker's rule of thumb was alive until proven dead. And second, because I wouldn't—couldn't—do that to Lara.

Lara didn't say anything for a beat, her eyes drawn to the indeterminate shelter of shadows around us. I tried my damnedest not to look, but it wasn't very long at all before my gaze slid to her profile.

The button curl of her nose. The bow of her lips. The freckles that charted constellations over her cheeks.

Beauty wasn't a survival skill except in the most figurative of ways, and so it was something I rarely took notice of beyond an objective assessment. But Lara . . . she was the kind of beauty I couldn't ignore. The kind that stopped me in my tracks.

It didn't steal my breath, but chambered it in my chest like a bullet to be fired. One that would obliterate the thin veneer of professionalism between us. Regardless of our past connection, she'd hired me to do a job—to find her sister—and that was all this should be. It was all it was supposed to be. *All it could be.*

A breeze swept around us, and Lara shivered.

"You should go back inside."

She stubbornly didn't move.

"I'm sorry about your mother. I didn't know she was . . . murdered."

A thread of tension pulled my spine taut. "It was a long time ago."

"Time is like a drug. It doesn't cure the disease, only lessens the symptoms." She folded her arms. "At least, in my experience."

There was a reason I didn't talk about Mom, but it didn't have anything to do with the circumstance of her death, only the aftermath. But maybe that was why I should share it. Because what had just happened in the tent almost completely ruptured my restraint.

I needed a reminder that the worst thing in my life wasn't not having Lara, but what could happen if I lost her.

"Before Stonewall and us, Mom was a biochemical engineer," I began, the growing darkness dragging me into the memory of a similarly dark night. "She was recruited by the Department of Defense to work on a top-secret project, and that's where she met Cassius. He was FBI."

"Wow." The shape of her lips should've been criminal, the way it broke into my senses and entered a thieving heat into my veins. "So, your dad . . ."

"Didn't always exile technology?" I chuckled. "No. Far from it. That's why he is the way he is. He knows just how . . . dangerous it can be."

"What were they working on?"

"I don't know exactly. They never spoke of it. And to guess . . . well, there are very few kinds of top-secret DOD projects that the government would need one of the nation's foremost biochemical scientists for."

"A weapon?" I could hear surprise elevate her voice.

"Or a defense against one."

The concepts of biochemical warfare and bioterrorism weren't new to the discussion of national defense. As time ticked on, it had only become more likely that bioagents would be the weapons of the future.

"Whatever it was, it didn't end well. At least in my parents' opinion. They both got out of the field and moved here. Off the grid. Away from that project. Their past." I paused, hearing a screech just before a dark, winged shadow of a bat zipped across the pale haze of the full moon. "At least they tried."

Lara shivered, her arm brushing against mine.

"I was fifteen. Cassius had taken Creed, Callum, and Colt out for storm-survival training. I was at the house with Mom, Colby, and Creighton." I remembered the smell of electricity in the air. The hush of the wind through the trees like a whispered warning. I was surprised to feel my throat start to tighten. "I was in the library, studying. I had a geography test the next day. Colby came running in, trying to hide from Creighton because she'd let her pet chicks loose in his room."

Lara laughed then, the sound forcing me to stop. Rich and decadent, just like the homemade hot chocolate Mom had loved to drink every night. And just as uncommon.

"You're telling me you never played pranks on your sister?" I couldn't help but ask.

"I . . ." Lara pulled her lips between her teeth and then expelled a smaller, sadder laugh. "No, I never really pranked Rachel. We were always on the same side."

Instantly, I regretted the question, and went back to my story.

"I was about to buffer their fight when Mom came running in. Something was wrong, I could see it. Even as a kid, you kind of know—can sense when something is really wrong." I lifted my hand

and ran it along my jaw like I could forcibly stop it from clenching. "She told me to take them into the storm cellar. It's underground, below the greenhouse."

My pulse marched steadily faster, and I listened to the deeper, slower breaths from the woman beside me, the heat of her lungs beginning to fog the chilled air.

"I thought it was the storm," I continued, a hoarseness entering my voice. "Now, when I look back, I remember how she sounded. How she looked. I remember the handgun at her side and the panic in her eyes. But that night, I was annoyed because I had to study, and Colby and Creighton were antagonizing each other and Mom wasn't doing anything about it. I was too . . . preoccupied that the reality didn't really register."

"You were fifteen," Lara repeated, like I hadn't heard it all before.

In the distance, lightning cracked through the dark sky, too far away to be anything but ornamental illumination.

"I took my siblings to the cellar and waited like she'd instructed. Even underground, we could still hear the storm play out like the rumble and tumble of a football stadium."

Thunder boomed in the distance, the sound soft by the time it reached us.

"It took a long time . . . too long, trying to keep Creighton and Colby off each other to realize she hadn't joined us."

And I remembered the moment I did.

"There was a boom, almost like thunder but not. And then two more of the same. It wasn't the storm. As soon as I opened the cellar door to find her, there were two loud cracks. They were gunshots, not thunder."

"Calder . . ." I felt her hand land on my arm, warm like the draw of a bonfire tugging me effortlessly and invisibly closer.

"I ordered Creighton and Colby to stay silent in the cellar. When I climbed out, I looked in through the kitchen and saw the masked men, all in black, all armed. As soon as they headed for the library, I went through the outside door to look for Mom."

The raindrops had been frigid on my face, their pelting like frozen buckshot on my skin, the pain nothing compared to the sight of her.

"She was face down on the ground in front of the house. I knew . . ." By fifteen, I'd hunted enough times to know when a living thing was dead.

"Oh, Calder." The thick hitch of sympathy in her voice anchored me to the present.

"Before I could go to her, the masked men came outside, so I ran back to the cellar . . ."

"You had to protect your siblings."

I nodded, slowly, because even now, a decade and a half later, I still wondered whether it had been the right choice.

"I grabbed a knife from the kitchen and went back to the cellar. We were in there for an hour before Cassius opened the door."

"God, Calder . . . I'm so sorry. I can't . . . I can't imagine." Her head swayed. "Why . . . Who were they? What did they want?"

"Something to do with her work for the government. I don't know if Cassius ever really knew—found out what they were looking for." And if he had, he wouldn't have said. It was safer if none of us knew.

In the aftermath, he'd insisted on cleaning up the library on his own, though there were books and papers everywhere. And even after he had it put back together, I'd come across him roaming the library shelves late at night, looking for something yet nothing in particular.

"That's horrible, Calder. I'm so sorry."

My chin dipped, and I shifted my weight. "That's the worst part for him. That he and Mom walked away from everything—that they abandoned that part of their life and everything that came along with it, and it still found them. And took her."

"And the police, did they try to find—"

"The police weren't involved," I said, realizing how that must sound to a veritable stranger. *Like we hadn't wanted to know who had murdered Mom or why.*

"W-what?"

"Cassius never called them. Never reported her death. He buried her on the ranch. Out on the bluff past Callum's Watchtower."

"I don't understand."

I didn't expect her to. Maybe that was why I didn't share this story often. After all this time, I wasn't worried like Cassius was that those men or others like them would still come looking.

"There are six of us and one of him. In almost every scenario, survival isn't about skills or strength, but simply about preparation and odds. And the odds of those men, or others, coming back to the ranch if word got out that Dr. Annemarie Stone had died or Cassius started digging around . . ." Another slow shake of my head was all I needed to complete the thought.

It was too great a risk.

"Is that why you call him Cassius?"

My inhale pierced the pristine night air. What did it matter what I called him? *What did it matter to her?*

I wanted to brush off the question, but when I looked at her, the beauty of empathy stained her irises and flushed her cheeks . . . Maybe beauty wasn't a tool of survival but instead the most unexpected weapon, the way it held me hostage, demanding a reply.

"I call him Cassius because I missed all the signs that night," I finally said, the howl of wolves echoing in the distance. "I missed all the signs of her panic. Of her fear. I missed that she didn't come in the cellar with us, which she would've done if it was a storm. I missed her gun at her side. I missed the chance to realize what was really going on and the danger we were in. And I missed my chance to help her. To save her—"

"Calder, no." Lara stepped in front of me, red hair flinging wildly in front of her face as she shook her head. "He wouldn't blame you—he couldn't. You were a kid—"

"It doesn't matter if he does or doesn't. I was old enough to survive in the wilderness on my own. Old enough to track and hunt and climb mountains on my own. Old enough to spend nights on end in the wilderness, with no food or shelter, and survive. Old enough to know better."

I saw the way Cassius looked at me after that night—or the way his regard had changed *because* of that night. He knew I'd found her. But my brothers and sister . . . he'd shielded from the sight, burying her as soon as the rain broke in the morning.

"But your siblings—"

"Were safe in the cellar."

"You don't know what would've happened. Maybe if you'd done anything different, it would've made it worse," she countered, then suddenly shuddered, stepping back with a press of her fingertips to her lips.

"Maybe," I said slowly, angling my head to get a better look at her now that darkness had claimed most of the sky. "Lara—"

"How . . . how do you live with that?" She forced a swallow. "How do you live with not knowing what would've happened if you'd done something different?"

The question had its hooks in far deeper than superficial curiosity; it was written in every line on her face.

Every muscle in my body tensed. *What was she carrying? What guilt? And for whom?* I wanted to ask, but I couldn't without giving her an answer first.

"You carry the uncertainty like every ship carries an anchor." My gaze netted around hers. "With time, you learn when it should hold you back and how to lift it and carry it with you when it shouldn't."

She let out a deep exhale, taking a beat to absorb my words.

"Is this about Rachel? Because this isn't your fault. Whatever she's involved in . . ."

"I know." She nodded too easily, and for some reason, my hand reached out and caught her before she could walk away.

"I meant what I said earlier. You carry too much for others. Too much for her."

Silver moonlight dashed through her eyes. "Somebody had to, Calder. Somebody had to be there for her when y—everyone else walked away."

There was no mistaking the almost-slip of her tongue. I was starting to realize the truth about our past—about my past with her sister—was another anchor I carried. One I had no reason to yet every desire to let go of.

"Lara—"

"What's our plan for tomorrow?" Her decisiveness returned as part of her self-defense. No one could let her down when she was the one making all the decisions. *When she wasn't letting anyone in.*

I ran my hand along the back of my neck. "Confirm whether or not Rachel is here."

"And if she's not?" There wasn't much *if* about it.

"We'll see what we can learn from the other participants. Maxwell mentioned targeting another couple for this 'garden.' If it's something Rachel was involved in, maybe we can figure out a way to get on her radar, too. Figure out what and where it is."

"Okay." She took a step back. "I'm going to go get ready for bed. What do you . . ."

"I'll wait out here until you're done."

"I meant about sleeping . . ."

"I'll sleep on top of the covers," I said matter-of-factly, going completely against my previous decision to stay outside. *Because she made me weak.*

"Okay." She paused and then turned back to the tent.

If I was lucky, I'd spend most of the night searching Maxwell's RV, and not next to the warm temptation of her.

Chapter 14

Lara

A strangled cry tore me from sleep. *My strangled cry.*

Panic seized my pounding chest. If Calder heard—if I woke him again with my nightmares—I wouldn't be able to escape his questions this time.

But there was no waking him . . . because there was no *him*. I looked at the bed beside me, the blanket practically pristine, and suspected he'd never been here at all.

Was it because of earlier? When he'd stopped me from falling, my heart had burst into my throat. Wild beats. Flooding heat. Rampant need. When was the last time I'd felt something like that? Something so consuming. So controlling. So aching. *When had I* ever *felt something like that?*

And why wasn't I surprised that it was with him?

"Calder?" I whispered loudly when he didn't appear after a minute.

Maybe he'd gone outside or to the bathroom. Maybe I should do the same.

There had to be a curfew exception to use the bathroom, right?

I slid from the thin camping mattress, grabbed the small flashlight provided by the bedside, and quietly slipped on my shoes. A quick peek outside the tent revealed no Calder, so I started in the bathroom's direction.

The closer I got, the more unreasonable that thought became. He was a Stone. A survivalist. The very last thing he needed in the wilderness was a hole for excrement dressed up as indoor plumbing.

Sure enough, I reached the bathrooms and saw both stalls were unoccupied.

Where was he?

I spun around. There weren't that many places he could go. Bathrooms. Another tent. The communal area.

Maxwell's RV.

No, he wouldn't . . . I breathed out a curse. *He would.*

Just as I turned, I heard the unmistakable crunch of footsteps nearby. A flashlight zipped over the ground. A steady, whistled tune to the piña colada song.

Ben.

I clicked off my flashlight and made a beeline for tent 7, ducking behind it to catch my breath.

Calder should've told me he was going to do this. Anger rather than caution instigated my next move.

Keeping my flashlight off, I started in the direction Calder had gone earlier, relying only on the pallid light of the moon to guide me.

Calder had said there was another path from the clearing—the Sanctuary—that led to Maxwell's RV.

I couldn't go back through the woods—I'd lose too much light. But he'd said the RV was along the periphery, so if I continued to follow the trees, I'd have to find it eventually.

I walked for several minutes, my pace slow to stay quiet, even slower as I paused at every rustle and crunch, worried Ben was following me.

Maybe I should've waited. Maybe Calder had had a good reason for not telling me what he was doing, where he was going. But before I could decide to turn around, the RV came into view, everything as still as a tomb.

What if he wasn't here?

I looked over my shoulder and then back to the camper.

What if Calder went somewhere else? To talk to his brother? What if I assumed wrong?

My pulse felt like a gong ringing in my head as I sidled up to the edge of the trees, crouching into their canopy of needles. I squinted at the RV, looking for the slightest hint of movement.

Nothing.

What if Calder wasn't here? *What if there was something inside that could lead us to Rachel?* I was already here; I should at least look.

My eyes did one last sweep of the clearing before I jogged toward the motor home.

"Shit," I muttered when I reached it, lifting my hand to the bottom of the window; they were too high to peer into.

I moved to the far side of the RV, using the behemoth structure to shield myself from the woods as I considered my next move. The windows were too high up, but if I could find something to stand on . . . I peered around. *If there was a thick branch or log . . . or that.*

Before I could think better of it, my foot was on the rubber rim of one of the RV's tires and I was hoisting myself up.

I should've thought better of it. *Like I should've thought better of trying to reach the speaker in the tent.*

I lifted myself level with the dark glass just long enough to see a brief flash of light blind me from inside before I realized there was nothing for me to hold on to.

A small sound blipped from my throat as I tried to flatten against the wall of the camper—to stabilize myself. But I couldn't.

Swearing under my breath, I stepped down, but the height, and then the uneven landing, threw me off balance.

My arms flung out as my foot caught on a branch or rock or something. "Shit," I whimpered as I pitched backward—straight into something hard and steady and *male.*

One arm latched around my waist. Another snaked up, and a hand sealed over my mouth.

Oh god—

"It's me," a smooth voice whispered, barely audible in my ear, just as my body tensed, preparing for a fight.

Calder.

I almost collapsed with relief. Maybe that was why he held me to him for another second. "Don't speak," he ordered softly, his arms disappearing like they were made of shadows.

Large fingers circled my wrist and led me behind him, wordlessly and cautiously, to the camper's door, opening it and pulling me inside.

"What the hell are you doing?" Calder growled angrily.

"Me?" I hissed. "I woke up and you were gone!"

"Not a reason to come looking for me," he chided and clicked on his tiny flashlight, walking deeper into the RV.

The luxury interior now soaked into my perception. Wood-paneled finishes. Stainless steel. Large TV. Leather seating.

The only nature Dr. Julia seemed to be getting in touch with was the refined kind.

"Why didn't you tell me you were coming back here tonight?" I followed him over to the small desk.

The narrow glaring of his eyes gave me my answer. *My safety.*

Calder pinned the small flashlight between his teeth, aiming it at the pile of folders he'd pulled out and must have abandoned when he'd heard me outside.

I picked up the top one and opened it. *Kevin Erickson and Shaina Marks.* Below the names were dates and notes on the couple from the day they arrived, through all their sessions, until the program finished.

Her patient notes. That was what he'd come for.

A quick scan revealed nothing out of the ordinary. Quoted statements. Personality impressions. Dynamics between the couple. Hot-button topics. Areas of strength. Areas of progress. Perceptions. Intimacy assessment.

Nothing. I closed the file, the burn of frustration beginning to claw at my chest until I noticed Calder's efficient movements.

He opened and scanned files like I did, taking them from the larger pile and setting them into a smaller one. Except there was a third stack on the desk. It was only two folders, but he'd clearly set them aside for a reason.

"What are these?" I whispered, but didn't wait for an answer, remembering he was holding the flashlight in his mouth, and picked up the one on top.

Amita Lafayette.

Only a single name. She must've been from one of the singles groups.

The contents of the file appeared to be the same as the previous one I'd examined. Maybe Calder was making two piles for singles and couples.

I picked up the next one.

Lindsay James and Brent Underwood.

Not a singles pile after all.

Calder added another folder to the taller pile and grabbed one more.

He flipped it open as I asked again, "What's the small pile for?"

Calder stilled, but not because of my question. He looked at me and angled the folder in my direction.

My hands tingled with a burst of adrenaline, the papers almost falling from my hands as I bent forward to look.

Rachel Crane.

She was here. She was at the retreat. Or had been. *This was our proof.*

I went to take my sister's folder, but he set it down, open, on the desk. Drawing the flashlight from his mouth, he muttered, "This." He pointed to a marking in the upper right-hand corner of the first page. Something I hadn't noticed before.

EC. The initials were circled. *EC. Was it a person? A diagnosis?*

Calder took the folder from my hands, laid it on top of Rachel's, and pointed to the name notation in the corner: *EC.*

"What's EC?" I asked like he had any more of an answer than I did.

"Only some of them have the marking."

Was it some kind of progress marker? Something special offered to them? Maybe it was something. Maybe it was nothing.

Calder reached for the untouched stack of folders while I picked Rachel's up off the table, feeling the first flag of guilt. To look inside . . . it was more than her protected medical record. It was personal. It was all the things she'd chosen not to share with me. *Her sister.* But if there was another clue to her whereabouts, I didn't have a choice.

I flipped open the cover.

Assessment: ADD, low self-esteem

I skipped a page or two into the report, my eye catching on *Past Influences.*

Patient reports relationship spirals began during college. The words *inciting trigger* were in all capitals and underlined.

Calder.

His name wasn't there, but I saw it all the same.

What kind of sister was I that the man I'd asked to help rescue her was also the one responsible for being her *inciting trigger*?

What kind of sister was I for desiring Calder on top of it? For admiring every inch of him? For warming to his slightest touch? For holding my breath whenever he came close? *For almost kissing him?*

"Lara." Calder put his hand on top of the file, drawing me back to the moment and blocking me from reading more. "Hold this."

He handed me the flashlight.

Then, like he'd done in the locker room, Calder slid out the heel of his left boot and pulled the smallest cell phone known to man from the hollowed-out slot.

He took photos of the names on every chart in the EC stack.

"We need to go," he said once he was finished. "All of them need to go back in that drawer."

I nodded, but the only thing I could think was that I needed to keep my sister's file. *What if there was something else inside it? More information on what happened to her?*

Realistically, I knew there wasn't. I also knew we had to put everything back the way he'd found it, otherwise Dr. Julia might notice. Yet none of those very real cautions stopped me from sliding the papers from Rachel's file, folding them, and sticking them in the waistband of my scrubs at my back.

Within minutes, Calder had led us back out of the RV.

He moved swiftly with me to the edge of the trees, stopping suddenly, listening, and then facing me.

"Hold the back of my shirt and stay silent," he murmured and waited for me to follow his instruction.

I gripped the fabric, feeling the heat of his body ebb like a tide to my fingertips. And then he guided us into the trees.

At first, I wondered how he knew where to go. How he could see. How he could move in almost complete silence. But the answer to all those questions was the same: He'd grown up a Stone. This was what his upbringing had prepared him for.

Just like this was what Rachel's upbringing . . . our upbringing . . . had caused: her lack of caution in caustic relationships and my overabundance of it, practically resigning myself to celibacy.

But what had she found here? What happened after she'd gone through therapy with Dr. Julia? *What was EC?*

Questions marched like an army of anxious ants through my mind, providing a distraction so dizzying, I hadn't been worried about getting caught sneaking around the campsite until Calder halted suddenly and I went crashing into him.

He left arm snaked back and held me close behind him. *Something wasn't right.*

Calder looked over his shoulder and mouthed, *Ben.*

My breath caught, air pinching the center of my chest as I heard what he did. The footsteps and the low whistle of what I now considered his theme song.

Heartbeats hurtled into my veins. We were near the bathrooms; the white structure was maybe a dozen or so feet away. If we could just get there, we would have an excuse, a reason to be out of our tents. But even a few feet was a few too far.

Ben's flashlight zigzagged like a bullet of light around us. He wasn't guarding—he was hunting.

Slowly, Calder shifted us a single step to the right, putting us between two tall pine trees, their low branches destroyed, probably by bears.

The light chewed closer and the whistling stopped. Everything stopped. And then the footsteps propelled in our direction.

He'd heard us.

Calder spun around, his body completely shielding me against the tree at my back.

I tried to focus on the smooth metronome of Calder's breathing. In and out. Warm and slow. Rise and fall. But Ben's footsteps got louder. Closer. Fear drilled into my bones, incessant and terrifying.

He was going to find us.

I felt the panic start to seep in. The paralysis. The response triggered by my trauma.

"Lara."

My gaze snapped up, finding Calder's in the dark and holding on to it for dear life.

"Do you trust me?" The question was hardly more than a wisp of air against my nose, over my cheeks, along the shell of my ear.

Calder drew his face closer, the friction of his short beard warming the side of my cheek, waiting for my answer.

Trust him? I didn't have much of a choice. I'd asked for his help. I'd maneuvered us here. I'd gone out searching in the middle of the night when this was the exact reason why he'd decided to go alone.

I didn't have much of a choice in trusting him.

But neither did I need one.

"Yes," I answered, terror coiling from my toes all the way to my throat as Ben's footsteps sounded right on top of us.

What would he do? Would we get kicked out? What if he realized we'd just broken into the doctor's RV? What if he found her notes—

Calder took my jaw in his hands.

Air burrowed into my lungs. Hot and electric. And then there was nothing else—not the forest, nor the fear, nor the past, nor the future. Only the tachycardiac tension spiraling at hundreds of pulses a minute between us.

"Trust me," he rasped, and I realized just how little space there was between my mouth and his . . . right before there was none.

The touch of his lips was like three hundred volts to my stagnant heart.

I would know. I'd delivered the life-saving shock countless times in the ER. Yet I hadn't recognized any signs of my almost-demise until he was kissing me.

I hadn't recognized the way his hands padded the sides of my face, grounding me for what was coming. I hadn't recognized the urgent tremble of his voice needing me to trust him and stand clear of his plan. And I hadn't recognized the beat of blaring silence that warned of impending electricity before his mouth delivered the life-saving shock.

I hadn't recognized how dead I was until Calder's kiss brought me back to life.

I wished it was pure electricity that jolted my lips to part. Just like I wished it was pure panic that made my heart beat against its seams or adrenaline that infused my cells with heat. But it was none of those things that sent my senses into uncontrolled abandon—only his kiss. *Only him.*

I was kissing Calder Stone. My sister's ex-boyfriend. In the middle of the Wyoming wilderness. And there was nothing I wanted more.

Meanwhile, his mouth was firm with purpose, restraint holding his lips tight and his body tense. *"Trust me."* His words held him back—his promise not to take anything more than absolutely required, and I should've accepted that, but I couldn't.

From the moment I saw him again after twelve years, a steady IV of ache had been dripping into my blood. Intoxicating me. Addicting me. Even though I knew the warning signs—understood the side effects—I wanted more anyway.

More of something I couldn't control. More of *this thing* that promised to control me. Maybe it was my wild core . . . or maybe it was simply wild.

I slid my tongue along the seam of his lips, pleading for him to set it free, and instantly it altered him.

The hand that was cuffed over my jaw and neck tightened. The firmness of his mouth hardened into ferocity, deceit turned into desperation. His chest rumbled against mine, the sound of a tree splitting in two, and then his mouth opened and his tongue delved for mine, and a kiss that had started as only a cover story became a tangled web neither of us could escape.

From protective to possessive, he plundered my mouth with a dangerous kind of control. Licking to the very depths, marking every corner. Like an unmarked wilderness, Calder mapped every inch of my lips and teeth and tongue as though it were a treasure he'd long searched for. A treasure he'd never thought he would find. Hold. *Taste.* A holy grail that was now his for the taking.

He angled my head, allowing his tongue deeper, every stroke like a spray of gasoline over the fire in my bones.

It had been so long since I'd been kissed—even longer since I'd felt anything that made me hungry for more.

I gripped the coarse fabric of his shirt, pulling him tighter. Every breath was a mixture of forest and midnight and masculine, heady how it mangled my senses like a weed of want.

But Calder's kiss . . . it was nothing like I'd expected. Nothing like what Rachel had hinted to me. Not that a person's kiss, or their experience, couldn't evolve over twelve years, but the parts Rachel had described to me weren't the details, but the tenor. Restrained. Reserved. Proper.

This kiss was born of those things but had grown into something more. Something ravenous and raw and possessive.

A knee pressed between my legs, and my back butted up against a tree. I was pinned. A prisoner to his untamed beast. A willing captive to this feral storm.

I didn't need more encouragement to grind on him. To use him to ease the ache that he'd caused.

It was cold out, yet I felt nothing but his heat. Nothing but the burn of something I couldn't stop. Even if I could, it might blow our cover, and because of that, I didn't have to admit that I didn't want to stop it at all.

"Fuck, Lara." His low groan entered my mouth with a quake, and a shift of his hips allowed me to feel the hard length of him against my leg.

"Hey!" The rough shout was like the slap of a cold wave straight to the chest, dousing the heat and knocking the air from my lungs. "What do you think you're doing?"

Ben approached, his roughshod steps smashing into the forest floor.

"Let me," Calder muttered as he slowly pulled away, making sure I was completely shielded by his big body. *And consequently, keeping me encased in its absorbing warmth.*

"Sorry, Ben. Went to the bathroom and then got . . . distracted," Calder said with a husky chuckle, giving off an air of ease the rest of him clearly didn't feel.

"It's past curfew. You need to be in your tent," Ben hissed, coming around to the side of us to where he could finally see me. *Like he wanted to see me.*

Bile rose in my throat when I saw his weapon was drawn. Even seeing us hadn't prompted him to holster it, as though he liked the subtle display of power.

"What can I say, except that we were listening to our wild cores?" Calder murmured, letting a wry playfulness into his voice.

"Yeah, well, there's a curfew for a reason. I told you, it gets dangerous out here." Ben waved his gun around like it was a wand that could make wolves and bears appear from the surrounding woods. In front of me, Calder went eerily still, watching him.

"I'm going to have to report you to Dr. Julia for breaking curfew." The barrel steadied on us. "There's going to be repercussions for not listening to me. There are rules here. You can't just do whatever—hey!"

Calder lunged, grabbed the barrel of Ben's weapon, and, with a flick of his wrist, emptied the chambered bullet and dropped the magazine to the ground.

It happened so fast that both Ben and I couldn't fully react until it was over and the gun was hollow and useless in his hand.

"What the hell? What the hell do you think you're doing?" the younger man blustered, scouring the ground for the fallen clip. "I wasn't going to shoot—"

"Never aim a weapon at something you don't plan on shooting," Calder warned, frost coating his voice. "If you tell them about curfew, I'll have to tell them you have no idea how to properly handle a weapon and you put our lives at risk."

Taking my hand, Calder led me away from the scene, at all points shielding me from the guard and his furious string of curses.

"I'm watching you," Ben swore, and I heard him ruffling frantically through the debris for the clip.

"Just keep walking," Calder said from behind me, his steady hands on my waist, guiding me through the forest back to our tent.

I didn't take a full breath until he zipped the flap shut with a single swipe of his arm.

"Do you think—"

"No, he's not going to say anything." Calder strode over to the table and picked up his reusable water bottle, uncapping it for a drink but pausing before lifting it to his mouth. "You shouldn't have come looking for me."

My slack jaw snapped shut. "You should've told me you planned on going to Maxwell's RV tonight."

"It wasn't going to take two people to search through her things."

"It would've gone faster."

His eyes flicked to mine, and their normally serene golden-green was now mottled with anger. "With greater risk."

He lifted the bottle to his lips and took several swigs. My eyes ran over him. He kept himself still partially facing away from me. My pulse fumbled, and my legs pressed tighter together.

He wasn't the only one still feeling the lingering effects of that kiss. Mine just weren't as visible.

"Calder—"

The water bottle landed with a *thunk* on the table.

"I'm going out to send a message to Callum. I'll be right back. Stay here."

This time, he didn't leave anything up for interpretation. Not his instruction. Not his anger. And definitely not the evidence of his attraction straining against the front of his pants.

Chapter 15

Lara

This time when I woke up, there was a depression on the other side of the bed. A fossil where the furious man had slept. Who knew, though, for how long?

I'd tried to wait it out while he went outside last night, but my eyelids couldn't hold their own. Despite their failure, I couldn't regret the hours of unblemished deep sleep that had claimed me.

It was the adrenaline crash that had tossed me into exhaustion. *Not the desire to relive that kiss in my dreams.*

Even now, my lips tingled, their nerves altered from the memory.

The mattress crunched as I sat up, and I remembered I'd shoved Dr. Julia's notes on Rachel underneath it when Calder left the tent again.

Should I have taken them? *Should I continue to read them?*

I reached for the papers but stopped when I heard footsteps approaching the tent. *And that distinct whistled tune.*

Crap. *Where was Calder?*

"Breakfast!" The yell had been preceded by what passed for knocking on the tent.

"Shit," I muttered, rising and brushing the wrinkles from my scrubs. My eyes zipped from side to side as though I could've missed my extra-large fake boyfriend in the small space. *Not possible.*

Looked like I was going to have to face Ben on my own.

Heart pounding, I went and unzipped the front flap just enough to be able to reach for our food.

"Morning," I said tightly, refusing to cower from the guard who'd gone on a small power trip last night, only to be thoroughly embarrassed by Calder.

His eyes turned squinty as I took the tray of food. "Where's Calder?"

"Bathroom." I tugged on the zipper to close the opening, only for his meaty hand to block its path.

"You know, breaking curfew is a serious violation . . ." Ben said slowly, the creep of his eyes like slime as it wandered over me.

"Well, holding your pee can lead to serious kidney damage or kidney failure, so as a doctor, I can't say I recommend doing it just to preserve some arbitrary curfew."

His eyes narrowed to slits, and then he shoved his hand against the zipper, pulling it out of my fingers and forcibly open.

"I could have Calder kicked out of the retreat."

"I was there, too."

A twisted smirk appeared. "Only if I say you were."

His tone . . . his meaning . . . I wanted to vomit.

"Well, I was. So it doesn't really matter what you say. It's not like I would stay without my boyfriend anyway," I said with a tight smile. "Now, if you could let go of my tent, I'd like to eat and get ready for the workshop this morning."

He didn't let go. He didn't even seem to have heard me, let alone care about what I'd said.

"I could give you plenty of reasons to stay." He leaned into the tent and reached for me.

And my brain short-circuited.

Panic traded the tent for the emergency room. The rustle of the forest for the beeps of machines. And the look on Ben's face for the desperate one on Ian's. The nerves that had been fried by trauma still weren't healed, sending me into paralysis rather than response.

He tried to grab my arm, and instinct jolted me into action. I stumbled back, everything on the tray shaking.

"I want you to leave," I said in my best life-or-death doctor voice, still hearing it tremble.

Get it together, Dr. Crane. How will you ever be back in the ER if you can't keep your cool?

"Now," I added, clinging to the spike of strength in the syllable.

Ben wasn't going to listen. I saw it in his face, in the stretch of his arm. "Are you sure—" He broke off with a cry.

A large hand locked on his wrist and twisted it at an unnatural, excruciating angle.

"She sounded very sure to me." Calder's voice felt like warm rain over my fear-frozen skin.

"Let me go," Ben ordered, but Calder didn't budge.

He lowered his head uncomfortably close to Ben's face. "Remember how I dismantled your weapon last night?" He didn't wait for his answer; of course Ben remembered. "That is what I will do to the next extremity that trespasses into her personal space."

"I could get you kicked out for this," Ben snarled, like we actually cared.

Calder leaned closer, and Ben, insecure as he was, tried to pull away.

"And I could have you dead, dismembered, and disappeared faster than you can say *wild core.*" Calder released him with that promise—that warning—and Ben tripped over his feet to get away.

"I want someone else delivering our meals, clothes . . . anything to the tent," Calder added before the other man completely fled. "Either you can make the request or I can."

Ben was practically fuming, but he finally thought better of saying anything else and turned and stomped away from our tent as fast as he could without breaking into a run.

Calder zipped the flap shut and looked at me. "You okay?"

"Yeah." I set the tray on the table, and the dishes would've clattered from my trembling if they weren't that soft, recyclable material.

"Lara." His palm landed on my shoulder, and all I could think about was the calloused heat of that very hand on my throat last night, holding me to the mercy of his mouth.

"I'm fine," I insisted, jerking away at the first squeeze of ache in my chest. "Where were you?" I sank into one of the chairs.

Calder took one of the bowls from the tray and brought it to me, a not-so-subtle instruction to eat. Pausing, he tipped his head and made sure no one was outside listening.

"Checking in with Callum."

I stirred the cinnamon oatmeal and took a few bites, though panic had demolished my appetite. "Anything on EC?"

The feathering of his jaw muscle was answer enough. "Not yet," he said, and catching my forced exhale of stressed frustration, added, "But he'll find something."

Before he could say more, the chime sounded through the speaker above, distracting us both.

"Good morning, Wild Ones," Dr. Julia's voice soothed through the tent. *"We will begin our morning session at the gathering place in five minutes. Please start heading there so we may begin on time."*

Calder took our bowls and set the garbage back on the tray. I watched his hands the whole time, remembering how they'd held me to him—held my mouth prisoner to his. Strong and immovable and as desperate as I was.

"We should go," Calder murmured, and I snapped my head up.

He was right, but we also should talk about what had happened last night.

Setting down what was left in my cup, I called to him just as he grabbed the zipper to open the tent. "Calder." He stopped but didn't turn. "We need to talk—"

"I'm sorry for kissing you," he said, his voice like sharp shards of stone grinding up the warmth of the memory. "It was our best chance at getting Ben to not question why we were out there. If I'd had more time—"

"Stop," I interrupted, almost desperate to not hear his regret. "I wanted to apologize." I swallowed over the lump in my throat. "For putting us in that position in the first place. It's my fault."

He didn't reply right away, the pulse of his jaw marking the passing seconds.

"I should've told you I was going. I'm sorry. I'm not used to working with a . . . partner." Our eyes locked. Mine, hopeful. His, hard.

"But I still shouldn't have kissed you," he repeated, like we needed the reminder.

"It's okay." *Was I giving permission or confessing to wanting more?*

Calder's jaw clenched, his eyes taking on that wild glint I'd caught only in the moonlight.

"Don't tell me it's okay that I kissed you," he said harshly. "Not if you don't want me to do it again."

And then the zipper sliced completely open and Calder disappeared through it, leaving me with my mouth gaping and my heart spilling wild, wanton beats into my veins.

So, I wasn't the only one who wanted him to do it again.

Calder paused a few paces up the trail, and at first, I thought he'd stopped only to wait for me to catch up, but then I heard it: the angry rumbling of a masculine voice approaching from the tent nearby.

"Goddammit, Sarah. What the fuck are we doing here? You told me camping. Not this bullshit—"

"I told you it was a camping retreat, so we could work on us—"

"Bullshit. You tricked me into coming here. You're so fucking worthless, you know that? I tell you to plan a trip, and this is what you come up with? I swear to God—" The man stopped as soon as he reached the path about thirty feet in front of Calder, noticing us immediately.

His eyes swiped over Calder first, then me. His prematurely thinning hair was almost as noticeable as his receding hairline, and judging from the rest of him, the trip he would've preferred involved shooting animals, drinking beer, and enjoying a healthy dose of toxic masculinity.

Behind him, a pale blonde came through the trees, her hair braided into two plaits and her cheeks flushed, though most likely not from the exertion. Not if their color had anything to do with the red rim of her eyes.

"Good morning," Calder said just as the other man was about to turn away, forcing him to greet us.

"Morning."

"I'm Calder. This is Lara." My fake boyfriend took charge of the situation, striding right up to the couple and not-so-subtly stopping partially between them.

"Trent." The shorter man reluctantly took Calder's hand and shook it.

It took several seconds for the blonde to finally speak, like she wasn't sure whether Trent was going to introduce her or she should introduce herself. *No.* It was as though she'd made the wrong choice too many times.

"I'm Sarah."

"Hi, Sarah. It's nice to meet you," I said, reaching my hand out for hers and giving Trent a taste of his own medicine. *And unimportance.*

"We should go. Wouldn't want to be *late*," Trent scoffed, his tone dripping with equal parts displeasure and mockery. Again, without thinking or waiting for his partner, he stalked ahead, leaving the three of us in his wake.

When he was a good several paces ahead, Sarah looked at me and said, "I'm sorry."

"Please," I begged her with a soft smile. "Don't apologize."

She gave me a grateful but unconvinced look. "This is just a lot for him . . . too much, maybe."

Her reply rattled my nerves for so many reasons, but the biggest was how it reminded me of Mom. And of Rachel.

It wasn't my place or my business to say anything, but the weight on my chest was wondering whether I could do more to help her—whether I could've done more to help my sister. Maybe if I'd kept speaking up, things would've been different. Maybe if I'd given her more reasons to hate me, she wouldn't have found herself dating so many men who made her hate herself.

Before I could help myself, I dipped my head lower and murmured, "Well, then maybe he should go find less."

Sarah's eyes went wide, and a smile she couldn't control spread over her face.

"Sarah!" Trent called but didn't even bother to stop, like he'd hollered for a wandering dog to catch up to him rather than a woman he cared about. I couldn't believe a man who acted like that was capable of love.

"Thank you," Sarah said softly, and sped to catch up to her partner.

"You okay?"

I turned to Calder and found him looking at me strangely. Only then did I notice that I'd banded my arms over my chest and how hard I was scowling.

"Yeah." I dropped my arms and shrugged like that was all it took to release the tension. "That's just the kind of guy my sister would date, and I just . . . I can't stand men like that."

"That's not a man, Lara. That's a piece of trash." With that simple yet true statement, Calder Stone continued toward the gathering place.

And I'd never wanted to kiss him more.

Chapter 16

CALDER

Rule #8: Rehearse for the worst-case scenario until it becomes routine.

Being in over my head wasn't the kind of thing I was used to. From free-climbing rock walls and hiking twenty miles a day in the Wyoming mountains to night hunts with Cassius and my older siblings—practicing stealth, evasion, and hunting—there were very few scenarios I'd admit to being unprepared for.

But kissing Lara Crane was one of them.

I'd made the right decision last night. As soon as I'd heard Ben's approach, our choices were limited, and every other option had the lowest probability of success. So I'd kissed her. *Fuck, had I kissed her.* And fuck me, had that kiss rewrote my DNA and destroyed me from the inside out. Not since childhood had a decision based on trained instinct still managed to feel so wrong.

Now my survival instincts screamed to pull away. To retreat. Like I'd been caught in a trap—a carefully concealed snare I hadn't seen coming. I needed to create distance before there was no escape. Before I revealed not only my weakness for wanting her but also risked the kind of devastation Cassius had barely survived.

Lara stopped beside me at the edge of the tree-rimmed clearing.

"Ready?" I grunted.

"Yeah," she said, but I heard the quickening of her breath and the hesitation in her voice, and felt the slight tremble of her body next to mine.

I reached back and took her hand, feeling the familiar jolt to my senses. I didn't have to hold her, but I needed to. Lingering rage over Ben's intrusion—his borderline assault and the pure panic he'd caused—had mangled all my better judgment. Mine and hers, apparently, as her fingers tightened in mine.

I led us into the clearing, following the direction Sarah and her partner had taken.

"Welcome, my dear wild ones." Maxwell stretched her arms wide. "Welcome to the gathering place where we will all come together this morning for our first group exercise."

Lara slowed as soon as we had a clear view of the space and the people in it. We both knew Rachel wasn't here, but it didn't stop Lara from scanning every person for her sister. But that was hope. The smallest light in the most impossible darkness.

"This way." I pulled Lara close to me, guiding her to an open spot and murmured, "She's not here. Stay focused."

The words might as well have been a gun to her head; her attention slammed forward, and she immediately engaged with every couple we passed.

"Please, if every couple could take a seat on one of the blankets I've placed down." Maxwell roamed the center of the arrangement like the guiding sun to her captive galaxy. "Matthew will be coming around with matcha-smoothie shots for anyone who would like one."

Not a chance.

I let Lara sit first, giving the stoic guard a firm *no* when he paused with a small tray of tiny recyclable cups of that same damn welcome smoothie. Once he moved on, I lowered to my knees behind Lara and carefully examined the other dozen couples, all of them younger; I'd say roughly their late twenties to late thirties. All with expressions varying from eager to bored to irritated.

"Welcome," Maxwell said again, with an edge in her voice.

Something must have happened at the Garden last night with Adam and it was affecting her. Yesterday's mask of pure calm was now striated with strain.

"Congratulations to all of you for making it through the introductory portion of Wilderness Within. As we've talked about in your private sessions, the part of you we're trying to reach—to activate—is the wild core. And the wild core can't be coaxed or lured out. It must be driven." She moved slowly around the circle as she spoke, meeting every pair of eyes. "I used to offer traditional couples' therapy many, many years ago. It was the kind of therapy that clawed for inches of relief over months and months, sometimes years, of treatment. It wasn't until I came here, until I felt the powerful connection of ourselves to nature, that I realized there was a better way. Not because it was faster, but because it was more honest."

There was a sound—a snort—that suspiciously came from the corner opposite Lara and me, where Trent and Sarah sat.

"When moisture evaporates and collects in the clouds, Mother Nature doesn't portion out raindrops a few at a time to make it more palatable for the land to absorb. No, she drenches the earth. She releases everything she has, and the earth takes it. It adapts. Absorbs. And in the same way, that is what we must do with our emotions and with those of our partner or partners. We must unleash the totality of our wild core, and our partner must adapt to those urges."

I disagreed. There was no adapting to the way I wanted Lara. No adapting to the urge to kiss her. To touch her. No adapting to the urge to strip her in the woods and take everything I could like I needed her to survive.

"So today we take another step in that process with our first session on intimacy."

Lara went as stiff as a statue, and if she'd turned to look, she would've seen that I'd done the same. *Some parts of me stiffer than others.*

Maxwell continued her revolution, stopping to look directly at us. "Now, if everyone could turn so you are facing your partner."

Lara scooted around on the blanket, her eyes colliding with mine, two verdant pools with uncertainty skimming their surface and something more fervent rippling underneath. Something that caused her pulse to trample along the smooth column of her neck.

She was too close again.

Every breath buried temptation into the depths of my lungs and metabolized my rigid restraint into raw need.

My jaw clamped together, my teeth interlocking to absorb the strain. *Dammit.* I needed to control the way I wanted her.

"Good. Now, ladies, I want you to move onto your partner's lap, straddling them in whatever way is most comfortable for you."

Straddle—*fuck*.

My thoughts echoed in Lara's eyes. She stared at me like a deer in headlights, and I like a buck in a hunter's sights; we both knew one more move might be our end.

But what choice did we have? Get up and leave?

Even if we faked some kind of scene or emergency, it would only keep us away from the chance to find the answers we needed.

I glanced at Maxwell, making sure her focus was elsewhere—and it was, on Sarah and Trent—before turning to Lara and mouthing *Your call.*

A breeze swept between us, catching some of her hair in its fingers and threading it across her neck.

And then her chin lowered. An acquiescence to our unfortunate circumstance.

"You were the one who signed us up for this," I grunted, thinking it would ease the tension woven into the air. It didn't.

Her eyes snapped to mine, the glitter of determination cutting through the uncertainty as she put her hand on my shoulder.

"Is that your way of telling me you can't handle it?" she taunted right back, but her words dissolved into a wholly different meaning when she swung her leg over mine and settled squarely in my lap.

On my thighs.

Against my cock.

The thin material of our pants wouldn't have been a problem for couples who were real couples. Feeling the heat of her core directly on me wouldn't have been a problem if we were real. Nor would knowing she could feel the growing length of my cock pressing—pulsing against her.

We weren't real, but this, though . . . this heat. Ache. Lust. Only a fool would claim *this* was all part of our deception.

Her weight settled, and the pressure—the heat on my dick—was incredible and so fucking dangerous, considering I'd been too close to this woman for the last four days to have any time to relieve it. Without warning, a low rumbling sound grated from my chest.

"Sorry," Lara whispered, and then did the worst thing possible: She started to shift from side to side, seeming to think she'd hurt me.

Not realizing her solution was salt in the wound.

She wiggled slightly front. A little back. A rocking that was pure torture. I would've rather spent fifty days and nights in the winter wilderness or faced a raging bison or a pack of wolves . . . I would've suffered any violent extreme of Mother Nature rather than the erotic temptation of her.

"Stop," I growled and gripped her hips, forcing her still.

"I—" She swallowed. "I'm sorry. I thought I was hurting you."

You were. You are.

"I'm fine. Just stop . . . moving," I ordered between clipped breaths, unable to steady my galloping pulse.

"Okay."

Fuck, she was warm—and soft. Her bare skin felt like silk under my fingertips where they'd trespassed under the edge of her top when I grabbed her. Touching her fed my hunger. Cannibalized my restraint. I wanted to rip off her clothes and mark every forbidden inch.

"We'll start the way every storm does: with the brewing." Maxwell's voice cut through the fog of lust. "Look into each other's eyes. Deeply. Let yourself see and be seen, as though you are opening the very door to your soul."

I dragged my eyes to Lara's, sinking into the sweet trap of her gaze, deeper into the same molten mire that had consumed what was supposed to have been a purely practical kiss.

"Now, feel the breath. Your inhale is their exhale. Their exhale, your inhale," Maxwell intoned with a hypnotic resonance. "Feel the exchange from the depths of your lungs—from the depths of your wild core. Your energy colliding with theirs. Transforming. Mating."

Lara shifted and my dick jerked. Her sharp inhale tore the breath from my chest, and her exhale—it didn't just settle back in my lungs, it settled her more fully on me. The heat of her pussy nestled my thick, raging cock, and all I could think was that this wasn't a mating of energy, but its swift and deadly combustion.

"Feel your wild core reaching for theirs. Giving and absorbing. Pulling and wanting. That's it . . . soak and savor in the wanting," Maxwell's voice lulled through the fugue. Encouraging something that needed no encouragement, only an excuse. "Feel the barriers dissolving between you. All those restraints and reservations . . . feel them melt away."

In spite of what she said, I tried to hold on to them. I tried to grip them like a rock in my hand, only to realize what I held was nothing more than a fistful of sand, the particles of resistance slipping right through my fingers.

"In the wild, you take fully. You give fully. It is the only way. The only true connection. The only path to pure passion."

Lara's grip tightened on my shoulders. My hands slid higher, burying completely against her bare torso. Our heads bent closer, breaths colliding.

"Now, I want you to tell your partner one thing they do that attracts your wild core—that ignites it."

This session, however long it was, wasn't going to be long enough for me to tell Lara all the things that made me ache for her in every way I shouldn't.

Lara pressed her hand to the side of my face, and the world stopped on its head.

"This," she murmured, pressing her fingers to the muscle on the side of my jaw. "The way it pulses . . . It's a wonder you haven't cracked."

Not a wonder. *A goddamn miracle.*

My gaze tracked over every inch of her face. The tint of her blush. The dust of her freckles. The heady pulse of hunger in her stare.

"Maybe I have," I murmured quietly, like it would stop her from hearing me; it wouldn't. Couldn't.

She sucked in a breath, her gaze widening, and I found myself toeing the same line both of us knew we shouldn't cross.

"It's your eyes. They're like Dopplers for your emotions. They show every calm. Every quickening. Every storm. Always have." All those years ago, I could read her emotions in the pools of her gaze, right down to all the times those pools had reflected disbelief when she heard her sister lie to me.

Her stomach trembled against my fingers, spurring them into a revolution of slow circles on her waist, tracing and teasing along the boundary of her pants. A revolution, all right . . . against all sanity.

"And what do they show now?"

Lust. Ache. Desire. The list could go on, but it was better left in silence. The situation we were in . . . the position . . . was already too precarious to confess what I saw in her eyes.

"Whatever it is," I began, my voice low and guttural, "I don't think I'll survive it." *And considering survival was what my family was known for . . .*

"Calder . . ." Lara murmured, and too late I realized what it was: *a plea.* One that came just before she rocked in my lap.

It was the slightest, shortest motion. One single roll of her hips to try to quench the ache between her thighs. And it struck me like a bolt of lightning. Pure, white-hot lust straight to my cock.

"Fuck," I grunted on a rough exhale.

There was no hiding—not even the chance for polite ignorance of—my erection. Not when, with a slight nudge of my hands, I bade her to do it again.

To grind against me. Her hips to mine. Her heat to my hardness. My mind to the brink of insanity. *Friction against the forbidden.*

"Feel the ache in your partner and nurture it. There is nothing more primal, more primordial, than physical connection. Than sexual satisfaction with a partner who knows your whole self."

With a broken exhale, Lara's forehead dipped to meet mine, our breaths battling—beating into one another.

Was everyone else like this? Completely oblivious to the group? Consumed by their partner?

Or was it just me? *Consumed by her . . .*

"This is the plateau you want to reach. An erotic equilibrium of all your senses . . ." Maxwell went on, her voice ebbing in and out of focus until it was nothing but an auditory fog.

"Lara . . ." My husky whisper tangled in her exhale as her forehead rested on mine.

My hands tightened on her waist, knowing I should stop her but only dragging her harder along my length.

It was a contradiction. A perilous exception to my rules. Like everything else I felt about her. Never before had my logic differed so drastically, so dangerously, from my instinct.

My hand slid higher, cupping over her bare ribs, my thumb tracing the edge of her bra, coaxing her to keep moving. To forget everyone else around us. To forget anyone could see our primal desire bleeding from every seam.

"Gentlemen, she should be your sole focus. Her wants. Her needs. This is the garden you must water before anything can grow . . ." The mention of *garden* caught my ear, but not enough to shake me from Lara's trance.

"Calder." Her whisper stamped her warning to my lips.

To move. To turn. To take control.

Dragging my other hand to her head, I brushed her hair back from her face and bracketed my palm to the side of her throat. Here, I could read her pulse. The rapid-fire Morse code that signaled for help. For relief. For another taste of this thing that neither of us seemed to be able to stop.

I angled my head to take her lips. There was nothing holding me back, nothing strong enough to keep me from kissing her again.

Nothing until a loud shout and cry spiked my adrenaline from pleasure to protection.

With one swift movement, I slid Lara off my lap and rose up on my knees in front of her, quickly tucking my cock into the waistband of my pants. Thankfully, everyone's attention, including Lara's, was on the commotion on the other side of the gathering space, where Trent was making a scene.

"This is fucking ridiculous. You get off when I get off—that's how things work." Trent's chauvinistic snarl wormed like a sour weed through the clearing as he shoved Sarah off him; she was in the process of moving, but he wanted her to feel small. Like he couldn't get away from her fast enough. He wanted that humiliation for her, and I wanted to introduce my fist to his face. Unfortunately, he was already gone, and Maxwell had swooped in to calm Sarah.

I turned to Lara. "You okay?"

Her blown-out pupils flared. *Okay* was a relative term.

"As you can see, this journey isn't for the faint of heart," Maxwell addressed the group, stealing everyone's focus from Trent's dramatic exit. "But with every great and wild relationship, there are speed bumps. Sometimes they slow you down to find something deeper and more meaningful. At other moments, they show you it's time to take a different course."

My brow furrowed as I listened—and watched.

Tracking a person's emotions was similar to tracking their physical location. The important clues were in the details. The trail of Maxwell's eyes, stealthily roaming around the group until she mentioned slowing down, then swiftly plummeting to the ground before resurfacing on

Sarah. The break in her projected facade that didn't go unnoticed. At least, not to me.

She was thinking of someone when she'd mentioned a speed bump. Possibly her relationship with Adam, given what I'd heard.

"We'll conclude this morning's session and get you into your reflection time a little early. Like before, please find somewhere secluded and quiet to reflect and journal about the feelings and emotions that this morning's session brought up for you."

I stood and offered my hand to Lara. She jerked her chin, a wordless instruction to look behind me.

Maxwell was talking to Sarah.

Taking Lara's hand, I quickly guided us in their direction.

"I would like to speak with you privately, Sarah, after this morning—" Maxwell stopped abruptly as we got close and looked to Lara and me. "Great work this morning, you two. I have to say, there are very few couples that I can feel a wild connection from the very start, but yours was all nails and teeth. Good job."

Dammit. Fortunately, Maxwell was too concerned with her wounded disciple to notice how uncomfortable her remarks made Lara and me.

I wished I could've said they were too off base, but it was more like they struck too close to home.

"I'd like to have another session with the both of you now. Matthew will take you to the Sanctuary, and I'll join you in a few minutes."

I managed a sound to acknowledge her as Matthew appeared to do her bidding and led us away.

Chapter 17

Lara

"Are you ever still?" Calder asked, turning from his seated position on the blanket in the Sanctuary.

"Not if I can help it." I took one more, defiant trek across the clearing where I'd been pacing, restless for Dr. Julia to arrive. *Or because not even thirty minutes ago, I was dry-humping my sister's ex-boyfriend in the middle of a wellness retreat and it hadn't fazed me.*

When I'd been on his lap, his hands on my skin, his hardness right where I needed him . . . I'd forgotten everything. Where we were. Who we were with. Who we were there for. It had all incinerated under the heat of our attraction.

"I wonder what Dr. Julia said to Sarah. Maybe we should've snuck back out and tried to listen," I blurted out, needing more space to breathe.

Calder's frown made his opinion about that idea clear. "Do you remember the hummingbird that got trapped in your garage?"

I blinked, the long-ago memory coming back suddenly. "Yeah."

It was spring semester, and one of my housemates had left the garage door open. The hummingbird had flown inside, and I couldn't get it to fly out. Just as I was trying to swat it out with a broom, Calder had pulled up with Rachel in the passenger seat; she'd wanted to borrow a skirt of mine.

While he'd jerry-rigged my roommate's tennis racket onto the end of a broom, Calder explained that hummingbirds are attracted to the color red and get drawn in by the red release handle on the garage-door motor. Then, with an abundance of patience, he coaxed the bird onto the racket frame, and after about fifteen minutes of trying, he carried it to freedom.

"Do you know what would've happened if I hadn't gotten it out?"

I had the sense that this was a trick question, but I answered anyway. "It would've become our garage pet."

The corner of his mouth twitched. "It would've died."

"What?" I jolted. "I'm sure it would've flown out eventually."

I knew I was wrong by the slow, nearly immovable shake of his head.

"When hummingbirds sense danger, their instinct is to fly up, not out. It would've continued to fly up into that corner of the garage to try and escape, land on the tracks of the garage door when it got tired, and then fly for the corner again until it exhausted itself to death."

"That's . . . horrible."

The tragedy of that scenario struck me first. For the small bird to die of exhaustion when a wide-open door was only a few feet away seemed . . . unbelievable.

"Always doing something doesn't mean it's the right thing."

My shoulders tensed, ready to reject his insinuation. "Doing something is better than doing nothing."

"Is it? For whom?" Before I could reply, he added, "Is flying endlessly upward better than stopping to take stock of the situation? Is the hummingbird only worth something because it kept putting in the effort until the effort killed it?"

Suddenly, the open sanctuary felt suffocating. Stuffy with things I didn't want to think about, let alone think he could see in me: a hummingbird that never stopped trying—that never stopped flying. *Until it almost killed me.*

A wash of guilt stained my mind as I wondered, for the umpteenth time, whether I'd caused this. Had Rachel ended up here because I'd made her feel like she wasn't doing enough?

"I think we need to put some distance between us," Calder said. "In front of Maxwell."

Of course. It made total sense, and I should 100 percent, completely agree, especially after what had just happened at the group session. My body was still thrumming from the heat of him—the hardness. I should welcome any reason for distance. *So why did it feel like he'd just ripped the rug right out from underneath me?*

The ball in my throat inflated. "What do you mean?"

"She mentioned targeting Sarah and Trent because they'd argued during their first session. If we can provoke the same reaction, we might find out what the Garden and EC is sooner."

"Yeah. That could work."

A sound drew Calder's attention, and I quickly joined him on the blanket as Dr. Julia's footsteps sounded along the path for a few seconds before she entered the clearing.

"Lara, Calder. Thank you for joining me." She came and sat in front of us, and I noticed a distinct dilation in her pupils. I wondered how many of those smoothie shots she'd had that morning, or if she'd made herself something stronger.

"I want to say, I was very impressed with your intimate work this morning. That is the kind of connection I like to see—to feel—in those sessions." Her gaze wove between Calder and me. "Tell me, Calder, did you feel the electric tether of your wild core to Lara's?"

Felt it or faked it? Because as much as I'd thought he'd felt it, he'd certainly become all business right after.

"Yes," he answered after a beat, and I searched for the lie seamed into his voice but came up empty.

It was still a lie, though. It had to be.

"Good." Dr. Julia beamed and looked to me, and I braced myself to answer the same question. "And you, Lara—I know you felt it, too," she continued, surprising me with the assumption. "You felt it, and you tried to resist it. Why?"

My skin prickled. *Had she figured out we were faking this?*

And then I felt Calder's strong fingers lacing mine into his hold. Without a word, he comforted me. Steadied me.

Be still, Lara. Stop flying up.

"I'm not sure," I murmured, and Dr. Julia took my hesitation as nervousness.

"Do you think it has something to do with your sister?"

My jaw went slack. I should be glad—glad the accusation hadn't hit closer to home. *Do you think it's because you aren't really together? Because you're faking this relationship to invade my retreat?*

Still, I couldn't bring myself to answer her.

"Calder, what do you think?" She drew him in. "Is your ex-girlfriend, Lara's sister, a barrier in your relationship?"

"Yes."

I couldn't help but flinch.

"This is a safe place, Lara. A sanctuary for your wildness. You can let it be free here."

I released my breath, the air forced out by the battering of my pulse, and leaned—*hard*—into what I could think if Calder were really mine.

"I hesitate because he never looked twice at me back when he dated my sister," I started slow, my feigned answer fueled by coals of dark, messy truths like a locomotive gaining speed. "I hesitate because I wonder if he thinks of her when he's with me. If he wishes he were with her instead."

It couldn't be the truth—in fact, it was probably the furthest thing from it: Calder had ended things with Rachel, not the other way around. But somewhere in the fiction, my deep-seated anger toward him for hurting her began to sprout.

"But mostly, I hesitate because I worry he'll treat me like he did her. That he'll realize I want too much or something too serious, and he'll leave me without caring what happens." The words tumbled out, unstoppable. Like trying to unfire a gun, I couldn't reel back the bullet through the air or press it back into the chamber, any more than I could stop my words from piercing skin and bones and soul. "I hesitate because I've seen how carelessly he can break a heart, and I don't want him to break mine."

When I'd finished, the air around us prickled with a static energy, unmoving but threatening to spark all the same.

"Good," Dr. Julia finally cooed. "Bravo, Lara. Bravo." In my periphery, she turned to Calder, but his stare didn't break from mine, shimmering and molten. "Calder, Lara's wild core has shared this vulnerability with you. Reached for you. How does what she said make you feel?"

Her question drifted into long seconds of silence.

"I'm sorry, but I haven't thought about your sister in any meaningful way in the last dozen years. And before that . . ." His jaw fired up. "I never looked twice at you back then because all it took was once."

My heart tripped and fell flat on its face, its rhythm returning only to the cadence of those words: *All it took was once.*

Five words and I forgot this was fake. How could I not when he stared at me like he wanted to rip my prior thoughts to shreds?

"Your sister and I dated for nine months, but it could've been nine years and I still never would've felt for her what I felt for you after only one look."

A small whimper escaped my chest, and as soon as I heard the sound, I stiffened. His words were affecting me too much—he was affecting me too much.

"Don't tell me it's okay to kiss you. Not if you don't want me to do it again."

"What is it, Calder? What are you holding back?"

Calder grimaced, a wild, tortured expression consuming his face. He was holding back, or trying to. His jaw anchored shut and his mouth pulled into a tight line, but even that wasn't enough to stop the honesty that came next. "As for how things ended," he rasped, "sometimes letting someone believe a lie is the only compassion you can offer."

My heart tumbled like a glass from a table, shattering in my chest and sending shards of heartbeats like shrapnel through my veins.

There was no responding to him before he rose abruptly and strode from the Sanctuary without another word. Like he was angry. Like we were *not real.*

"We need to put some distance between us in front of Maxwell."

The raging heat under my skin turned to ash. *Of course.* This was fake. Calder would never display emotion like that. This was all part of his plan—our plan. To make Dr. Julia think we had major problems, too. This was nothing more than a show, and like a fool, I'd been swept away in the performance—in the sweet promise. *"All it took was once."*

"Let him go," Dr. Julia said as she stood and placed a hand on my shoulder. "This is what happens in the Sanctuary. An unearthing of things we'd rather not think or talk about, but it's the only way to go deeper."

For the sake of the ruse, I swallowed, tasting nothing but bitterness in my mouth. "And if we're not meant to go deeper? What happens then?"

And more importantly, why did I suddenly care? Why did I care about what he said? And why did I want to know the truth of his words that were supposed to be only lies?

"We'll cross that bridge if we come to it," she said and tapped my shoulder. "Go reflect on what happened today, and be sure to give Calder time in solitude before you come together again to review your reflections."

She left me alone in the clearing, Matthew appearing less than a minute later to escort me back to the campsite.

When we reached the bathrooms, he left me to make my way to the tent on my own, mumbling something about needing to bring another couple to the Sanctuary. I wasn't far down the path before I caught Sarah coming out of her tent. Her face was beet red, and she repeatedly swiped the back of her hand over her cheeks. As I got closer, I heard the sobs she tried to stifle.

"Sarah," I called softly so Matthew and whoever else might be around wouldn't hear, and went over to her.

She turned and hiccuped. "Lara."

"What's wrong?" I took her hands in mine.

"I'm okay." Another hiccup. "This is just . . . a lot." Her gaze lowered. Participants weren't supposed to talk to each other about their relationships or their sessions.

"I know, but it's a process," I coaxed. "We're not meant to tackle everything on our own from the very beginning." I mirrored the same mothering tone Dr. Julia used, not because I wanted to deceive the poor woman in front of me, but because I worried about her the way I worried about my sister. Worried that her pain was being taken advantage of, her weakness abused for someone else's desires.

"You're right." Sarah's trembling breath rushed out, followed by a grateful smile. "Trent and I are . . . really having a hard time. He's just so selfish, and I try to please him but—" She caught herself. "Dr. Julia said pleasing each other is a two-way street and that I'm so deficient in . . . being pleased that I might need a special program."

It took everything I had to keep my voice steady as I asked, "A special program?"

She gave a sad laugh and placed her hand on top of mine. "Nothing that you need, don't worry. The way Calder looks at you . . . like he could eat you for every meal and still be starved." She clapped her hand over her mouth. "I'm sorry. I shouldn't have said that. It's just . . . Trent has never looked at me that way."

Because you've never been in a fake relationship with him, I thought but kept the falsehood to myself.

"So, she wants you to leave the retreat?"

Sarah nodded. "She said I need to gain confidence in myself, in my own needs and desires, and that's what the program specializes in. A community dedicated to women's pleasure. Can you imagine?" Her wistful sigh gutted me.

"What program is Dr. Julia referring you to?" I tried to focus her.

"She said it's very exclusive. Very private." She lowered her voice, her eyes sliding side to side with worry and uncertainty.

"Sarah—"

"I'm not sure I'm going to go. I'm not sure about anything right now. I'm sorry. I shouldn't have said anything. Dr. Julia said not to—"

Shit. My palms went damp. I was losing her. And suddenly, my desperation took over.

"I think my sister went there, that's why I'm asking," I said calmly, and the risk instantly paid off.

Her breath caught. "Really? She went to Eden's Children?"

Eden's Children.

EC.

My heart rocket-launched into my chest. "She . . . just got there, so I haven't heard from her."

Sarah nodded. "Dr. Julia said it was even more sequestered than this because of the intensity and . . . nature of the community." She bit her bottom lip. "I'm worried I'm going to get there and panic or freeze. She said I have to go with a completely open mind and a hunger for something better for myself. I know I'm nervous to be intimate with Trent, but to explore"—her voice lowered to a whisper—"sex with multiple partners . . . I'm worried I'm not ready."

Multiple partners? My pulse started to levy a low thudding sound in my ears.

"She was very up front about it, and all the legal consents, insurance, NDAs, and the costs involved, but that's not even what's holding me back. It's the kinds of sex and pleasure . . ." *Was this a self-help program or a sex club?* "But Dr. Julia said that's the point. That I'm not ready and that going will force me to be ready to embrace wild, unrestricted pleasure."

The words came from Sarah, but they were steeped in Dr. Julia's mindset.

Was it brainwashing? *Coercion?* Was it wrong, what Dr. Julia was suggesting? Sarah clearly had self-esteem and traumatic relationship problems.

Was Dr. Julia taking advantage of that to get her to this compound, or was it really something she believed would help?

"You have to do what's right for you," I told her firmly.

"She said Ben could take me tomorrow morning to the Garden."

Ben?!

"What's going on—" A low voice boomed through the trees, echoed by the heavy footfalls of Matthew's uneven gait.

I breezed through an excuse. "I was on my way back from the bathroom and I saw Sarah crying. I just wanted to make sure she was okay."

Matthew's stare chiseled into mine before he reluctantly accepted my explanation. "You should be out reflecting. Alone."

"Of course." I nodded, and after passing a reassuring smile in Sarah's direction, I turned and walked quickly toward my tent.

Chapter 18

Calder

Rule #7: Your survival kit should assume everything will go wrong, because eventually it will.

I let out a sharp, fast whistle, catching Lara's attention just before she reached the tent. Her head turned, eyes squinting through the trees, and I stepped out from behind the pine where I'd been waiting. As soon as she saw me, I saw the mess I'd made.

Fuck.

Fuck.

There were a dozen ways to end our meeting in an argument, but I'd chosen the path closest to the truth. Not for a logical reason. Or a rational one. Or a thoughtful one. But for an emotional one.

"I've seen how carelessly he can break a heart, and I don't want that to happen to me."

To hear the pain strangling her voice like a vine, to see the anger barbing her stare with thorns, and still to feel that surging, tidal pool of desire drowning us together . . . I couldn't take it.

I knew she blamed me for what had happened with Rachel. That I'd broken up with her. Hurt her irreparably. Though she'd never confirmed it until now. Still, I'd thought I was prepared to face her assumptions—her distorted version of the past—knowing it wasn't wrong, exactly, but neither was it wholly right. But I wasn't prepared for the worst-case scenario: *the way it made me feel.*

"This way." I charted a new path to the edge of the woods, never following the same path twice in case Matthew or Ben had an eye for broken branches and crushed leaves and the stories they told.

"Sorry about earlier," I said gruffly, turning once we'd cleared the trees, bottling up those feelings nice and tight in my chest; they'd only make things worse. "I didn't want Maxwell to think we were making progress. The sooner we start to break down in front of her, the sooner we'll get answers."

That response—unlike the ones in the Sanctuary—was rehearsed. Practiced on repeat between each chastisement. I had to put out the sparks of truth before they turned into a wildfire I couldn't control.

Lara's wince was quickly concealed; when it came to putting on a mask of control, we were both equally matched.

"I might already have some," Lara blurted out, the information popping from her throat like a shaken bottle of champagne. "I just ran into Sarah. She told me 'EC' is Eden's Children. Sarah said Dr. Julia wants to *refer* her to the advanced program to work on herself and her self-esteem. Alone."

My brows rose.

"She made it seem like the program was geared toward gaining . . . sexual confidence in various scenarios and with multiple partners."

Well, that wasn't exactly what I'd been expecting.

"She briefly mentioned some of the paperwork she'd have to sign and the costs involved, but she seemed more worried about . . . the other parts."

"Did she say where it was?"

Lara shook her head. "She told me Dr. Julia wants her to go as soon as possible—tomorrow morning. And she said Ben would take her."

Displeasure rumbled from my chest. "I don't like the sound of that."

"That's what I thought. I could see how someone like Sarah would be a good target for something like that and how she could be easily swayed." She paused here, a silent acknowledgment that Rachel would've been chosen and willing for similar reasons. Except Lara thought that reason was me, and I still felt the war being fought in my bones on whether it was my place to correct her.

What good would it do? Arguing about a decade-plus-old relationship? Sharing things her sister clearly wanted to keep private even if it had been at my expense?

What would the truth change?

The word *everything* echoed from somewhere deep in my chest, and I strove to ignore it.

"So what do we do now?" Her arms folded over her chest and her head swung side to side; *the hummingbird was back.* "Should we leave? Or confront Dr. Julia? Ask where the Garden is—"

"Slow down, hummingbird," I said without thinking. "Let me see what Callum can find out. We don't know anything about Eden's Children. If it's legit. If it's not. If we confront Maxwell and it spooks her, or her partner, I don't want to risk it."

Based on the limited information Lara had gleaned, I had a gut feeling about the kind of organization we were dealing with, but I didn't want to throw the c-word out just yet; for Lara's sake—and Rachel's—I hoped I was wrong.

"You should head back," I said, reaching for the heel of my boot and the cell phone hidden within. Lara stared, her silence heavy with protest. "You know they roam around the campsite to keep an eye on everyone and make sure we're reflecting alone. If they can't find either of us . . ."

Her lips pursed, but she finally clipped her chin in a nod.

"I'll let you know what he finds."

"Eden's Children," I said when my brother answered the phone.

"Hold on," Callum grunted. There was some shuffling and then a loud bang. "I'm dealing with something for Calder. Can you leave?"

"What about borrowing one of your drones—"

"I'm not getting involved in your prank war with Creighton," Callum interrupted our sister.

"But he spray-painted Donnie—"

"I don't give a fuck. Or a duck." That was as close to a joke as Callum would get—one that was barbed in cold antipathy.

"Fine. I'll ask Colt." *If she could find him.*

People were usually surprised to learn how solitary most of us were. They thought because we lived on a family compound, sequestered from society, that we must live close-knit, like the seven dwarves, whistling by the campfire every night while we roasted s'mores.

They couldn't be more wrong.

Mom had been the glue in that nuclear-knit family, holding together all the strings Cassius taught us were safer to keep separate. Once she was gone, we all unraveled. Some of us farther than others.

The following silence was broken by the march of Callum's hands over his keyboard and Twister's trot, nails clipping against the floor, as he followed Colby to the door; our animal-whispering sister was his second-favorite person after Callum. A few seconds later, I heard his door slam shut.

"You'd think living in my own damn house would send the message that I want to be left alone," he muttered. "I'm going to have to install a bigger lock."

"A bigger lock is only going to encourage her to pick it."

He cursed under his breath. "Then I'll install whatever Creighton has on the attic. She hasn't managed to get through that."

No, she just trained her duck to fly through his window. But I decided to forgo mentioning how much Donnie would probably enjoy the skylight in Callum's house or chasing down his drones. I'd called for a reason, and it wasn't to give Callum advice on how to manage his relationships. God knew, I was a pretty poor poster child for that right now.

"Anything come up?"

"How'd you learn the name?"

I flexed and released my fist. "Lara talked to one of the other women at the retreat who was invited to join."

Callum's silence wasn't promising.

"What is it?"

"Not much on the corporation. Ownership is obscured, but it was registered with the state about three years ago. Hold on." Another pause. "Well, Eden's Children is run by one Adam Eden."

"So that's who Maxwell is working with." The pieces were starting to come together.

"Calder . . ." I could hear his heavy exhale through the line. "The wilderness retreat was one thing, but this—Eden's Children—is giving me cult vibes."

Fuck. There was the c-word.

"What did you find?"

"The usual bare-bones markers. Plain website and stock photos advertising sexual confidence and well-being. No contact information. No address. Nothing but a few blog articles written by Maxwell, though she's only referenced as Dr. Julia."

In my experience with cults, which thankfully wasn't too much, their online footprint was hardly even an outline. It was for show. A house of cards. Just like their foundational belief system. The only thing that was real was how they sought to take advantage of people.

"There's an online form anyone who stumbles onto the website can fill out for more information, but I doubt it's ever been used," Callum continued. "The website didn't show up in my regular search, so they're probably using a program to stop search bots from crawling the site and sorting it into a search feed."

"Not surprising," I murmured. The few cases I'd taken involving a missing loved one who'd been recruited to join a cult had followed this same kind of online framework; they had enough of a presence to appear legitimate, but they didn't want cold leads or law enforcement to be able to find them easily. "And Adam Eden?"

"His bio is sparse, just a big quote about his feminine-empowerment philosophy and why he created Eden's Children."

Most cults fell into one of two categories: those containing a religious element and those that didn't. Almost all wielded a kind of self-improvement, "better life" fantasy as their main selling point, which could make it hard to distinguish between legitimate businesses with altruistic motives . . . and those that stepped over the line and abused the basic instinct of humans to want to be better.

"His photo is useless. I can already tell it's been run through one of those AI-enhancement programs, judging by that jawline. It's going to take me a while to figure out what he really looks like."

I grunted.

"I'll keep digging into him."

"Focus on finding a location." Finding the cult's base—"the Garden"—was my only priority right now. "I'll text you if we learn anything else."

"Another storm's hitting your area tonight."

"Thanks," I said, though even I could already see the dark clouds blotting out the mountain peaks in the not-so-very-far distance, towing a promise of thunderous tumult in their wake.

By the time I returned to the tent, I'd caught Ben and Matthew weaving through the woods with the dinner trays. Tonight, dinner was cut short for Maxwell's evening lecture; even she was worried about the reliability of the broadcast due to the arriving storm. The change in schedule meant that hours passed between when I'd talked to Callum and when I finally had the chance to reveal what he'd found.

"A cult?" Lara stared at me.

"Yes," I grunted. There was no easy way to share our suspicions, so I didn't sugarcoat it; it was better to rip off the Band-Aid and move on. "We can't say for certain—"

"But you think she was recruited to a cult—excuse me, a sex cult," she said in that stern doctor voice, the one that feigned calm even when she was unsteady inside.

I nodded slowly, watching every shade of green cascade through her eyes as she continued to metabolize the idea.

She paced the tent, worrying her bottom lip until all I could think about was kissing her to make it stop.

Looking at me over her shoulder, she finally spoke again. "We have to find her."

"We will. Just remember, right now, we have nothing to suggest Rachel is in danger—physical or life-threatening danger." Lara glared at me. "Think about what Sarah told you. It appears everyone who joins, joins willingly." Aside from one incident in Maxwell's former life, there was no indication that Eden's Children was harming anyone.

"So, you think there is a chance, in this world, that this sex cult *isn't* exploitative? That they aren't taking advantage of her?"

I gritted my teeth. I'd always made it a point to not argue possibilities. Decisions could only be made with what was *known*, not what was possible. But I couldn't argue with her. I couldn't be *objective* with her.

"No," I admitted roughly.

Lara flinched and then steeled her shoulders. "We can't let Sarah go."

"Sarah is an adult. We can't force her to do or not do something she wants—"

"We can. We can warn her, stop her. I can tell her the truth," she rioted, a hungry desperation seeming to drive her.

"Lara." I took her shoulders, demanding her attention. This wasn't about Sarah. Not really. This was about her sister, and Lara holding on to all this guilt for no damn reason, let alone a good one. "We're going to find Rachel. If they are going to take Sarah, we can follow them, rescue them both—"

"No." Her head shook, caught up in the storm of her mind. She grabbed my shirt like she wanted to shake me—like she needed to shake me—into hearing her. "I have to help her. Warn her. I won't use her as bait. I won't risk it—risk losing her, too. I can't. I can't lose—"

"Lara . . ." I caught her chin on the edges of my knuckles, pinning her head in place. "What is it?" I searched her face. "What aren't you telling me?"

Her throat bobbed, her eyelids drooping heavily. The pink swells of her lips parted, the warm rush of her breath tempting me to take a taste.

Everything she did tempted me to take another taste. Another kiss. When she looked at me. When she spoke to me. When she accused me of breaking her sister's heart. Every single thing made me want to cover her mouth with mine and show her that what I'd said earlier had been the truth.

It had only ever taken one look at her to completely undo me.

"Calder . . ." Lara swallowed again, her eyes glistening.

There was something else.

I wanted to catch the first tear that fell with my thumb. The second, with my tongue. I wanted to pull her resolute but weary frame against me and kiss away every pain. But instead, I forced myself to stay steady. To breathe steady. To ignore the white of her knuckles where she gripped my shirt, and instead focus on only her motionless stare.

One wrong move—one loud heartbeat—would break it.

The greatest skill a tracker could possess after an acute attention to detail was an enduring ability to be still. To let the answers come to him. To me.

It had never not worked. Until right now.

That storm Callum had warned was going to "hit" . . . well, it seemed he'd chosen that word with purpose. Thunder cracked then like a bat against a perfect pitch.

Lara jumped and then shuddered, dragging in a breath as she pulled away from me. "I need some air."

She was out of the tent before I could stop her, and there was no calling after her. Not now. Not after curfew.

Chapter 19

Lara

I sucked down giant gulps of air like I hadn't been breathing at all for the last four minutes.

In the distance, lightning scratched giant white tears through the onyx sky. A storm was close, but it wasn't quite here yet, and I needed to get out of that tent. Away from what Callum had found. Away from Calder's probing stare and a different truth it threatened to uncover.

A cult. Rachel had joined a cult. And Ian . . . *I'd lost them both—failed them both.*

"Lara." Calder came up behind me but stopped a pace away. I hated how he knew I needed the space.

"I'm sorry. I just need a minute," I managed.

"I'll take one with you," came his deep reply, and I shivered.

I could ask him to leave, but he wouldn't. And then there was the tiny, broken piece of me that didn't want to be alone.

It felt like he knew that, too.

My arms banded over my middle, my hands curling into the sides of my shirt.

Thunder boomed again. "They don't have storms like this in Phoenix," I said, watching the tapestry of the angry sky unfold.

I didn't want to talk about Rachel right now. Or the cult. Or what was going to happen. Or what I could've done—should've done. I kept . . . *losing* people. Because I wasn't enough. Because I hadn't done enough.

"How do you mean?"

"The storms in Phoenix, they're . . . empty." It took me a minute to decide on the right word. "Maybe it's the desert or the dry heat, but the thunderstorms always feel like they come from a place of desperation. Like they're trying to draw something from nothing."

"And here?"

I sucked in another breath, tasting the particles of pre-storm energy on my tongue.

"Here, they come because nature is . . . too full. Full of energy and charge and power. Too full to contain, so it has to be set free." I exhaled, closing my eyes as I added, "Don't tell Callum. I'm sure he'll disagree. My theory isn't backed by science."

"Callum would disagree even if it were," Calder replied ruefully. "Another example of something too full of . . . energy to contain."

Taking another deep breath, I confessed, "I miss this. The storms. The energy in the air. It's like . . . breathing in lightning. Energizing and grounding at the same time."

I was rambling, but I didn't care. Like the storm, I had too much pain bottled up inside to hold it all in.

"Not even nature can carry it all."

My pulse stumbled. We were talking about the weather—the quintessential superficial conversation starter. Except nothing about this felt superficial or quintessential at all.

"Yeah," my voice cracked.

"Do you miss Phoenix?"

No. The thought came unbidden.

"I don't know." And I didn't want to talk about this. So then why had I brought up Arizona in the first place? *Because I couldn't carry it all, either.*

"When do you have to go back?"

"Take the time for what it can be, Lara. Until the lawsuit is settled, we can't have you here anyway."

"I don't," I said, unsure whether my voice had ever sounded so small.

His head cocked to the side, and I could feel the rush of energy in my direction.

"What do you mean, you don't?"

My breathing sped up, carrying me like a runaway train back to those moments. Those split-second, life-changing moments that day in the emergency room. The sounds. The machines. The screams.

A shudder racked all the way along my spine, trembling the truth up to my lips.

Maybe it was the storm's crescendo. Maybe it was the vastness of Wyoming, which promised to swallow me up and rock me in its mountainous cradle. Or maybe it was just Calder. His steadiness laid like bedrock around me, silently promising to withstand the excess of my own storm if I would just let loose. *If I would just trust him.*

"I don't know if I still have a job," I said, annoyed that I sounded purposely evasive, but on the inside, it felt like I was trying to put together a jigsaw puzzle with my eyes closed and a noose around my neck, tightening with every connected piece. "I won't know if I still have a job until the lawsuit is settled."

I closed my eyes, wishing it was raindrops and not tears that dangled, cold and merciless, onto my cheeks. I hadn't talked to anyone outside the hospital—couldn't. HIPAA. Hospital policy. Lawyers.

But here . . .

"What happened?" His low voice carried from behind me. Just like the heat of him did.

Another bolt of lightning shredded the sky. Closer now.

"Someone died." The words were wrenched out. "Because of me." The pain, the guilt, almost took me to my knees.

He was quiet, and then I felt the warm grip of his palm on my shoulder, directing me to turn toward him.

"Tell me." There he was. The gorgeous *director*. Except I didn't hear a command from his lips, but a promise: *Let me help you carry this.*

"It was late—early, actually. 2:43 in the morning." When I blinked, I could still see the clock on the wall just as I'd seen it that night—and just like I'd had to include in what felt like endless recounts of my report. "A patient was brought in by ambulance. A young kid."

Not really. Ian wasn't that much younger than me, but he looked like he was. Like he'd only just dipped his toes into the vast pool of his life.

"The police were with him. I was told they'd pulled him off a sidewalk downtown because he was tripping. His pupils were dilated. He smelled like Brandon's trailer. He wasn't coherent. Mumbling. Stumbling. Hallucinating." Closing my eyes, I could see him now. Every detail. His clear blue eyes. The goldfinch tattoo on the side of his neck. "I went to take his vitals and told the nurse working with me to grab the NARCAN in case we had to administer. I followed protocol. I took his pulse. It was erratic but there, and he seemed to be drifting into a stupor."

I stopped blinking, recalling the whip and whirl of his heartbeat like a wild stallion that wouldn't settle.

"I told my nurse to start him on IV fluids, and at the first prick of the needle, he went wild. He grabbed the needle—grabbed her arm." I started to shake. Big racking shakes, with panic and fear detonating like I was still in that moment; the only difference was, in that moment, I'd kept the earthquake inside.

Calder's hand tightened on my shoulder, anchoring me back to him and the comfort of his steady gaze.

"The nurse, my friend Hailey, she started screaming. I yelled for help, but I couldn't wait, he was going to hurt her . . . I lunged across the hospital bed, forcing him back with my own weight. She got free and then he let out this . . . unearthly roar and then came for me."

My eyes shuttered, unable to hold up the wet weight of my tears as they fell. At that moment, I wouldn't have known it had started to rain, except that when I looked at Calder, I saw droplets staining him, too.

"He didn't look that strong, but the meth in his system . . ." I gritted my teeth. After how many times I'd had to go over this chain of events, it should've been easier to recount. "His elbow landed in my stomach, and then he grabbed my face and shoved me so hard I fell back, smacked my head against the wall." I winced, recalling how it had felt as though my skull had split in two. "I opened my eyes and looked at him . . . that last moment, I stared into his eyes . . . and then he went into cardiac arrest." I swallowed. "I tried . . . but it didn't matter. He was gone."

"That's what wakes you up at night," he murmured, his hand sliding from my shoulder to the side of my neck as though he saw I needed help holding up the weight of my guilt. "Ian."

My breath caught when he said his name, and I felt myself nod, wishing that the nightmare ended there. Unfortunately, it didn't.

"It turned out, he wasn't homeless. He was twenty-three and from a wealthy family local to Phoenix. He ran away because his parents wanted to send him to a rehab program and was staying with friends. They were at a bar and he snuck off, got too high, and then got kicked out. Anyway, his parents . . . they said I killed him." My throat was so tight, I could barely speak. "That because I'd restrained him and he'd tried to get free, it was too much strain on his heart."

"While he was high on meth? And what do they think the police or security would've done?" His voice was calm, yet his eyes were anything but.

"I know I did the right thing." A protest of bitter laughter bubbled out. "Funny how that doesn't seem to make a difference."

All the reports. The autopsy. The video footage. The witness accounts. Everything but a parent's grief had cleared me of wrongdoing.

"I couldn't save him," I said, not needing to speak loudly, because his face was right in front of mine.

Cool air dumped into my chest as Calder framed my face with both hands, my gaze hostage to his.

"I'm sorry."

I watched a fat droplet of rain land on the bridge of his nose and run down all the way to the tip. I was grateful for the rain. It made me feel like I wasn't crying alone.

And I was grateful for Calder because he didn't try to explain away my guilt or grief. He didn't try to soothe it with kind words or placating promises that this would get better.

Instead, his hand slid around the nape of my neck and pulled me to him, the other wrapping around my back like the root of a tree trunk, anchoring me to the warm bedrock of his embrace as sobs finally claimed me.

He held me in the rain. In the storm. And let it soak him, too.

"I couldn't save him," I repeated over and over into his chest, his steady heartbeat echoing back. *Thump, thump. I know. Thump, thump.*

It's okay.

I hadn't cried. Not like this. I'd been too afraid of what it would do—afraid it would drown me. But the way he held me, I knew he wouldn't drag me under, so I finally let the tears fall.

Time passed only by the deep breaths that filled my lungs with his rich, masculine scent. It dissolved in the rain, electrified by the storm, and dug its greedy fingers into my veins, holding on until the scales tipped from exhaling grief to inhaling him.

The entire time, I buried my face against the warmth of his chest and listened to his steady heartbeat. His hand drew slow circles in my hair at my nape, and his chin rested on top of my head.

By the time my cries subsided, the rain camouflaged the damage done to his shirt by my tears.

Hesitantly, I turned my head and angled it back. I couldn't cry anymore, but neither did I want to leave his embrace.

I couldn't have saved Ian. I couldn't have done enough to change his fate. But in this moment, there was something I could do to change mine.

"Calder," I murmured huskily.

Rain soaked our faces, but it was nothing compared to the way lust drenched his pupils, mine overflowing the same.

I dragged my tongue across my lips, clearing the water for the taste of him.

His head dipped lower. Closer. Resisting him—resisting us—was too much for nature to hold back, too.

And then a rip of lightning tore through the sky, illuminating the whole of his face. And there, his vivifying ache that haunted every ridge and dip, every muscle and crease, was so damningly obvious, as embedded in his expression as oxygen in his blood, that I knew what he'd said earlier was true.

"All it took was one look."

"Come on. We have to get inside," he ordered in a low voice.

He kept his arm around my shoulders as we jogged into the woods, Calder leading us by flashes of lightning back to our tent.

It was a downpour by the time he zipped us into shelter, both of us panting and our clothes soaked through.

For a moment, he stayed there, unmoving and facing the flap of the tent, like he wasn't sure that we were completely out of danger, or maybe it was because he knew that we definitely weren't.

Something in my chest twisted. The hungry ache that had throbbed in the woods now a sharp, wringing need.

"Calder . . ." I said softly and stepped closer to him.

The smallest movement sent a cascade of tension from his shoulders all the way down his spine. I imagined this was what it would look like if a human were able to turn to stone. Perfectly still. Entirely unbreakable.

I held my place. My breath. My heartbeat. Afraid if I didn't, his rules, his restraint, would get the better of us again. And then he slowly turned until our eyes met, like electricity to water.

The funny thing about electricity in water is that if the water is pure, the shock does nothing. It's when the water isn't pure—when the water is charged with impurities—that electricity can take hold.

Well, there was nothing pure about wanting my sister's ex-boyfriend.

Not. A. Single. Thing.

And maybe that was why what happened next wasn't a singular charge of electric current, but the complete electrocution of all our reservations.

I didn't know who moved first. All I knew was the moment we collided. My arms grounded around his neck, his hands bracketing my waist. Our mouths fused together, a detonation of lips and teeth and tongue into desire.

I kissed him frantically. Desperately. *Wildly.*

I'd lost so many people. I couldn't lose anyone else; I couldn't lose Calder. *Not tonight.*

"Fuck, Lara," he growled, his large hand sliding up to cradle my head, fingers firm in my hair. With a low, helpless groan, he angled my mouth and kissed me hard.

I couldn't lose Calder, but I did lose myself in that kiss. In the drive and slide of his tongue scorching my senses, in the hot sear of desire and destruction embedding all the way into my bones. I clung to him in the storm, scoring my nails against his scalp and anchoring myself to the broad hardness of his chest.

I'd never felt so not-in-control before—never so at the mercy of someone else—as I did in this kiss. The way he charted the spots that made me tremble and quake, tracked the spots that made me moan. I wasn't surprised by his surgical-level awareness of the minutiae of my undoing, but neither was I prepared for it.

"Please," I begged, uncertain what I was begging for exactly but knowing the only word to describe it was *more.*

A second later, Calder slid his hands to my ass and hauled me to him, with him, as he moved toward one of the chairs, sat in it, and pulled me onto his lap.

He could've been pulling me straight down to hell and I still wouldn't have protested. Not if it meant never breaking this kiss.

We dripped all over the chair. All over the floor. Our sopping clothes were stuck to us, and stuck us to each other. But the only thing I felt was the slide of his tongue along mine. The heat of his chest pressed to the painful points of my nipples. And the thick ridge of him intruding against my core.

Whether it was instinct or muscle memory from this morning, I started to rock against him. Along his length. And it wasn't like adding gasoline to a flame, but cartons of dynamite to a wildfire, pleasure ravaging through every inch of me.

"Fuck." Calder's husky rumble quaked over my skin as he slid his hand up under my shirt and pinned it to the damp skin of my waist, guiding my movement.

I wanted this—needed him. *My sister's ex-boyfriend.*

Calder's other hand returned to my nape, taking my wet hair and winding it like a rope around his fist. I didn't realize his intent until my head was being firmly arched back, baring my throat and the greedy thrum of my pulse to his lips.

"What are you doing to me?" he rasped, his breath hot where it blew over my damp skin.

Whatever answer he wanted, he was going to take it directly from my skin.

His teeth scraped over the erratic beats of my pulse, back and forth like a predator playing with his prey.

I whimpered, feeling his cock thicken, stoking the heat in my stomach that unraveled me from the inside out. "Please, Calder . . ." I squirmed against him, begging for more pressure. More friction. *More dynamite.*

The bracket of his hand cinched on my waist, stilling me. "Fuck," Calder muttered like a man losing his grip on reality.

He wasn't the only one.

Crazy or not. Cult or not. I needed from Calder exactly what Dr. Julia had said—I needed that part of him that let me take without worry, that let me be needy without fear of not being in control.

Breathing heavy, he took the bottom of my shirt and peeled it like wrapping paper from my torso and over my head; it landed with a wet *thwack* on the ground.

Calder held my gaze for a torturous second, my breasts coated in goose bumps, aching for the burn of his stare. And then his jaw fired, the tension like a bullet loaded in the chamber, ready to fire and ravage anything in its path.

I pressed my fingers to the knot of muscle like I could coax it to release, and in reply, he turned his head and sank his teeth into the meat of my palm until I gasped in delicious pain.

"Calder . . ."

He buried a savage sound into my palm, an incoherent confession of a need there were no words to describe, and then released my flesh, his hunger finding a new destination.

His chin lowered and leveled with my chest, my breasts so heavy and aching, I could've cried for his touch. But he didn't move—didn't touch. Instead, he stared, his pupils blown wide as my nipples drew into even tighter beads, begging for attention.

Sliding his palms to span my ribs, Calder let out a ragged breath and muttered, "God, how I've dreamed of you."

My unsteady pulse went into a riot, throwing my heart against the wall of my chest. I wanted to confess to dreaming of him, too, but lost my ability when he bent forward and pressed his lips to my sternum in a reverent kiss.

A slow, tender second elapsed before his teeth marked a fresh path toward my aching nipple, searing a sizzling agony to my skin.

My hands slid from his broad shoulders toward his neck, needing something to hold on to. Bracing for when his feral mouth reached my—

Boom!

Calder froze, his exhale the only part of him that ever reached my breast.

"Calder," I murmured, the fugue of my desire forced to clear.

Was that—no, that wasn't thunder. It was too sharp. Too piercing.

My stomach dropped. "Was that—"

"Shh," he warned with a finger to his lips and his head cocked, listening.

If there was something else to hear, I couldn't through the storm or over my pounding heart.

"Calder—" I broke off with a small cry as he rose, taking me with him as easily as if I were a rag doll. But he didn't take me far. Turning, he set me right where he'd been sitting.

His head jerked again, and I heard it, too: the sound of shouting in the distance.

"Stay here," Calder ordered and pulled free from my limp, panicked limbs.

"Wait—"

"Lara," he growled, his gaze piercing wildly into mine.

"Okay," I acquiesced with a nervous nod.

He picked up and handed me my top, a subtle message that the moment had officially ended.

He strode to his side of the bed and pulled out an . . . axe?

"Where did that come from?" I whispered.

"I made it this morning," he grunted. *So that was what he'd done during our reflection time: made an axe from a sharpened stone attached to a carved tree branch.*

Calder turned back to me, his gaze dropped for a split second, his entire body tensing. Glancing down, I realized I'd wadded my top into a ball in my lap rather than pulling it back on. *Crap.*

"I'll be back," he murmured before opening the flap. "Don't come looking for me." And then he was gone.

Wriggling back into my cold, wet top, I went to the entrance and drew down the zipper once more. Standing there, I looked for Calder in every flash of lightning and listened for whatever was going on through the cacophony of the storm.

The longer I listened, the more I heard the strains of an argument threading between the thunder. An argument that had involved a gun.

Calder had told me to stay back to protect me, but if I was here, who was going to protect him?

Chapter 20

Calder

Rule #22: Practice fighting from all positions and in all conditions. Conflict resolution doesn't wait for ideal circumstances.

The thunderstorm was too raucous for me to need to temper my movement; I could hardly hear my own footsteps from only six feet above them. The shouting, though, that came through loud and clear the closer I got to Trent and Sarah's tent.

And away from the greatest threat to me.

I tried to shove Lara from my mind. Everything from her confession about what had happened in Phoenix, both in the hospital and the aftermath, all the way up to the moment when we'd kissed.

Again.

Never had I felt such a lack of control than when it came to her—when it came to needing her. If it hadn't been for the unmistakable sound of a gunshot, there was no denying I would've broken some unspoken rule (and all the spoken ones) and fucked her in that chair.

Her. *The woman who thought I broke her sister's heart.*

What the hell was I thinking? I wasn't, that was the problem. But it was a problem for another day.

A light flashed ahead. Two of them. Flashlights, not lightning.

"Fuck you. Don't fucking touch me." The shouting grew louder, and definitely belonged to Trent.

"Don't make this harder than it has to be."

"Get your fucking hands off me."

I reached the small clearing of their tent just in time to see Trent shake Matthew's hold off his arm. Crouching behind a tree, I wiped the rain from my eyes and squinted at the scene in front of me.

Trent, Matthew, and Ben stood in triangle formation outside the tent, the light from inside illuminating all three of them, along with Sarah, who was huddled at the entrance. Her arms were wrapped around her middle and she was shaking. She also had a bright-red welt forming on her cheek. Someone had hit her, and I had a damn good guess as to who.

Matthew was managing the situation, his stance commanding. Ben, on the other hand, stood a little farther back, holding his weapon at his side. No one appeared injured, so the shot we'd heard must've been fired into the air as a warning.

"Trent, you need to come with me—" Matthew started.

"Is this really what you want?" Trent ignored him, his vitriol aimed at Sarah.

"I don't—"

Trent didn't wait for her to finish, lunging for her and shouting, "Bullshit! I know this is because of you. You told them to do this, you stupid fucking cunt—" The wind went out of him when Matthew landed a punch to his gut, sending Trent doubled over and onto his knees.

I'd be lying if I didn't feel a not-so-small burst of satisfaction seeing that asshole brought down a notch.

"Fucker—"

My satisfaction dimmed when Ben launched toward the downed man, taking advantage of easy prey. He swung the butt of his gun into Trent's face, who went sprawling into the muddy ground, and then nailed his boot into Trent's stomach. The beaten man curled into a ball, emitting a pained groan that was almost too low for me to hear.

"Enough," Matthew warned his partner.

Trent was clearly no longer a threat, but neither that nor Matthew's caution stopped him. Like a switch had been flipped, Ben grabbed a limp and moaning Trent by the back of his collar and punched the side of his head. If the first blow didn't completely knock him out, the next one would. But Ben wasn't going to stop there; I could see it in his eyes, a sadistic kind of savagery that was too evil to hide. He wasn't going to stop brutalizing him until Trent was dead.

I stepped out from behind the tree, my fist tightening on my weapon, my heart pumping for a fight. Two against one wasn't my favorite for odds, but I'd certainly fought in worse.

"Stop!" Sarah yelled and stepped out from the tent and I stilled, too, waiting to see whether my intervention was necessary.

Ben's head jerked to her. "Stop?" He laughed, and through the rain, his expression twisted. "Soon you'll be thanking me for knowing how to get rid of him and not leave a trace."

A coldness swept through me, and I carefully moved closer to them, my pace slower now that the rain had started to ease.

"Enough, Ben. This is done." Matthew grabbed his shoulder and shoved him back. Ben finally, begrudgingly, took the hint. "Go inside, Sarah," the guard ordered. "You don't have to worry about him anymore."

Bending, Matthew grabbed Trent and dragged him to the ATV I could now see parked beside the tent, draping the unconscious man over the back.

"What—where are you taking him?" Sarah demanded.

"He broke the rules for hitting you. It's protocol to remove violent participants from the retreat," Matthew replied as the ATV's engine coughed to life.

Ben couldn't resist adding, "Soon you'll learn not to question a man when he is taking care of you."

"But—"

"Get some rest. You'll be leaving for the Garden in the morning."

Shit.

Matthew revved the engine and then drove off, the headlights ping-ponging along his path through the woods.

Once Matthew and Trent were out of sight, Sarah's head collapsed into her hands, her shoulders shaking with loud sobs.

I straightened for a second time, my plan already decided; first, wait for Ben to leave. Then get Sarah, go back for Lara, and leave the campsite tonight. It was too risky to stay; we'd figure out where the Garden was another way.

Except Ben didn't leave.

"Sarah."

"Go away." She jerked from Ben's touch—the kind of thing that would only infuriate a man like him.

"Me? I just want to make you feel better after that asshole hit you. One day you'll thank me for knowing how to get rid of him."

"What?" Sarah backed away, whipping her head side to side. "No."

"Come on. Let me show you what a good orgasm can do for you. Think of it like an introduction to the Garden," he said, ignoring her.

Her sad face became stricken with horror. *With fear.* I didn't blame her.

Looked like my plan was going to be modified.

I took wide strides to make it quickly into the clearing, Sarah's loud gasp announcing my presence.

Ben whipped around, rage distorting his face.

"I think someone needs to teach you the meaning of no," I said, moving close enough for him to acknowledge the weapon at my side with the quick drop and rebound of his gaze.

"Go back to your tent. This doesn't concern you," he growled angrily.

"I disagree."

He lifted his gun carelessly—dangerously—aiming it right at me. "Get back—"

Sarah screamed, and I took advantage of the nanosecond of distraction. I dropped my makeshift axe to the ground and lunged for Ben's Colt. In a split second, I'd taken it from his grasp, dropped the mag to the ground, and whipped the body into the dark woods.

Humiliation was like steroids to the anger of small men.

"You fucker!" Ben snarled, crazed, as he swung at me. I ducked and avoided the punch, sending him stumbling and almost losing his balance. "I'm going to kill you for this. She's mine. She's supposed to be mine."

He spun around to face me, and a flash of lightning caught the switchblade now open at his side.

Dammit.

Ben charged again, but this time, as I sidestepped the arc of the blade, I slipped on the wet underbrush and didn't make it out of his way fast enough.

Fuck. The curse bloomed from the white-hot slice of pain.

I grabbed my side and quickly moved into a defensive position several feet away. Gritting my teeth, I pressed my fingers around the wound. The broad stroke of the knife left a superficial cut along my side, but no major damage. It fell into the *looked worse than it was* category, and therefore wasn't something I could worry about now.

"Ha," Ben cackled. "Just a taste of what I'm going to do to you."

"Look, Ben, it doesn't have to end this way. Just put the knife down and walk away. No one needs to get hurt," I said, my hands lifted like I'd be willing to surrender if he did.

"Says the man who's already wounded. You just know you're going to lose." Confidence inflated not only his threats but also his actions. He charged again so wildly, he should've been swinging for a home run, not trying to stab someone.

This time, I anticipated the terrain better, not only veering to the side but also spinning and driving my palm into the center of his back, sending him tripping forward and crashing to his knees.

Two steps brought me right back to my starting position—and the place where I'd dropped my weapon.

"You're either going to stop this now and walk away, or you're going to look like a fool. Again," I warned, picking up my axe.

I tried to give him an easy way out—again. For some reason, the bad guys never seemed to take it.

"Then I'll get rid of both of you and take your whore instead," he snarled and, with a look of pure insanity, turned for Sarah.

She screamed, and my arm swung in a sure, short arc, the axe slicing through the air and burying into his shoulder.

Ben roared and collapsed to his knees, grappling for the blade lodged in his flesh.

I didn't waste any time—I didn't have any of it to waste.

"I'm . . . going . . . to . . ." His threat sputtered into silence as I came up behind him, wrapped my arm around his neck, holding tight enough to send him into unconsciousness.

He dropped like a Slinky to the ground.

"Oh my god. Is he—oh my god . . ." Sarah cupped her hands over her mouth, her face oscillating between a shade of white and green.

"He's passed out, but he'll survive." Unfortunately.

Her head volleyed back and forth as I walked by her into the tent and ripped two strips of cloth from the bedsheet. I would've preferred a zip tie or cuffs, but beggars couldn't be choosers.

Yanking the blade from the meat of his shoulder, I wiped it clean on his shirt. Getting skewered by an axe was a dramatic injury, but I'd made sure it wouldn't be a lasting one. Nothing some antiseptic and stitches wouldn't heal in a few weeks. *Hopefully from the inside of a prison cell.*

Stuffing the first wad of cotton into Ben's mouth, I dragged him over to the closest tree, braided the second strip of fabric around his wrists, and then tied them behind the trunk.

It wouldn't hold him for long, but I only needed it to hold him for long enough.

Standing, I turned to tackle my next hurdle: the woman going into shock.

Making sure to keep myself between her and Ben, I approached her slowly, my hands raised in a *I mean no harm* gesture.

"Sarah, are you okay?" I asked. "I need to know if you're hurt at all," I said, but with no more success. "It's okay now. No one is going to hurt you. We're going to get you out of here."

I must've gotten close enough to pull her out of her stupor, because she jerked and stammered, "What . . . What . . ." And then turned pale. *Pass-out pale.*

Shit.

I reached for her, guiding her to the ground before she took herself there. "You're all right. We're going to get you out of here, okay? Lara and I."

"Calder!"

I stiffened and turned as Lara came through the trees, her wide eyes raking over the wreckage and stopping on Ben tied to the tree, blood trailing down his arm.

"He's alive, just unconscious," I informed her. "But we have to go before Matthew comes back."

"I don't—I don't understand what's happening," Sarah murmured, her head swaying like it was about to become untethered.

Lara beelined for her, crouching and taking her shoulders and turning her toward the light.

I leaned close and murmured just her for ears, "She's in shock. Trent hit her, and Matthew and Ben came to escort him off the retreat, but Ben got violent. He beat up Trent, and when Matthew stepped in and took Trent away, Ben tried to assault her."

Lara nodded somberly, her eyes narrowing on the wounded woman. "Did Dr. Julia give you another smoothie, Sarah?"

Damn. How had I missed that?

Sarah nodded weakly. "She said it would make me not nervous . . . for the change. But then I didn't want to, and she said I had to. That I needed it." Now that she was talking more, I could hear the alteration in her voice. "I signed and . . . and then when I told Trent . . . he hit me . . ."

"Okay. It's okay now. You're okay now." Lara blew out an exhale, and I could feel her anger pulsing underneath. "We're going to get out of here, okay?"

Sarah nodded again.

"Good. You're doing good."

Releasing her, Lara turned to me and lowered her voice. "How are we going to get out of here?"

"The highway is less than five miles. I'll call my brother to pick us up."

"I don't think she can walk five miles." She glanced over her shoulder, catching Sarah just as she swayed. "Not the way she is."

My jaw locked, my eyes darting around. "All right. Stay with her. I'll be right back."

This time, I knew she'd listen.

I moved much faster knowing Ben was restrained and Matthew was busy dealing with Trent. I doubted the beating Ben had given him was part of their plan, so Matthew was likely consulting with Maxwell on what to do. *Who would probably call Adam.*

I cut a direct path to Maxwell's RV and saw the ATV parked by the door, Trent still lying across the back. In the shuttered windows of the RV, I made out two shadows: one still and one moving.

They were in crisis mode. We didn't have much time.

The rain had worked itself down to a drizzle. Just enough to disguise my determined stride over to the ATV. Lifting the seat, I found a small maintenance toolbox and pulled out a screwdriver from the bag.

After backtracking to the tent, I found Lara and Sarah sitting inside.

"Time to go."

Lara gasped and stood. "Calder, you're injured."

Looking down, I winced at the dark-burgundy stain orbiting the cut in the fabric.

"It's fine. I'm fine. The rain is making it look worse," I brushed it off—along with the inappropriate fantasy of having her doctor me. "I have another way out, but we need to go. Now."

I glanced at the blonde, who was shaking and still deathly pale. We had to get her out of here.

Lara blanched but nodded.

To leave now was to give up our shot at getting any more information from anyone here. Even if I called the police and they arrived first thing in the morning, only three people knew what and where Eden's Children and the Garden was; none of them had any reason to talk and hours to destroy any evidence of what happened here tonight.

"This way."

Single file, we walked along the path to the Sanctuary, through the clearing, and then cut a hard left the way we'd been brought in to the camp.

Sure enough, partway down the ridge was Matthew's Jeep.

Our first stroke of luck was that it was unlocked. Unfortunately, the keys weren't inside. Fortunately, I hadn't expected them to be.

After getting Sarah and Lara settled in the back seat, I rounded to the driver's-side door and climbed in.

I'd just jammed the screwdriver into the ignition when Lara grabbed my shoulder.

"What if it alerts them?"

"It won't," I promised because I'd already accounted for that possibility.

Carefully, I turned the flathead to the "on" position, but not beyond it.

Putting the gearshift in reverse, I released the emergency brake and looked over my shoulder. Lara had her arm around Sarah and was calmly rubbing her arm. The distress she felt for the other woman was evident—to some, it might've been the only thing that was evident, but not to me.

Lara's shattered stare caught mine and I saw the personal pain she tried to hide. There was no going back now. Whatever chance we'd had here to figure out what had happened to Rachel was gone.

She lowered her head in a slow nod. A small plea to get us out of here.

In the span of a blink, I recalled the feel of her face in my hands. The brine of her tears on my tongue. And the way she'd caved into my embrace back in the woods—an embrace I both wished I could give her now and wasn't sure I'd ever be able to give her again.

Taking my foot off the brake, I pushed in the clutch and let the Jeep roll backward. It would've been easier to jump the engine, but with how close Maxwell's RV was, I didn't want the sound to alert them to our escape; I wanted to give us as much of a head start as possible.

So I decided to compression-start the engine . . . something I hadn't done in ages, and never in reverse.

I checked the speedometer, watching the dial tick up. I didn't need much speed, but I did need space. The dial hit 5 mph, then 10. I tempered it with the brake just above there, needing a little more distance . . .

Back and forth, my gaze shifted between the rearview and the speedometer, checking our path, monitoring our distance from the campsite, and our speed. As soon as we hit the mental marker I'd placed, I pressed harder on the brake, needing only a scrap of speed to shock the engine to life.

"There's going to be a bump," I warned Lara, waited a beat, mentally crossed my fingers, and then took my foot off the clutch. The engine protested the stress of the forced start with a violent jolt, then settled into a steady rumble.

Success.

Slowing, I checked on the women in the back and then shifted into first. Turning us forward, I followed my mental map through the BLM terrain and back to the Wilderness Within parking lot.

"We'll get my truck and go back to the ranch. She'll be safe there."

Chapter 21

Lara

My eyelids felt like they'd been stitched together when I went to open them. All of me, really, was stuck, like I'd been stitched straight onto the mattress as I slept . . . *at the Stone house.*

That was enough to pop my eyes open and free my heavy limbs. I sat up, maybe a little too quickly, as the final sequence of events of last night toppled through my mind like a series of dominos, one falling over into the next.

We'd made it back to the retreat's parking lot. Back to Calder's truck. I hadn't any energy left for the surprise when he dug his keys out from the dirt by the front wheel; he hadn't gone back to check that the doors were locked, but to hide his keys outside like he'd known we'd need them. Then driving back to Stonewall Ranch, Sarah trembling next to me—exhausted, drugged, and crying through currents of grief.

Sarah. I turned, my hand landing on the empty space in the bed beside me.

We'd shared Colby's room last night. Calder's sister had offered it up as soon as we walked through the front door, saying she would stay in Colton's room, the somewhere-in-the-middle brother who wasn't home.

I also had no energy to stymie the surge of disappointment when Calder didn't mention the Airstream. Not that I would've spent the night there with him; I needed to stay with Sarah. To make sure she was okay overnight and that she had a friendly face beside her when she woke up—clearly, something she'd already done, waking and leaving without my notice.

Had she talked to Calder already? Did she remember anything else from last night now that the drugs in her system were metabolized? Anything that could give us an idea where to find Rachel?

Pummeled with a dozen questions, I rose and heard the bed crinkle with the movement.

Dr. Julia's notes.

I lifted the mattress to see the papers from my sister's file folded underneath. My throat constricted as I recalled more from last night: the growing strains of the argument in the woods, hearing Sarah's scream through the trees. I had no idea what had prompted me to take the papers with me—what had prompted me to know we wouldn't be coming back. But I'd tucked them into my waistband before going in search of Calder and then stashed them here last night, under the mattress, when I'd stripped out of my soaked clothes.

I didn't have time to look at them now. I needed to find Sarah. And Calder.

While leaving Rachel's file under the mattress like a wound I couldn't heal, a different memory struck me: the blood on Calder's shirt, on his side. He was injured, and I . . . in the tumult of our escape, I'd completely forgotten because he hadn't acted hurt.

He'd said the injury was minor, but he wasn't the doctor. I was.

Next to the door sat the bag of clothes I'd packed for the retreat. Calder must've brought it in from his truck at some point last night. After quickly changing out of the dry sweats Colby had loaned me last night and into jeans and a tee, I headed for the door.

The first voice I heard was Sarah's unsteady one coming from the kitchen, and I assumed she was talking to Calder.

"Thank you so much—"

"No need to thank me," a weathered, deep voice responded.

Compared to the short greeting I'd received from the indomitable Cassius Stone, it was almost hard to believe the softer words I now heard in his worn tone were coming from the Stone patriarch himself.

Not that he wouldn't help someone. Cassius's family—and the work they did—was a testament to the charitable values he possessed, but he still didn't like outsiders. However, maybe Cassius saw in Sarah the face of another woman he hadn't been able to save—just like in her, I saw my sister.

"Good morning, Sarah. Mr. Stone," I said, entering the room and going to her side.

Cassius didn't return my greeting with anything more than a nod, but Sarah brightened when she saw me.

"Lara."

"How are you feeling this morning?" I asked, but I was already taking my own appraisal.

Sarah's color had returned. Her pupils were no longer blown out. The red welt Trent left on her cheek had faded slightly.

"I'm . . . okay." She tested the words.

The psychological and emotional damage, on the other hand, wouldn't dissipate as easily.

"Did you—oh," I stopped, noticing the empty plate bearing food crumbs and a trail of maple syrup.

"I made breakfast," Cassius said then, setting a plate on the island and sliding it in my direction. It was packed with eggs and bacon and pancakes, and my stomach growled. *Wow, that looked good.*

"Thank you." I swallowed and took a seat on the stool next to Sarah's, feeling like I'd been hit by a runaway train of hunger; it was crazy what stress and adrenaline could make you forget.

"Coffee?"

"Please."

As if on cue, Sarah picked up her mug and took another drink.

"I . . . I don't even know what to say, Lara. Thank you—"

"Isn't necessary." I reached out and took her hand, giving it a squeeze as she wiped her cheek with the back of her free hand. "There was no way we were going to let them take you."

She sniffled, and Cassius returned not only with my mug, steaming with coffee, but also with a box of tissues. My chest pinched when she couldn't even look at him as she took the box.

"Fresh cup of joe." The mug bookended my plate. "Not as good as my son's, but it gets the job done."

My brows rose as I reached for the cup. *So he knew about Calder's coffee habit.* There were a hundred reasons why that shouldn't be a big deal, but the way Calder had painted their strained relationship, it didn't fit that Cassius would know about his eldest's hobby, let alone sound like he cared about it.

"Thank you. It smells wonderful," I said over the rim just before the bitterness burned along my tongue. *Definitely not as good as Calder's.*

Somehow, in the course of a few cups, I'd learned what good coffee tasted like, and this . . . this wasn't it. This was the kind of coffee the hospital ran on. Funny how it didn't take long to realize what I'd been missing—and what I didn't want to go back to.

I stiffened and shifted in my seat, afraid that notion might take root somewhere else—somewhere not as easy to fix or as harmless to lose as a good cup of coffee.

"Calder went to talk to Callum," Cassius said, and only when I faced him did I realize I'd been looking over my shoulder—*looking for Calder like I was expecting him to walk in any minute.*

"Oh. Right." I reached for my plate, taking a big forkful of eggs and shoving them in my mouth before I gave away anything else.

Cassius stretched across the counter, taking Sarah's empty plate from her hands. "I'll take care of that," he said before she could try to clean up.

The longer I spent around Cassius, the harder it was not to appreciate the qualities he shared with his son. His protectiveness. His concern. His chivalry. *And his stubbornness.*

Barred from lifting a finger, Sarah turned and told me, "Calder came here first, but you were still sleeping, and he didn't want to wake you."

Or he wasn't ready to deal with me yet.

"What did he say?" I tried not to sound too desperate.

"He wanted to know how I was. How I'd slept. If there was anything else I could think of . . . or remember about what Dr. Julia told me about . . . that place." Shame hung from every syllable in her voice.

My fingers whitened where I held my fork. All I wanted was to hug her tight and tell her that none of this was her fault. Not how Trent had treated her. Not what had happened at the camp. Not for being manipulated, the weaknesses she'd confided to Dr. Julia then exploited for the benefit of this Adam Eden. All I wanted was to tell her all the things I wished I could've said to my sister.

As if sensing things were getting . . . emotional, Cassius cleared his throat. "If you'll excuse me. I want to feed the chickens before we leave."

Leave? I looked at Sarah. *How much had I missed?*

Sarah's eyes remained low until he was gone, and then she said in the quietest voice, "Trent never . . . in a million years . . . would've done dishes."

"You deserve more, Sarah. Better."

She nodded like she wanted to drive the thought deep where no small man could ever uproot it again and then looked to me. "Because of you, I have the chance to find it."

My throat tightened, her gratitude like salt in the wound of my sister's disappearance: healing, but painful all the same. "Where will you go?"

"I'm going to my parents' house in Virginia. I moved out here because of Trent . . ." She trailed off with a shudder. "Mr. Stone is taking me to the airport. I think it's best for me to go home for a little bit."

"Yeah, I think that would be really good," I agreed, offering her a smile.

"I'm so sorry, Lara. You told me about your sister, and I didn't understand why you were so quick to help me . . . a stranger . . . until Calder explained why you both were really at the retreat."

My stomach tumbled over itself.

"I guess it's proof of how terrible a judge I am of people, because I swear, seeing the two of you together was like something right out of a fantasy." Her breath caught—or maybe it was mine.

"I would do anything for my sister," I said, my tongue thick as it carved the words through my teeth.

Including putting myself at risk of falling for her ex-boyfriend.

Sarah hugged me then, so tight that she almost toppled her stool. "I'm sorry," she cried softly. "I wish I knew more to help you. I wish I hadn't panicked so soon and told Trent. Maybe then she would've told me more and I would be useful. God, I'm so useless—"

"Don't." I drew back and caught her hands in mine. "You stood up for yourself—fought for yourself. You're strong, Sarah. Not useless, okay? Don't carry the words of weak men forward with you. Please." I said the words wishing Rachel could've heard them, too.

Sarah let out a deep exhale, collecting herself before she said in a watery voice, "You're going to find her."

"I hope so."

"You will. You love her too much to give up. And Calder . . ."

Calder was being paid an as-yet-to-be-determined fee to not give up. *And he'd promised.*

"Sarah?" Cassius stepped into the doorway. "Do you want a few more minutes?"

She shook her head. "No. I don't want to keep the plane waiting. When I land, I promise I'll reimburse you whatever the flight cost—"

It occurred to me then just how much Sarah was leaving behind. While Calder had kept our IDs and credit cards safe, Sarah hadn't. She and Trent had left all their things just like they'd been instructed, which meant her wallet and license.

"How did you book a ticket?" I blurted out.

Sarah looked to Cassius, who explained. "I have a friend who has a private plane. He's going to fly Sarah back to Virginia."

Sarah hugged me again, her voice thick with emotion as she thanked me once more. "I just want to use the restroom, and then I'll be ready."

Cassius stepped aside to let her pass.

"Thank you for helping her. For helping me." I swallowed hard and slid down from the stool.

"No need to thank me for that," he said gruffly, taking my plate to the sink to clean like he'd done for Sarah.

"Then at least let me thank you for the delicious breakfast," I said, having eaten my entire plate.

His smile was clipped on one side and brief. "You're welcome. Though I'm sure I have a thing or two to learn about coffee-making."

"Well, I happen to know you have a son who'd be happy to teach you."

Cassius looked up from his suds-covered hands, and I felt like I'd just put my entire foot in my mouth. His expression hardened, but it was difficult to tell whether it was from anger or pain. "I don't know about that."

I should've let the conversation end there, but I didn't. "My mom, admittedly, didn't have very many rules, but she did always say it didn't hurt to ask."

"Knowing my son, it might."

Don't say anything. Don't get involved. Don't—

"Knowing your son, I think it would mean a lot." It would mean a bridge back to a relationship that was more than business, and that, in my opinion, would mean everything.

"Did he tell you that?" Cassius arched a brow and then shook his head, and for the first time, I thought he looked a little something like weary. "Calder took on too much after Annie died, including the responsibility for things that weren't his fault. Something I should've realized sooner. Done more to stop."

"Have you told him that?" I asked, but I knew he hadn't. Calder wouldn't believe, wouldn't feel like he did, if Cassius had.

"I should've. I should've a long time ago." He sighed and turned off the faucet, looking every inch like a man whose wife had been murdered, leaving him with six kids to raise. Every inch like a human being who, in the process of dealing with his own trauma, had made mistakes he didn't know how to fix. "But you know, once Calder makes up his mind . . ."

Oh, I knew.

Mr. Director.

But, to be honest, if I looked in the mirror right now, I would think the same of the woman staring back and how I'd treated my sister over the years.

I'd never wanted to hurt Rachel; everything I'd ever done and said was because I loved her. Because I thought she deserved so much better and couldn't stand that she couldn't see it. But now, it was hard not to wonder whether my own trauma had aggravated hers.

"Well, maybe start by asking him about the difference between filter and French press, and see where things go," I suggested warmly.

"Filter or French press," Cassius repeated like I'd just spoken Greek.

"Yeah."

He stared at me for a long second, and then his head jerked to the hall. A second later, I heard Sarah's footsteps approach, which Cassius seemed to catch sooner than I did.

"Do you want to take the four-wheeler up to Callum's?" he offered.

"I'd rather walk." Then I'd have some time to figure out what to say to Calder after last night. After that kiss.

With a nod, Cassius went to meet Sarah, and I followed to say goodbye.

After one more hug on the front porch, I watched her walk toward the old red Ford parked on the gravel, the truck looking like it hadn't been started in a decade and might not start at all.

Cassius paused beside me on the top step, his expression grim. "His mother's death isn't the only thing Calder's taken responsibility for that doesn't belong to him."

Chapter 22

LARA

The truck was long gone, Sarah on her way to safety and freedom, and I was still left wishing Cassius had given me time to ask what he'd meant. I doubted it could be about anything other than my sister, but how would he know what Rachel had been through? Why would he insist the blame shouldn't be laid at Calder's feet?

The thought dug like a splinter into my mind. The more I picked and pulled and tried to work it out, the deeper the notion of Calder's innocence was buried.

"Lara!"

My head snapped up, my gaze having fallen to my feet marching along the path between the Stone house and Callum's Watchtower. My gait faltered, seeing Calder walking toward me.

He didn't move like a man injured. At least, not physically. The darker shadow of his short beard, the hollows under his eyes, and the firm line of that oh-so-dangerous mouth told a different story.

We both slowed and then stopped. The foot and a half of space between us was almost comical, considering his tongue had been down my throat and I'd been grinding on his lap, on his thick arousal, last night.

"Are you okay?" I asked, searching for any sign otherwise.

"Fine. Are you?" His husky voice confirmed he hadn't slept as soundly as I had.

"Me? I'm not the one who was stabbed by a crazy man," I blurted out, to which he stared and folded his arms, clearly still expecting my answer. My lips pinched tight before I huffed, "Yes, I'm fine. I ate. Your dad made breakfast, and he just left to take Sarah to the airport."

Calder nodded. "She said she wanted to go home."

"It's for the best." My eyes dipped, catching the breeze ripple his shirt right where his blood had splotched his scrubs last night. "Can I take a look at your wound, please?"

"It was superficial. I sterilized and bandaged it. It's fine—"

"And as the medical professional, I'd like to confirm that."

Calder didn't budge. *Damned stubborn man.* The sun glinted harshly off his gold-chipped gaze, but I wasn't going to back down. After a minute, he blew out a hard exhale and, wincing at the effort, hauled up the edge of his shirt.

The V. Those abs . . . But as soon as my eyes locked on his wound, I went from internally drooling to doctor mode.

I went to him, spanning my hands over his abdomen and hearing his low hiss. *Forcing myself to ignore it.*

His skin was hot under my fingertips as I palpated around the three-inch-long cut.

"Lara—"

"I need to check for infection," I repeated, looking up to catch Calder's jaw as hard as flint and his gaze as sharp as steel. One wrong move and I might cause him to spark.

I leaned closer and carefully focused on my purpose.

The skin didn't look puffy or inflamed. No sign of infection or bruising from deeper internal damage. He'd used butterfly bandages to pull the sides of the gash together and hold them tight, but he hadn't used a bandage on top.

I squinted. "Did you put superglue over this?"

He grunted. "Easier than taping a bandage."

Fair. I swallowed, the doctor in me convinced he'd treated himself sufficiently, but the woman in me . . . the woman in me couldn't be convinced to stop touching him.

"Satisfied?"

I stilled, heat toppling over my skin. *Bad word choice.*

I straightened slowly, a breeze blowing, bending around us rather than going between. Like there was so much tension and ache piled up between me and Calder that not even the air had room to squeeze by.

All my life, I'd been following a path—one that had taken me away from the life my mother had led, kept me safe from the kinds of relationships that had failed her and made me self-sufficient and independent, but this time yesterday, I wouldn't have been able to tell you where I wanted that path to lead. Today . . . today, I knew exactly where I wanted it to go: right to the center of his warm embrace.

There were so many things we needed to talk about, but the only thing on my mind was those moments in the rain when he held me. Those minutes in the tent when we'd kissed. It wasn't just nature or desire; it was a natural disaster. Forceful. Unstoppable. It destroyed everything we said we were. *Every lie we'd told ourselves.*

How did I even begin to talk about something that had changed everything?

"Sarah didn't know anything else about Eden's Children," Calder said, saving me from sounding like a fool.

A fool who knew better.

My chest caved in on itself, hot hope deflating like a burst balloon. No matter what Cassius had hinted at, I *knew* this was the part of Calder that had sent my sister spiraling. The part that was stoic in the face of her wanting more. In the face of me wanting more.

I buttoned my arms over my front like they were a business suit, dressing me for a part I was reluctant to play.

"Did Callum find anything about its location?" I countered, at least confident I could match his cold practicality.

"No." Calder's *masseter* fired against his cheek, and he muttered, "We should walk. The sun's already pretty high, and you've got nothing on your face. The cool breeze is deceiving."

I followed his orders, but sensed he was holding back. "What is it?" I demanded.

Another pause. "The authorities just found Trent's body."

Trent's . . .

I stopped short and strangled the words from my throat. "He's dead?"

Cold crinkled over my skin, wrapping me in a frozen fabric of dread. Calder had said Trent was beat up pretty badly last night and that Matthew had taken him away, but not that he was dead.

Calder returned in front of me, his height blotting out the sun. "His body was recovered near a popular but difficult hiking trail in the park."

"What?" I choked out, confusion shredding my comprehension. "I don't understand. Did they leave him there without medical attention? The police should be able to see evidence of trauma—of the fight. If we tell them we know who attacked him and where—"

"His body was found at the bottom of a fifty-foot ravine. They won't find any evidence of what Ben did to him," Calder said tightly. "Or what they did to hide that evidence."

I pressed my hand to my stomach, feeling it cave and crumble. I'd seen countless traumatic injuries, from motorcycle accidents to stab wounds, come through the ER, but nothing had made me physically ill like hearing this. *A murder made to look like an accident.*

"Last night, after attacking Trent, Ben said something," Calder continued. "He told Sarah she would thank him one day for knowing how to get rid of Trent. I was focused on other things, but now . . ."

My eyes rounded. "You think . . . they've done this before?"

"Remember how Sarah mentioned she wasn't concerned with the waivers or taking out life insurance to join Eden's Children?"

"Yeah . . ." My eyes bulged. "No." My head swung side to side. "If they are *killing* people and getting paid for it, I think someone would've noticed by now."

I knew a little something about how insurance worked. Health insurance, life insurance . . . they were all the same. A business. A *for-profit* business that employed every trick in the book to *not* pay on claims.

"Killing people, yes. But death by misadventure . . . not much wiggle room."

Misadventure . . .

"Is that what they're calling kinky sex? Or is that what happens when you get a Christmas tree–shaped ornament stuck too far up—"

"It's what happens where the insured party voluntarily took a risk that resulted in their death, which"—he stretched out his arms—"happens a fair amount out here."

My gaze rolled along the peaks and valleys charting an EKG into the horizon, the whole picture coming into view. *A murder made to look like an accidental death.* "You think what they did to Trent . . ."

"I think they've done it before."

I lifted my hand to my throat, feeling my screaming pulse. "Did you . . . Did Callum find proof?"

"Creighton used to work closely with the coroner for Teton County. I told him about Trent's connection to Rachel's disappearance, so he's on his way there now to get a list of all the deceased whose deaths were ruled as 'death by misadventure' in the last three years." His *masseter* drummed against his cheek. "Sarah remembered the policy was with UnitedLife, so once we have those names, we can confirm with the company if they had policies for the deceased, and if Adam Eden was the beneficiary."

"Will that help us find Rachel?"

His voice sank. "Not directly."

"What if we called the police? Told them Trent's death wasn't an accident? Told them about the retreat—"

"We have no proof, Lara," he growled. "And if they decided to get rid of him—get rid of his body—I'm damn certain they got rid of any evidence back at the retreat. On top of that, the second we send law enforcement near there, Maxwell, the retreat, Eden's Children . . . they're going to pack up and disappear, and take Rachel with them."

"So we just keep the knowledge that they're killing people for insurance money to ourselves?"

"No, we keep digging into the *theory* that this is what they're doing while we keep looking for the compound. At some point, Maxwell is going to go back to the Garden."

My jaw dropped. "We can't wait another two weeks to figure out where Rachel is."

"We're not," Calder clipped and started walking toward the house again.

"Then how are we going to find them?" I jogged to catch up.

"Eden didn't just wave a wand and a compound appeared. Not in the wilderness. There are certain nonnegotiable components needed to live somewhere, even in the wilderness. Water. Shelter. Energy. Food. If they're living off the grid, some of those things can be found or foraged, but energy can't be. They'd need some way to create it outside of the power grid, and the cheapest way to do that is solar."

My brows knotted. "So Callum's going to send a drone out looking for solar panels in the forest?"

Calder sent me a flat look over his shoulder. "No," he grunted and kept moving. "When we were getting in the Jeep to go to the retreat, I noticed solar panels on the roof of the Wilderness Within building. They were the same brand as the ones Callum put on his house: Peak Energy."

"And you think they bought the same ones for Eden's Children?"

"I think it's highly likely," he muttered.

"Even if they did, what are the chances they'll have records after everything Eden's Children has done to remain hidden?"

"They'll have to. Solar panels are highly regulated by the government for tax purposes. They'll have to have a record of the purchase to him or Eden's Children if they want the tax credit. Once we find that, I'll be able to follow the trail."

"We." I stiffened and corrected him, "We'll be able to follow the trail."

I stared at his back—at the give and tug of his *trapezius* and *deltoids* as he walked away—and then, against my better judgment, I insisted, "Wherever she is, I'm coming with you to find her."

Calder spun around, a surprising amount of anger on his face. "Lara, did you just hear what I said? They might be *killing* people for life insurance money; they definitely killed a man because he knew too much—"

"I don't care. I'll be careful. I'll do what you tell me to do. Stay where you tell me to stay. Be silent. Be still." I charged forward until I was in front of him again, fury jutting my chin out toward his towering form. "But what I won't do is stay behind. Not after everything—"

"And if I don't give you a choice?"

I sucked in a breath. True, Calder had not only the opportunity but also the skills to simply take the information and slip into the wilderness and leave me behind . . . Rage fringed my view in red. He wouldn't. He couldn't. I wouldn't let him.

"Is that really what you'd do? Just up and leave me?" I dared him to admit it—dared his stubbornness to go toe to toe with mine.

Heat bubbled off him like molten tar, sticking to my skin, staining my veins, and hardening me to him with every passing moment. Gold-green eyes bored into mine as though he could stake me to the ground right here, right now, and not have to worry about answering.

"Dammit, Lara." His hands rose to frame my face, and I swore with his exhale, I felt the crumbling of his reservations.

He wouldn't go without me. He wouldn't leave me. My lashes fluttered against my cheeks as his head lowered. *He was going to kiss me.*

I welcomed the warmth of his breath on my skin, the press of his fingers on my face. I welcomed the way, even when we were arguing, his touch chased the tension from my body.

But instead of his mouth touching mine, it was his forehead that pressed to my own, and a strained groan that caressed my lips instead.

"I'll do whatever I have to to keep you safe . . . even if you hate me for it."

Hot and cold crashed like two oceans meeting inside me, churning and lurching my senses until I didn't know up from down.

How could I both ache for someone to care about me the way he did but also hate him for it?

I jerked out of his hold, anger toppling all rationality. "Is that what you told Rachel when you left her? Because I can promise you, it didn't help her at all."

I spun around and stalked back to the house, burying the brief glimpse of pain I'd caught when it marred his beautiful face.

It was hard to think of Calder Stone as the kind of man who could be wounded, but the look on his face, the one imprinted onto the backs of my eyelids, was evidence that I'd accomplished the impossible feat. Like David taking down Goliath.

Only, by the time I closed Colby's bedroom door behind me, I worried it wasn't a giant I'd taken down with my harsh words, but a good man.

Chapter 23

Lara

Rachel had always said I had a long fuse attached to a big bomb; it was the foil to her very, very short fuse and tiny little explosions. And between what had happened in Phoenix, realizing my sister was missing, having to work with Calder to find her, having to fake (but not) my very real attraction to him, learning Rachel had joined a cult, telling Calder what happened with Ian, *kissing* him, having to escape with Sarah, and figuring out that cult was killing people for insurance money . . . my fuse had been whittled terminally short.

Mortally short.

And hearing Calder try to push me away . . . The bomb had let my barbed words fly.

But now wasn't a good time to apologize. I was still too . . . everything. Too upset. Too worried. Too angry, scared, aching . . . to tempt fate and face Calder again.

"I'll do whatever I have to do to keep you safe . . . even if you hate me for it."

Part of me wished I could hate him for it. But there was no hating Calder Stone. Even back then, after Rachel had called me sobbing, telling me they'd broken up. Crying and repeating over and over that he didn't care. That she couldn't make him care. That it was all her fault. The only person I'd hated in those moments was myself for the tiny, nagging question *But what if it was her fault?*

I'd felt horrible, but I'd also been a witness to the truth behind her tears. The lies she'd told him more and more frequently. The excuses, the cover stories she'd roped me into.

No matter how hard I'd tried, no matter how upset she'd been or the path her life had taken, I never could fit *who* I knew Calder to be, the guy who came at the drop of a hat to track down a cat or rescue a hummingbird, with the man who'd broken my sister's heart.

But even if what I'd accused held a fragment of truth, Calder didn't deserve my vitriol. Not for his well-justified intention to protect me. I'd lashed out because it was easier than having to admit I was too afraid to demand a harder conversation.

I paced Colby's room—unable to be still—and looked over her amazing landscape photographs hanging on the walls. I knew they were hers because they had the same energy as the ones in Calder's Airstream.

And then there were the photos of the animals. Her animals.

Donnie. Duke. Boris. Bonnie. Cy. Winston. Minx.

The duck with his broken wing. A cat with one leg. Another with one eye. Two baby mice. A dog with a wheelchair attached to his back legs. A malnourished horse. The wall was covered in her rescue stories. And as I glanced at the bed, I wondered whether Sarah and I were the newest additions to her list.

No, Rachel needed rescuing, not me. I walked to the corner of the bed and began to strip the sheets.

There was nothing more for me here, and I certainly wasn't going to impose on Calder's family's hospitality for another night when I had a perfectly wonderful place to stay at the B and B, a place that would keep me well beyond the arm's length Calder had put between us.

I piled the pillowcases on the floor, but when I pulled back the duvet and top sheet, the wrinkled papers slid out from the mattress.

Rachel's file.

I took the crushed papers and set them, folded, on the nightstand. Now—here, of all places—wasn't the time to read them. But as I went back to stripping the bed, a name stuck out like a sore blue thumb between the water-splotched crinkles.

Allen Hendricks.

I wished I could unsee it, but I couldn't. Just like I couldn't stop myself from peeling the paper wider.

Allen Hendricks had been the star quarterback for the University of Wyoming officially, and unofficially was the team's MVM: *most valuable manwhore.*

Swearing not to read any more than this single paragraph, I scanned over Dr. Julia's notes.

Claims to always have had issues with self-esteem. Notes examples from high school of exaggerated attempts to gain attention. Feels that became a negative cycle in college when Hendricks rejected her in a moment of actual need. Believes that is what prompted her to search out that same personality in future partners to try and elicit and achieve the response she was looking for back then. Patient very emotional at this point. Will continue discussion during next session. Preliminary assessment is ideal candidate for advanced treatment at the Garden.

It was only supposed to be one paragraph, but before I knew it, I'd flipped the page to read what Rachel had told her next, and my heart, currently beating in my throat, dropped into the pit of my stomach; the remaining pages were completely water-damaged from the rain last night.

I sank onto the edge of the bed, confusion tearing at the seams of my sanity. Rachel and I had told each other everything. With Mom and how she'd lived, it had always felt like it was the two of us against the world. *So why hadn't she told me about . . . whatever had happened with Allen?*

I tried to think back, tried to remember any fragment of conversation or mention of the guy, but aside from the frat parties she'd lied to Calder about—Allen being a member of one of those frats—my memory was a giant blank space.

Maybe because after all this time, only my memories of Calder had survived.

I jumped at the knock on the door.

"Lara?"

I recognized Colby's voice.

"Come in," I called, folding up the damaged papers and setting them back on the nightstand.

Colby stepped into the room, and I was struck again by how perfectly the color of her eyes matched Calder's; they must've gotten the green-gold shade from their mom, because Cassius's stare was as blue as Wyoming's big sky.

She wore an athletic tank and fitted cargo pants, though the material looked stretchy and breathable, and a pair of hiking boots. Her hair was strapped in a high ponytail, her face makeup-free.

"How are you feeling? Do you need anything?"

"No," I said, shaking my head. "You've already done more than enough. Your whole family."

"Please." She smiled. "We're happy to help anyone Calder . . . is helping."

The way she hesitated made me wary, but the last thing I wanted to talk about was her brother. I wanted some distance to clear my head—and my feelings—and let the adrenaline high of the last several days flush from my system. Maybe then, when I talked to him, I wouldn't have the simultaneous urge to strangle and kiss him again at the same time.

"Well, I'll be out of your hair—out of your room soon. Actually, maybe I'll just head back to my B and B until Calder has any new information." That was the kind of space I was talking about, even if it came with the healthy dose of fear that he'd find the location of the Garden and go looking for Rachel without me.

"Oh." She looked disappointed.

"Is everything okay?"

"Not really." Her shoulder leaned into the doorframe and with a frown, she confessed, "Creighton has duck-napped Donnie and is sending me on a wild goose—wild duck chase to find him with ridiculous clues." She unfolded and held out a scrawled note in her fingers. "I was hoping you could help me."

She wanted my help?

I blinked, stupefied.

She was from a family of trackers. There were at least four more of them who had not only the most extensive training in tracking and locating anything from humans to animals, but also certainly more experience than me.

"I don't think I'll be able to—" I stopped and stared, my jaw falling as quickly as my eyes snapped up. "He left you clues in *Latin?*"

Primum. Ostium silvae.

"Did no one tell you? Creighton is the Stone everyone should leave unturned," she grumbled, folding her arms. "But I worry about what would happen if he never got unturned." She bit into her bottom lip, and right then, I saw the woman who'd rescued every weak and wounded animal on that wall. The one who had no fear for how they'd lash out because of their injuries. The one who was determined to love them until they were healed. "Anyway, do you know what it says?"

I almost blurted out to just check Google Translate, but then I remembered that my cell phone lived in a metal box on the front porch. Even if it didn't, I severely doubted Wi-Fi or cellular data existed in this house.

"Callum refuses to get involved, and I can't find Calder." I winced when she mentioned *that* brother. It was probably my fault she couldn't find him. "I thought maybe, because you're a doctor . . ."

I gulped. "Well, *primum* means *first. Ostium* . . . is *an opening*. The Latin word for *mouth* is *os*. So it could mean *entrance* or *opening*, and *silvae*, if it's a derivative of *silva*, well, *silva* means *forest*."

Her squeal barely forewarned of the arms that wrapped around my neck in the tightest of hugs. "Thank you so much." Her relief was effusive . . . and contagious. "I know you were thinking of going back to your B and B, but would you mind coming with me? I know where the mouth of the forest is, but I also know there's only going to be another clue waiting for me."

I paused but really had no reason to say no. I had nothing to do back at the B and B except worry about Rachel and ruminate over my last conversation with Calder, who was apparently MIA, so even attempting to apologize right now was out of the question.

"Sure," I said with a small smile. "I'm happy to help."

At least one Stone wanted me involved in a search and rescue mission.

—

Sure enough, the first clue had taken us to the edge of the forest where there was a half-moon glen. Colby had said all their hide-and-seek games as kids always started from here. In the center, pinned to a stake in the ground, was the second clue.

Secundo. Viscera lacus.

Second. The bowels of the lake.

At one time, there'd been a river that cut through Stonewall Ranch, gouging a trench in the mountains and leaving behind, as its only remnant, an oblong lake I matched to the map in Calder's RV: Lima Bean Lake. Underneath a small shelter was a rack of canoes and paddleboards, and for a second, it struck me how many thousands upon thousands of visitors came to the Tetons every year and filled up Jenny Lake, paying for the exact same activities that the Stone family had grown up enjoying in privacy.

Colby scanned the perimeter with binoculars and pointed to the far side, the third clue tethered to a fishing hook on the farthest pebbled shore.

The lake led to a stretch of boulders, the boulders led into the fields, and the field turned us back into the forest.

For two hours, we followed Creighton's clues, searching for Colby's missing pet. Along the way, I was introduced to some of the celebrities framed in her room. Boris, the one-eared bunny; Minx, the three-legged cat; and Cy, short for Cyclops, Minx's brother. *You could guess how his name came about.*

The search took us to what felt like the far ends of the ranch property, though realistically, we couldn't have walked more than a few miles. She pointed out Callum's house, not realizing I'd already been there, and a rock wall she told me they called Free Fall, which led into a rambling story about how they'd all trained to climb it, as reaching the top was a rite of passage in the Stone family. Then there was a tree house she'd built with Cassius, and an old barn that housed a few horses and, apparently, her brother Colton when he didn't want to be found.

"It had to be the Doritos," Colby muttered, stomping through the brush toward some tree the final clue referred to.

"Doritos?"

"Donnie's weakness is Doritos, and I've tried to hide that from Creighton, but he must've figured it out, because he's tried to catch Donnie before. Many times. But Donnie knows Creighton is enemy number one." She sighed, stepping over a fallen tree trunk. "The only way he would've been caught is Doritos."

"A duck that likes Doritos?"

"We all have our weaknesses." She winked at me, and my throat felt strangled shut.

I wished my weakness was Doritos and not her oldest brother.

"Aha!" She jogged over to some brush and pulled off the next clue, tacked to a tree trunk.

"Is this the tree?"

"No, but we're close . . ." She trailed off, and when she held the paper to me, I saw the fumes coming from her ears.

Trees are tall.
Creighton is the winner.
Colby is too small.
To save Donnie from becoming dinner.

My brows popped up. The tone of his clues was devolving.

"He won't really eat him," Colby assured me . . . and maybe herself, too. "But once we find Donnie . . ." She flew a hot stream of fury through her lips. "I'm going to burn his little black book on a pile of his expensive tea leaves."

She angled toward the sky, shading her eyes with her hand.

"Black book?" I followed.

"Where he keeps track of all his booty calls."

"Men still do that?"

"Creighton isn't 'men.' Creighton is . . . a moron. Brilliant. Eccentric. But one hundred percent moron," she informed me, her narrowed eyes swinging from treetop to treetop. "I don't understand how women are attracted to him." She winced. "I guess I don't really want to, either, but that book has all the information on women who want to be his booty calls."

"How do you even know about it?"

She sighed. "Well, one time, I wanted Donnie to steal Creighton's diary from his room, but I didn't realize the black book *wasn't* his diary until Donnie stole it. Unfortunately, I was so grossed out by what I was not expecting to find that I immediately threw it back into Creighton's room rather than swallowing down the urge to vomit and using the information for an elite prank."

It didn't take much imagination to think of all the ways Colby could've wreaked a little havoc on her brother's love life with the contact information of his "booty calls."

"Donnie!" Colby screeched and sprinted over the hazard-laden forest floor like it was paved flat until she reached a towering pine about twenty feet ahead of us.

My gaze climbed the trunk. Higher. And higher. *And higher.* Sure enough, from one of the top-most branches hung a large cage housing a very cranky duck, who squawked with what sounded like recognition on hearing Colby call his name.

Walking around the entirety of the trunk, she turned back to me and blurted out, "Shitballs."

It would've been funny if there weren't a duck hanging from a tree.

"Do you have to climb to get him?"

She shook her head. "No, but that's what he wanted me to do first. *Jerk,*" she muttered under her breath and then pointed to the knot of rope securing the wooden cage to the thick branch above. "He cut the rope. So even if I climbed to the top, I couldn't lower the cage safely to the ground, and I won't be able to reach to open the latch." Following the movement of her finger, I saw that the hook keeping the cage closed was on the side farthest from the tree.

"So how does he expect you to free—" I stopped because she was already reaching into her backpack.

"I'm going to shoot the latch." She grinned and my mouth fell open.

"You're going to shoot that tiny little hook?" *And not hit the duck?*

Her smile stretched wider as she moved into position. "Creighton knows I'm the best marksman in the family." She raised her handgun and closed one eye. "It annoys him, but that's why he set this up this way. A test to prove I'm still the best."

Well, I was glad she was sure—I flinched when her gun fired and the cage went spinning. Donnie didn't like the Tilt-A-Whirl, but she ignored his quacks. When the cage slowed, she mumbled a curse. Her shot had nicked the latch but not enough to open it.

I looked back at Colby, and she murmured softly, "Always fire between breaths." I watched her exhale depress her upper body until there was nothing left but pure stillness.

This time, I didn't jerk when she fired at the cage. It spun again, but now with success. Her shot hit the latch and the bottom of the cage dropped out and Donnie took to the skies.

Or at least, he coasted through the trees, slowly descending as he reached the edge of the woods.

"Is he okay?"

"He's fine. I left a whole bag of Doritos out for him back at his pool." She holstered her weapon and returned it to her backpack.

"I can't believe you made that shot," I murmured, severely impressed.

"Thanks." She beamed and we started in the direction of the escaped duck. "If you're sticking around, I'm happy to teach you. Even Calder will tell you I'm the best shot in the family."

I swallowed an instant surge of bitterness. She had no idea just how little her oldest brother actually wanted to tell me.

As soon as we cleared the trees, Colby held up her hand. "Wait." Her head cocked. "Do you hear that?"

I listened, and then, hearing nothing, closed my eyes and listened again.

"Come with me." She didn't leave me much choice before taking off in a direction that was kind of close to the way we'd come.

I caught up and kept close. Donnie waddled off as soon as we reached the fields, and that was when I heard what Colby was talking about. A rhythmic sound that echoed to the tune of a heartbeat. *Thump, thump.* Pause. *Thump, thump.* And it was coming from the partially restored barn.

"Colton?" Colby called, jogging toward the structure and disappearing inside for a solid minute before I reached the open barn door, stopping to catch my breath.

Or so I thought.

As it turned out, there was going to be no catching of breath, when inside the barn was a shirtless, sweaty Calder, one wrapped hand resting on top of a punching bag that hung suspended from a thick beam, the heavy weight still swaying from the impact of his last punch.

Biceps brachii. Triceps brachii. Deltoids. Pectorals. Rectus abdominus. This time, the Latin left clues that brought me right back to where I'd started: dangerously attracted to my sister's ex-boyfriend.

"You shouldn't be boxing with a stab wound," I said, watching him go still.

Calder straightened his spine and his shoulders to roll back. He swiveled his head to me, and his jaw locked familiarly into place. Sweat beaded on his brow, and his short hair glistened in the lowering sunlight that filtered through the distorted planks of the barn.

"It's a cut, and it's still sealed shut," he ground out, sounding like he had just as much experience exerting himself while injured as I had in treating emergency wounds.

His chest rose and fell rapidly from exertion, the pace just as quick as when he'd held me. Touched me. Kissed me.

At my side, my fingers twitched, itching to ground themselves to him. To slide over muscle and sinew, ligaments and bones, and absorb every inch of the man who looked as chiseled as if he'd been carved from his namesake.

A horse neighed.

"I know, Achilles. I know I should've brought treats," Colby murmured, walking over to the closest stall and letting the horse nibble in her hand as she glanced at the neighboring empty stall. "I guess Colton isn't back." She returned to her interrogation, worry marking a blip in her brow, obviously having hoped to find a different Stone inside the barn, pummeling the heavy bag.

"No." Calder reached down and grabbed his water bottle, downing several swigs as I approached. "What are you doing out here?" He grabbed a towel and began to pat himself down.

"Creighton duck-napped Donnie, so we were—" Colby stopped short, realizing the question hadn't been directed at her, then noticing the way Calder was looking—glaring—at me. "You know what, I'm going to check the back pasture for Colt and Ajax."

"He's not—" Calder tried to stop her, but there was no point; she was already gone. And it was just the two of us again.

Chapter 24

Calder

Rule #28: Silence is a tool, not a weakness. When you're hunting or being hunted, the one who breaks first usually loses.

My sister wasn't going to find Colton outside, and she knew that as well as I did. But man, could Colby read a room. *Unfortunately for me.* It was times like these I wished she had the social aptitude of Creighton, who'd stay in a conversation just to see how insufferable he could get.

"Colby needed my help deciphering the clues to finding Donnie," Lara said, looking like she expected me to tell her to leave.

"Deciphering? Why? Did he write them in Latin?" I joked, and her only reaction was a blank stare. "Seriously?" I dropped my arm and let my head shake. "Of course he wrote them in Latin."

Creighton would tell you he'd learned Latin because it was the foundation of many prevalent languages (because he was loath to use the word *romance* even in this context), but in my mind, Latin appealed to him because it was considered "dead," and that was how my brother liked to think of himself on the inside. Dry, droll, and dead.

"I'm not sure if they were correct or properly conjugated, but they were definitely in Latin," Lara said, moving closer, and suddenly, the giant barn started to feel like the size of a matchbox. And just as hot.

"Is that what you told my sister?"

I blew out a slow breath, her words like an invisible undercut to my gut. They say sticks and stones and all that, but this woman's sharp tongue could break a man. Cut him into a thousand guilty pieces. And knowing what she believed about our past, I didn't blame her for it.

"Knowing Creighton, I'm sure they were." I dragged my towel over my face and then hauled on my shirt, feeling her gaze crawl over me like the heat of an ember starving to ignite. "Well, I'll leave you to your hunt." I reached for my water bottle, preparing to walk outside and dump the cold contents over my head.

I'd almost made it to the barn doors when Lara called, "Calder, wait."

Damn me. And damn my feet for stopping for her. *My heart, too.*

"I want to apologize for what I said earlier," Lara started again, regret fused to her voice. "I'm just frustrated and tired and emotional and . . . a lot of things, but that didn't justify—"

"Stop." I whipped around. "Don't apologize for how you feel. Ever."

"Except I don't feel that way," she insisted, wringing her hands and reminding me of how strong her fingers were when they'd pulled me to her; to feel someone need me like that, the way she had, was something so powerful and vulnerable at the same time. Exactly the reason why I'd avoided anything like it until now.

But Lara Crane was just as unavoidable as the storms that barreled over the plains and bowled down over the mountains. And equally as earth-shaking.

"I know you're just trying to protect me, and I know, whatever happened back then, you wouldn't have intentionally hurt my sister. I know how she was. How emotional and . . . difficult she could be. And I know the way she treated you probably wasn't—"

"Enough," I cut her off with the kind of rudeness I didn't even reserve for Creighton. I couldn't let her keep going—I'd already let myself go too far. Told her things that should've stayed in the past. Kissed her . . . touched her . . . when I should've kept my hands to myself.

There was more than the truth about her sister that was separating us. I knew I'd ended things honestly and couldn't regret that. What really kept me from Lara was the way she made me feel, and the memory of what losing Mom had done to Cassius.

I locked my gaze to Lara's, ignoring every emotion I saw and every instinct of mine to reach for her.

"It's in the past," I continued, my voice clear as it trod over the grave of my buried-alive heart. "Emotions can run high in the middle of a case, especially after what happened last night." Quickly realizing there were two *very* different sets of events I'd just left open to interpretation, I added, "Seeing Sarah like that, and thinking about your sister . . . there's nothing to apologize for. It's par for the course."

Said the man who'd spent the last hour and a half beating on Colton's heavy bag because being a good man was at war with being a better man.

"And is making out with your clients par for the course, too?"

Dammit.

"No, it's not," I said through locked teeth, though parts of me wanted to make it par for our course. "That was well outside the bounds of our professional relationship. Professionalism isn't just a rule. It's a code. A contract of trust, and one that I . . . muddied."

Just holding her in the rain had broken every rule she deserved to have kept in place.

"I think both of us were involved in the muddying."

I couldn't stop the shudder that hit me, recalling how perfect she'd looked in my lap. How perfect she'd felt grinding on my cock. *And how fucking wrong it was to take advantage of her right now.*

"You have my word it won't happen again." It couldn't. For a million and one reasons, the most important one being survival. *Mine.*

I could account for a hundred different scenarios. Plan for a dozen different kinds of danger or injuries. But this . . . her . . . the havoc she'd wreak if I only had a taste . . . I didn't know what was worse: having her and having her leave, or *having* her the way my parents had had each other and knowing it could be lost.

"And if I want it to?"

"Don't," I ground out.

Colby chose that moment to return, sliding the door wide open behind me and propping her hip on the edge. "Looks like another storm is rolling through."

The record should show that her statement came *before* she'd taken a good look at Lara and me.

"Yeah, you both should head back to the house." I extended my arm as though waiting for the two of them to do just that. "Cassius probably has dinner ready."

The mention of food spurred my sister and her grumbling stomach into action. As she strode by me, her head swiveled so she could keep her intrigued stare anchored in my direction.

"Yeah. We'll get out of your hair." She linked her arm with Lara, who'd managed to wipe the anger from her expression but not the flush from her face.

I watched the two of them leave. Waited. Convinced myself I was going to have dinner in the Airstream. *Alone.* And I did good on that resolution, making it back to my RV and through a refreshingly cold shower without reneging. I fixed a basic turkey sub and took a seat at the table without second-guessing my decision. But when I pulled over my crossword puzzle, all I saw was the word *PHILTRUM*, and then the woman whose lips had given me the answer.

Cursing the crossword, cursing myself, and cursing my damn dick, I wrapped up the sub to eat another day, threw on my jacket, and jogged through the light rain down to the house.

"Look what the cat dragged in," Colby teased, her smile wide as I entered the dining room behind Cyclops.

I grunted, raking my eyes around the table until they found Lara.

For the size of my family, dinner was functioning at half capacity. Cassius sat in his seat at the head, Colby and Lara on one side of him, and Creighton on the other. Aside from Lara, this was the typical attendance to an evening meal. If Creed was around, which wasn't often, he joined—not that he said much. Colton came in spurts but preferred to spend his time with the horses and taking out his aggression inside the barn; Lara took his place at the table tonight. And Callum . . . forget it. At least, that was my opinion, but Cassius set a place for him regardless.

He set a place for all of us, regardless.

"I could smell the barbecue all the way up the hill," I lied and drew out the chair next to Creighton, who chuffed at my lie. If I were anyone else, he would've called me out on it, but me, Cassius, and Creed were the only ones regularly spared from his rancor. Probably because we were the only ones he wouldn't get a rise out of.

I took a second glance at his right arm, noticing a tattoo I swore wasn't there last week. Coffee-making was my hobby, and tattooing himself was Creighton's. He was covered in them, though always somehow found room for more.

"Barbecue chicken and sweet potato bowls." Colby handed me the fixings, one after another, to make my own.

Sweet potatoes were grown in the garden. Barbecue sauce was Dad's secret recipe. And chicken came free-range from another ranch a few miles down the road. Years ago, Cassius had bought chickens for *this* purpose, but as soon as Colby had named them all, there was no way in hell she was going to let them become dinner.

Creighton leaned over as soon as my plate was filled and murmured loud enough for everyone to hear, "If it were up to me, we could've been having duck."

Colby's expression flatlined and she gave him the finger.

Cassius made a sound halfway between a sigh and a chuckle and redirected the conversation. "So, Lara, how do you like Phoenix?"

Pain lanced my chest, and I shoved a bite of food in my mouth. I didn't want to think about her going back to Arizona, but I should. Better to get the ache over with now.

"It's . . . nice."

"Nice?" Colby prodded, scooting back as Cyclops jumped into her lap. Cassius sent the cat a glare but said nothing. "Have you been to the Grand Canyon? I don't think it's too far . . ."

"It's about five-ish hours, so not too far, but I haven't gone. Most of my coworkers have and rave about it, I just . . ." Her head angled and her smile tightened. "Lately, my version of a day trip is going up the elevator to the ortho floor at the hospital. I haven't really explored much at all, which is embarrassing, but I work a lot. Too much, probably."

"What made you want to move down to the heat?" Cassius's bias for his home for the last four decades was making a strong showing.

"I wouldn't say it was a choice. It was where I was accepted for my residency, so I went. I enjoyed where I worked and the people I worked with, so I stayed when I finished." Her shoulders gave a little shrug. "Not a great reason, unfortunately."

"But your sister has been living up here still? Since college?" The mention of Rachel instantly hung a cloud over her, one I wished I could just rip away.

Why was he asking about Rachel? I stopped eating and leveled Cassius with a hard glare, waiting for him to acknowledge my silent warning to lay off the topic.

"She moved around a bit, too, but eventually ended up back here."

"Wait, Dad, how do you know where they went to college?" Colby butted in, her head cocked at a wild angle.

Cassius stilled and sat back, unsettled. Maybe because he wasn't used to being the one questioned.

"We went to University of Wyoming together. Rachel graduated with me, and Lara two years after," I said, hoping to put an end to the conversation.

Colby's head whipped toward me, her eyes wide for what I was sure was a Colby-only reason.

"Do you think you'll stick around once Calder finds your sister?"

Goddammit.

"Cassius," I warned, my fork clattering to my plate.

Cassius wasn't particularly known for his tact. I wished I could say it came from avoiding most forms of society for the last thirty-odd years, but that would be a lie. The man was a survivalist through and through. A born prepper. Situations were stripped bare of emotion so they could be thoughtfully evaluated and choices made accordingly.

He had the decency to grimace. A surprising consolation, in my experience.

"My apologies, Lara."

"You don't have to answer—"

"No, it's okay," she interrupted, and based on the look she shot me, I got the message that Cassius was going to get his answer for no other reason than to aggravate me. "I don't know. I'm still waiting to hear if I even still have a job at my hospital in Arizona, but even if I do . . ." She paused for a second, scooping another bite of food onto her fork. "Even if I do, I'm not sure that's enough to hold me there. I'm not sure it ever was. I was just working too much to realize it."

Her regret-laden voice gutted me. The guilt she carried for her patient was only a symptom of the guilt she felt for Rachel. For being absent. For not realizing where her sister's insecurities had taken her. For having her own way of dealing with the trauma of their unstable childhood and now believing it had compounded her sister's misfortunes.

That wasn't the truth. It was just a story told by the mind in its weakest moment. One sharp enough to bury into her subconscious.

I glanced at Cassius because I knew what that was like. How a thought could embed itself like a splinter under the skin, after a while, healed in so deep, the moments of pain seemed like less of a problem than tearing through the flesh to get it out.

"Avoidance is rarely an adequate method of dealing with a problem." Creighton entered the conversation with his usual brand of brutally blasé remarks.

"Creighton—"

"Unless that problem is a tornado. Then you definitely want to run. Ask Callum."

"Jesus, Creighton." Colby's balled-up napkin went flying and smacked him in the head.

Picking up the soiled napkin with two fingers, Creighton deposited it next to his plate. "Very mature." He raked his hand through his long hair, somehow making the dark circles under his eyes look more severe.

"Says the man insulting our handicapped brother."

"Callum would've appreciated the humor." Creighton's eyes darted rapidly through the group, daring anyone to disagree, which, unfortunately, none of us could.

Callum's humor existed in only the very darkest corners of his mind, if it existed at all. Similar to Creighton. You'd think the traumas they'd gone through, while very different, would've given them more common ground than a morbid sense of levity.

"Well, Lara, I think you should stick around. I could teach you how to shoot. We could even use Creighton for target practice," Colby said, her voice and her smile both sickly sweet as she rose and started grabbing plates. "Anyone want coffee? Except you, Creighton."

"And here I thought you'd relish the chance to poison me," he returned with a hint of a smirk.

Colby's eyes narrowed. "You're too toxic to be poisoned."

"I'll take that as a compliment."

"You would," she huffed and went to pick up Lara's plate, but Lara grabbed it first.

"Please, let me help you," she insisted, then reached across the table for mine.

"I'll take a decaf," came Cassius's request.

"I'm good, thanks." After dialing in the intricacies of my pour-over ritual, I couldn't stomach Cassius's decades-old drip machine. Especially right now, when Colby's words were still ringing in my head: *"I think you should stick around."*

My hand reached for the side of my jaw, working over the muscle in long rubs. *I wouldn't survive Lara Crane sticking around.*

"You know, Calder," Cassius said, and I didn't miss the way his eyes flicked to Lara's retreating form. *Shit.* Was he going to ask me about her? Did he know—had I given away—"The kitchen could use an upgrade in the coffee department. I was wondering if you could . . . show me the difference between filter and French press?"

I pushed back in my chair, staring at my father like he'd grown a second head.

Cassius had always been the authority. Always the answer. *Always the end.* He knew how he wanted things done, and there was rarely a time when I could disagree with his way or his rules. So to have him ask for *my* expertise on making coffee when he'd been perfectly satisfied with his drip machine from the beginning of time . . . *And the way he'd looked at Lara before he'd done it.*

My nostrils flared with my sudden breath.

It was one thing for her to destabilize me. My mind. My emotions. My desires. It was another for that to ripple over into this. Into Colby. Into Cassius. *My family.*

Get a grip, Calder. He's just asking about coffee, I reprimanded myself. "Yeah," I clipped. "Sure." And then I stood. "But I think I'm going to head out. Good night."

I almost made it out of the room without hearing Creighton: "Looks like someone has his panties in a bunch. I guess I'll have to forgive her for translating my Latin."

Chapter 25

Lara

"I remember your sister," Colby blurted out as soon as we were alone.

My hands, filled with bowls, paused halfway in the giant farmhouse sink. I'd honestly assumed Colby knew who I was—who I was to Calder, and why I'd come here in the first place. But then again, it was equally plausible she didn't. *This was business for him, after all.*

"Oh?" I tried to sound nonchalant. "I didn't realize you met Rachel when she was here." She would've had to have been, what? *Eleven? Twelve?*

"No. Not officially." She bit her bottom lip, scrubbing the dishes roughly, water splashing onto the counter like she wasn't really paying attention. "I saw them walking at a distance."

My heartbeat steadily climbed into my throat, giving a tremor to my voice. "They dated in college."

Her wild scrubbing screeched—or *sloshed*—to a halt, and she turned to me, gaping. "Wait, they were *dating*?"

Had that not been mentioned? Judging by the look on her face, I guessed not.

"Yes . . ." I grabbed a towel to help her dry.

"Calder and your sister?" she repeated.

Taking the first clean plate from her, I said with emphasis, *"Yes."* And then managed to feign a weak laugh. "Calder brought her here to . . . end things. It was a long time ago. It doesn't matter now."

"Lara." Colby shook her head slowly. The kind of horror-movie slow, like I'd just unknowingly made out with the murderer. "No."

"No? What do you mean?"

"I mean, you've been here—are here. You know we don't really do well with strangers. Calder wouldn't bring someone here to end their relationship."

My mouth opened, lined with a million explanations for *why* Calder would do that, knowing my sister, but then I shelved them all for the simpler "Well, he did."

"No, Lara, he didn't," she insisted, and my head spun, confused as to why she was being so persistent about this. "I'm sorry. I didn't just see them walking. I mean, I did see them walking, because they walked right by the tree house we passed earlier, and I happened to be inside it, so I heard them talking, *completely unintentionally*, which I'll admit is not the norm for me."

"You . . . heard them?" I choked, my heart thrashing against my chest.

"Your sister was sobbing about some other guy. Ethan—no, Aaron, maybe?"

Thank God I wasn't holding a dish right then, because I would've dropped it.

"Allen?"

"Yes! That's it. Allen."

The ground started to feel like a balance board, tipping and rocking underneath me in every direction. *Breathe, Lara. Focus.*

"I couldn't make out much because I was up pretty high and she was crying pretty hard, but she was definitely upset at Allen, not Calder. I had no idea . . . I guess maybe I wouldn't have had any idea if they were dating, but my brother definitely wasn't breaking up with her."

My brain felt like a spilled jar of marbles, thoughts rolling in every direction, faster than I could catch them.

Whatever had happened between Rachel and Allen had to do with the night she'd come here.

Calder had known about it this entire time, and not only had he not told me, he also hadn't defended himself when I'd accused him.

And Rachel . . . had lied to me.

Air whooshed at the fresh burst of pain in my chest, anger and guilt melding into double-sided torture.

"Calder tends to accept responsibility for things that aren't his fault." I reeled when Cassius's words slammed to the front of my mind.

Did he know the truth, too?

Did everyone know the truth except me?

"Did you hear why she was upset? What Allen did?" I asked. At this point, Colby was pretty much the only person I trusted to tell me the truth.

"It just sounded like she was in trouble and that was why Calder brought her here. It's really the only reason Calder would bring anyone here," she answered honestly.

"Yeah," I croaked bitterly. "It's why I'm here." I dropped the towel on the counter, fresh anger clawing over my skin.

"Oh, no." Her head whipped wildly. "You're not here because you're in trouble, Lara. You're here because you *are* trouble . . . for him."

Trouble . . . for Calder.

"I have to go. I'm sorry," I said, bolting for the door.

Calder had no idea what kind of trouble was headed his way.

The storm that coalesced over the sequestered ranch was fresh with fury. The hollow winds sharpened through the mountain peaks, cutting my cheeks with cold. Peals of thunder erased the sound of my footsteps on the gravel while a gossamer of lightning seemed to rend open the whole sphere of the sky. It was as though Mother Nature, like the rest of us, had lost her shit at the end of a hard day.

The disquiet spurred my walk to the Airstream, my tears masked by the torrent of rain.

What happened that night?

And why had Rachel lied to me about it?

Like something that's too hot to the touch to tell whether it's hot or cold, anger and pain churned inside me to the point where it was impossible to know where one emotion stopped and the other began. Even the burn of my legs up the last hill didn't make a dent in the band of hurt ratcheting through my chest.

The cracks of lightning reflected off the Airstream's polished silver exterior as I approached the door, looking like some kind of alchemy had occurred within. Wiping the coating of rain from my face with the end of my equally wet sleeve, I banged loudly on the door.

There was a shuffle, and a second later it swung open, Calder looking far too large for the frame and glaring out like a reincarnation of Zeus, wondering who dared to bother him on Mount Olympus.

It was a poor consolation that he was still dressed from dinner, in dark jeans that fit snug on his hips and a tee hanging like a stage 5 clinger to the topography of his shoulders and chest as his arms stretched across the doorframe.

"Lara? What the hell are you doing?" He went to pull me inside, but I stepped out of his reach.

"I want answers." I backed into the familiar madness of the rain.

"So do I," he growled, stepping outside like the survivalist he was: one utterly unaffected by a little water. "And as soon as Cal—"

"I'm not talking about now. I'm talking about what happened the night you brought her here."

"Lara, that was twelve—"

"I know about Allen," I blurted out, and the look on his face screamed *Ding, ding, ding! You hit a nerve.*

"How?"

"I saw the name in Dr. Julia's notes from her sessions with Rachel." When his brows rose, I offered, "I took them from her RV that night because I didn't think . . . She never deserved my sister's trust."

"What did they say?"

I scowled. "Why? So you can decide what lie to tell me?"

His jaw locked. "I've never lied to you."

"You're right. You just carefully decide how much of the truth to reveal so you can *direct* the situation." I hated the bitterness that soaked into my voice, but I couldn't stop it any more than I could stop the rain from soaking my clothes.

"Dammit, Lara—"

"And don't tell me you don't know, Calder. Even Colby knew about Allen."

Rain shivered off his skin as he winced. "What?"

"Colby heard you that night. She was in the tree house when you and Rachel walked by," I said, his eyes rounding as the words tumbled out. "She told me Rachel was upset about *Allen*, not with you. Colby looked at me like I had three eyes when I told her you two were dating." I sucked in a breath, not needing air when there was so much agony oxygenating my blood. "I don't understand, Calder."

"Lara, it's not my place—"

"Not your place?" I was shaking now, furious because all I wanted to do was reach out and rip the truth from his perfectly formed lips. And afraid that if I touched him, instead of shaking him, I wouldn't be able to resist pulling him close and sinking myself into his heat. "It wasn't just her relationship, Calder. It was yours, too. She came to you. You have the right to share what happened; that doesn't just belong to my sister."

He dropped his head back, closing his eyes and letting the rain soak his face. When his face lowered again, rain had slicked every taut line of muscle. "Rachel and I had broken up the week before. Things weren't working out and we both knew it."

"So why did you bring her here?"

Air pushed through the tight line of his lips, and for a second, I thought I was never going to win this fight. Before I could think better of it, I stepped forward and grabbed his shirt, clutching him to me as I whispered, "Please, Calder. What happened to my sister?"

His jaw popped and I felt the tension start to seep from him, his deep rasp reaching my ears.

"I brought her here because she was pregnant with Allen's baby."

A tornado could've swept me off to Oz and it would've been less shocking.

Rachel.

Pregnant.

"Lara." His hands reached me even before his rumbling growl, holding me steady as I started to sway, overloaded by every single aspect of the revelation.

Pregnant.

My sister had been pregnant. With someone's baby, who wasn't Calder's.

And she hadn't told me.

My mind was scorched, thoughts flying like flaming batons, and every one I caught burned worse than the last.

I knew Rachel had gone out with friends plenty of times without Calder. Bars. Frat parties. Everything that wasn't his scene. Had they all been to see Allen? Was it one time? Had Allen—I shuddered.

I'd thought I was prepared for anything. For God's sake, I knew how to bring a trauma victim back to life. But I wasn't prepared for the moment when I was the one crashing out.

Why hadn't she told me?

"Lara."

Calder's hands framed my face, the bracket of warmth a shock to my system. I blinked slowly, my eyes wading in and out of focus on his face. On the worry in his glinting gaze. And then I felt it—the calm he created. Like he'd drawn me into the eye of my own storm, destruction and calamity whipping around but unable to touch me.

Slowly, I let out every molecule of oxygen in my lungs and said, "Tell me what happened, Calder."

He moved his hands to my shoulders like he was trying to let go of me but couldn't. Water shivered off the scruff of his beard as his jaw tensed and then finally unlocked for the truth.

"A few days after we broke up, she called me . . . very upset. Panicked." For Calder to describe her that way, I knew exactly the state my sister had been in. "The things she was saying, I thought she might be in trouble, so I picked her up and brought her here. Somewhere safe."

"Please, tell me he didn't . . ." I couldn't even finish the statement, feeling the entirety of my Hippocratic oath start to unravel at the thought of someone hurting my sister.

"No. He didn't hurt her," he said quickly, and his expression blanched. "She told me they'd been hooking up for several weeks, and she was pregnant."

Oh, Rachel . . .

Guilt sat like a stone in my throat, but before I could chip away at it with an apology, he continued. "She told him about the baby, and he didn't take it well. He wanted her to get rid of it, and after that, he started denying it was his."

The expression on my face must've belied the question in the back of my mind, because Calder answered it. "Rachel and I hadn't slept together in over a month, so we both knew the baby wasn't mine."

And all I could think was *Why?* But I swallowed it down. It didn't matter now.

"After she argued with Allen and he told her he wanted nothing to do with her, she panicked and called me. I brought her to the ranch and she told me everything."

Sure, it had been over a decade, but the way he said it, it was like hearing his girlfriend had been cheating on him hadn't had much of an effect back then, either.

Who was I kidding? Calder had been raised a tracker. A man to seek answers obscured by surroundings. To eliminate emotion in favor of only the essential senses. I would be a fool to think he hadn't at the very least suspected Rachel wasn't faithful.

There were many things in life I'd resigned myself to not understanding, but how my sister could cheat on a man like Calder would forever remain at the top of my list.

"Why didn't she tell me?" I whispered, not really expecting him to have an answer but not surprised when he did.

"Sometimes we love people too much to be able to bear the thought of letting them down."

I felt the words weigh like lead in the marrow of my bones. I wouldn't have judged her or been angry with her, but I knew that didn't matter in the same way that Calder's innocence in his mom's death didn't change the way he viewed his role or how it had affected his relationship with Cassius.

Rachel hadn't come to me because she thought I would've judged her. For cheating on Calder. For getting pregnant with a complete asshole like Allen. And that was my fault.

How many times had I told her I wished Mom hadn't been so desperate for love? That I wished she'd would've been more conscious of her worth rather than settling for guys who didn't deserve her?

How many things had I said to Rachel in the fugue of hormonal teenage years that I'd never considered what kind of effect they would've had when my sister ended up in the same position?

"I guess the way Allen spoke, she thought he wanted to be with her."

I bit into the side of my cheek hard enough to taste blood. No wonder she hadn't told me. I would've quickly disabused her of that notion. Allen Hendricks had wanted sex. Mostly with women who were considered off limits. In fact, I was pretty sure I'd heard a rumor that he'd been involved with one of his married professors on campus not that long after all this must've happened.

"At the very least, she thought he'd be there because of the baby."

The baby.

"What happened to the baby?"

"There was no baby," he replied before I even had the chance to think of anything else. "I went with her to the doctor the following week, and they did blood work; the at-home tests she took were both false positives. She was never pregnant."

I sucked in a breath, inhaling the cool rain onto the tip of my tongue. *No baby.*

Whatever fractures were present on my heart split fully open. For deep, gasping moments, all I could think about was the pain Rachel would've been in. To think she was pregnant . . . She'd always talked about becoming a mom. And for Allen to shut her out . . . I knew my sister. Her whole world would've revolved around that baby the moment she knew she was going to have one. There was nothing she would've clung to more than the unconditional love from the person growing inside her. To find out it was a faulty test . . .

Calder cleared his throat, his eyes falling for a moment before he offered, "In some ways, I think hearing that was worse than when Allen abandoned her."

The last piece of what happened sank into my brain, painting a whole new picture of what I'd thought had happened—*what Rachel told me happened.*

She'd told me about her breakup with Calder after she knew there was no baby, and the more I tried to remember that decade-old conversation, the more my sister's cries and harsh words had come in generalities, ones I'd filled in the specifics of with Calder's name when it couldn't have been further from the truth.

"Why didn't you tell me?" My head swayed, disbelief setting it adrift. "Why did you let me think this whole time that it was your fault—"

"Because it was a long time ago and she wasn't the only guilty one in our relationship. And because it wouldn't make a difference to dredge it up with Rachel missing."

I grabbed his shirt, now completely wet from the storm. My fingers curled into the cold fabric—and into the heat of his chest. But it was a different storm that caught us in its wrath. A different storm that split molecules in the air and made the earth feel like clouds and the sky as heavy as stone. That made lightning rock the ground and thunder brighten the skies.

A storm born of the tension gathering between Calder and me with nowhere else to go. *Nowhere else to hide.*

"And after?" We both knew what *after* meant.

After we realized this attraction between us. After we kissed. After I told him about Phoenix and Ian. *After we'd almost torn each other apart in our tent.*

Calder's nostrils flared, like I was Eve standing in front of him and offering him the apple.

"After . . ." His voice was serrated with the same ache burning in his lust-filled stare. "After, it was easier if you hated me."

"What was easier?"

His palms framed my face. "To stop myself from doing this."

And then his mouth sealed over mine.

Chapter 26

CALDER

Rule #1: The essence of survival is preparation.

There would be no surviving this. No surviving Lara.

All night, I'd cursed myself for my weakness. My irrationality. *My irresponsibility.* Maybe it wouldn't have changed anything, or maybe we would've gotten answers faster. Maybe we would've found Rachel already. Now I'd never know because I was too distracted by wanting her. Too hungry for her to realize where it would lead—to the past. To breaking all the rules I'd made to keep me from this very moment. The *Fuck It* moment where I gave in to everything we'd both been fighting.

"I don't want you to stop," she panted against my mouth.

There was nothing that could have prepared me for the way I wanted her, nor the way my body reacted to just one taste.

"I can't stop," I grunted, sinking my tongue into the depths of her mouth. "Not anymore."

Lightning. Thunder. Rain.

Rules. Guilt. Danger.

There was no force of nature that could stop me from having her. Taking her.

My hands slid into her slick hair, angling her head as I stepped forward, my foot sinking and sliding in the mud. She inched back, both of us unsteady until I had her back against the RV.

I should've felt guilty to press her against the cold, wet metal, but she didn't even shiver. If she burned even a fraction of the way I did, the cool shower was welcome.

"Calder," she pleaded, her arms sliding around my waist.

Her kiss was heat and electricity. Sunshine and lightning. Satiation and starvation all at the same time. And for all the ways she stood her ground, nothing compared to the honor I felt when she held fast to me and melted into my arms.

Rain slicked her mouth, my lips moving at an angle so my tongue could tangle and slide along hers. And she gave it right back, moaning and stroking her tongue to mine as her fingers clawed at my soaked shirt. Our kiss became as wild as the storm. Thrashing. Soaking. Striking.

She tugged at my shirt—yanked to drag it up my torso. The scratch of her nails made my skin tingle.

"Lara," I growled, skating my teeth along her jawline.

"I don't want to go inside," she panted, her gaze swimming as it focused on mine. "I don't want softness or a bed." She pressed her fingertips to my cheeks. "I don't want you to fuck me by the rules, Calder."

Goddamn if that didn't turn my cock to instant stone.

I grabbed her chin, holding her face hardly a breath in front of mine. "Then how do you want me to fuck you, Tomb Raider?"

I wanted her so damn bad, it came like a hurricane through my system, flooding and destroying every sense for its own satisfaction.

Her bruised lips parted on a sudden breath.

"Like the way you're looking at me now, Wild Man. Like it's the only thing that's going to keep you alive."

Fuck me.

Fuck my rules.

Fuck everything.

My mouth landed savagely back on hers, kissing her like I wanted to leave a mark. Like I wanted to leave tracks over her lips and skin so I could find my way back to this moment again and again and again.

Her pleas became a heady chant of moans in my ear as my teeth and tongue roamed and ravaged their way to the side of her neck. I'd just gotten a taste of the intoxicating glug of her pulse when I felt her fingers at the waist of my jeans.

She'd given up on my shirt. Everything was too wet to remove easily. Or quickly. And her frustration had become audible.

"Please, Calder."

I straightened and brushed her hand aside, my gaze roaming over her. Every inch of her was soaked. Her hair. Her eyelashes. Her shirt. My cock throbbed when I saw the peaks of her nipples, hard and begging, outlined in the wet fabric.

Goddamn, she was perfect. Fire drenched in rain and want. Her hair streaked like lava over her shoulders. Her nipples pebbled tight on her rapidly moving chest, raindrops falling off the tight tips every time she let out a shuddering exhale.

Sliding my utility knife from my pocket, the blade streaked open like a flash of lightning. Lara's gaze dropped, as I ordered, "Turn around. Hands on the Airstream."

Her pupils blew wide for a split second, but she obeyed wordlessly. *Wantonly.* As soon as her palms were flat against the metal, she widened her stance, presenting me with her perfect ass.

"The things you do to me . . ." I trailed off and palmed one globe, satisfied when I heard a husky moan escape her throat.

God, I should take this slower. Strip her. Taste her. Get on my knees and bury my tongue in her pussy—

"Stop thinking and fuck me, Wild Man." Her breathy order injected another measure of lust in my veins, as if I wasn't already overdosing.

With a growl, I grabbed the waist of her jeans. "Wild or not, there is still one rule for you out here. That hasn't changed." Desire flushed over her skin. "Tell me what it is."

She hummed and whimpered, "Obey."

"Obey who?" I tightened my grip and flexed my hips against her ass.

"Obey you."

"Obey me when?"

She tried to move against me again, her desperation turning me on just as much as what she repeated: "Obey you when we're in the wilderness."

"That's right," I cooed and then rumbled low, "Now, stay still."

With a hard yank, I jerked her ass back so she was bent forward and stabilized by the RV. Shoving her shirt up, I pressed the flat of my knife to her skin, watching her body shudder just as much as I felt it.

"Fuck, Calder . . ."

"Still," I reminded her roughly and slid the knife lower, hooking the tip under the waist of her jeans. Angling the blade, I cut the seam that went straight down the curve of her ass in a single motion, the fabric gaping to show me her black thong.

Two swift cuts and I severed that, too.

"Does that make you wet? When I cut your clothes off to fuck you?"

"God, yes." Her head hung as I sheathed my knife and returned it to my back pocket. The whole time I stared at her, watched her shift her weight, trying to ease her ache.

"And how about this?" I wound the string of her thong around my fingers and reeled it slowly from between her thighs, hearing her choked breaths as the fabric rubbed right along her clit as I pulled it free. "You don't have to answer. I can see it does."

The only piece of clothing that wasn't soaked from the rain was soaked with something else as I balled it in my fingers, desire clawing at the inside of my chest.

"Calder—"

"Spread your legs wider," I interrupted, dropping the fabric into the mud and reaching for the zipper of my jeans. "Show me just how wild you want me."

She almost slipped with how fast she moved, and I grabbed her waist, steadying her.

"Careful," I ordered, returning to work open my jeans.

I watched rain skate down her spine and disappear into the seam of her ass. Knowing it collected lower, where she was already hot and worked up, made my dick throb, and made the groan that ripped from my chest impossible to contain when I finally pulled my cock free.

Lara tilted her head over her shoulder, trying to look at me. As soon as I caught her gaze, I grabbed her ass with one hand and delved two fingers between her thighs. It was impossible for them not to sink straight into her pussy. She was so slick and hot and tight. *So tight.*

"Fuck, Lara." I pumped my fingers inside her, feeling her muscles tighten and draw me deeper.

"God, Calder. Fuck me," she half cried, half begged. "Do you need an anatomy lesson for how it works?"

A burst of thunder quaked around us then, and I stilled with my fingers inside her heat. I waited for the earth's trembling to stop, so I knew I was only feeling hers as I inched forward until my cock brushed along the seam of her ass. *Letting her feel just what she was begging for.*

I smiled at the sudden catch of her breath.

"This *is* your anatomy lesson. If I don't stretch you before I fuck you, then this is going to be a one-time thing. And I don't know about you, but I plan on *surviving* all night inside you."

"Jesus," she whimpered as I started to scissor my fingers in her heat, widening muscles that only wanted to bear down and bury me inside her.

"Now, widen your legs." *Obey me.*

Her fingers curled into the metal, her arms taut like she was trying to puncture holes through my walls to give her something to hold on to.

I stared down between us, feeling everything start to slow like the storm had created a ripple in time. Or maybe we had. My thumb rubbed back and forth on her back, massaging her wet skin. Raindrops trickled down her spine and dripped down her ass. If they made it to my fingers, I wouldn't have known. The only slickness I felt was her.

"Please, Calder," she panted, her weight starting to shift.

"*Wild* doesn't always mean *savage*, Tomb Raider. Sometimes *wild* just means *brutal*." I imparted the knowledge with a curl of my fingers along her front wall until I found her G-spot and she cried out. "*Unrelenting.*" I pressed over it again, feeling her knees buckle and then give.

As soon as she stabilized, she rocked into my hand and against my cock, bright white charging through my vision. With a grunt, I released her hip and fisted my length, letting out a hiss.

"And *unexpected*," Lara added huskily, cheekiness oozing through her fugue of desire. I slid my fingers out of her pussy, about to add a third to the mix when she spoke again, softer this time. "Please, Calder. I need you."

It was that last part that was my undoing. I'd never been able to say no when she needed me. Even when it was wrong. Against the rules. Even when it was dangerous. And this moment would be no different.

"How many rules are you going to make me break, Tomb Raider?" I growled, already reaching for my cock.

I grabbed hold of my length. My skin was on fire, my cock stretched and pulsing, spilling out of my grip. So thick it felt like a crime to make her take me, but a death sentence if she didn't.

She looked over her shoulder, her blown-out pupils swallowing mine. "All of them, Wild Man."

Another time I'd confess there were none left to break. Another time when my throat wasn't clogged with ache and my tongue leaden with lust.

Holding her slick skin, I stepped between her legs and slid my cock down the seam of her ass, all the way until my crown brushed against her heat.

Lightning forms because the electric charges in both the cloud and the ground become too great for space to insulate. Too much to contain. Just like the ache and want building between Lara and me.

As soon as my cock touched the warm welcome of her slick cunt, a bolt of unmetered need charged along my spine. White-hot electricity rained over my skin. Blotted my vision. Burned my lungs.

One touch sent me over the edge. Electrified me. *Destroyed me.* One touch and I thrust forward, burying myself to the hilt inside her.

Lara screamed at the invasion, from pleasure and pain, but I couldn't stop. I could barely breathe as her tight heat enveloped me. Pulled me deeper. And strangled every rational thought from my mind. She felt so good. Too good. Rule-breaking good.

Holding her hips, I drove into her slick pussy. Again and again. Harder. Faster. And each time, she took me deep with a garbled cry. Each time, her muscles squeezed and fluttered, begging just as much as her moans for more. And then the storm became us. Skin cracked against wet skin. My groans rumbled the ground. Her cries drenched the air.

"Oh god, yes," she panted, and it unraveled my control.

"Fuck, Lara. *So fucking tight.*" And then I was not only brutal and unrelenting, but feral, too.

The rain made everything slick. Us. The RV. The ground.

Mouths. Hands. Limbs.

Everything was messy. Messy and wild and savage.

And all I could think was that she was everything. Everything I'd ever wanted, from that very first look. And like many storms that had torn through my life, I knew I wouldn't be able to walk away from this one without some serious destruction.

"Calder . . ."

Her feet started to slide, my thrusts lifting her onto her toes. She clawed at the Airstream, but even that wasn't stable. Not in the rain. Not in the wild. Her hands slipped and my arm snaked around her front, catching her just before she pitched forward.

"Fuck," I swore, gasping for breath and scrambling for something more stable. There was nothing—nothing but the ground. "Hold on."

Her chest heaved against my arm as I gritted my teeth and slid out of her.

"Knees on the ground, Tomb Raider," I ordered over her whimpering. "Time to get your hands dirty."

I'd hardly spoken the words before she obeyed, mud squishing under her knees and against her palms. I savored the sight of her ass prone in the air, and then my heart stopped when she went down on her elbows. Lightning flashed, illuminating her slick, swollen folds, and I broke.

Now she was the savage one. Brutal. Unrelenting. *Wild* the way she made me want her, and tomorrow, I'd feel the pain from how hard I dropped to my knees, but tonight, the only thing I could feel was the exquisite tightness of her waiting cunt taking all of me back inside her.

The heat was just as devastating as the first time, but the angle . . . Stars exploded in my vision as I sank deeper.

"Yes, Calder. *Yes.*" She pushed back into my thrusts. "More."

I felt like a beast, rutting over her in the mud in the middle of a thunderstorm. My ex-girlfriend's sister. My wild fantasy. But I was *her* beast when I fucked her, and she'd begged for more.

I slid my hand up her spine and gathered the wet strands of her hair, turning and turning my wrist until there was a distinct arch of her back. "This was what you wanted, Tomb Raider. A wild man. Fucking you to survive."

Tomorrow I'd apologize for the bruises that would mark her and the soreness that would stain her muscles.

The sky above lit with greater frequency, like it wanted me to see what I was doing to her. Like it wanted me to see what she was doing to me. And I did. I couldn't look away from where we were joined. From where my thick cock, swollen and bursting with veins, moved in and out of her body.

I'd always known Mother Nature to be something I couldn't control. Something that existed outside of me that I had to respect. For the first time, I realized the wildness I existed in also existed inside me.

A wildness for her that couldn't be contained. That was utterly essential. That couldn't be stopped.

"Fuck," I panted raggedly, feeling her body start to ripple and fracture around me. Every thrust was met with more resistance. With louder whimpers. With greater trembling. Pressure pooled at the base of my spine, my own release crackling at the very limits of what my body could contain. My cock felt ready to split open, and it was only the tightness of her cunt that kept me together.

"God, Calder. God, yes," she choked out, her fingers clawing at the mud. "I can't."

Her whole body started to sink as I slammed into her. *There was no coming back from this,* I thought as I gripped her hair tighter, afraid if I let go, she'd collapse to the ground.

"You can," I coaxed roughly, feeling her grow even wetter on my cock.

Lara didn't need permission, but she wanted it. She was determined and strong and capable, in every moment of every day, so it wasn't just an honor—it was the greatest turn-on when she trusted me and turned her determination into deference. When she handed me the reins to her body—to her pleasure—and begged me to take control.

"Come for me and scream loud," I ordered. "No one can hear you but the mountains and me."

Rain cascaded down her back. I heard her lungs dredge the last of her breath, and then her body seized as her release swept her away.

My fingers dug into her hips, knowing I'd leave a bruise, but it was the only way to stop her from bucking off my cock when her climax tore through her. Her core clenched wildly around me, pulling me, milking me, sinking into me to seat me deeper. And her scream . . . it sliced through the atmosphere as a strike of lightning turned night into day.

And that was all it took.

One bright moment for me to see how beautifully she came apart for my own release to explode. My roar stitched itself like thunder to her lightning, booming as my cock erupted, filling her all the way to the depths of her womb.

For several long minutes, my cock pulsed inside her. Like I hadn't orgasmed in the last dozen years since we'd first met. Of course, I had, but goddamn, it didn't feel that way. My hips rocked slow, like I could fuck her forever. Like I never wanted to stop.

It was incredible.

Somewhere deep inside my chest, I knew it would be like this. Had known from the first time I saw her—from the first time it stirred something in me that went against the rules. That went against everything I should feel. It wasn't just something—it was *the* thing I tried to ignore but couldn't. The thing that drove me to break up with her sister. But that was the last thing she needed to hear right now. That was my guilt to carry. Not hers.

At some point, I started to hear the storm over our breathing and noticed the goose bumps painted on her back; it was time to go inside. Carefully, I slid out of her and drew her body up from the ground, feeling her shiver as I pulled her against me.

"Wild enough for you?" I rumbled and pressed my lips to her hair, feeling her melt into me. "Time for a hot shower."

As I carried her to the door, her small moan of anticipation had my cock stirring all over again.

Chapter 27

LARA

"You made a mess," I murmured as Calder set me on my feet in the bathroom, stepping away to turn on the shower.

A collage of muddy footprints and murky puddles stained our path through the Airstream, and I felt a twinge of guilt for insisting we stay out in the storm.

"You wanted me to," he said and straightened, letting the shower door shut so it could start to steam.

Our eyes locked, and I felt my skin start to prickle again. What had just happened . . . what we'd done . . . I couldn't even savor it because I simply ached too much for it to happen again. I knew where my priorities should lie. I knew I should be focused on my sister. Worried about what was happening to her. Worried about what *had* happened to her.

Worried, worried, worried about everyone but myself. Because, of course, I was fine. I was a doctor. I was stable. I had a good job. A good life.

I'd lost a patient. Been attacked in a place I thought I was safe. I'd buried my own fears and insecurities so deep, I didn't even know how to unearth them, let alone give myself the freedom to treat them. I'd been alone for so long, too busy caring for everyone else—

"Hey," Calder rumbled and I blinked as his hands cupped my face. "Not here. Not tonight."

Air whooshed from my chest, sinking into the safety of his promise.

Calder was a buoy in the middle of my storm. Someone I could trust to keep me afloat when I just didn't have the strength. Someone who could hold my weight and my worries without judgment. Someone who made me feel safe enough to not have to carry everything all the time.

"Yeah." I tipped toward him, my hands splaying onto his chest.

He looked over his shoulder and then back to me. "Let's get you clean." When he stepped back, my arms fell to my sides, and I saw the muddy handprints left on his shirt.

"You, too."

I caught a whiff of a smile on those dangerous lips before he reached in his pocket and I heard the gentle click of his knife sliding open.

"Are you going to ruin all these clothes, Wild Man?" I murmured when he brought the blade to my chest, using his free hand as a buffer against my skin.

He stilled at the nickname, his jaw muscle feathering his cheek. Slowly, his eyes lifted to mine, and that familiar tension metabolized the space between us. Oxygen ladened with ache. "Do you want me to stop?"

My heart thudded so hard, he had to have felt its lurch.

"No." *I never wanted him to stop.* But that kind of thinking didn't belong here. Tonight. It might not belong here at all, which was why I couldn't think about it now.

He cut through my shirt with one swipe, the cotton releasing not even a whimper against the blade, and then peeled it off my shoulders in seconds.

"I need to get me one of those," I murmured when his hands went to my pants. When his eyes lifted, I added, "I cut off my fair share of clothes."

He frowned so harshly, I would've laughed if the reason for it didn't make my stomach somersault. *So it was possible for Calder Stone to be jealous.*

"In the ER," I murmured, but it didn't seem to make a difference; a grunt was his only reply.

Flicking open the fly of my jeans, Calder stripped the muddy shreds from my legs, leaving me in front of him, naked except for my black bra. I waited for the embarrassment to come, but it never did. I stood in a pile of shredded clothes, covered in mud and dirt and rain and *him*, and the only thing I felt was power. Like Venus rising from the sea, I'd risen from the storm.

And then I felt something leak down my thigh. Not rain. Something warm and sticky and wild.

Crap.

"Calder, I'm on the pill," I blurted out, needing him to know.

He balled my clothes in one hand and straightened with a jerky movement. "I know."

"You know?"

"I saw the blister pack you packed in your bag for the retreat." I shouldn't have been surprised. *Preparedness* was synonymous with Stone. He caught my chin in his fingers, lifting my face to his and lowering his voice. "Know your terrain, your target, and your limits."

"So now I'm a target?" I breathed out.

His eyes smoldered. "No. You're the one who never left my sight."

And like he'd just reached that invisible line of no return again, he let me go and took a towel from the small cabinet, setting it on the counter for me. I removed my bra, unable to take my eyes off him as he reached in the shower and checked the water.

"It's warm," he said, and moved aside.

"Calder—"

"Take your time. I'll shower when you're done," he said sternly, as though reminding himself the shower wasn't big enough for two.

He strode out of the bathroom and closed the partition behind him, giving me only the briefest glimpse of his wet shirt tented in front of his groin.

I stepped into the stream with a smile on my face and closed my eyes, my sore muscles soaking in the delicious heat. The Airstream had surprisingly decent water pressure, but even that couldn't tempt me to linger. So I soaped the dirt and muck from my skin, then made quick work of washing my hair.

All those years ago, I could've only fantasized about a night like this, and now that I'd had it, I didn't care what havoc Calder wrought on my body as long as it came from him.

I shut off the water and pulled the towel from the counter, drying myself and then wrapping it around me. Whatever calm I'd found slipped away when I opened the door into the Airstream.

Calder stood by the entrance, hips resting on the kitchen counter, and his face lowered toward the mug of coffee clutched in his hands. He looked like Rodin's *Thinker*, but the Survivalist Edit. The mud had dried hard into his shirt, his jeans well on their way to the same fate. Everything stiff on him. Him included.

And my mouth started to water.

It couldn't have been more than a second or two that I took to simply admire him before he sensed me. "There's coffee if you want it and a T-shirt for you on the bed," he said and straightened. "It'll be big."

He came toward me, and I saw he'd removed his boots and cleaned the mud from the floors while I'd been in the shower.

"It'll be perfect," I murmured, knowing it was his.

"I'll be out in a minute. Make yourself at home."

I couldn't help but steal another look as the door closed to the bathroom again, catching him haul his shirt off his back with a single hand.

His shower was just as quick as mine. Meanwhile, I'd savored the coffee but left his tee folded on the bed. Next to it, I reclined on my stomach—naked—working on his crossword.

My chest moved at a shallow pace, listening to his heavy steps in the bathroom, waiting for the slide of the partition opening. When it did, my breath caught.

One step. Two.

"Lara," he growled when he saw me, and my pulse revved into gear.

I took a bracing inhale and pushed myself up, taking his crossword with me in my lap as I turned. He stood just outside the bathroom, eyes dark and filled with lust stars.

"I was working on your puzzle." *Naked.*

His fist flexed, his hot gaze roaming over my face. My chest. My legs. There was no hiding the way I responded—the way I wanted him. And there was no mistaking how he was trying to hold back. Again.

I understood. It was . . . rough out there. Now I felt every step, every movement, in my core, the tender muscles so completely used, and I knew I would for days. But I wanted more. I wanted this whole night, if that was all I was going to get. And I knew he wanted the same.

"I'm stuck on a word. Four letters. Begins with an *f*."

His nostrils flared and he took a step closer, and then another, his silence intoxicating.

"The prompt is . . . what my *wild core* wants."

Calder reached the bedroom, his hands rising to frame the entrance as he stared down at me. This close, I lost my attempt—my ability—to be coy. Outside, in the storm, had been reckless abandonment. Now all I wanted was to drink in the sight of him up close. I wanted to fill in all the gaps of stolen glances and brief touches. I wanted to memorize every inch of him, not with my mind, but with my fingers and tongue.

"What you need is for me to let you rest."

A tiny smile teased the corners of my mouth. I loved Gentleman Calder and his rules. Almost as much as I loved breaking them.

"Me?" I slanted my head, savoring the chiseled abdomen in front of me, right at eye level, watching every ragged exhale cut the lines of his stomach deeper. "You're the one who's injured."

His stare flicked to his bandage. "A flesh wound."

It was a little more than that, but I held my tongue and instead let my gaze continue to roam.

"I used to think you were perfect," I said and reached a hand out, trailing a single finger along the center. The *linea alba*.

I swore the doorframe creaked under his punishing grip. "'Used to'?"

Perfect was an understatement, I realized now as I followed every dip and line, every bulge and muscle.

"Back in college," I said, squeezing my legs a little tighter as the ache between them started to swell. "I would study for anatomy, and I would picture you." Heat bloomed in my cheeks, but I didn't care. I wasn't embarrassed to admit I'd crushed on him; I was turned on by it. By sharing this piece of myself I hadn't shared with anyone.

"What anatomy did you picture?" He lifted an innocent eyebrow.

Two could play at that game.

Biting my lip, I rose onto my knees, the crossword falling to the side, and scooted to the edge of the bed. His expression was feral as I came eye level with him, his towel straining over his cock like it was holding on by a single thread.

"Neck and shoulders," I replied, dragging my tongue over my lips. Instantly, his jaw clenched. "Oh, and your *masseter*." I lifted a hand and pressed my fingers to the bulging muscle. "It was always firing every time I saw you. Always tense."

It pulsed under my fingertips, and then he rumbled, "It wasn't the only part of me that was tense around you."

I couldn't look away from his eyes and the way they splintered with untold truths. "Calder—"

"What else?"

I wanted to probe, but I also didn't want to talk about my sister any more tonight, which invariably was where that conversation would lead. So instead, I slid my fingers along the side of his neck, feeling the hammer of his pulse against my fingertips.

"This. *Sternocleidomastoid. Thyroid* and *cricoid cartilage*." I traced over his Adam's apple and then swept down to his collarbone. *"Trapezius. Deltoid. Biceps."* His skin felt like molten metal, hot and hard and impossibly smooth. *"Pectorals. Rectus abdominus."* His abs tensed as my hand climbed down their ladder, careful to avoid his wound. "I used to think you had more than was anatomically possible."

"Do I?" he rasped, his gaze lethal as it followed the path of my hand.

"Technically, no," I answered, trailing my fingers to the V that cut in at his hips, and then dancing along the edge of the towel.

"So what do you think about me now?"

"I think . . ." I drew my lip into my teeth and hooked my fingers into his towel. "I think I still haven't seen all of you, Wild Man."

Leaning closer, Calder's hand covered mine, *directing* it to release the fabric and let it fall to the ground.

There was no explanation for the way my lungs ceased to work and how my tongue felt like it weighed a thousand pounds. Even *godly* didn't seem to do justice to the specimen of man in front of me, though something otherworldly seemed appropriate to describe his massive cock. The length jutted from a nest of dark hair, hanging low under its own weight. He was so long and thick . . . maybe it was a good thing I hadn't been able to see much outside, or once again I would've wondered if he—*we* were anatomically possible.

"Now you've seen all of me, Dr. Crane . . . what do you think?" he demanded again, and I swore his cock swelled the longer I stared.

"Now I think . . ." My eyes swung to his. "Now I think I need to touch you."

There was hardly any space between us, but still Calder caught my wrist before I could reach him. "Calder—"

"You spent months studying my anatomy," he said gruffly, eyes glittering with lust. "Now it's my turn to study yours."

In a flash of movement, he tugged me to him, swept his other arm around the back of my knees, and pulled my legs out from underneath me.

I fell back into the softness of the bed with something that started as a laugh and ended as a moan as he climbed over me. He was mountainous like this, looming above me, hard and ridged and breathtaking, pinning my hand above my head. His muscles rippled, strong and powerful and *poised*, like a predator about to devour his prey.

"Calder . . ." I rubbed my thighs together, loving the way he took the control I offered without making me feel weak.

His head lowered gradually, holding just a second above my lips before he claimed my mouth. The kiss was slow and deep. Outside had been a surgery. Demanding. Necessary. Life changing. But this . . . the deep strokes of his tongue, the exploration, the cataloging of which spots made me moan and which drew me to shiver . . . what was happening right now was an autopsy. A systematic dismantling of my erogeny for his study. And the man doing it was a different Calder. The slow and in-control Calder. The reserved and determined Calder. The Calder with the hungry eyes and slow touch that promised to peel me apart cell by cell before he put me back together.

"Calder." It was a question and an answer all wrapped in one breathless plea.

He nipped at my upper lip, and I felt the pad of his finger press just above. *"Philtrum."*

I sucked in a breath. "You remembered."

He traced my lips and then took hold of my chin. "I'd never forget a single thing about you."

And just like that, a blanket of goose bumps layered over my skin, my nipples pebbled, and a familiar heat flooded my veins. My core ached for him. Throbbed to the point of pain.

My eyes drifted shut as he pressed his mouth back to my jaw. My cheek. My neck. *"Sternocleidomastoid. Thyroid cartilage."* My throat bobbed as he covered each spot with slow, languorous kisses. *"Clavicle.*

Sternum." The heat of his breath warmed his path, and as it reached my breast, I felt myself arching toward him, aching for that touch.

"What's this, Dr. Crane?" he taunted, dragging his finger in a circle around the swell of flesh.

"Breast." The word rushed out.

"And this?"

My eyes snapped open as he flicked my nipple. *"Areola."* My reward was the heat of his mouth sealing over the sensitive peak. Instantly, I grabbed the back of his head, clutching him to me as his tongue swirled and teased.

He kneaded my begging flesh, plumping me to his mouth like a man starved.

"God, Calder," I panted and gasped at the scrape of his teeth. Their sharp bite. And then the fast, soothing flick of his tongue.

For long minutes, I dissolved into an offering of whimpers and moans, a tithe to the torture of his mouth on one breast and then the other. He didn't stop—not even to breathe, it seemed—as he savored every bit of pleasure from my body. Savored every inch of me until I started to squirm, my core so slick and needy for more.

I never knew anatomy lessons could be like this.

"Please." I reached for his shoulders in some poor attempt to pull that mouth of his back to mine.

Instead, he moved in the other direction.

Calder bent between my thighs, and I'd never felt more on display than in that moment. He pushed my legs wide and spread my pussy open for his attention. A rush of heat welcomed his gaze, and all I could do was stare, his expression a masterpiece in salivation.

"Calder—"

"Don't," he ordered, his eyes gold daggers slicing into mine. "I don't need help with this one."

Oh god.

My arms started to shake, but I couldn't look away. Not when I needed to brace myself for every touch that was to come.

"Clitoris," he said as the pad of his thumb skated over the swollen bundle, sending me into a cascade of shivers. His low groan caught my attention, and he slid two fingers along my entrance. "Damn, that made you wet," he rumbled and brought his fingers to his mouth, sucking them clean. "So wet for me, Dr. Crane." And then he helped himself to seconds.

Gasping, I clutched the blankets at my sides. "Enough," I panted, my nails scoring into his sheets. "Calder, please—"

"Shh." He gave his head a slow shake, but his eyes didn't leave my core. "I'm not done with my lesson yet."

Air heaved from my chest, taking a strangled cry with it. "Calder—"

I didn't get a second warning before his mouth covered me, and my eyes rolled back into a sea of white-hot stars. Sounds rammed their way from my chest out through my throat. I grabbed for his head. I needed him close—closer. I needed the heat of his mouth, the dip and swirl of his tongue, the suffocating pull of his lips on my clit. I needed more of it all.

I'd asked him to be wild, and in turn he was making me insane. But I was doing the same to him.

Calder devoured me like he couldn't get enough. Not just of my sex, but of me. Of this moment. Of my hums and quivers. Of my pleas and desire. Somewhere in the onslaught, I'd hooked my legs over his shoulders and held on, with a prayer that I'd survive the way he consumed me. The scrape and tug of his teeth. The hit of his tongue. His lips tugged on my clit, and my hips pushed forward, arching for more.

Pleasure seeped from every pore, swelling with every stroke of his tongue and surging with every pull of his lips. By the time he paused his assault to let me come up for air, my head wouldn't stop spinning.

"Who knew anatomy lessons tasted so good?" he growled, then sucked my clit hard and let it pop free. "There's just one last thing . . ." His fingers picked up where his words had trailed off, sliding through my tight, sore muscles, preparing them for what was to come.

"Calder!"

"There it is." His curled fingers stroked over my sensitive front wall, the nerves there humming on edge. "G marks the spot, Tomb Raider."

His mouth found my clit again, and I was a goner. My pleasure spots hunted, tracked, *found* by the wild man I'd always wanted.

"Yes!" I cried as my orgasm knocked the air from my chest, crashing my body into a spiral of tremors, surging and gushing around him. Fast. Demanding. Destructive. The only thing I could do was hold on to him so it wouldn't swallow me whole.

My chest heaved. My heart raced. And as the waves subsided, the first thing that registered was Calder's deep, dragging groans as his tongue mopped up every ounce of my desire. It was everything . . . and not enough.

"Don't stop," I begged breathlessly, a big enough part of me afraid he'd try to be chivalrous again.

But the narrowed eyes that looked up and caught my gaze contained nothing of his golden chivalry—only that dark, savage hunger. As he rose over me, the light from the kitchen created a halo around him.

"I can never seem to stop myself when it comes to you. Not when I've wanted you for so long." His voice was resignation seeded with raw hunger, and my legs simply fell apart, leaving me spread and bare to his gaze because I didn't have the strength to do more.

Calder splayed his hand on my stomach, giving him a front-row feel to my quivering as he fisted his thickness with his free hand, hardly able to close his grip as he guided himself to my entrance.

The tension in that moment was combustive, my whole body braced to take him again. His voice cut through the hazy fugue. "Open your eyes, Tomb Raider," he ordered, and my lids snapped open. I hadn't even realized they'd drifted shut. "Watch me fuck you."

My eyes dropped to the space between my legs, and the blunt head of his cock pushed into my slit. My body instantly tensed, wanting but resistant to the invasion again.

He was so big, so thick, my core squeezed and tightened to slow him down, but he didn't let up, and I didn't want him to. Inch after inch of his massive organ pushed inside me, permanently altering my anatomy with the size of his own.

"That's it, Lara." His rough praise soothed me through the greedy pain. "Fuck, you feel so good, stretching for me again. Fuck . . ."

"Calder, please," I begged, even though it felt like he was splitting me in two. I wanted to be split. To be severed. To be ripped from the cold, lonely cage I'd lived in for . . . forever. And I wanted this wild man to be the one to do it.

"God, yes," he groaned when he finally reached the hilt, and I struggled to breathe, feeling so full of him that it was like there was no room for oxygen. "Tell me, Doctor, is this how the anatomy is supposed to fit?"

I shuddered and breathed, "I'm not sure *fit* is the word for this." Stuffed *was more like it.*

His low laugh rippled all the way inside me, and then he was moving. Drawing back and sinking deep. It would be a mistake to think his movements were tender or gentle. They were as gentle as a scalpel through skin. As tender as a needle into my vein. They were precise. Calculated for pleasure. Able to harm me or heal me at the discretion of the man wielding them.

His palm flattened hard on my stomach, pinning me to the bed and to the drive of his cock. In and out. Again and again. I felt every inch, every ridge, every pulse of his thick erection as it rhythmically dismantled what remained of my insides. Piece by piece. Thrust by thrust.

The feral noises he made as he fucked me sounded like they were cut raw from his chest and implanted into my own.

"And what is the word for when I can see my cock move in your stomach?" He drove deep, my G-spot fizzling with the friction.

"Not possible," I choked out in a rush.

"You've said that about me before, Dr. Crane," he growled and thrust again, my hips bowing off the bed to meet his. "And again, you're wrong."

All the soreness disappeared in the face of wanting him. My legs hooked around his waist and my hips rose to meet the drive of his. And then I broke his rules again, lifting my eyes up over the sheen of sweat on his chest to look at his face. There was a wildness there, woven into the strain in his jaw and the hunger in his eyes. A wildness that he didn't suppress, but harnessed in the way he fucked me.

And then his gaze met mine and there was something in it—something I recognized. Not from tonight. Not from today or yesterday. Not from the time we'd spent together over the last two weeks, but from twelve years ago. And suddenly, the bond to that memory was as solid as steel.

Calder had looked at me back then. Like this. He'd wanted me back then. *It was wrong.* But now, nothing had ever felt more right.

"Lara." My name sounded different this time. Worn and ragged and undone.

"You wanted me back then," I said between scattered breaths.

It was the hard pulse of his jaw that confessed his answer and tipped me off to the truth—one the gentleman in him wanted to deny but the *man* in him couldn't.

A wicked, wild look swept through his eyes, and he reached for my clit, rolling and pinching the thrumming bud until I bucked, crying out desperately for release. And then his thrusts picked up. Faster. Harder. His hips slammed into mine, the force blinding with pleasure and shaking my entire body.

But the entire time, his eyes never left mine. *This* was his reply. His admission. *That he'd always been looking at me.*

And I spiraled from that look. Higher and higher. Pleasure spooled my body tighter to the brink of insanity or destruction, whichever came first. Calder fucked me until I couldn't see straight. Until my insides were rearranged and my heart learned a new beat. Until I wasn't begging or cursing, but praying to his name like the god I'd always envisioned him to be.

"I want you to come for me now." His deep, drawn direction was my undoing. I came apart with a scream and convulsed around him. Under him. For him.

And he watched. He fucked and watched as I unraveled to his command, and then he finally drove fast and buried deep, a rough groan dislodging from his lips as he came. Without the rain and the storm and the onslaught to my senses, I could feel everything. The swell of his cock before he climaxed. The hard pump of his length. The hot rush of his cum.

And then I felt more. I felt the warmth of his breath on my cheek. The soft brush of his lips on mine. The tender way he turned my limbs so I lay on top of him. And finally, the thump of his heart under my cheek and the strong press of his fingers as they slid through mine.

For the first time in far too long, my eyes drifted shut, and there were no nightmares waiting to chase away my sleep.

Chapter 28

Lara

I'd slept soundly. A victory that was short-lived when I opened my eyes to a loss. The bed was empty beside me and the bedroom door open. I could smell the hot coffee steaming from the kitchen counter and hear every thump of my heart in the silence of the empty Airstream.

Calder hadn't just left the bed—he'd left the Airstream entirely.

I hated the way my heart plummeted, not even bothering to pull a parachute before crashing into my stomach.

There could be a million good reasons for why he wasn't here. A million good reasons anchored not only by how he'd worshipped me in a deliciously brutal way last night, but how he'd tenderly cared for me afterward. But of course, none of those million were the first that came to mind.

The first thought that took root was that Calder regretted what had happened. Why wouldn't it be? For eighteen years, I'd watched a string of men leave my mom's heart high and dry, and I followed that with another decade in the front row seat to my sister's stack of heartbreak. *A stack including the man who'd just fucked my brains out last night.* Okay, maybe not my brains, but definitely my insides, I thought as instant soreness slowed my slide out from the covers.

I didn't have examples of relationships, only cautionary tales.

Scooting to the end of the bed, I found a pile of clothes for me waiting there. *Only Calder Stone could turn disappearing the morning after into a gentlemanly feat.*

As I dressed, I cataloged the bites and bruises he'd left scattered on my skin. They were nothing compared to the invisible mark he'd left inside my chest.

Was it because of Rachel? Because of what I'd demanded he tell me? Or was it something else?

Was it the same thing that made him pull away from my sister?

While I'd learned a lot about their past last night, Calder hadn't done more than gloss over why he'd broken up with Rachel. And he definitely hadn't explained what he'd done to make her lie to me about it.

"Because she wasn't the only guilty one in our relationship."

I tensed. Those words had gone in and out last night, my head overflowing with too many other massive bombshells to latch on to them, but now, they sank their teeth into my mind.

Calder wasn't the reason why my sister's world had shattered. Dr. Julia's notes, shaded in by Calder's knowledge, made that clear. But just because he wasn't the reason she'd broken didn't mean he hadn't contributed to her cracks.

And he'd admitted it to me.

"He was so distant, Lara. The harder I pulled, the more he pushed. The more I needed him, the less he cared." Rachel's sobs plagued my memory. Was she talking about Calder or Allen? And if she was talking about Calder, should I have known better? *Should I have known this was coming?*

A noise outside pulled me from my spiraling thoughts. The sound of Calder's truck starting outside. If my heart hadn't already fallen to my stomach, it would've buried itself there now. Right under a nice thick blanket of hot fury.

He was leaving. Without me. *The very thing he promised not to do.*

Like. Hell. He. Was.

I stormed out from the bedroom, grabbing my bag from where it was neatly placed on the table like I was just supposed to take my things, leave a tip for good dick, and see myself out. I dug inside for the folded check I'd brought with me and filled it in for $50,000.

Sure enough, I stepped outside to the very worst of my assumptions.

Calder, dressed in his tracking uniform of dark-green pants, a black jacket, and utility boots, packing camping gear into the bed of his truck. His running truck. And for a second, the only emotion that consumed me was regret.

Regret that he was only mine for a night. Regret that I'd turned all the words he'd said to me *while we were undercover* into trophies. Into marks of meaning on my heart. And regret that I could look at him now, watching him in the process of leaving me, and still wish I could have just a little more time with him.

It didn't take him long to realize I was there. Survival instinct and all that.

"Lara." His low greeting sent a traitorous hum through my veins as his eyes raked over me. *Like he had X-ray vision to all those marks he'd left on me.* And it made my heart angrier.

"You found her. You know where the cult is." They weren't questions.

"Yes."

A cocktail of emotions too potent to describe injected into my veins.

"How dare you?" I handed him the tone I reserved for only the gravest of reprimands in the hospital, where a repeated mistake could risk a patient's life.

"Excuse me?"

His calmness aggravated me. I strode close enough for my head to fog for a second when the scent of strong coffee and masculine musk hit my nostrils. I quickly shook it off and banded my arms over my chest, a barricade against breathing him in too deep.

"What was your plan? Fuck me into a coma so I wouldn't notice when you left me behind to find Rachel?" I barked out a laugh. "I mean, I heard you when you said you wouldn't do anything to put me in danger. I guess it's my own fault for not realizing there would ever be a scenario where you could justify fucking someone to keep them safe."

His stillness made my skin prickle. The smooth flow of his breath. The unwavering hook of his gaze. But the flex of his jaw—that spelled out in Morse code that I'd struck a nerve. Or several.

Methodically, Calder turned and shut the tailgate on his truck, the latch sliding into place like a loaded gun. And then he was in front of me, his steadiness swallowing me up and holding me prisoner.

"Who said I was leaving without you?"

My heart tripped over a pebble of hope. "You didn't have to say it. What was your rule? Track the person, not their footprints? You left me asleep in your bed. Clothes, coffee, and my bag waiting for me for whenever I woke up. Meanwhile, you're dressed and loading up your gear. I have to assume you've heard from your brother. That you know where Rachel is. So unless you were planning on hooking up the Airstream and literally hauling me along with you . . ."

He inched closer until his chest brushed my arms. "I was planning on letting you sleep for as long as I could while I got everything ready. You were exhausted after last night."

My mouth dried, a new kind of regret starting to seep in.

"I grabbed a pair of Colby's hiking boots for you and brought the rest of your things from the house because I knew you'd want to leave as soon as possible," he said, his gaze unwavering. "And because if I stayed until you woke, we wouldn't have left that bed today."

Butterflies swept through my stomach like a fluttering hurricane. "So you weren't leaving without me?" I said, not trying to hide the huskiness in my voice.

He cupped my cheek, the tender touch turning dominating as that hold slid to my neck. "I promised you I wouldn't."

There was something quite unbreakable about a promise made by Calder Stone.

Heat flooded my cheeks, and I felt like an ass. A vulnerable ass. My arms lowered to my sides, taking with them the last holds on my defenses.

"You also said you'd do anything to keep me safe."

I didn't know what to make of his soft laugh, and I didn't have much time to think about it because he grabbed my arm and lifted my hand up—the one holding the check. Air sucked into my lungs as he peeled apart my fingers and pulled free the crushed paper.

His nostrils flared as soon as he saw what it was.

"Calder—" I stopped when a lighter appeared in his other hand, a flame sparking.

Wordlessly, he held the check to the fire and let it catch. "I was wrong." The paper charred a quick trail to his fingers. "If I'd wanted to keep you safe, I never would've let you come to the diner with me."

Calder didn't even flinch when the fire chewed between his fingertips and he opened them to a stain of ash.

"So why did you?"

His gaze lifted and settled onto mine, a look sweeping over him that answered me with words he refused to say. *Words I ached to hear.* But before I could ask . . . or beg . . . he stepped back and jerked his chin in the direction of the Airstream.

"Go get your things, Tomb Raider, before I bend you over my tailgate and ruin another pair of your pants."

And just like that, the ache I had for him ignited once more, careless of the desperation I had to find my sister.

"You can't ruin these. They're all I have."

His mouth quirked on one side as it descended close to my ear, and he murmured, "You say that like I care."

We were pulling out of the drive and heading north not even ten minutes later, the Tetons rising into a cloudless blue sky off to the right.

"I'm sorry about earlier," I offered. "I'm not good at this. I'm not good at letting people in."

"I live in an Airstream that only parks for long stretches in the Wyoming wilderness. I don't think that makes me great at it, either." His sideways stare caught mine and I smiled.

My phone vibrated twice from inside my purse, the sensation surprising to me after so many days either without it or without service.

The screen was filled with a bunch of random alerts from the weather app and from my email, but it was the missed call and voicemail that launched my heart into my throat.

"Crap," I murmured and swiped to open the message.

"Everything okay?"

"It's the hospital." I tapped on the message and put the phone up to my ear, Dr. Morgan's low drawl coming in clear.

"Dr. Crane. I wanted to call and let you know that Sunrise's internal review of the case has closed, and you've officially been cleared of all wrongdoing. I will be back in touch in a few days once we decide our next steps."

The voicemail ended, and even though it should've been good news, my chest struggled to release my breath.

"Lara." A large hand closed over mine, making me realize my fingers had balled into a fist in my lap.

"The hospital's investigation into what happened in the ER is closed. They cleared me of any wrongdoing," I repeated almost hollowly.

His hand squeezed mine. "Isn't that a good thing?"

"It . . . I don't know." I fought to swallow. "I guess. It just . . . I guess it just feels like if I'd done everything right, Ian would still be alive."

Calder hummed. "Feelings aren't always the best indicator of fact."

"I know." I stared blankly out the window, focusing too much on the comfort I derived from the simple gesture of his hand holding mine. *When was the last time anyone had comforted me?*

When was the last time I'd let someone in enough to know I needed comforting?

My mind went to that night at the retreat when I'd broken down in his arms and told him what had happened in the ER that day. Maybe I wasn't that bad at letting people in after all. Or maybe it was just him.

God, I shouldn't be thinking about him like that. Like he was . . . *everything I'd wanted all these years?*

Flushed at the thought, I sat up and reached for my coffee, effectively loosening his hand from mine. "Did Callum find the location from the solar panels?"

Calder cleared his throat and then let out a grunt of disbelief. "Yeah."

He slowed as the road turned to gravel and shifted the truck into all-wheel drive; the amount of rain over the last couple of days had not only turned the road into mud, but as we climbed higher in elevation and deeper into the woods, scattered limbs of trees turned into obstacles.

"And they just gave him the information?"

"Well . . . yeah." Calder winced. "The guy who owns the company is an amateur storm chaser and a huge fan of Callum's, so when he explained why we needed the information, he sent over the delivery coordinates. There were two. One matched the Wilderness Within building, and the other was about another mile ahead on this road, but the compound is deeper into those woods." He pointed out my window, catching my eyes on the swivel.

I sat up straighter. "How far?" I squinted like I'd be able to see it.

"Eight miles, so we have a bit of a hike."

Thankfully, my coffee was only on the way to my mouth, not inside it, or I would've choked. "Eight miles?"

"This road is the last place the delivery truck could reach. I'm guessing the panels were off-loaded into Matthew's Jeep or some kind of four-wheeler to get it to the compound buildings. Eden probably thought it isolated him, too. Controlling the final delivery."

"Did one of Callum's drones locate it?"

Calder gave a slow nod. "Last night."

"I thought it was too risky with the lightning?"

The whiskers of his beard fluttered. "I made it worth his while to take the risk, so we could have answers," he said, and then continued talking like I couldn't read between the lines. I knew how expensive and custom that type of equipment was, so whatever Calder had promised to pay or reimburse if the drone got struck by a bolt of lightning had to have been significant. *And he'd done it for me.*

"And it was able to see—get images in the storm?"

"It was a thermal drone. They're smaller and faster, and nighttime is ideal to pick up heat signatures and go unnoticed." Calder paused when one of the tires spun in the mud, making us swerve for a split second before finding traction again. "Now that we have the location, he sent out another drone this morning for imaging. By the time we hike close, I'll have an idea of what we're looking at."

"So, we go to the drop-off location and then hike to the compound?"

He frowned, his eyes narrowing. "Well, that was the plan."

"Was . . ." Ahead of us, a huge tree had fallen from the storm, the trunk spanning the width of the road.

Calder slowed and then angled his truck off the shoulder. "Looks like we're hiking from here."

Chapter 29

Calder

Rule #6: Information is as vital as water. Know your terrain, your target, and your limits before you set foot on a trail.

Eden's Children had chosen the drop site with precision—a nondescript clearing where the unpaved forest service road ended in a turnaround. Beyond, there was nothing but eight miles of arbor-laden wilderness between the road and the compound.

"You okay?" I turned as soon as I heard her stumble. I frowned when she sank all her weight on her right foot for a second.

While I was glad that Lara and Colby wore the same size shoe, my sister's hiking boots had been broken in for her, not for Lara, so our eight-mile trek was bound to cause some discomfort.

"Yeah. Fine. Just caught my foot on a rock." *Fine* had a very broad definition, given how she limped a little on her next step. It wasn't serious, but it still could've merited a break, had she wanted one. But if there was one thing Lara Crane never seemed to give herself, it was a break.

Not in school. Not when it came to taking care of her mom. Not when it came to her work. And not now, when all she wanted was to save her sister.

"I'm good, Wild Man," she insisted, worried I'd slowed my pace because of her.

I wanted to insist we stop for a minute, but I held back. If she needed to stop, I wanted her to trust me enough to tell me. I wanted her to let me in, and to do that, I couldn't keep her at arm's length.

For as long as I could remember, that was how I'd kept the people I loved safe. By directing their safety from a distance, keeping them far enough away so I could never be distracted by my own feelings. But with Lara, just the thought of keeping her away from me was more dangerous than any other distraction.

We walked another quarter mile, her slightly uneven pace haunting mine over the rugged terrain.

"How do you know which way to go?" It wasn't quite a request for a break, but I'd take the opening.

Slowing next to the nearest towering pine, I made sure we stood shaded from the high afternoon sun as I pulled off my pack. Sixty pounds—no more, no less—and everything we'd need to survive out here for weeks, rather than a single night or two, as was my plan.

Nature didn't care about plans and she didn't care about your survival, so planning for the worst was always the best move.

I handed her the canteen of water and then reached for my phone. There was no cell service out here, but that wasn't what the phone was for. I opened the screen to the advanced map app that showed watersheds, topographical and elevation data, and had cost a small fortune but was priceless in practice. *A shortcut,* Cassius would say, knowing he'd taught us all to memorize that data when we had access to it before a hike and how to read the landscape when we didn't.

"Here is the location of Eden's Children." I tilted my phone and pointed to the green pin that marked the coordinates I'd entered.

Having the location of the compound was only half the battle. Even with a pretty pin, it wasn't like I could just ask for walking directions through the mountains.

"High elevation. Low elevation." I indicated the different colors, yellow and green. "The compound is positioned at the end of this valley between these two ridge systems." The peaks of which were marked in yellow, the valley bordered by the low green lines. "Given the terrain, there are three viable approach routes. The first is this."

Tapping on another filter, a pale-blue haze descended on part of the map.

"This is the most obvious path from the drop point. It follows the watershed and given its relative flatness, probably the route they most commonly use, and therefore the riskiest for us to take." I flipped off the watershed filter. "The second route over the western ridge is the shortest, but not only would we be exposed and visible for miles, it would take us longer to reach the site because of the change in elevation."

"So we're going this way." She reached in front of me, her hand laying gently over mine as she traced a line from our red dot, through the deepest part of the valley, and then up to the green mark.

"A maze of deadfall and boulder fields. Not easy hiking, but shielded by the forests on each ridge and a path they'd probably consider impassable."

The forest was dense along the ridge, the trees a natural canopy that would shield us from observation and the sun. Hiking straight through the peak of the afternoon wasn't ideal, making it one more factor I'd taken into consideration when planning our route.

"What's that?" she asked when the red dot marking our location flashed purple.

"Satellite transmission. Never hike alone unless you absolutely have to." *Rule #2.* "Callum is tracking our progress. We'll make camp here." I indicated a spot in the ridge almost directly below the location of the compound. "And then I'll turn on the satellite link and Callum will send over the drone images."

"And then we'll hike to the cult?" She handed me back the water.

"One step at a time, Tomb Raider." I brought the container to my mouth, the liquid almost hitting the wrong pipe when she swiped her tongue over her bottom lip, pulling it between her teeth with worry.

I didn't take much time to think before I palmed her neck, pushed her chin up with my thumb, and covered her mouth with mine. The kiss was to quell her worry. To crimp the fuse before it ignited agitation in her mind. It wasn't because I'd been starving for a taste of her from the moment I'd left her in my bed. And it definitely wasn't because her voicemail from the hospital had opened an unwelcome can of worms in my mind.

Her sister might have been here, but the rest of her life was in Phoenix. And now wasn't the time to think about what that meant. So I kissed her like it could root her. Not to a place, but to me.

With a moan, Lara's lips parted, our tongues instantly tangling. My mind already had the topography of her mouth burned to memory. The paths to stroke her pleasure higher and the places to make it simmer low. There was one destination, but the paths to get there were as numerous as the time I wanted to take exploring them all.

I kissed her deeper. Harder. I lost myself for a moment in the ache I had for her before the caw of a hawk above reminded me where we were—*what I was doing.*

"Trust me," I murmured over her lips, not as a command but a plea.

Trust me to find her. Trust me to take care of you.

"Okay." Her eyes were still hooded, her head still angled for more, but if I gave it to her, I wouldn't be able to stop.

"We need to keep moving," I said as I pulled my head up, my gaze roaming over her upturned face one more time before I stepped back and hefted my pack back onto my shoulders. "Ready?"

"Are you?" She countered with a husky voice.

For the wilderness? "Yeah."

For her? Never.

For the successive three miles, we moved at a decent pace along the east ridge, using what shade we could. When the trees thinned into a scree field—the unstable, jagged rocks too treacherous and too exposed to cross—I led us down into the valley and along the stream.

About a mile along the bubbling water, a large Douglas fir had recently fallen across the stream, branches still protruding and sap still seeping from the destroyed bark.

"We'll cross over the trunk but I need to remove some of the branches first," I told her. Sliding my pack from my back, I unzipped the top pocket, pulled out a protein bar, and handed it to her, along with the water bottle. "Eat this and hydrate." When her brows rose, I let my voice sink low. "What is my rule?"

At the reminder, she obeyed, her cheeks stained with a blush.

Sliding my CRKT knife from its sheath on the strap of my bag, I went to work cutting through the branches all the way to the other side. When I'd finished, I turned back to find Lara hoisting herself onto the tree with my sixty pounds of gear on her back.

Dammit. I didn't even spare a second to curse out loud before jogging back across, making it to her just in time to catch her as she swayed.

"I didn't realize that was so heavy." She stared at me, wide-eyed with the realization I'd been hiking with it all this time.

"What are you doing?" I growled.

"I did what you said. I ate and drank, and then I saw you were done, so I thought I should come to you."

I gritted my teeth and grunted, making a mental note to be more specific when I needed her to stay in one spot.

"I'll take that." Sinking my hand to her waist, I used the other to grab the top handle of my pack, taking the weight from her shoulders. "Follow me. You can hold on to the pack if you need for balance."

Two minutes later, we were across the stream and on the western edge of the valley. Two and a half relatively easy miles later, we hit the hardest part of our hike—twelve-hundred feet of elevation gain across a mile-long boulder field. I mapped out the most stable path through the granite chaos and told Lara to follow my every step.

Once we'd cleared the boulder field, there was a small leveling of the terrain and an area shielded by a cluster of jack pines that provided both a windbreak and some canopy. An ideal campsite.

"Sit and finish the water." I guided Lara toward a stray boulder underneath a tree.

"That was . . . intense," Lara said after a beat, and I heard her cap the water bottle as I removed my shelter system from my pack. "How far is the compound from here?"

"Not far. About a ten-minute hike up the ridge." I pointed in the direction. "The trees should give us enough cover down here."

"Do you want help setting up the tent?"

"Not a tent." I flapped open the ten-by-eight sheet of military-grade silnylon, the top printed with a muted camouflage pattern. The material weighed less than a pound, yet had a hydrostatic head rating of 3,000mm—enough to handle anything short of a Wyoming deluge. "Tents are visual targets, make noise in wind, and restrict peripheral awareness."

"Oh" was all she replied, watching me unravel next the seventy-five-foot 550 paracord; stakes or poles left distinct marks in the soil and recognizable geometric patterns from a distance.

"How are you feeling?" I asked, approaching the tree she sat under to use as my first anchor.

"Exhausted, but fine." She moved her feet out of the way when I got close and winced. "For the most part, fine. I think Colby's shoes are breaking my feet in rather than the other way around."

"I've got a first aid kit in my bag with some bandages and salve for blisters. Give me one sec," I said and reached over her, tying the paracord around the trunk in a modified tension-less hitch—a knot that applied no direct pressure to the bark, leaving both no damage and no visible marks.

"My body isn't used to mountains," she offered as I pulled the first aid supplies from my pack, adding, when I handed them to her, "It's not used to much of anything up here."

Our eyes connected for a second before I turned away and secured the cover to two more trees around the clearing. But even that couldn't keep the questions that gnawed at me at bay.

"When does the hospital want you to come back?" I asked gruffly, masking my agitation at the thought of her leaving by setting up the groundsheet with a layer of pine boughs; the recent storms had left more than enough already sacrificed on the ground.

"I don't know." I caught her heavy sigh. "They said . . . Just because I was cleared of any wrongdoing doesn't mean they want me back. It's all politics—perception. Because Ian's father is a senator, it might be a bigger boon in the long run to let me go so there's no bad blood between him and the organization."

"That's bullshit," I muttered. "You didn't do anything wrong. You tried to save him."

"Is that Tyvek?"

I nodded, giving the sheet of house wrap a few good shakes until it laid flat over the pine boughs. "It's virtually silent when weighted, breathable enough to prevent condensation, and reflective enough to preserve body heat." *A perfect base.*

"Wow."

"Survival is different than recreational camping. Especially in situations when you don't necessarily want to be found." Returning to my pack, I pulled out my sleeping pad, a specially treated closed-cell foam mat rolled into a ball roughly the size of a cantaloupe and laid it out.

"To be honest, the longer I sit with the possibility, the more I have to wonder if I even want to go back."

"Because of what happened?" I probed gently, and when she didn't answer, I added, "No one would blame you if you didn't."

"Maybe, but I don't think it's that. I think it's . . . everything else. Or the lack of it." She swiped her tongue across her bottom lip, her downcast eyes lifting to mine. "The longer I'm away, the harder it feels to explain even to myself why I stayed there. I mean, I loved Sunrise. I love the people I work with, but that's all I have there. Work. And even when I had the opportunity to create more, I didn't."

My throat went tight, crowded with all the things I wanted to say and all the reasons I shouldn't. I wanted to be let into her life—I didn't want to be responsible for changing the course of it.

"My mom was responsible for teaching us about gardening. About plants and herbs. What was safe to eat and what wasn't. How to grow year-round," I said, pulling out my weapon and satellite phone from my pack and then moving in front of Lara. "She always told us that what we watered would grow. Didn't occur to me she wasn't talking just about plants until I was having to explain it to Creighton and Colby."

Crouching, I gently lifted one foot and then the other, examining her handiwork on the bandages around her ankles and toes. *Like she wasn't a doctor.* I looked up and found her eyes and started to tip forward. Maybe it was natural the way I wanted her in moments without reason. Natural the way gravity doesn't give you a choice before pulling you in.

"Calder . . ." She exhaled softly.

And then the sat phone vibrated.

Callum.

Chapter 30

LARA

Guilt pierced my chest over the fact that it took a single, significant second after his phone buzzed for the need to find Rachel to surmount the brutal ache I had for the man in front of me. The one who'd cut a precise path through the mountains, stitched our way through a forest of trees, and led us across a stream with the expertise of a surgeon. All I wanted was to spend time with him, but now, like then, the need to protect my sister surpassed everything.

While Calder went to his phone, I quickly slipped my socks and Colby's hiking boots back on, ignoring the protest of my aching feet.

"Is it the photos?" I asked and went to stand next to him, my front pressed to his side.

He tilted the Garmin sat phone so I could see the screen and what waited on the ridge above us.

"Here is their main entrance." Calder pointed to two small squares and a thin line of gate connecting them. Outside the gates were several parked vehicles. Two trucks and two four-wheelers. Panning and zooming to a different spot, he added, "It looks like the whole thing is encircled by a wooden perimeter fence except for this side, where we're coming from."

Because they thought the access we'd taken would be too involved for anyone to attempt.

Anyone except Calder Stone.

"These are probably living quarters for higher-ranking members. The smallest buildings usually are." Six square structures lined the un-fenced edge of the compound, one larger than the rest. The camera caught the glare off their solar panels. "The biggest building is usually communal space for meetings, dining, and administrative." He zoomed in on the building with the largest rectangular footprint, making it easier to see that it was a large A-frame.

"That looks like a greenhouse." I pointed to the white-capped structure in the corner, and Calder nodded. "Where do you think they're keeping Rachel?"

"Probably one of these buildings." He panned over to the farthest side of the compound, where there were two more buildings of medium size. "Once the sun starts to set, he'll send the drone for a closer sweep."

I felt the urge to take the lead and insist we should go investigate now. I felt it and I swallowed it, asking instead, "What's our plan?"

Calder shut off the phone and turned to me, his eyes glittering in the low-hanging sun. "I know you want to storm the gates, Tomb Raider, but I promised I'd find your sister. I promised you I'd get her out of this safely, and that's what I'm going to do, but we have to do it my way."

"I know," I murmured, feeling his knuckles catch under my chin and something even stronger catch in my chest.

Even though my anxious heart wanted something different, I'd always been on Calder's side of this argument. Calm and careful when it came to my patients. Now I stood on the other side of the proverbial hospital bed. Now I was the loved one who wanted to rashly swoop in like loving my sister was enough to mitigate every risk of acting irrationally.

"The sun starts to set in a little over an hour. We have to be back here before then, so I can get a fire going before dark. Dusk will mask the smoke and not highlight the flame." He picked up his weapon and clipped it at the small of his back. "We'll hike up to the edge of the compound and get a lay of the land. What buildings are what. Who is where. Any kind of idea of what happens in the span of a day." He paused. "Surveillance. Knowing Rachel's location is only half the battle—a losing half, if we can't get to her and get her out of there safely."

Again, I felt the instinct to insist on a plan of my own—to search every building under the cover of night until we found my sister and got her out of there. And the urge softened. Settled. *Soothed.*

"Do you think they're . . . armed?"

Calder frowned. "Even their wilderness retreat came with armed guards."

My stomach rolled into a knot.

Even bandaged, my blisters protested for every step. But I'd long ago perfected the art of ignoring my own needs—food, sleep, a bathroom break—when it came to saving someone's life. A determination that only deepened when that someone was Rachel.

Calder paused on the slope ahead of me, crouching and bringing his head closer to mine. "Stay silent and stay behind me. If I tell you to stay put, you stay. If I tell you to run, you go back to the camp, you grab the sat phone, you find a hiding place beyond the boulder field, and you call Callum. His is the only number saved. Understand?"

Collected, commanding Calder was back.

"Yeah," I murmured, something twisting tighter in my chest as he looked at me.

And then his arm snaked out and he hauled my mouth to his in a hard kiss. Lips and tongues combusted for a single second, the explosion of a supernova before he yanked away.

"Promise me," he said, his tone ragged like it was the first time he'd trekked over those words. *The first time he'd encountered a scenario where there was more that he cared about at risk.*

"I promise." The twist between my ribs loosened, and we started up the last few yards of the climb.

If I wasn't convinced this place would end up on a Netflix cult documentary one day, I could've admired the way the Eden's Children compound was built. The log cabin structures. The solar power. The cistern for water. An entire self-sufficient community left to its own devices.

When we reached the edge of the ridge, a thicket of trees allowed us to safely peer into the compound. I followed Calder's lead, staying flat to the ground as we observed a man in dark-green scrubs enter the larger cabin to our left. From our vantage point between the two cabins, we watched a group of three women pass through the center of the compound. My heart immediately rocketed into my throat, thinking one of them was Rachel. It wasn't.

After a few minutes of little activity, Calder motioned and we moved around the perimeter. Keeping low, we were bathed mostly in shadow all the way to the end of the six larger cabins. Beyond them, we had a wide view into the center of the compound.

Two more men in green carried a large wooden podium and set it up in the middle of the grassy space. Behind them, two women in the same blue-gray Wilderness Within uniforms began arranging cushions into orderly rows, and I immediately thought of Rachel putting on those clothes. Going to the retreat to find herself, and instead being manipulated into someone else's twisted fantasy.

A bell chimed from the large A-frame to our right—the same sound Dr. Julia played through our tent's speakers. Calder and I looked at each other, having the same thought. *Was Eden's Children kept to the same schedule we'd been on at the retreat?*

Moments later, the doors of the big building opened and two dozen women filed out, some smiling and laughing together. Others silent, looking to each other nervously. All in the same uniform. I squinted and looked for my sister. Even at a distance I'd see her. I'd know her. And she wasn't there.

The group went to the lawn and filed into rows, taking a seat on their knees and resting their hands on the tops of their thighs. It was a little thing, but it made my stomach turn.

Breathe, Lara.

Men in green exited from the cabins and headed toward the gathering. Everyone on the compound appeared to be congregating in the center of it, and all I could think of was Dr. Julia's evening meditations.

I jerked when Calder touched my elbow. He tilted his head toward the A-frame: *Time to move.*

We slipped behind the large building, pressed against its back. Behind the A-frame was a greenhouse, a row of composting toilets, and two large rainwater cisterns.

We crept from the A-frame to the next building. On our right, an eight-foot wooden fence, the ends sharpened and threatening. On our left, the windowless building, a boon now but a worry for later.

Calder slowed and peered around the corner. After a beat, he crooked his finger for me to look. From here, we could see almost everything: the metal entrance gate to our far right, the cabins encircling the center, the A-frame's front with a massive sign above the door, EDEN carved into it.

In the center of the lawn, all the women were seated, the six men in green forming a row behind them. And then a man stepped onto the podium. He had longer, wavy hair, a classically handsome face with a straight nose, hard cheekbones, and a wide smile for his crowd. He was one of those men who sat comfortably in the category of *Aged Well.* Wearing all-white scrubs, he stood apart from everyone else, leaving no doubt to who he was. *Adam Eden.*

Tension rippled through Calder as the cult leader started to speak. "Good evening, my beautiful children. Another day, another courageous step toward your authentic nature. We bring the day to a close the way we always do, with a gentle reflection on why we are all here and our purpose."

While I listened, Calder's attention shaded in the details of the compound. The buildings. The people. *The threats.*

"Look around you. Feel the energy in this sacred space. This isn't like the world you left behind. Out there, they sold you the greatest lie: that your feminine essence is a weakness to overcome. But the truth—the truth is that essence is power. A primal power. Passionate power. A power that we are here to cultivate. To nurture and grow. Society fears this power. That's why they've convinced you to suppress it. They've taught you shame. They've taught you to distrust your instincts. They've convinced you that your greatest gift—your feminine energy—is somehow a liability. Here, we strip away those lies." Eden stepped down from the podium then and began to walk through the rows of women, many of them—too many—looking up at him with adoring eyes.

My jaw couldn't have fallen farther as I watched the women eat up his words like they were forbidden fruit. He touched the faces of some. Bent to kiss the heads of others . . . And they were enrapt by him. Too worshipful to see the way he looked at them—like they were a buffet he'd created for no one but himself.

"This journey isn't easy. Your conditioning runs deep. Your ego will fight to maintain its illusions of control. It will tell you not to trust your wild core. To not trust the men who are here to strengthen your gifts. Some days, you'll want to retreat back to the comfortable prison of societal expectations. But I make you this promise: Trust this process. Surrender to me, and let me nurture your wild core, and in just three months, you'll experience a level of adoration, abundance, and authentic power that most women will never know in their lifetimes."

Calder squeezed my elbow again. I turned as the metal gate opened, and Dr. Julia walked through it, followed by Matthew. Both of them looked on edge. My head whipped back to the cult leader. As soon as he saw Dr. Julia, his hand fell away from the woman he'd been admiring in front of him and he calmly strode back to the podium.

"Our evening meditation ends here. Now it's time to go back to your rooms and reflect on your journey. On your desires. On your wild core."

Calder nudged me again. *Time to go.* We quickly backtracked along the same path toward the cabins.

"Those who will have the ritual of release tonight will find your doors marked and instructions on your bed."

I pressed my fist to my mouth, trying to swallow the urge to vomit. Calder must've sensed it, because as soon as we reached the cloak of trees where we'd entered the compound, he hauled me to his chest, holding me as I shook. With anger. With rage. With fear. With pain.

"I've got you," Calder said, so quietly he could've actually just mouthed it next to my ear.

Closing my eyes, I nodded into his chest, knowing we had to go.

Calder didn't get a chance to pull away before determined footsteps invaded the quiet around us. His arms tightened, only allowing me to turn my head and watch.

Dr. Julia entered the small clearing between the last two cabins. She looked completely different from the picture of serenity who had greeted us at the retreat.

Moments later, Adam Eden joined her. "You need to calm down, Julia. We're safe here, my darling wife—"

Wife? Calder and I shared a look.

"Safe? What if they find him? What if that couple or Sarah sends people after us? This is your fault," Dr. Julia returned, twisting her hair in her hands as she paced in front of him. "You were the one who wanted more when I told you it was too soon. You always want more, James—"

James! Calder's chest swallowed my gasp and dampened the detonation of my pulse. *Had James Braun become Adam Eden?*

I looked to Calder for confirmation that I hadn't imagined her slip, but his gaze didn't stray from the other couple. In fact, he hadn't moved a single muscle, shown any reaction to the information at all.

"I'm sorry. I'm sorry, Adam," Dr. Julia quickly said, her voice hushed and distinctly trembling.

"Did you do this on purpose?" Adam demanded, stepping into her path.

Dr. Julia's hand slapped to her chest. "On purpose—"

"You know this is how the wildness works." He clasped her face, not waiting for her to finish. "You don't have to be jealous of them. Just like I don't have to be jealous of Matthew—"

"Matthew and I aren't—"

"It's okay, Julia." Again, he didn't bother to hear her out. "He's yours to have. All of them are. He can have you and I can watch . . ."

Clearly, there had been a time when that arrangement would've interested her, but now she turned her head away from him, seeming weary at the thought.

"I don't think we should stay here, Adam. I think we need to leave."

"Shh." He pressed a kiss to her forehead. "We're safe here. Protected. We don't need to run anymore."

"Adam—"

"Why don't you go rest, darling." He slid his hands to her shoulders, gently massaging them. "It's been a stressful few days. Frustrating. And you've done so well. Been so strong. You deserve time to rest."

She looked up at him. "Adam, I want you with me tonight."

I felt the smallest twinge of guilt, intruding on what was clearly a private moment between them. But it was only for a second, and then he spoke, and guilt was replaced with something else.

"Of course." He nodded and smiled, and for a second, she looked impossibly relieved. Right up until he said, "I'll be with you when I'm finished with Brielle."

My head snapped up, my gaze finding Calder's hardened stare. I knew what he was thinking. Brielle was young. Too young. *And where was she?* I hadn't seen her in the group.

"I'm your wife, *Adam.*" His name came out almost like an accusation.

"You are my Lilith, and they are my Eves," he corrected. Was the biblical reference meant as a comfort or as a threat? An assurance that she was the first and most important, or a warning that he could banish her from the Garden if she didn't obey? "You know this is how my garden works, my love. I will come to you when I'm finished, and then tomorrow I will have them worship you. Whichever of them you want to join us, you'll have your pick."

Her silence didn't deter him. I doubted much of anything deterred a narcissist.

"Maybe Tara. I know she worked well with us before. She's been very . . . eager to please me while you've been at the retreat." Bile rose in my throat, and it was only Calder's hand that suddenly gripped mine that stopped me from vomiting when he added, "Or what about Rachel? She's been very . . . timid during her initiation, even when I have her watch me with the others. Normally, that opens them up; it certainly did for Brielle, but everyone is different during initiation. Some flowers take longer to bloom." He hummed. "Maybe she needs your feminine touch to awaken her wild core again. I know how much you enjoy cultivating the troubled ones."

I squeezed my eyes shut, feeling like I was sitting in the front row to my sister's very own nightmare.

"That's it. I'll have Rachel brought to us after morning meditation, and we will both worship you." Adam cupped her face and kissed her forehead, the gesture sickening. "Now, go back to our temple and rest. I'll be there soon."

Adam left, heading across the compound. The minimal lights on the buildings made the white of his scrubs glow. Had he picked white because it made him feel like a doctor? Like he was actually sexually healing these women by manipulating them? Or had he picked white to seem more like God?

Probably both.

All I saw was the reflection of his narcissism in the pristine facade of his abuse. Passing off cheating on his wife like it was a benefit to her.

Roping her into his sexual fantasies as though they were choreographed for her pleasure.

Relationships, whether with one partner or multiple, only worked when there was a foundation of trust. It was obvious Dr. Julia's trust in her husband had loosened. Meanwhile, Adam Eden was twisting its slack around her neck.

Calder kept still—and kept me still—waiting for Dr. Julia to leave, but instead, her head turned as Matthew appeared from the shadows, his voice haunting.

"You deserve better, Julia."

"Don't start with me, Matthew," she begged, more tired than anything. "Not tonight."

"Tell me what I can do."

"Just find him, Matthew. Just find him," she asked and then turned and walked away.

Who was "him"?

Calder released me, and I looked up at him in horror. By now, they had to have realized we'd given them fake names and hadn't left our IDs in our locker. *Were they looking for us? Was she talking about Calder?*

The question—like so many others—plagued me during the silent trek back to our campsite.

Chapter 31

Lara

"Adam Eden is James Braun," Calder said without skipping a beat as soon as we were back at our campsite.

"I can't believe it," I murmured, taking the fresh pouch of water and a protein bar he offered me; there were no Michelin stars out here, only a growing galaxy of real ones. "I thought maybe I misheard her . . ."

"You didn't," he grunted. "I recognized him from the picture Callum found of Braun from his law firm. Older now. Longer hair. But the same person, no question."

That was why he'd flinched when Eden appeared . . . and not when Dr. Julia called him James.

As much of a revelation as it was, it paled in comparison to hearing them talk about my sister.

"She's here," I murmured, almost in a daze, watching him finish a message on his phone; I assumed to Callum, confirming that Braun and Eden were the same.

My tongue turned to lead, and dread coiled like a snake about to strike in my stomach. *Rachel was here. We'd found her.*

What had they done?

"I just can't believe . . ." That was it. That was the whole statement. I couldn't believe. It was somehow exactly what I'd been expecting but nothing I could've prepared for. *Like watching Ian flatline.* "We can't—I can't let them—" I broke off, tearing at the laces on my boots. My stomach turned as I recalled what he'd said about her, about them.

"I know," came Calder's low reply as he crouched in front of me, framing his hands on the sides of my knees. "We won't."

Even his promise couldn't loosen the grip of fear around my throat.

"What are we going to do?" I heard myself whisper. I wasn't just ceding to his direction anymore—I was begging for it.

"We're going to get Rachel out of there," he said. "But first, you're going to eat."

I was too . . . too many things to feel hungry. Even the bar in my hand looked like more than I could stomach, but I opened it and began to eat anyway.

Satisfied that I wasn't going to stress-starve myself, Calder returned to his meticulous process of creating our campfire. Three strikes of his flint on the pile of deadwood and a flame ebbed to life.

"Do you think they're holding her in that building without the windows?"

"No. That was for food and storage. There were additional units for climate control on the back of the building," he replied.

My mouth rounded, drawing his brief but hot attention. "Where do you think she is? How are we going to find her before tomorrow?"

I'd been too focused on the group on the lawn—looking for Rachel and then watching the horror show of that man manipulating all those women—to look at anything else.

Sliding open his phone, Calder pulled up the aerial image again and zoomed in. "Here's where we were. I think Rachel is in this building." He held it in front of me and pointed to the building right behind the one we'd stopped at. "I think that's where all the women stay."

"So why wasn't she out there with the rest of the group? And I didn't see Brielle, either."

"They probably keep the new arrivals, the ones going through *initiation*, separated from the rest of the women. They'd want to make sure they're adequately indoctrinated before letting them absorb into the larger group."

My stomach turned again, and I almost gagged. "So how do we get to her?" I forced the question out.

Calder panned again on the image, brow furrowing in thought. Hearing the crinkle of the empty protein bar wrapper in my fist, he immediately set his phone to the side and took the garbage from my hand and stuffed it into his pack.

"It's too risky to get to her where she's staying. Even if I could map out a path, without observing the patrol of the guards to know for sure where they are going to be, it's not . . . ideal."

"Calder—"

"The men are armed, Lara," he interrupted, his eyes darkening. "Not all of them. I saw three at the gathering with weapons. I'm assuming they rotate between security and—" He caught himself. Not that it mattered.

"Between security and the women," I finished thickly.

Calder grimaced but nodded.

"So what is your plan?" I asked, my voice hardly more than a sound, the answer screaming through my bones.

"I want to wait until they bring her to Eden's cabin. Then she'll be separated and alone while the rest of them are at the morning meditation."

My breath seesawed in and out of my lungs. He had good rationale for his plan, but I hated the idea that the safest place to rescue Rachel from was the middle of the lions' den.

"It's the only time the rest of them, including security, are in one place. They'll bring her to his cabin and head to the lawn. His cabin is more secluded than the rest, so it should be straightforward to slip in and get her. Even if Eden only talks for fifteen minutes, that should be plenty of time," he said, and his jaw flexed so hard, it was a miracle it didn't crack.

The fire popped, and Calder straightened and went to tend to the flame, but even then, his shoulders didn't relax.

"What is it?" I rose and went to him. When I placed my hand on his arm, his muscles quaked. "What are you worried about?"

Chin lowered, Calder looked at me, his expression taut. "You."

"What? I'll be fine," I lied through my teeth; I couldn't make that kind of promise, no matter how much I wanted to. "I'll do whatever you tell me, but if it's as easy as you say—"

"I'm not worried about you getting in, Lara. I'm worried about what happens once you're there."

"I don't understand."

"You saw them, Lara. None of those women are being held against their will. There are more of them than guards. They weren't handcuffed or under duress—"

"No, they were brainwashed," I countered, prickly. "And probably drugged."

"And I want you to be prepared that Rachel might be, too." His words were harsh, but they needed to be. Like alcohol on an open wound, the idea burned into my brain. I knew I was saving her, but what if she didn't? *What if I went into that cabin tomorrow and instead met a woman who didn't want to leave?*

I tensed. I'd considered a lot of things in the last twenty-four hours, but somehow I hadn't considered this. That when we found her, she might not want to be rescued.

I echoed a sentiment we'd shared before. "I'll do whatever I have to to keep her safe . . . even if she hates me for it."

I hadn't realized my chin had drifted down until his fingers came to rest underneath it. "I hope it doesn't come to that."

"Me, too." My head angled, searching for his mouth. For his steadiness and his savagery. For the way that, for those brief moments when we were together, it was only my own desires at the front of my mind, and it was with a man who made me feel safe enough to be taken care of.

But instead of kissing me, Calder let out a deep groan and drew back. "You should get some sleep," he said gruffly, turning back to the fire. "I'm going to wait and make sure the fire goes out."

My feet refused. And my body. *And my heart.*

"Calder." He turned, and I saw it again—*that guilt he'd mentioned but hadn't explained.* "What did you mean when you said Rachel wasn't the only guilty one in your relationship?"

He jerked like I'd struck a nerve, and I knew exactly what that looked like.

"We both made mistakes, that's all."

"Everybody makes mistakes, Calder. Doing the wrong thing isn't the same as thinking you haven't done enough."

His hand balled at his side. "I don't want you to have to carry this."

"Calder." I took his big hand in both of mine, disbelief pummeling my chest. "Stop being bad at letting me in."

He hung his head, the angle of his jaw hardening, a picture of perfect torture. "I meant what I said. I've meant everything I said, Lara." I blinked and his hands cupped my cheeks, his head held above mine, and his eyes pooling into dark orbs. "All it took was one look. One look and I wanted you in a way I'd never felt for your sister."

Oh god. All the oxygen evacuated from my lungs.

He tried to turn away, and I reached for his face.

"Calder . . ." My palm to his cheek, I turned him to look at me.

"I thought it was a fluke. An anomaly. I wasn't going to make a rash decision on an anomaly, especially when I wasn't an expert at relationships. I wanted you, and I thought it would pass; I thought it did pass when we didn't see you much. But then every time . . ." His massive body shuddered. "Every time it was like being hit with the same drug over and over again. And then the same withdrawal."

My lips peeled apart. "You wanted me?"

"I was drawn to you. *Wanting* implies I had a choice." His thumb notched in my chin as firmly as his words sank into my heart. "But I'm not—I would never disrespect your sister. Things weren't working for a dozen other reasons, but I don't doubt my own distance and turmoil was what drove her to Allen."

"You knew?"

When his chin lowered, my heart broke to hear that he'd known Rachel was cheating on him. Even I hadn't known. I knew there were times she'd lied about where she was . . . lied that she was with me. Maybe I was naive, but I'd had no idea it was because she was seeing someone else.

"I'm sorry."

"There's nothing to be sorry for, Lara. Knowing was only confirmation that I should've ended things sooner." He sighed deeply. "Maybe if I understood sooner how I felt, things wouldn't have gone the way they did."

"You can't blame yourself that she got involved with him."

"I wanted you the way I should've wanted her, and even if I didn't say it, I'd be a fool to tell myself it didn't have an effect." A harsh breath blew through his lips. "When I told Rachel I wanted to break up, it was a sigh of relief for both of us. We both knew things weren't working, but I still cared about her. Enough to decide there was no good to come from telling her how I felt about you. Honestly, I didn't even know how I felt about you. I just knew I felt something I couldn't shake. So we parted as friends with our own secrets; she had Allen, and I had you."

"Please don't say you feel guilty for not telling her, Calder. It wouldn't have done any good," I blurted out. "You were her first call. In spite of everything, she still turned to you." *Instead of me.*

His mouth drew tight. "But after she learned there was no baby, that changed."

"How?" I swayed toward him.

"I tried to console her. To be there for her. I told her you would be there for her, too, but it wasn't enough."

"I don't understand."

"She wanted us to get back together, Lara," Calder said hoarsely, his eyes snapping to mine. "She begged me in the parking lot of the hospital as she sobbed in my arms. She was so attached to that baby, to the idea of having a family . . . I don't . . . I tried to calm her. To tell her she would have plenty of support. Plenty of people who'd help and be there for her. That she'd find someone else. That this wasn't the end of her chances to have a baby."

Oh, Rachel.

"She wouldn't . . . accept it." His throat bobbed. "She started blaming herself for why we ended, saying it was because she was nervous about commitment and that Allen had been fun and easy but a mistake, and she knew that now. And all she wanted was a baby and a family and someone who'd care for her the way I had. But it was when she kept apologizing . . . wanting to take responsibility for something that wasn't her fault. I couldn't . . ."

My heart stilled to slow, heavy beats that pushed my next words out. "So you told her the truth."

The quake and ripple of his body, the heaviness of his breath—it all gave me the answer.

"I didn't know what else to do except be honest." His throat worked to try to swallow. "I wanted her to stop blaming herself. I wanted her to just breathe for a damn minute and realize what she was asking for from me wasn't what she wanted, either—wasn't what she deserved.

"She deserved someone who felt for her what I felt for you. Who ached to be near her the way I ached to be near you. Someone who knew after only minutes around her that his life was changed. That something had changed in him. I hoped—" He blew out a breath. "It doesn't matter what I hoped. What happened was, I made it worse. The only thing she wanted from me after that was for me to find someone else to take her back to campus because she never wanted to see me again." His jaw pulsed. "So I called Cassius to give her a ride."

I didn't know my heart could break in so many places. For my sister. For Calder. For everything that could've been . . . and wasn't.

"How do we not feel guilty when our best for someone wasn't enough?" I asked because I didn't have an answer. I still carried the weight of the man who'd died in my emergency room despite every attempt to save him.

Now it made sense why Rachel had never wanted to talk about him. Why she'd let me think Calder was the reason for how everything turned out . . . or maybe why she was too hurt to correct my assumption.

"I wanted you then, too, Calder," I confessed, needing him to know. "More than admiring your anatomy. My crush on you was like a contagion. Something that altered my DNA. A bar that was set by a man I couldn't have."

"When you kept your distance, I assumed Rachel told you everything, and you wanted nothing to do with me."

How different things might've been if she had.

"Is that why you never said anything to me?" I asked, spreading my hands over his chest.

His gaze dimmed. "No." His voice dipped lower. "I didn't say anything because I didn't know what to say. I didn't know what I felt, but I was afraid—" He broke off and swallowed hard. "I was afraid whatever it was, could be what Mom and Cassius had. And even then, even five years later, he was hollow. Even now . . ."

Right then, I knew the most traumatic thing about his mother's murder hadn't been finding her body or thinking he could've saved her, it was all of that in the context of watching Cassius's grief consume him.

"I didn't water what I felt because I was afraid of what would grow."

My fingers curled over the thud of his pulse like I could hold his heart in my hand and take the pain away.

"And now?"

He let out a harsh breath. "Now I want you too much to be afraid of anything except not having you." He slid his finger along my cheek. "And what about you? Do you feel guilty for wanting me now?"

"Maybe I take too much responsibility for my sister and for what's happened to her, but I also take responsibility for my feelings. I've never felt guilty for wanting you. Not then, in secret. And not now, out loud."

His nose brushed mine, and a low sound rumbled from his chest. A weight relaxing. "How loud?"

The coarse texture of his voice coaxed a hot shiver up my spine. "Fuck me, Calder, and find out."

Chapter 32

Calder

Rule #40: The person you love becomes a potential weapon against you in the wrong hands. Protect them by keeping some secrets, even from them.

Smoke and sweetness filled my nostrils. The last embers of the fire were out, but a whole different flame had ignited.

"Fuck me, Calder, and find out."

Tipping her head, I kissed her the way I always had. I kissed her like a man who'd started dreaming of her a dozen years ago and never stopped.

Back then, the timing wasn't right. Not with her sister. Not with my mom's death. What I felt—what we felt—was nothing more than a seed that had been planted and gone into dormancy, waiting for the right time to bloom.

Now, it more than bloomed.

I groaned as Lara's arms slid around my neck, pressing herself to me like the last thing separating us was finally gone.

Tonight, there was no storm but us. No rain except the drench of desire in our blood. No lightning but the white-hot heat of every touch. No thunder except the booming inside my chest.

The harder I kissed her, the louder she moaned. Wordless pleas escaped her throat as her hands started to roam over me. My shoulders. My sides. My waist.

"Fuck, Lara," I hissed as her palm sank straight to the front of my pants, cupping the heavy weight of my cock through the fabric.

"I want to taste you," she said, dragging her mouth along my neck until her lips landed on my jaw muscle. "I want to feel you go wild in my mouth."

I groaned, helpless as she worked open my pants. A second later, her hand was sliding along my bare length and cupping my balls. I'd barely reeled the stars in my vision back into orbit before she dropped to her knees in front of me.

I met her upturned eyes, losing my mind at the sight of her blown-out pupils, flushed cheeks, and swollen lips.

Reaching down, I cupped her cheek. "Open wide."

Her jaw dropped.

Fisting my girth, I guided myself through her lips, and she closed them like a fucking Venus flytrap, sucking me deeper.

My eyes rolled into my head, pleasure shooting like a rocket down to the base of my spine. She shouldn't have been on her knees. Not on the rocky ground. Not after a full day of hiking. Not tonight.

But I was only a man. I was only a man with the most beautiful woman I'd ever known choking on the length of my dick. Threading my fingers through her hair, I palmed the back of her head and started to thrust.

In and out. Deeper. And deeper.

"God, you're so fucking perfect," I cooed, watching my wet cock stretch and disappear into her mouth.

I listened for her stunted breaths, her sputters over the drying crackle of embers. I felt the pulse along the back of her throat every time I hit it.

Without instruction, Lara angled her head. She knew the anatomy. She knew exactly how to take me deeper. And she fucking did it. Pleasure wrapped a hard fist around the base of my spine, tightening and tightening—

"Fuck," I grunted and jerked out of her mouth.

Before she could protest, I hauled her into my arms, lifting her under her knees.

"Don't you dare take me to the tent," she murmured, her lips red and swollen from stretching around my length.

My dick pulsed, and I growled, "Not a tent." Spinning, I set her down in front of the boulder she'd sat on earlier today.

I kept her facing me only long enough to undo the front of her pants. They got to stay intact because they were the only ones she had.

"Lay down," I ordered and turned her toward the large rock, making sure she laid herself carefully onto the surface, which was still warm from the fire. "Let's see how wet you are, Tomb Raider. How wild you want me."

Grabbing a fistful of the waist of her pants, I had them and her underwear down at her ankles in one firm tug. Dropping to my knees, I eyed her swollen folds, her seam slick and dripping in the moonlight.

"God, you kill me with this." I pressed one finger in deep, and as soon as I heard the catch of her breath, I yanked it out and covered her with my mouth.

On my knees, I tongued her pussy until she whimpered and thrashed and bucked against the rock. Until she soaked my lips and chin and her desire started to run down the rock she lay on.

Until she begged for me like she hadn't just waited twelve years for me, but waited twelve years to come, too.

She tried to reach for me, and with one hand, I grabbed both her wrists and pinned them to her lower back.

"Fuck, Lara," I growled, sucking her clit as my cock started to weep.

She was perfect. So fucking perfect.

"Please, Calder," she cried, trembling.

"Not yet." I pulled her clit between my lips and sucked hard, hearing her choked breaths as soon as I released the pressure. "You promised me loud. I want to hear you come loud, and then you can take my cock."

If I'd survive long enough.

Even now, I reached for my throbbing length, jerking it hard in my hand because I needed some relief.

"Yes, Calder . . ." she moaned, pushing back against my mouth.

I pushed my tongue through her seam, tasting inside her, and then found her swollen clit again. Sucking hard, I listened for her gasp. Her cry. And then I thrashed the aching bud with my tongue, sending her flying over the edge.

Her scream echoed all the way to the bottom of the ridge—utterly animalistic to anyone and anything that heard it—and the sweet rush of her orgasm flooded my lips.

With a roar, I shot to my feet, my fist continuing to pump my thick cock right up until I fed the fat tip into her entrance. Pure pleasure seared through me as I tunneled into her release. Blinding. Suffocating. The feel of her contracting around my cock the most wild, incredible thing I'd ever felt—I'd ever let myself feel.

"Fuck, that's it, Lara. Let me in," I growled, burying into her clenching muscles.

It was hard to concentrate on anything except the squeeze of her tight, wet, hot pussy. Hard to concentrate on anything except the most destructive pleasure I'd ever known, ripping and thrashing its way through me. But even as my own orgasm clawed at the inside of my stomach, I managed to focus on her. The trembling of her limbs, the bucking of her hips. The way her arms thrashed against my grip, but I wouldn't release her.

"You wanted me like this. Wild and fucking you," I bit out roughly. I wouldn't let her run from the pleasure that was coming.

"Please . . ." she panted breathlessly.

I knew every thrust brushed her throbbing clit against the rough rock face. Every pulse brushed me against her G-spot. Her incoherent cries spilled like a landslide from her lips, begging for something she couldn't put words to.

"And I want you like this. Trembling and writhing because you don't think you can take more of me." I forced the words out, feeling every contraction, every wet, hot wring of her body milking me. "I want you like this, knowing I'll always take care of you."

Almost instantly, she went over the edge into another climax. I pinned her to the boulder and fucked her as she split and shattered around me.

She screamed, a sound of pure anguish and ache, and came again from the invasion of my cock. Her rippling muscles spasmed tighter, the waves of pleasure rendering her limbless under me.

Lara sagged against the rock, her legs giving way and impaling me even deeper inside her. A place that made me see stars and that made her—

"Fuck." I released her limp arms and grabbed her hips, and I lost it.

My grip tightened and angled her higher for me. The only instinct I had now was primal. A mindless, wild urge to fuck her until we left marks in the stone, just as indelibly as she'd left a mark on me.

"Fuck, Lara," I chanted, driving into the soaking wet depths of her, my hips smacking against her ass with each thrust. Once. Twice.

Head tipped back, my groan rocketed into the night sky as I came. Pulse after wet, hot pulse, I filled her until there was nothing left of me, either. Nothing except the way I wanted her. The way I—

Carefully, I slid out of her. Peeling her jelly limbs off the rock, she whimpered and sagged against me. I carried her under the shelter and cleaned us both before making sure she was settled under the blanket. I checked once more to make sure the fire had gone out and then slid onto the bed beside her, pulling her to my chest.

"I've got you," I murmured against her hair, listening to the soft sound of her sleeping breaths in return.

I couldn't take her pain or her worries or her weights from her, and I wouldn't want to. For all the same reasons I wouldn't let Colby beat me on our climbs. We don't learn to survive in life by being spared its hardships. But I would hold her while she held them. Protect her while she fought her fears and soothe her while her worries cast her adrift.

I had one last confession for her. This time, I wasn't going to wait twelve years to tell her how I felt, but I was going to wait until we found her sister. Until no other emotion or situation could make her question my love for her.

Chapter 33

Lara

"Damn."

I lifted my head, pausing mid-tie on my left boot. "What is it?"

Calder stared intently at the sat phone, the hard lines of his face sharpening. I rose and went to him, careful of my loose lace.

"Calder—"

"Callum got a hold of the private investigator hired by Hannah's parents. Apparently, he found two other women who were in relationships with Braun that transformed into a threesome with Maxwell. They said he was very controlling, though not usually violent. Things ended when he wanted them to move to Wyoming with him on a property he'd just purchased."

Eden's Children. I banded my arms. "Why didn't they come forward?"

"There was nothing to accuse him of. The relationships were consensual."

"So he started targeting Dr. Julia's clients." *Women who were more vulnerable and easier prey to his coercion.*

"Hannah's boyfriend, Jack, told the PI that he thought Braun might have letters Hannah wrote to him. Before he could find any proof of what happened, Maxwell and Braun disappeared."

"I wonder if they wanted Hannah to come out here with them and she refused."

I could only imagine what it would be like for someone yearning for attention, to receive it from a man who captivated like Braun—like *Eden* had captivated his crowd yesterday, only for him to take that twisted love away. Or threaten to if she wouldn't leave.

I forced myself to keep breathing, focusing on tying my boot and not giving in to the urge to vomit.

All I wanted was to get back up there and get my sister. When I rose, Calder was right in front of me.

"What's the rule out here?" he murmured, taking my face between his palms.

"Obey."

He started to pull away, and then, like he couldn't help himself, his mouth came down on mine, warm and possessive, like the dawn reclaiming what had previously belonged to the night.

It was more than an ache for him that I felt that morning. It was an ache for us. For what came after this was all over. An ache for something that was wholly my own.

"Let's go." And then he was striding around our shelter like if he didn't walk away now, he wouldn't be able to.

Familiarity and adrenaline made the climb to the compound quicker, and before I knew it, we were at the edge of the trees. Calder looked at me, waiting for my ready. I nodded and he rose from his crouched position and headed along the wooded canopy until he reached the third cabin down where he'd be able to see the center of the compound.

He moved from the trees with the stealth of a panther, prowling to the back of the structure and flattening himself to it. My breath stuck in my lungs as he drew his weapon from the holster at his back, keeping it pointed at the ground as he peered around the corner and then turned back to me, giving me the go.

Heart thudding like cannon fire into my chest, I darted for the door to the cabin. Even though it wasn't visible from the congregation area, the door was still exposed to the interior of the compound. If anyone wasn't at the morning congregation . . . was walking around . . . but there was no one to see me. Calder made sure of that.

My hand was slick as I grabbed the doorknob, flinging it open like I'd expected it to be barricaded, the ease of its movement tempering my hope.

No one was being held prisoner or by force. They were here because they actually believed him.

I froze as soon as I saw my sister perched on the edge of the massive bed, her knuckles white where they gripped the blankets.

"Rachel." I forced myself to breathe deep, the scent of baby oil clogging my nostrils.

Disbelief and confusion warred over her face.

"Lara?" Her dilated pupils took a second to focus on me, and I quelled the fresh burst of rage. *She was drugged.* "What are you doing here?" She stood suddenly—too suddenly—and started to sway.

Forgetting the open door, I went to her and grabbed her shoulders, and she stared at me like I'd just become real. "Lara." She cupped her hand over her mouth, and a sob broke from her chest.

"It's me. I'm here." I pulled her into my arms, holding her tight. "I came for you. I came to bring you home." The words felt thick in my throat.

"I'm sorry," she croaked into my chest. "I'm s-so sorry."

"Don't apologize. This isn't your fault. Not at all." I scraped through her hair to draw her head back. "None of this is your fault."

She stared at me, her lip quivering. "I thought it was something good. I thought Dr. Julia was helping—I believed—"

"Shh. I know. I know what they did," I promised, but I couldn't explain everything to her now. "But we have to go now, okay?"

"How did you find me?"

I turned us toward the exit and stopped short. Matthew stood in the doorway.

No.

"You have to let us go," I said, keeping Rachel behind me, protected with one arm. The other lifted like the flat of my hand could stop a man like him. "Please. Eden drugged her because she doesn't want to be here. Please, just let us go."

His eyes narrowed as he stepped into the cabin.

Shit.

I scanned around us, but to get to any of the windows meant going toward him, not away.

I stepped back into my sister, feeling her stumble slightly. "Please, I'm begging you, Matthew. Please let us go."

He stopped, and I thought it was because of what I'd said. It wasn't. There was some noise outside. His head cocked toward it, and then he drew his weapon.

Rachel whimpered, and I felt blindly for her arm, giving it a squeeze.

Think, Lara.

I had Calder's knife with me. He said it was in case Rachel was restrained, but I knew there were other "in cases" it was for, too. I could try to get it, but I knew I wouldn't be fast enough. Not against a man with a gun. I wasn't like Calder; I didn't have an expertise in weapons, but I did know the adage to *never bring a knife to a gunfight.*

Maybe if I rushed him, hit his low center of gravity, it would knock him off balance enough for Rachel to get by. If she could make it behind the cabin, Calder would see her—help her.

Matthew's head snapped back to me. I started to bend, the balls of my feet pressing hard into the ground.

"Rachel, find Calder—"

"Wait," Matthew uttered harshly, and disbelief grabbed me by the throat as he lifted his hands in surrender. "I'm not going to hurt you."

What? I didn't move. This couldn't be real. He had to be lying. It was a trick to stop me. He holstered his weapon and with his other hand brought a finger of silence to his mouth.

What was going on?

I froze, balancing on the fulcrum of trust, waiting for his next move to prove whether or not I could believe him.

He kept his head turned slightly—listening—for another second and then strode toward me so quickly, I wasn't sure I could've stopped him even if I had been prepared. But he wasn't coming for us. He veered to the right, motioning wordlessly for us to follow him.

Where does he want us to go? And why—I looked back to the front door, now hearing the voices he had, and they were getting closer.

Taking my sister's wrist, I went with my gut. I followed the large guard through a door on the side of the bed into the bathroom. There were two showers on the back wall, and Matthew went straight for the one on the left. Opening the glass door, he stepped inside. There wasn't time to wonder what he was doing before he grabbed one of the shower nozzles—one that existed in the left shower but not the right—and twisted it.

A latch popped, and a hidden door opened to the outside.

Holy shit.

I didn't want to think about why Adam Eden needed this kind of exit from his own cabin because I had a feeling he wasn't the one who used it.

Matthew peered through the door. Left and then right, and then looked back to me, motioning that it was clear.

All I wanted to know was why he was helping us. *Was it for Dr. Julia? Did he realize what Adam was doing to her? Was he trying to get her out, too?* As much as I wanted to know, my sister was my only priority.

I led us through the shower, going as quickly as her unsteady steps made possible.

"Go," Matthew clipped when he saw me start to thank him, then went back inside Eden's cabin, the door closing up its invisible seam.

Voices—commotion—reached a crescendo from inside the cabin. *Was it Adam? Had he found Matthew? Would he tell him which way we went?* I squeezed Rachel's hand and buried the hammer of my heart the way I did when a patient coded. Panicking wouldn't bring them back to life. Chasing unknowable questions wouldn't restart their heart. And worrying what was coming for my sister and me wouldn't help us get away any faster.

"This way." I pulled her into the trees.

I pressed my hand to the rough bark of each trunk, pushing off them like it helped us move faster. Whether it was the drugs in her system, the fear, or both, my sister hardly made a sound behind me. I looked back to her only once and saw tears streaming down her face; after that, I knew I couldn't look again until we were truly safe.

Once we were far enough onto the ridge, I stopped and brought us to a crouch.

"Wait here for a second." She nodded, and I stood again, climbing back up the ridge to look for Calder.

I searched for him through the trees, expecting him to appear by my side any second like the silent hunter he was, but he never did. He should've been right behind us. That was the plan. He kept a lookout on the cabin, and once I led Rachel out, he would rendezvous with us here on the ridge to go back—*Oh god.*

Calder was waiting for me to bring Rachel out the front. He didn't know about the secret back door. He didn't know we were safe. *He didn't know Matthew entered the cabin to help us, not harm us.*

I lurched forward and a shot rang out, the distinct echo cascading down the slope.

"Whatever happens, get back to the shelter. If I'm not with you, call Callum."

Calder . . . I brought my fist to my mouth and bit into my knuckle, my heart bleeding beats like it was being ripped from my chest.

Obey.

Save Rachel.

Spinning, I rushed back to my sister. She was shaking.

"Lara—"

"It's okay," I told her, burying my own sob. "Just follow me. We have a shelter lower on the ridge. We'll be safe there."

Taking her hand, I followed the path Calder had marked with single broken branches on trees.

Who had fired that shot? Was it Calder? Every step, every crunch of the underbrush, morphed into that lethal sound. The kind of situation that would force him to draw his weapon wouldn't be a good one; he avoided that kind of force whenever possible. But the alternative, that it wasn't him . . .

My heart stopped just as the pattern of the tarp materialized ahead.

Obey. Save Rachel. Call Callum. Calder's words drove me forward, and I led my sister into our shelter.

"Lara . . ." She looked up at me in a daze as I guided her down to the sleeping pad. "You went to Calder?"

The vise around my throat tightened. "I didn't know where else to go," I told her even though what I really meant was *he was the only one that I could think of.*

The only one I'd ever thought of.

"Lara . . ."

"Shh," I cooed and rested her head on Calder's pillow. When she was steady, I pressed my fingers to her neck and checked her pulse. Slow and stable.

Reaching for the sat phone, I called the only programmed number.

"Everyone okay?" Callum's weathered voice answered.

"It's Lara," I replied, somehow knowing it was an answer to his question. *If Calder was okay, I wouldn't be calling.*

"Your sister?"

"She's with me. They gave her some kind of sedative"—I looked over my shoulder—"so she's sleeping right now." It was a miracle we'd made it here before the drugs had taken full effect.

"Okay. Police and park rangers are on their way. Unless the campsite is compromised, don't move."

"But Calder—"

"Don't worry about Calder. He'll survive."

Survive.

The sentiment was meant to be calming. A relief. But all I felt was nauseous. All Calder had ever done was survive. The wilderness. The solitude. The loss. The responsibility. And he'd done it alone.

"I have the sat phone with me. If anyone gets close to the camp, call me," I clipped. "I'm going to look for Calder."

"Lara—" Two gunshots tumbled in tandem down the ridge.

"I'm going." Those words ended the call.

I hung up on Callum and crouched by my sister's side.

"Rach, I'm going to find Calder. Just rest here, okay?"

Her head moved in a slow bob.

"I'll be right back." I pressed my lips to her forehead. Above me, the whir of Callum's drone echoed closer. If I could at least get back up to the ridge and see what was going on—see if Calder was okay.

I reached the edge of the shelter when I heard them—a single set of footsteps rushing down the ridge.

Calder.

The gait was uneven. *He was injured.*

My heart leaped just as quickly as my feet. I sprinted out from under the canopy, my pulse banging as I scanned for him. My mind filtered movable from immovable, blurring the stable forest setting and sharpening on the flutter of movement between the trunks.

"Calder!" I took two steps in his direction and stopped as he appeared through the last of the trees.

Oh god. *No.*

Ice-cold fear dumped into my veins as I stared at the battered man in disbelief. I blinked twice, but neither time revealed Calder, only the slow sneer of a man I never thought I'd see again.

"Find him." Dr. Julia's orders whispered in the back of my mind. She hadn't been talking about Trent or Calder. She'd been talking about him. The man in front of me. The man who'd been tied unconscious to a tree the last time I'd seen him.

"Ben."

"It's my lucky day." His mouth contorted into a snarl. "I came here for what I'm owed, and I found something better."

Chapter 34

Calder

Rule #31: Learn to see what doesn't belong. The human presence creates patterns that disrupt the natural world.

Eden's voice settled like a funk in the air.

"Good morning, my children. We begin another day ready and willing to succumb to our wild core . . ."

I pressed my back to the side of the cabin and scanned the crowd of women, Eden at their helm. Behind the rows of seated women, the six guards, including Matthew, stood. His focus, though, wasn't on the charismatic leader, but on Maxwell who stood next to him, looking just as unsettled as she had last night, making me suspect she was equal parts accomplice and victim.

Everyone was accounted for. I looked back to Eden's cabin, where Lara had entered moments earlier, my entire body buzzing.

I wished there was another way to go about my plan. Unfortunately, Eden's cabin was situated with the door faced away from the center of the compound, meaning the only way to confirm the coast was clear was to separate from Lara and watch—protect from a distance.

Movement caught the corner of my eye. I turned and my eyes tracked a figure climbing over the entrance gate like a wolf sneaking into a henhouse.

Ben.

What the fuck.

I strode back into the trees and then started to jog toward the gate. *What the hell was he doing here?* Nothing good, was the only answer I had. If he went for Eden's cabin—if he saw Lara again—I couldn't let that happen.

My feet fell quickly across the forest floor. Decades of experience, of training with Cassius, made my path swift and silent. I rounded the back of Eden's cabin and advanced on the front gate. Even at a distance, Ben looked the worse for wear, and not all of that *worse* was from me. He must've come to and escaped the retreat before Matthew could do something about him.

I pulled my weapon as I reached the gate, scanning up and along the wall, but saw no sign of him. I was long past resolving anything with this man without at least a threat of serious force.

I crouched. His boots crushed some yellow grass and left a deeper imprint where he'd landed when he'd climbed over, the tread leading in a lighter pattern toward the opposite side of the compound—toward the building where the women stayed. I gritted my teeth. As long as he wasn't heading for Eden's cabin, I'd deal with him later. My first priority was Lara and her sister, and they should've been out by now.

I squinted at the door to Eden's cabin. *Dammit.* Lara had left it open. I itched to go and close it, but the closer I got, the less I'd be able to see.

Minutes ticked by, each one draining the life out of me as I waited for them to leave the cabin. *Come on, Lara.* My fingers drummed against my leg. Waiting.

Waiting.

Fuck waiting.

Moving back along the perimeter, I lost sight of the center congregation and all my plans. My rules. *For her.* Striding up the steps, I slipped right through the open entrance and quickly shut the door behind me.

The cabin was empty. Bed. Table. Chairs. No sign of Lara or Rachel. *What the hell . . .* My head whipped around like they were hiding in plain sight.

"Lara?"

A grinding sound came from the back room—the bathroom. I continued forward and drew my Glock.

A moment later, the door swung wide and Matthew filled the frame. Our arms aiming at the same time.

Staring down the barrel of a gun was never how I liked to start a conversation. Even less so when it was clear Lara and her sister weren't here, and Matthew was most likely the reason.

"Drop it," the guard from the retreat ordered.

He looked both haggard and hateful. Dark circles under his eyes and wrinkled clothes, but an anger bright with life in his stare.

"I can't do that, Matthew," I said calmly. "Where are Lara and Rachel?"

"Gone," he ground out. "Just like you need to be."

My finger slid to the trigger, having to take the threat at face value.

"I'm not leaving without them." My own anger electrified my skin. If anything had happened to them—to her—there was no corner of this earth I would leave unturned to find who was responsible and make them pay.

I heard his teeth grind together. "They're gone. You need to go. Now," he snapped, his teeth clacking together and his eyes darting behind me.

I didn't fall for the distraction, in case that was all it was. *Once your gun is raised, you never take your eye off the target.* A moment later, the door swung open and the distraction became real.

Adam Eden, with Maxwell right behind him, stopped in the doorway, his eyes whipping back and forth between me and Matthew.

"What the hell is going on here, Matthew? Who the hell is this?" Eden demanded, and as soon as Matthew heard his name, his target quickly switched to the older man.

What the . . .

"Matthew!" Maxwell swayed behind Eden, who roughly shoved her back. She fell backward, hitting her head on one of the posts of the railing along the stairs.

"Whoa, whoa, whoa. Hold on a second." Keeping my Glock aimed, I put myself squarely between Matthew and Eden, hoping that would stop him from shooting the older man. "Let's all take a breath," I said quickly, looking at Matthew and then lifting my free hand in Eden's direction. My preference was always to defuse a situation, not escalate it.

"What's going on here?" Eden snarled, blocking the doorway with his frame. "Who are you?"

"I'm Calder Stone, and I was hired by Rachel Crane's family to bring her home." There was no reason to hide my purpose now. "I'm happy to go about my business without interfering with yours."

Eden stepped into his cabin, calmer now that another one of his guards had appeared behind him. "This is private property. You're trespassing, and the wilderness out here . . . it doesn't take kindly to trespassers."

So he planned to kill me and dump my body over that ridge. *Understood.*

"And you have some questions to answer for back in California, Mr. Braun." I didn't have very many cards to play, but at least that one struck a nerve.

"Thankfully, California can't find me here." His smile was cold just before he turned to the guard behind him. "Take care of both of them."

Matthew's finger tightened on the trigger.

My head tilted, warning the other man with the smallest shake. "Don't do it. You can still walk away and leave. Leave it all behind."

"I'll never walk away from this," Matthew said, his voice hollow and his eyes haunted, reminding me for a split second of Cassius after Mom's death. "Not until he pays for Hannah."

Hannah.

Matthew wasn't a guard or a participant in Eden's Children—he was a vigilante. He was Hannah's boyfriend. The one who'd told the PI that there were letters. *The one who'd tracked them across state lines and joined a cult to find them.*

"No!" I lunged, but it was too late.

Matthew pivoted his gun an inch to the right and fired just before I slammed into him. Eden stared at the flashes sprouting from the barrel, not realizing he was the target until red bloomed through his white shirt.

Shit.

Eden fell into the doorframe and slid to the ground. Over Maxwell's unconscious body, the second guard fumbled for his weapon.

"Let me go! He deserves to die!"

Matthew and I struggled on the floor. Gritting my teeth, I drew back just enough to let him think I was letting up and then let my hand fly, clocking him in the side of the head with the butt of my gun. He'd have a nice lump there tomorrow, but the alternative was becoming a lump himself. Dead because of his own devastation.

"Master Eden—"

"Kill them," the leader sputtered, blood seeping between his fingers where it rested over the open wound. He didn't have enough strength to put solid pressure on the wound, which was what it needed.

Breathing heavily, I shook my head slowly when the guard looked at me. "Don't do it," I verbalized in case the message wasn't clear.

Unfortunately, clear is rarely a deterrent to crazy.

I fired a nanosecond before he did, the slug hitting his shoulder, sending it whipping back and his weapon spinning from his hand.

The guard screamed in pain. Worse than his idol who probably wouldn't survive the shots Matthew had buried into his gut.

I grabbed Matthew's gun, dropped the mag and stuffed it in my back pocket. Next, I pulled a towel from the corner of the bed and went to triage Eden. The second guard looked at me with equal parts fury and fear, undecided which to fuel.

I helped him make the decision. "You can either die trying, or you can actually help him and live." He nodded frantically, choosing the *live* option. I pressed the towel over Eden's middle, the man waking slightly to the pain before it swallowed him up again. Police and rangers were already on their way, though I doubted he was going to make it. Eden deserved no less than to live to see justice for all of his victims served.

"Press here as hard as you can."

The man did as I said but asked, "What about me?"

Unbelievable.

"You'll live." I'd aimed for the meaty part of the shoulder, and the bullet had cleared straight through muscle and tissue. He'd be good as new in a few weeks; the same couldn't be said for his leader.

I checked Maxwell's pulse on my way out, confirming she, too, was okay.

I went first for the second guard's gun, emptying the bullet in the chamber and then adding the mag to my pocket. By my calculation, at least two other men here had weapons. The last thing I needed was someone to take up the unattended Glocks and join the hunting party.

Around me, pandemonium was starting.

Matthew had used a silencer, but the guard and I hadn't. I slipped around the corner of the building as footsteps barreled toward the cabin. Following the perimeter, I dipped into the woods just as the sounds of sirens started to creep through the trees.

Chapter 35

LARA

He looked like Ian, but the only drug responsible for the crazed look in his eyes was hatred.

My sympathetic nervous system screamed *fight or flight*. Flight wasn't an option. He didn't know Rachel was practically unconscious, and I would fight until my very last breath to keep this deranged man from getting to her.

"You should've picked me when you had the chance," he sneered and came closer.

I lifted my hands and rooted my feet. It would be a mistake to move now when Ben's gun was pointed straight at me and his finger was on the trigger. Even if he didn't follow Calder's rule to never aim a gun at something you didn't intend to shoot, I wasn't going to take the chance. Even if the sound almost stirred Rachel and she made a noise.

"You're making a mistake," I said, aiming for the calm tone Calder used.

"Shut up," he snapped as his heavy boots trod down to me. "On your knees."

My throat constricted. I didn't dare defy him, but I didn't rush to comply, either. Taking my time, I sank one knee to the ground and then the other. *Think, Lara. What can you use?*

"I'm going to fuck that whore mouth of yours first. Teach you to say no to me," Ben snapped, stopping about a foot and a half in front of me and reaching for the waist of his pants.

I gagged, feeling something digging into my thigh. *Calder's knife.* Hope seared through my chest.

All I had to do was wait for him to get close enough to use it. *Well, he certainly planned on doing that.* Bile rose in my throat, knowing what that would entail, but I had to. I had to survive. I had to protect my sister.

I waited, feeling my muscles start to vibrate with adrenaline as he came closer, one hand opening the flap of his slacks, the other keeping his gun aimed at me.

"God, I need this," he groaned and freed himself.

Though I'd probably seen hundreds of men's cocks at this point, I found in that moment there was a distinct difference in observing the anatomy of a patient and seeing the sad erection of a man who was about to assault me.

He came right in front of me, a sick grin on his face. I turned my face away and pulled the blade from my pocket.

"Don't you fucking look away from me." He grabbed my hair and yanked my head straight. Pain burst through my skull, and then the cold butt of his gun was pressed to the side of my head.

This was it. I was going to have only one chance to deflect his gun and sink the knife into his femoral artery. If I was lucky, by the time he realized what happened and could reach for me or try to shoot me, he'd already be slipping into unconsciousness.

One chance, and it involved putting his disgusting penis in my mouth.

"Open wide." He yanked my head back, obscuring my view even more from the inside of his thigh. "Bite me, and I'll blow your brains out."

I stared up at him, his skinny member floating in my vision. I was sorely tempted to ignore his warning, but I wouldn't. Not because I wanted to obey him, though he'd think that, but because I had a better plan. A better pain in store for him than a damaged penis.

"Fuck you," I spat.

Rage shriveled his features. "Fucking—"

"Lara!" a voice boomed from the ridge.

Ben spun around. *Distracted.* And I moved. The knife flicked open and I drove it into the inside of his upper thigh at the same moment Calder fired.

Ben's wide, shocked eyes came toward me as he fell forward like a sack of bricks. Yanking the knife free, I lunged to the side so he wouldn't fall on top of me.

"Lara!" I heard him yelling, but it was muted under the thudding of my heart. I stared at the fallen man, face down in the leaves. I knew he was dead. I felt it. Just as surely as I felt the sticky heat of his blood on my hand, the dark heme coating the tip of the silver blade all the way to my forearm.

"Lara."

Calder cupped my cheeks, forcing my eyes to his. Forcing my mind to the moment.

"Are you all right?" he asked, turning my head and scanning over my body like whatever my answer was wouldn't have made a difference.

"Yeah," I said, my voice not sounding like my own and my eyes drawn back to my hand.

His curse was muffled as he took the knife from my hand and dropped it to the ground, then used his own shirt to wipe the blood from my skin.

"I've got you," he murmured, pulling me tight to his chest. Only against his strength did I feel how bad I was shaking. "You're safe."

Calder couldn't have held me for long, but he did manage to pick me up and carry me under the shelter, sitting me next to Rachel and using a wipe to clean the rest of Ben's blood from my hands.

Before I knew it, a helicopter thumped above us and two park rangers had made their way down the ridge to our shelter. They helped stabilize my sister, who was too knocked out to even wake up as Calder and one of the rangers secured her on a sled and pulled her back up the ridge where the paramedics were waiting.

Thankfully, Adam Eden was already on the medevac before the group of us reached the compound from our campsite. The blades whipped higher, and I was glad I wasn't the surgeon on call to treat Adam Eden, though I doubted he would make it even with every attempt to save his life.

Just like Ben.

My attacker was dead before he'd hit the ground. The rangers hadn't even attempted to help him, and when we left the shelter, Calder had already covered his body with a tarp from his bag so I wouldn't have to see it. They'd come back later to remove the body, and with a few more stormy nights, even the ground wouldn't have any trace left of his blood.

"Follow my finger," I instructed, holding up my index finger and moving it in front of Matthew's face.

With the medevac gone, there were only two people available with advanced medical training: me and one of the other women who'd been a nurse before joining Eden's Children. Both of us had flipped into emergency-response mode. I asked for the first aid kit from the rangers and, after confirming no serious damage, instructed her to bandage the guard with the gunshot wound to his shoulder. Meanwhile, I went to evaluate Matthew and Dr. Julia for any sign of concussion or brain injury.

Dr. Julia was shaken, but the least injured—at least physically—of the two. Emotionally, I wasn't sure even her professional training was strong enough to unpack all the trauma Adam Eden had heaped on her for decades.

Matthew, on the other hand, I found sitting on the steps outside Adam's cabin, staring off like he was hoping to see a ghost.

"He made Hannah write him letters. That's how I realized what was happening. I found an unfinished one in her room where she wrote about being nervous to leave school and move out here." Matthew spoke, though I wasn't sure he was really talking to me but instead just . . . getting it out.

On the hike back to the compound, Calder revealed Matthew was Hannah's boyfriend who'd joined Dr. Julia and Wilderness Within to get justice for Hannah, and I shared how Matthew had helped Rachel and me escape.

"I confronted Hannah. I told her they weren't helping her. That they didn't care about her. I told her I loved her and I wanted to marry her."

My throat tightened as I checked the lump on his head.

"She wouldn't believe me. She went back and told them what happened—what I said. They were furious that I knew—that I found out. She called me when she left Dr. Julia's office. I'd never heard her so upset. She said they didn't want her. They didn't love her. That it was my fault. I'd made them not love her. I told her I loved her, but it wasn't enough." He paused then, emotion clogging his voice. "The next morning, they found her."

I ran through the cognitive tests for any signs of a concussion, all negative.

"You told the investigator about the letters."

Slowly, he nodded. "Then they disappeared, so I came here to find them."

"She didn't recognize you?"

"Dr. Julia?" He shook his head. "I transferred in sophomore year on a soccer scholarship. I never met her, and in college, I went by my middle name, Jack. My dad's name is Matthew," he said by way of explanation.

"You didn't find the letters?"

He shook his head like that was the worst part of all this. "I think I came out here knowing I wouldn't find them. Deep down, I knew it would come to this." *To killing them.* "I wish there was something worse than death for him."

He looked up at me, desperate for something to relieve his pain.

"There is," I said, and stepped back. "The life Hannah would've wanted you to live."

The heartbroken man stared at me long and hard, then hung his head and sobbed.

Satisfied that he showed no sign of brain injury, I left him to sit with his grief. My own emotions were already at their bursting point, and I needed to make sure everyone else was okay.

After checking on the nurse and the bandage she'd applied, I returned to Rachel's side. They'd laid her on a shady patch of grass. Kneeling next to the sled, I took her hand in mine, anchoring myself to its warmth.

"You're okay now," I murmured and bent over her, kissing her forehead.

When I looked up, my gaze swam into focus on the people congregated in the grassy middle of the buildings.

Calder had joined the police and rangers as they rounded up everyone else in the compound and began interviewing them. The irony of the scene struck me. All of the women were in the same area where Eden ministered to them on their knees. Some were crying. Others were holding each other in shock. Only now, they weren't kneeling. They were standing.

Warmth fizzled along my spine, my gaze searching for the source. *For him.*

Calder finished talking to the officer he stood with and then came over. Dirt and blood caked to his clothes, same as mine, and that only made me pull him harder to me.

His lips went to the top of my head. "You okay?"

"Yeah." There were so many other things I wanted to say—to tell him—but my body was nose-diving into an adrenaline crash, and all I wanted was to close my eyes and never leave his arms.

I got my wish for a few minutes. Nothing but the breeze invaded our embrace until the cavalry arrived.

Another police SUV and an ambulance drove through the gates. Behind them, Cassius's truck slowed to an idle just outside the perimeter.

"Time to go," he murmured, and released me. Looking down at Rachel and then over to the ambulance where Dr. Julia and the man with the shoulder injury were already being loaded into the back, Calder asked, "Do you want to take Rachel to the hospital?"

"No." The sedatives they'd given her would wear off in a couple of hours. Until then, my sister had her own personal doctor to look after her.

Nodding, Calder went over to the EMTs and handled the conversation and the natural pushback that came when anyone refused formal medical assessment. It would've been easier if I had gone and told them I was a doctor, but right here, right now, I wasn't a doctor. The last of my honed authority had seeped out from me the moment I'd walked away from Matthew.

Now I was a victim who'd killed my attacker. I was a sister who was both exhausted and relieved, worried for Rachel and wanting to weep that I'd found her at the same time. And I was a woman, wanting nothing more than to let go of the weight I carried and be taken care of by the man who always protected me. The man I loved.

"Let's go home," Calder said when he returned. Crouching and lifting Rachel into his arms, we headed for Cassius's truck.

Home had never sounded so good. Nor so right.

Chapter 36

CALDER

Rule #41.

I drove behind Cassius down the mountain.

Lara had chosen to stay with Rachel in Cassius's truck, and now that I was alone, all I could think about was seeing Lara on her knees in the woods, Ben standing in front of her, a gun to her head. That was all I needed to see, all I ever needed to see. It wasn't my life that flashed before my eyes—it was my love.

And I was an idiot for not telling her sooner. Now the confession pulsed in my chest like a grenade clutched in my hand, threatening to blow. I didn't care if it was too much or too soon. I didn't care if she wanted to leave to go back to Arizona. I would do anything and go anywhere as long as it was for her. But I had to hold all that to myself until I could talk to her alone again.

As soon as Cassius pulled up to the house, he didn't wait for me before lifting Rachel from the back seat and carrying her inside. *Into his room.*

"Are you sure, Cassius? I'm sure Colby—"

"She'll stay here as long as she needs." For a man who was skeptical of anyone who stepped onto our property, his tune had taken a complete 180 turn when it came to Rachel.

"Thank you," Lara said and adjusted the pillow under her sister's head. "I'm just going to shower and lay with her until she wakes up. I don't want her to be afraid."

I nodded. "Do you want me to sit with her while you—"

"I'll sit with her," Cassius declared, entering his room with a large weighted blanket from downstairs. He unfolded it and laid it over Rachel, arranging it with a degree of care that shocked me.

Cassius did care, could be caring . . . in his own way. But I'd only seen him like this very few times in my life, either when Mom was pregnant or once when Colby was sick with the flu. I folded my arms, watching him make sure every inch of her was covered.

Maybe seeing Rachel like this had brought back memories of Mom. Not that the circumstances were even close to the same, but here was a woman he could help, in a way he hadn't been able to for Mom.

I looked to Lara. It was up to her to decide, though it didn't sound like Cassius was really giving either of us a choice.

She bit her lip, hesitating for only a second before agreeing. "Thank you, Cassius."

He didn't do more than grunt as Lara and I stepped out of the room. As soon as the door closed, she sagged into my arms.

"Calder . . ."

"I've got you," I promised, cupping her head even as she angled it back, her eyes swimming with a thousand emotions. In the last hours spent saving her sister, saving herself, caring for the wounded, and looking over Rachel, Lara hadn't let herself process all the emotions that came with being a victim.

"Kiss me."

She never needed to ask me for that.

I slid my hand to her face, and her fingers curled into my shirt. Our mouths collided in a hot and heavy mess, our bodies banging into the walls of the hall. Tongues and teeth tore at each other, not soft or gentle, but savage, in search of safety. Knowing she was okay. Knowing I was okay. Knowing we still had each other.

At the first quake of her knees, I hauled her up into my arms, my mouth never breaking from hers as I pinned her back to the wall. I couldn't think about where this was going or where I should have been taking it. All I could focus on was the kiss. On her. The sweet heat of her mouth. The hunger of mine. *She was safe. She was mine. I loved her.*

"Lara." I tore my mouth away, the words sitting right on the tip of my tongue. "I—"

"And they say I'm the savage," Creighton's deep voice mocked, and I turned, only to be greeted by my brother's smirk. "At least I put up a sign."

According to Colby, one time she'd gone to visit him at his apartment in town, there was a piece of paper nailed to the door that read COITUS IN PROGRESS.

Lara ducked into my chest, and I carefully lowered her feet to the ground.

"Creighton—"

"Who's in Dad's room?" he demanded, his scowl deepening.

"Lara's sister, Rachel," I answered. "We found her this morning. She's resting." He didn't need the details.

A deep crease of confusion furrowed his brow. More than me, Creighton looked completely boggled by our father's decision to offer up his bedroom to a virtual stranger.

"Interesting," he remarked, dragging stained fingers through his long hair and then disappearing into his room.

Lara caught her breath, resting her head on my chest.

"Tell me what I can do," I said, trailing my knuckles gently along her cheek.

She lifted her eyes to mine. "I killed him, didn't I?"

"No." My jaw locked. "He was dead before he could bleed out."

Was it the truth? Honestly, I didn't know and I wasn't sure even the best medical examiner would be able to determine which injury had been the cause of death: the two slugs I'd fired into him, center mass, or the traumatic blood loss from where she'd stabbed him.

"You're sure?"

I nodded. I hadn't taken an oath to save lives, and I didn't have a problem killing when the circumstances warranted, and for those things alone, I would assume the responsibility for Ben's death.

"I wanted to kill him, though," she confessed in the smallest whisper, not sounding like she felt guilty for the thought but to prove she was strong enough to have it.

"I know." I kissed her forehead. "It's over now. You're both safe."

She angled her head higher, her mouth orbiting for another kiss, but then she drew back. "I need to shower and get back to my sister," she said softly.

"Yeah." *Of course.* This . . . us . . . was a priority, but it would have to wait. I would have to wait and live with the tightness in my chest for several more hours.

I couldn't take my hand from hers as I guided her to the bathroom she'd used the other night. "I'm going to check in with Callum."

And I needed to figure out how to tell Lara how I felt . . . and what the hell I would do if she didn't want to stay. Not because I couldn't leave. I could. I could live anywhere. But the possibility had just then occurred to me: What if she didn't want me to come with her?

She turned in the doorway and I kissed her again. "I'll have Colby bring you some clothes."

"Thank you."

My hand wore a path along my beard as I walked to Callum's. He hadn't followed through on his threat to change the locks on his door, so I let myself inside to Twister's welcoming committee.

Stationed in his chair at his computers, Callum greeted me without turning. "You're alive."

"Yeah." I went to stand by him, Twister circling my feet. "Thanks for all your help . . . with this."

Callum didn't take gratitude well. Actually, he preferred to not take it at all by ignoring the sentiment. "I wasn't expecting to hear Lara's voice on the phone this morning, worried about you. Is the great Calder Stone losing his touch?"

She worried about me. I tried not to let the thought sink in too deep. It didn't change the reality that her life was back in Phoenix.

"Things didn't go as expected."

"That's one way of explaining two dead bodies," he mumbled. "Can't say I'm surprised that Eden and Braun were the same person."

"Neither was I. But realizing Maxwell's bodyguard, Matthew, was Hannah's boyfriend was not on my bingo card."

His hands stopped moving on his keyboard, and he finally looked at me. "Her boyfriend went to work for them? I thought his name was Jack."

"His middle name is Jack. He wanted to find proof of what Eden was doing to women." I'd come across a lot over the years in the retrieval business, but from memory, this quest for vengeance certainly topped the charts.

"No shit." Callum blew out a breath, his hands flying over the keys before he grabbed his mouse, panning over a storm cell. "Talk about the long game."

I grunted and briefly recounted what had happened when Lara found her sister.

I wasn't sure what was more tragic—what had happened to the young girl, or that her boyfriend had spent years tracking down the people responsible to bring them to justice, only to sacrifice himself to their end.

"So that was how Lara made it back to camp without you." My brother shook his head. "I tried to tell her there was no way you weren't okay."

The unbidden compliment surprised me, but responding to it would only make Callum more miserly with his emotion. I didn't need the vote of confidence, but I had to believe if he could acknowledge it in others, one day, he'd do it for himself.

"After we left Wilderness Within, Matthew worried his window of opportunity was closing, so he decided to kill Eden instead," I began and told him what happened once I'd entered the cabin.

"So, Eden isn't dead? I thought for sure he was the one under the tarp."

"You saw?"

He shrugged. "I already had a drone out there in case. When Lara said she was going to look for you, I figured something went wrong, so I sent it low in case I could be of any help." And there was the bitterness curling at the edge of his voice.

"It was the other guard from the retreat. Ben." Even though he was dead, I still felt rage thinking about him. "He went after Lara."

"Understood." Out here, we preferred pacifism but accepted killing on principle. "Well, if you're wondering, I finished looking into the UnitedLife angle. They've paid out on ten *death by misadventure* claims to Adam Eden over the last three years, totaling almost eight million dollars."

I shook my head. "Guess we found where the money was coming from."

"I'll send what I found to the police. I'm sure once they process all the records from Wilderness Within, they'll find some matching names."

"I wonder if their partners even know they died or if he just told them they left the compound," I mused.

"Were the women hurt?"

I swallowed. "Not physically, no, but I can't help but think this was just as bad." There wasn't much that curdled my stomach. Not in my line of work. But opening up the storage building with one of the officers and seeing shelves lined with baby oil and K-Y Jelly, condoms, and sex toys, and sedatives. Lots of sedatives . . .

Callum grunted. "The kind of man that manipulates women into a sex cult is the kind of man who doesn't even know how to find the clit."

An unexpected chuckle erupted from my chest, and I stared at my brother. It was a glimmer of the old Callum who had spoken, and he realized it.

"Well, I guess the case is closed, then."

I'd never felt so reticent about the idea before. It was always finished with one case and onto the next. *I'd never wanted more time with anyone before.*

"Unless there's something else you need?" he said tersely, scorching any evidence that his former lighthearted nature still existed underneath all his wounds.

One step at a time.

"No."

Callum whipped his chair around me, rolling toward the side door of his house. "Then I've got a cell to monitor." He grabbed a ball cap from the bottom of the coatrack, catching it the wrong way and sending the pole tumbling to the ground, hats and coats littering the floor. "Fuck." Twister barked and ran through the casualties.

"Here—"

"Leave it," Callum snapped. "Just leave it." And then he pushed outside and disappeared down the ramp.

I wouldn't just leave it. I righted the coatrack and replaced every item except one.

I picked up the cowboy hat Callum had worn on every storm chase back when he was the infamous tornado wrangler, and I left it on top of his keyboard so he'd have to deal with it when he got back.

At some point, he couldn't keep running from the storm.

I'd avoided the house for as long as I could. First, touching base with the rangers and police. Then checking on the status of Maxwell and the other women. All the while, the pull to go back to her—to talk to her—burned in my veins. But this was one scenario where I wouldn't be *the Director* but a distraction when Lara needed to be with her sister. So, instead of going back to the house, I went to Free Fall.

This time, it wasn't a race, but a restoration. Every grip. Every hold. Every calculated movement. It wasn't an exercise in climbing the rock face, but in facing the condition of my heart.

For someone who tracked things for a living—who was paid to notice what others couldn't—somehow I'd both observed yet completely missed every sign that I was falling in love with Lara Crane. Or maybe I hadn't wanted to see them. Had tried not to see them.

Before, my idea of love was the torture in Cassius's eyes when he saw Mom's lifeless body. When he passed from day to day, knowing surviving each one meant facing another without her. My idea of love was colored over in shades of grief.

It wasn't until Lara was on her knees in front of Ben that I saw the path, clear as day, that my heart had walked out of my chest and attached itself to her. It wasn't a choice. It was a force of nature, *too full to contain*, that struck with a bolt of lightning and then seeped like a torrent of rain into my bones.

I couldn't help the way I felt about her any more than I could control a thunderstorm.

I scaled the wall with deliberate slowness, feeling only a single sentiment sweat from every pore, strain from every muscle, and flow through every vein. I was in love with her. And not only would I do anything to save her, but I would also do anything to not live without her.

I pulled myself up to the ledge, turned, and sat. I'd seen this same skyline in every season of every stage of my life, changing but somehow always the same world to be explored. Until today.

Today, everything to the color-steeped horizon and beyond wasn't a world I wanted to explore, but a world I wanted to share. And for the first time in my adult life, the choice of what to do or what came next wasn't wholly mine to make.

A door opened and shut on the second floor, and I looked up from my crossword. After showering and changing in the Airstream, I'd finally returned to the house, puzzle in hand. By then, Cassius had made dinner and a foiled plate of leftovers greeted me on the kitchen counter.

Firm footsteps settled with familiarity on the staircase.

How many nights had I heard those same footfalls when I'd been burning the midnight oil, cooped up in the library reading or studying?

Cassius appeared in the doorway, his gaze ravaged as it found mine.

"Everything okay?" I set my puzzle down, the pen rolling off to the side. "She wake up at all?"

"For a little. Still pretty groggy, but ate a few bites of my chicken." Cassius's crispy hot chicken could tempt someone back from the dead—it was that good.

It was the first and only home-cooked food Callum would eat after his accident. The first meal Colton had wanted when we brought him home from prison. The only meal Creighton had deigned to learn how to cook. And the meal Colby requested for every birthday, holiday, and fourth Sunday of the month.

Not that we had very many guests or friends at the ranch, but Cassius had never made it for anyone but family before.

"She's sleeping now."

"She's going to be okay." After I spoke, I realized the words could've been about either Rachel or Lara, and directed to either Cassius or me.

"Physically, yes."

"She's strong. She'll get through this," I said, my head drawn back to the crackling fire.

I might not have been in contact with my ex since college, but the time I had known her, especially those moments at the end, left no doubt that Rachel Crane would survive this. Maybe not without help. Maybe not without some time. But in spite of the flaws of her younger self, she was a fighter.

"In my experience, the heaviest weights we carry are the ones no one asked us to. The ones we were never responsible for."

The words settled like a band around my chest. I snapped my gaze back to Cassius and stared at him. Was he talking about Rachel, or was he talking about me?

After a moment, I decided it was both. Stones weren't good at letting people in. Literally or figuratively. But I wanted to be better. *I wanted to be better for Lara.* And maybe Cassius wanted to be better, too.

Abandoning my puzzle, I stood. "Want some coffee?"

I wasn't sure I'd ever seen my father's shoulders lower quite like they did in that moment. "Would love some."

I followed him to the kitchen like I'd done all those nights as a kid, when he'd whip up Mom's favorite cocoa drink and make me swear to keep the recipe a secret.

The first thing I did when we reached the kitchen was walk over, unplug his ancient coffee maker from the wall, and toss it in the trash.

"Take it you aren't going to use that."

"I offered coffee, not muddy swill," I said, hearing a hint of his chuckle.

"And what am I supposed to do tomorrow morning?"

I smiled. "I've got an extra French press in the Airstream I'll bring down."

I'd gotten it for Creighton for Christmas, but then he started avoiding coffee and opting for tea. However, without it now, I'd have to improvise. Thankfully, I'd been taught how to survive when not having the right tools was the standard.

I filled the kettle and started to heat it on the stove.

"So, what happens now, Calder?"

I knew that question. That tone.

"I told the police we'd go give statements tomorrow," I said, scooping coffee grounds into a glass carafe until it looked like a pile of dirt. "I'm figuring Rachel will be well enough to want to go back to her place as well."

The water hissed and I flipped off the burner, pouring it over the mound of coffee and using a knife to stir it together. *Three minutes.*

"And Lara?"

I stopped stirring for one long, painful second. Of course he knew. Trying to hide how I felt about her would be like trying to cover the tracks of Bigfoot with a four-leaf clover. "I'd assume she's going to stay with her sister and then go back to Phoenix. Back to her life." Statistically speaking, it was the most likely scenario.

"Is that what you want?"

I was sure Callum's radar could've picked up the storm that went through me right then. No, it wasn't what I wanted, but what the hell right did I have to say? To ask her to stay?

If I were . . . someone else, someone who hadn't been raised by the man interrogating me, I would've claimed this was just another case successfully closed and that Lara was just another loved one. But Stones weren't liars.

"I'm not sure what I want matters right now."

After grabbing two mugs, I lined a fresh piece of cheesecloth over the top of the carafe and carefully strained the coffee into each cup. I handed Cassius his mug and went to the garbage to dump out the used grounds, hoping the banging would encourage him to let this go.

It didn't.

"Calder. There's a difference between being a survivalist and an isolationist." Cassius's voice deepened, and I raised an eyebrow and my coffee to my mouth, trying to remember the last time I'd been taught a lesson by my father. "The difference is choice. The world doesn't give a survivalist a choice. You either have the tools to survive on your own or you don't. But an isolationist . . ." He exhaled. "An isolationist doesn't give the world a choice—a chance. I raised you to be the former, and after what happened to your mom, I don't think I made it clear that we were never meant to be the latter."

"You seem to be pretty content being isolated out here."

Cassius's jaw hardened—*his masseter.* I noticed it now because she'd noticed it in me. Maybe his rules weren't the only thing Cassius had given me.

"Rule 41."

I frowned. "Rule 41?" There were only forty.

"Rule 41. Love makes you vulnerable, but isolation makes you weak. Choose your attachments carefully, but don't live without them," Cassius instructed, his voice dropping even farther as he added wearily, "We all have our demons, Calder. Don't let mine become yours."

Chapter 37

LARA

My sister stirred, and I lifted my head as her eyes opened. "Lara?"

Tucked into the middle of Cassius's bed, she looked so small. Too small for all the things she carried.

"Hey," I said sleepily, lifting my head from the side of the bed. While there was definitely enough space for me to have slept next to my sister last night, I'd instead fallen asleep in the recliner that Cassius had pulled next to the bed for either me or him to sit in. "I'm here."

"Where . . ."

"You're safe." I squeezed her hand, watching her absorb what I'd said. Even when she'd woken up yesterday afternoon and ate, she'd still been so groggy from the cocktail of sedatives. She'd asked what had happened, but could barely keep her eyes open to wait for an answer—one the meds would probably make her forget anyway.

This morning, though, all that was cleared.

"Can you tell me what happened?"

"Rach . . ."

"Please." She looked up, her green eyes glistening. "I need to know."

Carefully, I walked her through what happened yesterday morning. Being brought to one of the cabins during the morning meditation where I'd found her. Matthew helping us escape. Hiding at the campsite until the authorities arrived. I left out what happened with Ben. Today wasn't the day for that conversation.

"Oh, Lara. I'm so sorry—" Rachel's shock cracked open into grief, and I immediately slid onto the bed and held her to me.

"Don't apologize, Rach. Please." I cupped her face, brushing her hair back. "None of this is your fault."

Her shoulders shook with quiet, gasping sobs, and even though I told her not to, all she would repeat was her apology. So I let her. I held her and I let her grieve for what had happened and for what she'd hoped, because sometimes, that was all you could do.

I hugged her until her breathing finally started to calm and she drew back to look at me. "I just wanted to be better—to feel better about myself. To do better for myself."

"I know, and they took advantage of that. They took advantage of you and all those other women, and they won't ever do it again."

"Something wasn't right. I knew something wasn't right," she said, wiping tears from her face. "But I wanted it to be right, Lara. For once. I needed it to be right . . ."

"You're going to get through this—we're going to get through this," I promised and handed her a glass of water.

She took the glass, but the way she stared at it . . . She was seeing something else.

"What is it?"

"They gave me a smoothie in a cup like this for breakfast. That's the last thing before everything gets fuzzy."

I frowned. Well, they were certainly consistent with their delivery method.

"They mixed a sedative in the drink. Those drugs can cause retrograde amnesia, so you forget some of what happened before they take effect," I explained, and she brought the cup to her lips like she wanted to swallow down the memory before it made her sick.

"Where are the other women?"

"Getting the help they need," I assured her.

"And Dr. Julia? Adam?"

"Dr. Julia was arrested, along with the rest of the men of Eden's Children, and Adam is in the hospital. But, Rach . . . his name wasn't Adam." Her eyes only grew rounder as I elaborated on James Braun's journey to becoming Adam Eden, and those he'd preyed on and sacrificed along the way. Including, by the end, even Dr. Julia.

"I just . . . It almost still feels like I'm dreaming. That none of this is real—could be real."

"I'm sorry."

She shook her head. "I can't believe . . . you found me. I can't believe you went to Calder."

I braced, heart pounding, knowing we had to get to this part eventually.

"I didn't know where else to go."

Her face was drawn as she admitted, "I know how that feels."

Allen. The baby. I wanted to ask, but less than one day after being rescued from a cult wasn't the time to dredge up the past, no matter how much it had shaped our future.

"How did he find me?"

I blew out a breath, unsure whether the story made me want to laugh or cry. "First, he tracked down Brandon, who told us about Wilderness Within, and then I called and pretended we were a couple so they would let us join."

Rachel's jaw dropped just as a knock sounded on the door.

"Can I . . ." I checked with her, and once I had her go ahead, I called, "Come in."

I'd thought about this moment a surprising number of times in the last twenty-four hours. The moment when I'd be in the room with the two of them again. My sister and Calder.

A moment I feared would bring me right back to college and the knot in my stomach and the worry that I'd looked at him too long. That my sister would discover my crush. Moments when I was on the outside of their relationship and stealing glimpses in. *Stealing fantasies of him.*

"Rachel," Calder said, keeping his distance from the bed and from us. "Glad to see you're okay." There was kindness in his voice, a gentleness with how he looked at her. But no intensity. No heat. *Nothing like his gaze when he turned to me.* "Lara."

"Thank you, Calder," Rachel blurted out. "Thank you for helping my sister and saving me." She bit into her lip as it quivered, but wouldn't let emotion stop her from saying everything she wanted to say. "I owe you more than a thank-you, and for much more than this."

"The thank-you is more than enough," he murmured and then cleared his throat. "I'm sorry to have to ask, but the police are here and want to get statements from us about what happened yesterday. If you don't feel up to it, I can have them come back—"

"No," she insisted, sitting taller. "I'm okay."

"I can tell them to come up here, if it's more comfortable," Calder offered as Rachel slid her legs off the bed.

She looked grateful, but refused. "Thanks, but I think I'd rather talk to the police from somewhere other than your dad's bed."

Calder and I shared a small smile between us, and then I took my sister's hand and we followed him downstairs.

I was surprised Cassius had even wanted the police at his house, but when I mentioned it to Calder, apparently, Cassius had insisted; he hadn't wanted my sister to have to go down to the station after what she'd been through.

That was how the Stones were, I realized. Hard to crack through, but once you did, they closed ranks around you like a fortress.

It took almost three hours before the two detectives finished interviewing the three of us, both unable to hide their amazement when Calder explained how we'd discovered not only the Eden's Children compound but also the truth about the man leading it.

After they'd left, Rachel wanted to go for a walk, and I did, too. I'd made sure to be in a separate room when I recounted what happened with Ben and how I stabbed him so my sister wouldn't hear, but once I was done, even I wanted to be outside and let the fresh air clear the band from around my chest.

Colby volunteered to take us on a loop through the ranch. Between her pointing out the "sites" on the homestead, the tree house, the huge tire swing, the garden, and then introducing Rach to all her rescue animals along the way, it was an easy way to while away the time.

By the time we got back, Cassius had made dinner, and it wasn't until after we ate that my sister and I ended up being alone again in Cassius's bedroom.

"I should probably go back to my apartment. I shouldn't be staying—sleeping—in his bed—"

"There's no rush. Give yourself a few days. Please," I begged. "I think Cassius might chain you here if I don't." I winced, wondering whether that had come out as wrong as I now thought it did.

Judging by the bright-red stains on my sister's cheeks, that answer was a solid yes.

"Do you want something to read? I can grab a book from the library. Or a crossword? Calder has a whole stack in his Airstream. Or I can play an audiobook for you—"

"Lara."

My heart dropped into my rib cage at her tone.

"Are you and Calder . . ."

She didn't have a word and neither did I, but whatever the right word was, my answer was still the same.

"Yes."

I was surprised how easy it was to say. Sure, there were a dozen reasons, not the least of which was a dozen years, why my answer shouldn't have been a problem, but I still worried. I worried because, at one point in time, she'd wanted to be with him. I worried because he would've been a safe bet for her, and I didn't want her to resent me for it.

I worried, but I wasn't sorry. I wasn't ashamed. And I wasn't guilty.

"Are you upset?"

"No, of course not," she blew out the answer so quickly and easily, my chest caved with relief. Her lip trembled, and she looked about to cry again as she added, "If anyone has the right to be upset, it's you."

"What?" I sat next to her on the bed.

"Because I lied to you about him." Her voice cracked and she blinked back tears. "Back in college, I told you a lot of horrible things, and I let you think they were about Calder, but they weren't."

"They were about Allen."

Her breath tripped. "How did you know?"

My throat constricted to the point that I couldn't swallow. "When we were at the retreat, we went through Dr. Julia's files. It mentioned Allen, so I made Calder tell me the truth." My voice dwindled to a whisper. "I'm so sorry."

She wouldn't—couldn't—look at me for several moments, and when she finally did, it was like she wanted to cry but just had nothing left.

"I'm the one who should be sorry." She took my hand in hers, both of us squeezing until our knuckles were white. "I should've told you the truth, but I was . . . a mess. I was searching for something . . . 'love in all the wrong places,' isn't that what they say? It felt like I was searching for love on the wrong planet." She sighed and shook her head. "I wasn't good to Calder or to you. And knowing that he helped you find me, after what I'd done, how I'd treated him—and the things I kept from you, the secrets I made you keep, the lies I let you believe . . ." The weight of guilt seemed to pile up on her shoulders.

"It's all in the past."

Somehow that only made her grow sadder. "I was horrible back then. Confused. Careless." Her sad laugh gutted me. "I guess I'm not much better now—"

I took her hand and pulled it into my lap. "Rach, you wanted to be better. That's why you went to that retreat. Because you wanted better for yourself. Don't let what they did diminish that."

Her chin bobbed slowly like it was still floating on uncertainty. "But Calder, if he told you the truth, then you know how he felt about you back then." She lowered her head, a tear landing on top of my hand where it held hers. "And if I hadn't said what I did, maybe the two of you—"

"Please." I gave her hand a shake. "Don't do that. If you go back to maybes, then so do I. Maybe if I'd been more open with you, you wouldn't have felt like you had to keep secrets from me. Maybe if I'd faced my own trauma from Mom, you wouldn't have felt like I was judging you. Maybe if you hadn't felt like you couldn't come to me, you wouldn't have gone to that retreat—"

"Okay!" she interrupted, frantic when she saw how it all could spiral. "I get it. I'm still sorry though."

"I am, too." We hugged tight. "But now, all I want is a future to look forward to. For the both of us."

"Do you love him?"

I inhaled sharply. Old Lara would've ducked away at the question, but now, all those times I never let her in had only encouraged my sister to do the same.

"I . . ." I swallowed. "Yes."

"Good." She smiled, and though it was weak and a little tremulous, it was the first full smile I'd seen on her face since we'd rescued her. She hugged me then, holding me tight, and murmured, "I know you, Lara. Make sure you let him love you back."

—

I closed the door softly behind me, turning to find Cassius sitting on the steps. Waiting.

"Is she okay?" he asked and rose, crossing his arms, not unlike his oldest son did when he was trying to conceal his worry.

"Yeah. Just getting in bed." I stopped in front of him. "Thank you, Cassius. For everything you've done for her. For us."

Something nondescript streaked through his eyes, bright but brief, before it disappeared. "Of course. Anything you need. It's the least I could do—" He stopped and cleared his throat. "It's the least I could do for what you've done for my son. I know Stones can be . . . hard to crack open."

My brows lifted, but he didn't elaborate. Offering me a muttered good night, he strode down the hall to the room where he was staying. It used to be Calder's room before being turned into Cassius's map-making studio. Inside was a small couch where Cassius had been sleeping. I was shocked he fit on it, let alone comfortably, but he wouldn't sleep downstairs—not because Calder had taken the large sofa in the living room, but because he wanted to be able to watch the door to his room and be there if my sister needed anything.

Downstairs, I found Calder in front of the fire. Pausing at the doorway, I just stared at him for a minute like I used to do all those years ago, when neither him nor my sister were looking. I'd stare and name the muscles. The bones. I'd cling to the facade of anatomy rather than admit the depth of my attraction. Now I didn't have to do that.

"Lara." He turned, his eyes dark.

"What is it?"

"Eden didn't make it through surgery."

I grimaced, a mix of emotions hitting me. "I don't know whether to be happy he's gone or sad he'll never see justice for what he did. Sad he'll never see my sister thrive in spite of what happened."

"It's okay to be both." His easy answer loosened the tension in my chest. "Are you going to bed?"

I looked up at him and shook my head. "No. I'm going home with you."

Calder took my hand as we walked to the Airstream, our pace unhurried under the million-star midnight sky. There was no storm terrorizing tonight. Maybe Mother Nature knew there'd been enough terror over the last few days.

With every step, I heard my sister's words echo: *"Let him love you back."*

Maybe that was what I was doing—what I'd been doing this whole time. Every time I let him lead. Every time I took his orders. Every time I sank into the shelter of vulnerability and obedience . . . I was letting him love me. I was trusting him to love me. To lead me. To take charge.

It wasn't about control. It was because he was intentional. With his words. With his actions. With the whole of his character. And he'd always been like that. He'd always acted with purpose and made decisions with calm clarity.

That was why it was so easy to fall in love with him. Because, for someone who'd always carried everything on her own, he made it easy to step out of survival mode. Out of life and death. He made it easy to step into a space where there was room to breathe. To feel. To live for myself. *To love.*

"Calder." I slowed to a stop, forcing him to stop with me before we'd reached the Airstream. His gaze met mine, and I felt the moment start to settle around it. Still. Calm. Magnetic. There was so much I wanted to say. We'd talked about what had happened at the compound, but just the facts. "Thank you for saving me."

Now there was a storm, but only in his eyes. He released my hand, and his shoulders bunched and his arms flexed as he reached for my neck, nesting my face in his hold.

"When I saw you there . . ." He didn't need to finish. I knew exactly the moment he meant. "There is nothing I wouldn't do for you. Not then. Not now. Not ever."

For some reason, it hit different when a man who was capable of doing *a lot* of things—many of them of a violent nature—said those words.

"Calder." I lost myself in his stare. "I love you."

It hadn't been safe to say those words.

It hadn't been safe to say them first.

It hadn't been safe to let love in.

Until him.

Now I could say them without worry. Without vulnerability. Because I could trust him to be who he'd always been: the man who made me feel safe enough to be me.

His voice came out raspy, the texture of bark on an oak tree, like it had been holding something living inside him for ages. "I love you, too, Tomb Raider."

I shuddered as his thumbs brushed my cheeks, and then I tipped my mouth to his. The tenderness of his kiss quickly unraveled and unearthed that wildness hidden under his calm exterior. This time, there was no rain or thunder, no danger or risk. There was nothing but a hundred stars and a million possibilities all around us.

I locked my arms around his neck, and he deepened the kiss, his big arms wrapping around me and his hands grabbing my ass. I melted into him. Into his warmth. His strength. Into the promise of his mouth.

"So, what happens now?" I murmured against his lips when we came up for air.

His gaze danced over my face. "Whatever you want." His forehead rested on mine, so when he turned his head, mine turned with him. "I can go anywhere," he said, both of us looking at his Airstream. "I will go anywhere with you."

My heart volleyed up into my throat. I was falling even more in love with a man who could both lead and know when to follow.

And how could I argue? He could, and did, go anywhere for business. He could easily come back with me to Phoenix and take cases from there without seemingly any change to his lifestyle. But there would be a change, and I'd been with him long enough to know what it was.

His RV was parked here, and whether he wanted to admit it or not, this was his home base. *His home.* And his family . . . as dispersed and independent as they all might have been at times . . . was here.

Did I even have a job to go back to in Phoenix? And even if I did, did I want to go back to it?

It wasn't a simple question, or one that needed a decision tonight. Though, deep down, I felt as if the simple answer had been buried inside my chest for a long time.

"Right now, the only place I want to be is here. With you."

He dropped his lips back to mine, kissing me roughly, hungrily, leaving no doubt exactly where he wanted to be.

This time, I didn't even care when he started cutting off my clothes.

Chapter 38

Lara

"Are you sure this is what you want?" I stood with my sister on the front porch of the Stone house.

She gave me a small smile. It had been six days since we'd rescued her from the cult, and every day the wound it had left on her healed a little more. Six days we'd spent in the haven of the ranch. Walking. Gardening. Cooking. Playing with Colby's animals. Sitting by the house's fire with hot cocoa every night. And talking. So much talking.

I told her what had happened in the ER with Ian. She gave me her version of what had happened with Brandon. We talked about Mom. We talked about college. About Calder and Allen and her pregnancy scare. I told her more details about how we'd found her, and I told her about Ben.

She wasn't the only one who'd been healing over the past six days, and I wished she'd stay longer.

While Cassius hadn't resorted to chains like I'd joked, he'd certainly done the bulk of convincing her to stay a few more days when she wanted to leave on day four. I wanted to worry that she was rushing things, but I also understood why she wanted to go.

Staying felt like staying put. And if there was one thing my sister had done in the face of every hurdle she'd been through, it was that she hadn't stopped moving forward. Even if it hadn't been exactly in the right direction.

I had a feeling it was, now.

"I need to learn how to take care of myself," Rach murmured and reached for my hand, giving it a squeeze. "And I think you could do with more time not having to take care of everyone around you." Her smile widened slightly as she looked at me. "Being loved looks good on you."

"One day, it will look good on you, too," I promised her, refusing to hear anything to the contrary as I pulled her in for a hug.

She'd said her goodbyes to the rest of the family, including Calder, who then dispersed to give the two of us a private moment together. I'd offered to take her to the airport, but she said Cassius was going to and she didn't seem to want to change that.

She'd told me how grateful she was to him and Calder for everything they'd done, but I had a feeling it had taken her some time to work up the courage to be able to say it in person, which was what she wanted to use the drive to do.

"Thanks again for loaning me your apartment." I didn't like that she was going so far, but my place in Phoenix was super safe, and the lease was still mine for another ten months whether I was there or not.

"You'll love it." I remembered how good it had felt when I moved there.

There'd been a honeymoon phase when I enjoyed my residency, enjoying a place where I wasn't reminded about Mom's death or the difficulties in my and Rachel's relationship. Maybe it wouldn't be good for her forever. Selfishly, I hoped at some point, the mountains would call her back, too. But for right now, it would be good. It would be what she needed.

"Have you heard from the hospital?" Rachel pulled back and combed her fingers through her hair. I loved to see its natural curl. She'd always straightened it or tamed it into loose beach waves—she'd always made it into something for someone else. Not anymore.

"Not yet."

She sighed. "What are you waiting for, Lara?"

"What do you mean? For them to call me about my job?"

"I mean, why don't you call them?"

My mouth opened and shut. "Because they have to decide if they still want me."

I still hadn't heard anything after Dr. Morgan had notified me that the internal investigation had cleared me, but maybe they were waiting until the lawsuit was settled to see how much the incident had cost them.

"When they call me, then I can decide what I want to do."

She shook her head and laughed, the wind taking one of her curls across her face.

"What?"

Leading me by the hand, we walked off the porch and to the end of the house, where she stopped us, facing toward the hill where the Airstream was parked.

"Why are you waiting for them when you already know what you want to do?"

My heart stumbled, unsteady beats rushing into my veins. Maybe I did know. Maybe I had known for some time. Maybe I was still having a hard time letting go of the person I'd been all these years, who took care of everyone else before even considering what I wanted.

"Thank you," I told her and hugged her again.

We separated when the front door opened and closed. Cassius stepped off the porch, his face shadowed under a cowboy hat.

"Ready?"

Rachel hugged me tightly again.

"I love you," I told her, hanging on to her fingers until the last moment.

"I love you, too."

"Call me when you land," I added as she approached Cassius's truck.

She looked over her shoulder. "Call the hospital."

I smiled and waved, watching them until the truck disappeared on the drive before reaching for my phone.

She was right. I'd known I didn't belong in Phoenix the moment I'd set foot back in the mountains.

"Calder?"

My entire body hummed after the voicemail I'd just left for Dr. Morgan. I didn't know why it had taken me so long. To just admit I didn't want to go back. Maybe I thought it would be easier if they were the ones to terminate my contract. Maybe I felt like I owed them something after what had happened with Ian.

But I wasn't the guilty one. I'd done my job. I'd tried to save him, and he'd almost killed me. And as soon as I'd said the words *formal resignation*, I realized what haunted me deeply about that day in the ER.

It wasn't that Ian had died, though there was natural guilt with that. It was that I could have. He came for me. He hurt me. He could've killed me, and I would've died without living. Without loving.

"Everything okay?" Calder stepped out of the Airstream, shirtless and devastating, and I almost forgot my plan. Almost.

"I have another case for you," I said, pinning some worry to my voice.

"What?" He came toward me.

"Another case." I fought hard not to laugh at the blank confusion on his face. "There's a doctor who's gone missing from a hospital in Phoenix. Red hair. Short." I smiled as recognition started to dawn. "They said she called and quit her job today, left a message that she was never coming back to Arizona, and they think she's now lost in the mountains in Wyoming."

He stopped in front of me, the warmth of his eyes tracking every inch of my face. "Really?" he rumbled, and I heard the hope—the ache—in his voice.

Biting my lip, I nodded slowly. "Really."

With a big shudder, his hands framed my waist and hauled me against him. "What's my reward for finding her?" His mouth lowered, but I pulled back enough to look him in the eyes and smile.

"You get to keep her."

Epilogue

Lara

One month later

"Did Creed have another case?"

"Huh?" Calder looked up in the middle of unfolding the crossword he'd brought to our picnic.

"He was packing up his truck when we left the camper, but I thought he'd finished the case on the reservation last week."

"He has . . . something."

I arched my brows. "Is everything okay?"

Calder frowned. "Not sure," he said, then sighed. "He said there was something he had to take care of back in Riverton and that he'd be gone another week or two."

"Oh. Interesting," I murmured, swiping my toes through the cold, clear surface of the lake. I'd known Creed for only a few weeks now, but it would take only days for anyone to realize the former military man's purpose was set in stone. His life revolved around business and he worked like a machine, receiving orders and then executing them. No emotion, no questions involved. So for him to return somewhere after a case was finished . . .

"Yeah, that's what I said," Calder grunted. "Apparently, he also asked Callum to look into one of the police officers on the reservation."

My eyes widened. "Does he suspect some kind of foul play?" I swiped my foot through the water again.

"No . . ." Calder trailed off and grimaced, drawing a pen from his pocket. "It's a female police officer."

This time, my mouth just shaped the O without making a sound.

"Yeah," Calder murmured, his gaze meeting mine. "Now, are we going to do this puzzle or not?"

My smile went full bloom. "Fire away, Wild Man."

His stare glittered on me for one hot, lingering second before looking at the paper and reading off the first clue. "'Nineties sitcom where a neurotic interior designer moves in with her gay best friend. His name.' Four letters—"

"Will!" I called out, excited. "Did you not watch *Will & Grace*?"

"No." His brows scrunched.

"What?" I gaped, my splashing stopping short. Even after a month of waking up to Calder every day, I couldn't stop the flutters in my stomach when his eyes caught mine.

It still didn't feel real. Not here. Not on the shores of Lima Bean Lake, the water so clear, so blue, it was like liquefied sky buried in the skin of the earth. Not surrounded by sky-scraping mountain peaks stitched with autumn-hewn treetops.

Here, underneath a million-star sky at night and next to the man I'd fantasized about for over a decade, it felt too good to be true.

"I can't believe you've never seen it. We're going to have to watch it." I pointed at him. "Add that to the list."

I wasn't in Wyoming long before I commandeered one of Calder's beloved case notebooks and labeled it *A Survivalist's Guide to Pop Culture*. Inside was a running list of all the shows and movies and experiences Calder's childhood had skipped. We were slowly making our way through them all.

Just like we were slowly figuring out our life together.

His eyes narrowed, but he didn't move. I cocked my head and then kicked my foot in his direction, sending a spray of water toward our picnic blanket.

In a nanosecond, he was up. Coming for me. I laughed—squealed—when I found myself hauled over his shoulder and carted back to the blanket.

"If you know all the answers, Tomb Raider, then you finish the puzzle," he said, depositing me in the center and handing me the crossword and pen.

"Fine." I jutted out my chin. "So, Will from *Will & Grace*. Next is . . . 'TV series about an obsessive, charming young man who stalks his love interests and intervenes'—oh, that one's easy." I looked up at Calder, who returned my stare with a blank one. "Really?" I leaned forward, bringing my face close to his. "You have to have seen a commercial . . . an ad . . ." *Still nothing.* I huffed. "The answer is *You*."

"Me?"

"No. *You*. The show is called *You*."

"The show is called Calder Stone?" he said, feigning confusion.

I shot him an unentertained stare. "No, it's called *Costello*," I deadpanned, knowing he would at least get that classic comedy-duo reference.

Grinning, he grabbed my chin and pulled my mouth to his for a kiss. His tongue slid along my lips, striking heat over my skin.

"Stop trying to distract me," I ordered, pulling away before he made me forget my own name. "Here. Eat some charcuterie." I pushed the board in his direction, a few pieces of cheese and some grapes left.

Cassius had thoughtfully made up the board for us when Calder mentioned he was taking me on a picnic to Lima Bean Lake. I hadn't been back to—let alone enjoyed—the idyllic haven since I'd helped Colby on her Donnie scavenger hunt.

"Finish it, then," Calder said with a grin, sitting back on his haunches and popping a grape into his mouth. *Did he make everything look hot?* Yes. Yes, he did. More importantly, though, he looked happy.

Like he'd found a piece of himself that had been lost. Not just with me but with his father. With his siblings. And I'd never loved him more.

"Next." I counted the open boxes and then found the clue. "Five letters. 'Tie the knot.'"

"Marry."

My eyes jumped to his, my throat tightening.

"You didn't say I couldn't help," he teased huskily.

"No," I murmured. "I didn't."

Jotting the letters into their spots, I quickly moved on before my thoughts got ahead of me.

"'Abbreviation for Maine.'"

"Me."

"M-E," I spelled out.

"No, Lara. *Me.*"

"You?" I chuckled, carving the letters onto the paper. "Is this another Abbott and Costello joke? I think you've exhausted your—" The pen slid from my fingers.

Calder wasn't sitting on his haunches. He was on his knees.

One knee.

With a ring box open in his hands. I stared at the emerald-cut diamond, a giant glittering star cushioned in a black velvet sky.

"Will. You. Marry. Me?" he murmured, and I lifted my eyes to his before dropping them to the crossword, all the dots connecting into a constellation.

Will You Marry Me. The answers were lined up in perfect formation in the puzzle.

"You made this." I lifted my head and slid the paper from my lap, rising up on my knees so our faces were level.

We'd done countless crossword puzzles together over the last month, so I never would've guessed—never would've thought—this one was rigged. *I guess that was the point.*

"Callum did. I've never heard of those shows before," he admitted, with that same gruffness he's always taken with me when he was trying to hide the depths of his want. When he was nervous he'd never have me then. *And that I might say no to him now.* "I love you, Lara. I've loved you from that very first look."

My cheeks burned. My thudding heart rumbled goose bumps over my skin. *This couldn't be real,* I thought as I reached for him, anchoring my palms to the hard heat of his chest. I wanted to look at the ring—to stare and appreciate every expensive facet of it—but all I could see was him. Love lustrous in his eyes. Need feathering the corner of his jaw.

He took my wrist and dragged my left hand to his mouth, kissing the middle of my palm as he said roughly, "Marry me, Lara."

"Are you asking or ordering me?" I teased through an unsteady breath.

He bit into my trembling flesh, and I shivered violently, my heart thrashing in my chest.

"Whichever gets you to say yes faster."

"I love you, Calder," I murmured, a watery smile stretching my cheeks as I lifted my face to his. "And yes, I will marry you."

The metal band was warm as he slid it along my finger, the diamond a welcome weight on my hand.

I would've liked to admire the ring he'd chosen, but that was going to have to wait, because as soon as it was settled on my finger, his mouth claimed mine.

"Were you worried I wasn't going to say yes?" I panted several minutes later as he hauled me to straddle his lap.

"No," he growled, divesting me of my top.

"No?" My laughed choked off into a moan as he cupped my breast.

He leaned his head back, his lust-rimmed gaze finding mine. "Why would I be worried about you saying yes when I know how to make you scream it?"

And then he did just that.

ACKNOWLEDGMENTS

Thank you for reading *Tracked*! For so long, I would watch all the crime-solving drama TV shows with the hunky hero (or team of heroes) saving the day and wish there was more of a love story. And then one day, I realized I didn't have to wait for the show to give me a love story—I could write one for them on my own.

Thank you to my agent, Josi, for believing in this book and working your magic! You are the best!

Thank you to Maria and Megan at Montlake for being so welcoming and friendly. For ten years, I've done everything for my books myself, so to say it was nerve racking to enter into a partnership is an understatement. But from our very first meeting, you made me feel nothing but comfortable and considered. Working with the both of you as a team has been a dream!

Thanks to my husband for always believing in me and being my hero every single day. And for accepting that I have no interest in any TV show where there isn't some kind of crime being solved. Thanks to my family and friends who have supported me along this journey. I'm so blessed and honored to have you by my side.

ABOUT THE AUTHOR

Logo © 2025 Nickolas Kossup

Rebecca Sharp is the author of over sixty novels of contemporary romance in a variety of genres. From new adult to extreme sports romance and forbidden romance to romantic comedies, her books feature strong heroines, hot alphas, unique love stories, and always a happily ever after. She is also a dentist in Pennsylvania, and when she is not seeing patients or writing, Rebecca loves to snowboard, cook, and travel with her amazing husband, affectionately referred to as Mr. *GQ*. She loves to hear from readers. For more information, visit www.drrebeccasharp.com.